RUNESCAPE®

THE GIFT OF GUTHIX

RUNESCAPE®

THE GIFT OF GUTHIX

ERIN M. EVANS

JAGEX®

TITAN BOOKS

RUNESCAPE: THE GIFT OF GUTHIX
Print edition ISBN: 9781803365213
Electronic edition ISBN: 9781803369235

Published by Titan Books
A division of Titan Publishing Group Ltd
144 Southwark Street, London SE1 0UP
www.titanbooks.com

First edition: May 2024
2 4 6 8 10 9 7 5 3 1

Cover illustration: Mark Montague and Terence Abbott.

A CIP catalogue record for this title is available
from the British Library.

Printed and bound by CPI Group (UK) Ltd, Croydon CR0 4YY.

To all the ones who never stop.

PART I
THE FOUNDING

I should have seen this as a sign of things to come, but I hoped that in free rein they might see the harmful impact for themselves, and gain enlightenment from their destructive impulses.

—THE WORDS OF GUTHIX

ONE

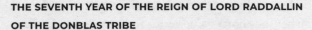

Ilme came to the shore of the Wolf Clan's summer encampment on a cold tide, two lies in her mouth and a gifted green cloak wrapped around her shoulders.

Master Endel regarded her with a scrutiny so thorough that panic curled in Ilme's stomach—he had surely figured her out. But he only refastened the silver brooch, shaped like a crescent moon, to sit higher on her shoulder and brushed something off the fabric there. He gestured at her long brown braid.

"Do something about your hair," he said, almost pleading. "Look less… guileless. We're aiming for 'aloof'. For… 'youthful wisdom'."

Ilme undid the plait and cast a sideways glance at Endel's apprentice, Azris, her dark hair piled in a knot of loops at the crown of her head. Ilme thought of Endel's second apprentice, a girl called Eritona, her rows of braids sleek against her elegant head.

Eritona was not here as she had fallen ill and remained behind—but everyone knew the Moon Clan travelled in groups of three and no one would accept them as mages from the Lunar Isle if they didn't. So Master Endel had needed a replacement and Ilme, guileless and unwise, would have to suit.

She raked her fingers through her brown hair and felt worry twist her stomach again. Eritona had fallen ill at the very time Ilme needed to go north. Someone might have poisoned her. Someone might have made certain Ilme was the one who followed Master Endel north, and if that came out—

"Fortunately," Master Endel said, as the ship swayed beneath them, "my understanding of the Fremennik suggests that the jarl will leave you be. They don't value youth and he will assume your magical aptitude makes you untrustworthy."

Azris cast a sceptical glance at Ilme. "Master, won't that mean he'll assume *you're* untrustworthy?"

Master Endel waved this away. "I don't intend to become the jarl's confidante—only to solve a mutual problem."

"I still don't understand how having a rune cache is a problem."

"Because you are not Fremennik. And you are not of the Moon Clan, but since here you are supposed to be an initiate of the Moon Clan—" here he gestured to himself, to his own borrowed green robes, "—you should just accept that it's the case."

This was the first lie: they were not from the Moon Clan, far up across the Northern Sea, where those mages hid themselves. The Moon Clan didn't believe in runes. Rune magic was what had caused all the world's problems before—putting magic in the hands of anyone who could grasp it, regardless of their worth. If you were pure-minded and dedicated, then magic would come to you just as it did for the Moon Clan. Magic they did not teach to outsiders. Not willingly anyway.

But the Fremennik were the Moon Clan's warrior cousins, in a way, and when there was a question of magic, the Moon Clan were the ones they would naturally reach out to—not the upstart court of a warlord of the south. So when Master Endel heard the rumours of rune essence found in the far north, this had been the plan he'd settled on.

"Are there male mages among the Moon Clan?" Ilme asked, trying to twist her hair up like Azris's. "I heard they're all women."

"I heard they're all demon-worshippers," Azris chimed in.

Master Endel sighed. He was a small man, narrow-shouldered and trim-bearded, but what he lacked in physical presence he made up for in wit and wisdom. "Azris, if you are going to become a wizard, you are going to have to be less credulous. The Moon Clan are not demon-worshippers. They are Guthixians. More or less," he added.

Master Endel, like most of the wizards Ilme had met including Azris, knew the names of spells and their methods of casting, the lore of the days before the God Wars shattered everything humanity knew. Like some, he had access to the stores of ancient runes, cached or collected, from which powerful magics could be formed.

But in his youth Endel had travelled to the Lunar Isle, the solitary refuge of the Moon Clan mages. He had slipped past the Moon Clan's guards, and had gone down into their sacred rune essence mine—too holy to touch—and come out with rune essence and a scar in his ribs. He found a way to shape that essence into runes—daring strange and ephemeral plumes of elemental power to force them into shape—and travelled far and wide to scrape together more remnants of essence.

But no one, not even the fabled mages of the Moon Clan, were like the wizards of old, shaping runes of power and combining the gleaming stones into spells at a whim. The last time Endel had done anything extraordinary had been a terrific burst of flame that he'd spent a fistful of fire runes to create, which had sealed the Donblas Tribe's success against the Caracalli in the earliest days of their campaign. Ilme had been eight when that had happened.

"The Fremennik as a rule do not work magic," Master Endel said, as the sailors started loading things into the boat meant to ferry them to shore. "They don't understand it. They fear it. So, if the rumours of the cache in the mountains are true, they will want to be rid of it. We're going to solve their problem for them, and the jarl can pretend it was all his own plan. You are to *embody* an initiate of the Moon Clan: polished. Superior. Distant. Presence is a great magic. Both of you, remember what we're doing here is of the utmost importance. If they have found a cache of runes, or even rune essence from the ages before, that will greatly benefit Lord Raddallin and thereby each of us. Ilme, leave the bags!"

"Yes, Master Endel," Ilme said, taking off the pack she'd slung across her narrow chest, navigating around the half-pinned knot of her hair. She did not, however put back her scribe's kit. That would not leave her side. She was careful, but it would only take one slip for the second lie to come out, and that would be very, *very* bad.

The sailors called that the boat was ready, and Master Endel gave the two young women one more assessment. "Azris, stop looking like you've smelt something unpleasant. Ilme, just… put the braid back. Come on."

Ilme climbed down the side of the ship, settling in beside Azris on the leaky boat, and looked out across the last stretch of water. A great longhouse stood on the ridge overlooking the wide pebbled beach, the most prominent building in this seasonal village. But even that was built of skins and timber and slabs of peat. A dozen smaller structures surrounded it, like a gaggle of ducklings, but only the longhouse poured cook-smoke up into the cloudy air.

Below the longhouse the Fremennik had gathered on the beach itself, weapons in hand, their agitation and wariness so intense it seemed to stir the choppy waves between the little boat and the shore. Longships rested to the left of her, sleek bulks of wood ready to launch into attack. In their little boat, one sailor rowed and one waved a green cloth, like a flag of peace. This didn't diminish the Fremennik's wariness—Ilme wondered if they'd been tricked by false signs before.

Ilme made herself take a deep breath.

"I hear they sacrifice people," Azris whispered to her, eyes on the Fremennik. "Put them on the fire and roast them alive. For demons. Maybe the Moon Clan don't worship demons, but the Fremennik do. Everyone knows that."

Ilme had heard this as well, but hoped it was a less credible rumour than the cache. "Master Endel said they were Guthixians," Ilme whispered back. "Why would Guthixians roast people?"

Azris gave Ilme's re-plaited braid a rough tug. "They're maniacs. Who knows why they do anything?"

That was nonsense—Ilme was only sixteen and there was a lot she hadn't seen and didn't know, but if there was one thing she understood completely it was that people always had reasons for what they did. They might be foolish reasons, they might be dangerous reasons, and they might be reasons that people themselves didn't know outright—but they were there. You could predict most things, if you listened and watched and uncovered the reasons.

Master Endel sat at the prow of the boat—polished, superior, and distant. When the boat hit the shore, he didn't wait, but began walking up the beach toward the jarl. Azris climbed out after him, and Ilme followed, splashing through the icy shallows. By the time she'd made her way up the sliding stones of the beach, wet and stumbling, there was no hope of her embodying anything so fine as a mage of the Lunar Isle.

But Master Endel had already begun the lie to great effect. He approached the warriors on the beach, as unconcerned and steady as a ship cutting through calm water.

"I have come from across the Northern Sea to seek the counsel of Jarl Viljar," he announced. "There is a disturbance in the magic of Gielinor and the Moon Clan wishes to resolve it to maintain the safety of all."

The warriors glanced sideways at a pair of men—both young, both stern-faced, the same heavy brows, the same sharp noses. *Brothers*, Ilme thought. One was whip thin, with a pale beard and dark, sharp eyes. He wore a tunic embroidered with ferocious, beastly faces and a pectoral shaped like a sharp-toothed, horned face framed by axes. Over his shoulders he wore a wolf pelt, the hood fashioned so the wolf's snout stuck out over his forehead, and summoning pouches hung around his waist. The other was dark-haired, his shaggy mane of brown hair flowing into his beard and down his furry shoulders. Two torques of braided silver were stacked on his thick neck, and he wore a helmet figured to look like a sneering, horned demon.

Ilme sucked in a breath.

"I might know what you speak of," the dark-haired man said, not looking away from Master Endel. "What business is it of the Moon Clan?"

"Are we not the guardians of magic in this world?" Master Endel asked. "As much as I would never claim an axe, I don't believe you wish to claim the runes. Will you take me to the jarl?"

The Fremennik muttered at this, and the pale-haired man made a sharp gesture. The dark-haired one spared the briefest of glances at Azris and Ilme, arranged on either side of Master Endel as they had practised, before saying, "We are not meant to interfere with the gods or their doings. Guthix has given us all we need to master our fates."

"Which is why he has sent us to root out your conundrum," Master Endel said. "Take me to your father."

It was a neat trick, Ilme thought, as the men both paused, gazes flicking away from Master Endel. Who else could this pair be but the jarl's sons, looking so alike and speaking with such authority? But they clearly hadn't expected it to be so obvious; maybe they forgot how much they looked alike when one was light and one was dark. Now, Endel seemed far more a master of his art.

"I am Reigo Viljarsson," the dark-haired man said. "This is my brother, Ott. If you are going to claim hospitality for the Moon Clan, then you will follow me and observe the rites."

This was not in Master Endel's plans—the hope was that they would recover the cache and leave as quickly as possible, no more than a day later, not lingering to let the Wolf Clan poke at their lie. But Master Endel was a quick-thinker, and he wanted the rune cache.

"Of course," he said. "I have seen the paths and I forget to walk them. Lead on."

The pale man started to object, but his brother shot him a look of irritation, and gestured for two warriors to flank Master Endel and guide him up the beach.

"Demon rites," Azris whispered. Ilme watched Reigo and his ferocious helm lead the way up to the great longhouse.

The warriors fell in, and no one said what Ilme and Azris should do. No one had even acknowledged them. Ilme looked back at their abandoned luggage on the shoreline.

"Did you have a dream about this?" a voice asked. "Is that why you came?"

Ilme looked back and saw that one person hadn't followed—a boy with yellow hair covering his ears, freckles, and dark, piercing eyes. He couldn't have been more than twelve or thirteen, all elbows and angles and potential.

Azris lifted her chin in a fine mimicry of Master Endel. "We don't discuss the visions."

"We didn't," Ilme said, remembering the fine points of the lie. "We haven't taken our final vows." Was that right? Did Moon Clan mages take vows? Tests?

Azris shot her a dark look, as if Ilme had insulted *her*. "Anyway, it's not your business, boy. Take the bags."

The boy snorted. "Take them yourself, apprentice."

Ilme stepped between them. "I'm Ilme. This is Azris. What's your name?"

That question made a dark cloud pass over the boy's face. "Gunnar Viljarsson."

"*You're* the jarl's son?" Azris asked.

There was no hiding the scepticism in her tone, and his posture shifted into a mimicry of his brothers'. "He's got three of us. Carry your own bags."

"Well met," Ilme said, giving him a courteous bow, and the boy relaxed a little. "Do you know where we're meant to go now? Do we follow Master Endel?"

Gunnar frowned. "What else would you do?"

Ilme shrugged, nodding back at their supplies. "Put the bags somewhere. Prepare the beds. Like you said, we're apprentices."

"But you're guests first," Gunnar said. "What do *you* do to seal the guest rites?" He eyed them both. "Is it true you poison visitors and make them tell you all their secrets, and only let them stay if they survive?"

"What?" Azris cried. "That's absurd."

He shrugged. "It's what they say."

"We just don't want to do anything wrong," Ilme said, thinking she ought to avoid the Lunar Isle if even a breath of that were true. "It would reflect poorly on our master and insult your father." She thought of his brothers' temper, the boy's bluster. "And we'd get in trouble," she added, a gamble.

It paid off. Gunnar, clearly used to being overlooked until he made a mistake, made a face. "I can't believe you came all this way and don't even know how to do the guest rites. Come on. Bring your bags up to the longhouse and someone will put them in a tent."

"Can you even imagine that little twig being a jarl's son?" Azris whispered as Ilme picked up the bags. "He doesn't look the part at all."

Not yet, Ilme thought. But that was Azris—she saw the surface of the water and never wondered what was churning beneath it. The moment and not what followed after it. Gunnar was only a boy, and so clearly *through* with being a boy. That was dangerous—someone could *use* that.

Ilme felt a little sorry for him and found she hoped nobody else noticed how usable he might be.

"I wonder if he knows where it is," Ilme whispered, as they climbed back up the beach.

"Where what is?"

"The cache. They don't want to talk about it with us," she went on, "but I bet they *have* talked about it. And they don't pay him any mind. I'll bet he's heard things."

"And I'll bet if you ask him, he'll go running to his father," Azris said. "And then we'll be in trouble. Sacrificed to the demons—did you see that helmet?"

Azris wasn't wrong. But if Ilme asked Gunnar, she might find out first. She might be useful enough to keep Master Endel from asking her too many questions...

Gunnar didn't offer to take any of the bags, but walked up the path, his posture slumping again. He pointed to a spot beside the great double doors of the longhouse, and then sloped inside without waiting for them. Ilme deposited everything except her scribe's kit, and followed Azris and Gunnar in.

Inside, the longhouse was warm and crowded. There were no humans roasting on the fires, no blood sacrifices draining on the tables. Instead, Ilme watched the Fremennik turn clay pots perched on the fire's edge with deft hands, dipping in wooden spoons to test barley porridge and boiled fish, spiky and fragrant with strange herbs. Others shifted domed loaves of bread around the fire's edge.

There was, however, a demon at the end of the hall.

At the far, rounded end of the building, the jarl's throne sat in the grasp of a monster—a horned man with a gaping mouth reached claw-like hands around the seat. Its eyes were dark mirrors, reflecting the firelight, the shadow of its maw beyond the throne a doorway into nothing. For a moment, it seemed to breathe, cold air bristling the hairs tugged loose from Ilme's braid. Azris seized her arm with a hissed curse.

"Shut the door," Gunnar said. "You're making a draft."

Ilme blinked, the spell shattered. It was a carving, a creature of painted wood and polished stone. She reached back and pulled the door snug in its frame.

"Demon worshippers," Azris whispered.

The jarl sat on the throne between the clutching hands of the horned man. He was as pale as Ott, as big as Reigo, and as surly-looking as Gunnar. Through the thick pelt of his hair and beard, Ilme marked scars carving his skin—a ruler who'd seen battle. She glanced around the longhouse, marked other injuries, other scars—a clan that saw a lot of battle, she amended.

Shields hung on the long wall painted with figures that seemed twisted and wide-eyed. It took Ilme a moment to recognise them—a salmon, a mammoth, a wolf, a falcon, a seal—

"You sit there," Gunnar said, pointing at a table against the long wall, beneath the seal shield.

"Our master's up there," Azris said. Master Endel stood before Jarl Viljar and his chosen warriors, and from where they now stood, Ilme could see a large green stone set between them. Reigo and Ott had settled down on a bench beside the throne, as the other warriors found seats nearer to the fire.

"You sit here because you're children," Gunnar said flatly, then after a moment, he sat first, seething.

"Children?" Azris demanded. "I'm nineteen!"

Gunnar's freckled nose wrinkled in disgust, as if Azris had just admitted something shameful. "If you weren't children," he pointed out, "your master would have introduced you. And he didn't. So you sit here."

There was no further arguing with the jarl's son: the buzzing blare of horns split the chaos of the longhouse, the Fremennik falling silent as Jarl Viljar stood before the stone and raised his arms, beginning a deep, throaty chant.

"There it is," Azris murmured. "Sacrificial altar. Mark my words. I bet that summoner-son brings the demons in and they eat them alive."

"You said they did it on the fires," Ilme pointed out, but she couldn't tear her eyes from the chanting jarl and the terrible face behind him. She leaned over to Gunnar. "What is he saying?"

"It's the old tongue," the boy said. "I don't know all of it. It's a prayer to Guthix, for strength and fortune in battle."

Ilme nearly asked Gunnar to repeat himself—Guthix was a god of creation, of balance and promise. Order and responsibility. Not battle and blood and strength. But she peered closer at the green stone before the jarl's throne and saw the faintly etched lines of teardrops covering the sharp-edged surface. The Tear of Guthix, as inarguably present as it was in the hanging talismans of the druids' grove near her aunt's hold or the stained glass of the wooden-walled shrine in Falador.

As Viljar chanted, warriors came forward, laying their axes, spears and bows against the stone with bowed heads, the clang and scrape of the weapons folding into the jarl's chanting. Ilme eyed the older sons, Reigo and Ott, seated on the wall, their faces still tight and scornful. Ilme wondered which of them was meant to succeed Jarl Viljar, and which of them would *actually* do so, regardless of the jarl's wishes.

Then she glanced at the jarl, his scarred face, and reconsidered. This was not a man who would back down easily.

But there were scores of hard faces, scarred and bearded and painted. "Have you had a war?" she whispered to Gunnar.

Again he looked at her, as if she were making fun of him. "We crushed the Seal Clan last season. They are under Jarl Viljar's control now."

Ilme glanced over her head at the row of shields. "That's what all these are? Your... vassals?"

"Guthix!" Viljar bellowed, cutting off Gunnar's answer. "When you stir, gods tremble! Where you walked, bounty blooms! You have raised mountains and leashed demons! You have granted the Wolf Clan the fiercest of warriors, the strongest of blades, the fruit of the field and the forest, and in turn we give these to our honoured guest—food, shelter, protection—that he might carry the word of the Wolf Clan back to his home."

You're safe while you're here, Ilme thought. *But tell everyone what a threat we are.*

"This is weirder than a sacrifice," Azris breathed. "It feels blasphemous. Why are they doing this *now*? Why are they talking about weapons?"

Viljar glanced down at Master Endel. "You are meant to lay your weapons on the stone," his voice full of his sons' disdain. "To grant your aid. But since the Moon Clan bear no weapons but their magic..."

Master Endel held up his hands as if offering to lay them on the stone. But Viljar waved this away, with the same nose wrinkle of disgust as his son. He beckoned to the Fremennik beside the fire, and pointed Endel to the bench beside his throne.

A woman came up bearing a clay plate of fish, barley and bread, offering it to Viljar. A man then carried over an empty plate, which he gave to Endel. Viljar spooned food from his own plate to Endel's and gestured at him to eat.

The ritual complete, food was distributed through the longhouse, though there was still order and ritual here—Ilme charted the hierarchy of the Wolf Clan one dish at a time and watched as Ott reached for a plate, clearly handed to his brother first, a look of disgust flitting over his face. She saw Jarl Viljar spot it too, and frown deeply.

You're observant, her aunt had said, only a month after Ilme had come to the hold, a month after the death of her father, *I can use that.*

Her aunt had something of the same keenness as the jarl, some of that same iron in her actions, rigid and uncompromising. She was the first person besides Ilme's mother to realise she had a knack for reading people. But she had not asked what Ilme observed in her, any more than she'd asked if Ilme wanted to serve her.

Ilme, Azris, and Gunnar were among the last to eat, but there was still plenty. Ilme kept trying to catch Master Endel's eye— but for the honoured guest there were more hosts to greet, more mead to drink, and no one seemed to remember that she and Azris were here as well. Ilme slipped a notebook and a stylus from her bag, marking down a few quick notes to herself about the Fremennik.

"What are you writing?" Gunnar asked.

Nothing she'd marked down was private, so she showed Gunnar the page. "I take notes for Master Endel," she explained, and this much was not a lie. "You're right—we don't do things the same, and it'd be better if no one embarrassed themselves later."

Gunnar scoffed. "You don't need to *write* it. Just do it." But she left the page open so he could read sidelong, still pretending he didn't care.

"This is taking forever," Azris said. She leaned across Ilme to speak to Gunnar. "How long do we have to stay?"

He blinked at her. "You… don't? The rites are over. You've eaten."

"That was it?" Azris said. She shook her head. "Fine. Can you just show us where we're staying?"

This was clearly not what Gunnar wanted to do, but he searched the room as if looking for a replacement, and found instead the jarl's stern gaze upon him. He hunched down again, before slipping from the bench. "Fine."

Outside, the sky was still bright white as the sun bled through the cloud cover, but the brightness had dipped, angling toward sunset. They followed Gunnar through the camp to a tent near the shore. Casks and boxes stood against its wall—it had been a storage building, Ilme thought, before they arrived.

"Are we *all* in here?" Azris sniffed. "Fine. I'm going to read and go to bed. Don't make any noise," she added to Ilme.

"I want to walk around a bit," Ilme said. "I'll be quiet when I come back."

"Suit yourself," Azris said. "Don't get thrown on any altars." She ducked behind the door of skins. Ilme turned to Gunnar, who studied her with that same scowl.

"*She* seems like a wizard," he said. "You don't."

"What do you mean?"

"I mean, she's rude and self-important," Gunnar said, bluntly. "That's what all the stories say. Wizards take magic and don't give a care for what it costs. Who it hurts." He paused. "Mages, I mean.

Is that rude if I call you a wizard?"

"No." Ilme thought back over the long course of history—through god wars and the fall of kingdoms, the gain and loss of magic. A long enough time, great enough changes, that anyone could be a villain. But having power certainly helped.

"That feels like most people with power," she said. "But… yeah, wizards too. Although, I do know some nice ones." She thought of Eritona, sick-abed, and hoped she was all right. They weren't friends, Ilme knew, but Eritona wasn't cutting like Azris, and she let Ilme look through her books. Though it was also easy to imagine her waking and saying that her stomach-ache had started when someone gave her a bitter cup of mead, and all eyes turning to the girl who replaced her…

Gunnar eyed her. "So are you a hopeless wizard then? Or a just a really tricky one?"

Ilme brought her thoughts back to the present. "I'm not really either. Mostly I just write things down," she said. "Azris is Master Endel's proper apprentice."

Do what you're good at, her aunt had said. *Listen, watch, keep track. Report. Be still and silent and take it all in.*

Ilme hesitated. What was the difference between manipulating someone and understanding them enough to predict them? She worried sometimes she didn't know. But she thought in that moment that Gunnar deserved a little kindness, a little reminder that he wasn't alone.

"I don't… enjoy it very much," she admitted, and the words gave her a frisson of panic. It was very close to admitting the second lie. "I think I'd like to be a wizard. It's very interesting. But I'm no jarl's son," she added lightly, "so I take my lot."

Gunnar was silent a moment. "Yeah, well… I don't like being the jarl's son very much."

"Would you like to switch places?" she teased.

He rolled his eyes. "I think people *might* notice."

"I don't really envy you, though. You've got a lot of expectations on you." Ilme considered before daring a little further, "Your father reminds me of my aunt a little. I feel like if I were her heir I'd wake up feeling like I'd failed already. You're doing a lot better than I would."

Gunnar heaved a sigh. "He doesn't *have* an heir. He won't just choose Reigo and be done. I'd rather leave anyway, explore the world. Do something interesting. But I can't. He might choose me. I have to stay here and *wait*."

He might choose no one, Ilme thought. She hesitated, and then offered him the only gift she had: "What about your other brother? Ott?"

"Ott?" he said, confused. "Wolf Clan doesn't have summoner-jarls."

"If your father takes too long… if he doesn't choose…" Ilme said. "Just a… mage's sense, I guess. He seems to want the throne most. And I think you know your father might never choose, so that won't be peaceful." She shrugged. "I suppose if you wanted to slip away before Ott did anything, he probably wouldn't chase you. You could both get what you want."

Gunnar blinked at her. "He'll probably choose Reigo anyway." He kicked a rock down the short cliff, staring out at the sea. Then he seemed to make up his mind and turned to her. "Do you want to see something?"

"Depends," Ilme said. "What sort of something?"

Gunnar glanced past her at the longhouse. "You came about the rift. The rune stuff. I know where it is. We could go see it now." When she hesitated, he added, "You're done, but they're going to go late into the night. If you didn't know. He's got to drink a lot of mead."

"I don't think Master Endel knew that either," she said. "Is it far?"

Gunnar gave her boots an appraising look. "Dunno. You live on the island. Nothing's far to you. Are you gonna give up if it's too far?"

"Are you going to make me walk five leagues to see a quarry?"

He grinned at her. "Oh, it's better than a quarry. But you have to climb."

✦ ✦ ✦

Ilme was sweating by the time they reached the top of the cliff, the light growing orange with the setting sun. Several times she had nearly asked to turn back, but the chance to see the rune essence cache before Master Endel was too precious. And if she could bring back information—good information—she might have a little more reprieve.

Ilme looked back the way they'd come—the longhouse and the camp full of torches seemed so tiny. "How did you find this place?"

"Egg hunting," Gunnar said. "Seabirds nest in the cliffs. Come on."

This high up, snow still crusted the rocks where the shadows lay deep and unshifting. The sweat on Ilme's skin chilled quickly and she pulled her new green cloak closer around her shoulders as she followed Gunnar up a path that curved around the next steep rise. It came out into a flat field, the snow lying like lace over patches of green-grey grass. Ahead, there was a dark crack in the earth.

Something in Ilme shivered, something very unlike the cold.

Ilme peered down at the crack in the earth. "How... How big is it? The cave or... what is it?"

"Come on," he said again, reaching back to take her hand, and for a moment he felt so much younger than her, so very far from where she stood. "Just follow me," he said, seeing her discomfort. "I'll go first."

Gunnar showed her where to put her feet, what to hold onto as she descended into the dark space. A faint, warm breeze gusted up from the cleft, like the breath of a giant beast and she thought of the demonic face in the longhouse and wondered where its likeness had come from.

"Do you have a light?" Ilme asked.

He snorted. "You don't need one."

That shiver built inside her as she descended one careful drop at a time, as if something were stirring deep down, waking from dormancy. It was unsettling—like dark things in the water, and no one to name them. Ilme liked safety, liked predictability. That some unnameable part of her was reacting to the strange cave felt terrifying.

Maybe it means there's more down here than Master Endel thought, she told herself. *Maybe enough to take some for yourself.* That would certainly gain her a reprieve…

The light above shrank quickly as they descended, a tiny window to the world… but then the darkness didn't close around her the way she'd expected. A faint light filled it, a soft, hazy glow that came from all around. When she stepped off at last to land at the bottom of the shaft, she found she could see Gunnar without any trouble.

And every inch of her skin felt as if it were humming.

"What is that?" she asked, her breath coming too fast. "What's doing that?"

"You're not scared are you?" Gunnar asked. "You shouldn't be. I'll protect you. I can… I think I could kill it. If I had to." He straightened, shoulders out, as if he could be as big and muscular as his brother.

His words didn't make sense, but Ilme couldn't order her thoughts to tell him so. She laid a hand against the wall of the cave, the same way she might lay a hand against the flank of a strange horse. The wall was only stone, but that unsettling *tug* on her senses didn't stop. "You don't feel it?" she whispered.

"Feel what? The rock?"

You need to get out of here, she told herself.

A cold voice that sounded like her aunt's cut through the worry. *If you leave without seeing anything, you will lose your chance. That jarl will never let you near here if he has his way.*

Gunnar grabbed her arm again, tugging her into the dim tunnel. "Come on. Don't be scared."

It was like a dream. The strange glow in the air, the winding crack of a path, the boy with his golden hair shining like a torch as he pulled her on and on. The echoing pull in her, like a song she didn't know, in a tongue too ancient and foreign for her to understand. And Ilme, who had always been so skilled at knowing what lay in others, who read their fears like a book, suddenly wasn't sure of what lay inside herself.

The path opened into a wide cave, faint sounds of water echoing off walls lost in the dim light, and Gunnar stopped, dropping her hand and setting his own hand on the knife he wore. The stones here glimmered, pulling harder on her. No… not all the stones. She reached for one, felt the lurch in her chest toward it. It was smooth, silky almost, but so ordinary looking.

"Is this—" Ilme began. But Gunnar hushed her and pointed into the shadows.

In the darkness, two great luminous eyes opened, and something massive shifted into motion. She knew she ought to run, ought to flee that huge creature, but shock stopped her feet from responding.

"Well," a great, sonorous voice said, strangely gentle despite the size of the speaker, "you've returned, little mortal. And what have you brought? Hm? I hope you don't mean her as an offering—not at all to my taste." A deep rounded laugh boomed through the cave as the speaker pulled itself forward.

Ilme blinked, unable to make herself speak. It was a frog—a frog as tall as a longhouse, patterned with pale green and dull purple patches, a droplet like a tear outlined in vibrant blue between its bulging eyes.

A guardian, Ilme thought feeling lightheaded. *A Guardian of Guthix.* They were said to stand over places of great power, great magic. Wardens of the sleeping god's gifts.

I could kill it, Gunnar had blustered. And all Ilme could think was, *I wouldn't let you.*

Gunnar didn't answer the creature, suddenly shy. It hitched itself forward, gazed on Ilme. "Welcome, child," the guardian said. "I am Zorya." It blinked its enormous eyes at her. "Have you come to reclaim the gifts? To bind again the rune magic?"

"How... How long have you been here?" The question was out of Ilme's mouth without thinking—what did it matter? What should she say?

Zorya's throat pulsed, a deep thrum echoing in the cave. "Mmmm, long enough. Because here you are, Ilme! And here I am, and here are the gifts of Guthix! You have great works ahead of you!"

"How... How do you know my name?" she said, small and fragile. This was not Master Endel's tricks, not the jarl's show of power. If the guardian knew her name, what else did he know?

Zorya thrummed. "Because it's your name, of course. Now: how much do you know about rune magic? Where should we begin?"

"I..." Ilme swallowed. "I don't think I'm the one you're looking for. My master—"

"Your master is not here," Zorya pointed out. "You are. But let him come—let them all come. After centuries of upheaval the world is in balance. Great changes are upon you! Humanity has been like the tadpole in the mud, but now it must grow its legs and take to the new world! I am so very delighted to be able to help you."

"Is that what the god wants?" Ilme asked, numbly.

Zorya's thrumming held a strange hesitancy this time. "I think so," he said.

Ilme shivered once more and hesitantly picked up one of the stones. "Is there enough rune essence to make a difference?" she asked. "How much did our ancestors cache here?"

Zorya thrummed again, and this time it sounded like laughter. "Oh dear, little mortal! This isn't some dead soul's treasure trove. It is the gift of Guthix."

Ilme shook her head. "I don't understand."

The enormous frog lowered itself, to peer at her. "This will be a mine. A rune essence mine. A vein that runs deep into the ground. I have guarded it against the legions of Bandos and the seeking hands of worse things. There is enough here to carry you through the next age and beyond. Enough to teach humans magic once again."

For a moment, Ilme couldn't breathe. A whole cave of rune essence—she thought of all the spells Master Endel and Azris went on about, the way things had been so long ago. Rune essence condensed into runes: if you didn't have to scrounge and steal scraps of essence, if you had an endless mine, then you could have endless runes, endless magic.

She imagined herself, briefly, casting walls of fire and dizzying spirals of magic to tangle an enemy's mind. She imagined herself, facing down her aunt—

"It's customary," the guardian went on, "to bring an offering." The pale sac of his throat pulsed again. "I'm rather fond of sweets," he added, meaningfully.

✦ ✦ ✦

When Ilme closed her eyes, Zorya's own great glowing eyes filled her mind, the resonance of the rune essence humming in her core. All through the night and the next days, all the way back to Falador on the other side of the mountains.

Master Endel hadn't been pleased that she'd gone off with the jarl's son, but when she brought tales of a Guardian of Guthix and the rune essence she'd taken from the cave, his manner changed. When he went to inspect the cave with Jarl Viljar, Endel expressed no surprise at the guardian, none of the excited energy he'd shown when Ilme showed him the rune essence she'd found. Polished, superior, and distant as he visited Zorya and offered up a thick, syrupy bean cake unasked. The guardian had been delighted.

"I will manage this for you, jarl," Endel said. "You need not trouble yourselves with the rune essence." There would be agreements of passage for Endel and his agents to travel to the mines, of course, the hospitality of the Wolf Clan bought with goods and gold.

"Master," Ilme asked, when the Wolf Clan's cold shores had faded from view. "What happens if they realise that it's not all Moon Clan mages coming for the rune essence?"

Master Endel waved this away. "The Moon Clan is very busy and hires outlanders to cart stone. What's surprising about that? Anyway, if the jarl finds out, he will still be glad to have this dealt with and all the weapons and goods it gained him. He has his eyes on the northern island clans and what he can gain there—he's not looking south." All the polish was gone, his voice bouncing with energy and joy. "Lord Raddallin will be pleased," he told her. "We have quite a homecoming ahead of us."

TWO

———◆———

L ord Raddallin was not pleased.

"Explain to me how this is to our benefit," he said, once Master Endel had told the story of the voyage and rune essence discovery, reading Ilme's report almost word for word. "You have been gone for months in search of runes, and what you have to show for it are…" He gestured at the rune essence laid on the table before him. "Rocks?"

Master Endel was not a large man, but beside Raddallin, all men looked small. The lord of the Donblas Tribe was a tower, a fortress unto himself; even when sitting down at the table in his war room, he filled the space and drew the eye.

When Raddallin claimed he would raise Asgarnia from the ashes of history, that he would unite the tribes into a kingdom, it seemed inevitable.

To some people, Ilme amended. There were many tribes in Asgarnia, many warlords, and even though Raddallin had succeeded in uniting the Eastern tribes against the nearby kingdom of Misthalin, he had not exactly brought all of them to heel. But, tucked as she was in the shadows of the war room, she said nothing of the sort.

"Not rocks, my lord," Endel said. "Rune essence. A mine of rune essence that only we know about. With this, you can make *new* runes—any runes. It is far more valuable than a cache of already crafted runes."

In the court of Falador more than anywhere, Ilme thought, Endel's ambition stood out, like grasping vines trailing all his words. He had come from Misthalin, frustrated at its rigidity and disinterest in his studies toward rebuilding rune magic, and found Raddallin full of all the ambition Misthalin had thwarted in Endel. It bloomed in him now, as if Raddallin were the sun.

She knew Raddallin was not dismissing Endel—he wanted to understand how things had changed, wanted to meet Endel where he stood now: excited about what seemed like a pile of gravel. But others at the table were not so open.

"Have you not already sources of power to craft runes from, Master Endel? Is that not your entire role here?" Beside the would-be king, Adolar, Grand Master of the White Knights, was a pale reflection, all bone and blond hair. He wore his armour as if he were born in the shell of it, and all the severity of his god, the bright lord Saradomin, seemed to radiate from his expression and clamp down on his shoulders in equal measure.

Ilme could imagine Adolar in another place, another time, ruling a tribe of his own with a fist of iron. *Not a great ruler,* Ilme thought. If Adolar stood in Raddallin's place, no ambitious wizards or powerful chieftains would turn toward him—he was all he would ever be. He would hold the reins of power firmly, but never be so bold as to reach farther, to ask *what else can I achieve?* Where Raddallin drew the eye and stirred a need to be recognised in people, Adolar merely made one feel as if he were already disappointed in them.

Adolar's White Knights had once been fully allied with the Kingdom of Misthalin. Once, the White Knights had counselled Lord Raddallin to swear fealty to Misthalin, to its strong army and its clever wizards scraping magic from the corners of the world.

Another sign Lord Raddallin is destined for something greater, Ilme thought, continuing to write down the words they were speaking from the dim corner of the room. *The Saradominists have bent to him.*

Master Endel turned to Adolar. "The sources I have cultivated are dangerous and difficult to draw from. And, more importantly, limited—they can only be what they are already. If you want fire, I must take from the fire. If you want ice, I must take from the ice.

"But the rune essence is unbound—it can become anything. It can become many things at once. Easily and without risk."

Adolar poked at the grey and unassuming stones. "This?"

"Think of it," Endel said, eyes only on Raddallin. "Your armies supported by spells of power in combat. Falador, not just a warlord's holding but a fortress of renown, a shining city on the mountain built as easily as breathing."

"Easily as breathing? That would be quite something," a woman's mocking voice called out, and dread poured over Ilme.

Sanafin Valzin, Marshal of Falador, First Lord of the Kinshra, swept into the hall like a raven diving from a high perch. Her boots clicked against the stone floors, her scabbard clinking against her sword belt. Her close-cropped black hair shone like a feathered helmet, her blue eyes gleaming in a pale face. Where Adolar was severity itself, Valzin was all deftness and motion. Here was the reason Raddallin defied Misthalin and the White Knights. Here was the first spark in the fire of his campaign. Here was the fire that lit Raddallin's own ambition.

She made Ilme's nerves itch, never certain what Sanafin Valzin was really doing.

In this, Ilme was not alone. Adolar looked up with a scowl and Master Endel did not turn but made fists of his hands. Only Raddallin seemed at ease, a little annoyed perhaps, but also a little amused.

"Sana," he chided, "you're late."

"My apologies, my lord," she said, dropping into a bow. "Your Black Knights were busy teaching the Massama Tribe to mind their manners."

"Lord Keerdan?" Adolar said frowning. "He said she would accept Lord Raddallin's rule."

"Yes well, it also seems he's saying similar things to Moranna of the Narvra. To the tune of a hundred fresh spears. Pity he doesn't have them anymore." She grinned at Adolar. "Don't fret. Now we're even. I missed the Kareivis Tribe talking to Misthalin, and you missed Lord Keerdan. And you—"she turned to Endel,"—have been busy."

"Since you did not join us, Marshal," Endel said stiffly, "you shall have to wait until I am finished—"

Valzin waved this away. "I read your scribe's notes on the way up. I have the broad strokes." She smiled at Ilme, who froze, suddenly visible. That, too, was Valzin—you never knew what she was watching. It benefitted Lord Raddallin to have an ally that moved in unexpected ways... but there were rumours among the White Knights that Sanafin Valzin wasn't loyal to Raddallin, but to the dark powers of her god, Zamorak.

If that were the case, Ilme thought, Valzin was doing an admirable job of obscuring herself. To all eyes, she was Raddallin's most devoted advisor. By all actions, too. And you could find the same whispers about the White Knights, their loyalty to their god and Misthalin, their former master. There was gossip everywhere.

"Now then," Valzin went on to Endel, "you don't have a way to create runes from the rune essence. You need the altars built in ages past to create so much as a puff of wind, let alone this easily-as-breathing crafted city-fortress."

"I was getting to the altars," Endel began.

"Perhaps get to them now," Raddallin said, patiently.

Endel blew out a breath. "To bring this plan to fruition, we would need to find and restore the rune altars—sites scattered across Gielinor which were said to be built by a Fremennik seer called... Never mind. You don't need the history. They were built and later destroyed. Restoring them is the most efficient, safest, and simplest way to create new runes. We have detailed information on how they should work."

"Once they're fixed," Valzin said.

"Where are these rune altars?" Raddallin asked.

"Scattered across Gielinor. We would need to mount an expedition to locate them."

"For which you need an escort," Valzin said, taking a seat at the table almost directly opposite Ilme, on Raddallin's farther side. "Which is to be? Adolar's knights or mine?"

Adolar stiffened. "I dislike the idea of taking forces away from Falador. The White Knights are needed *here*."

"Interesting," Valzin said. "That suggests to me at least, that you *also* have concerns about this venture. I can't imagine you saying the Kinshra should be sent after sources of great magic if you thought they were likely to be everything Endel's hoping for."

Adolar sniffed. "You're baiting me, Marshal."

"Never," she said, with a smirk. She turned to Endel. "What you're looking for has been lost and probably broken for ages. If you find the altars, do you know how to fix them?"

"I don't expect it to be complex," Endel said, eyeing Grand Master Adolar as if weighing Valzin's casual accusation. "Their locations are referenced in Julyan's *Catalogue of Ancient Advancements*. Once we locate the first, I have records of the rituals done in ancient times to create them—restoration will take some experimentation, but it should fall together."

"And then you can make runes?" Raddallin asked.

The barest hesitation, and then, "I believe so."

"But you don't *know*," Adolar surmised.

"To be fair," Valzin added, "how *could* one know if they have the ability to refresh a lost holy site?" She smiled at Endel, and it put Ilme in mind of a cat. "One presumes if you find the altars, if you repair them, you can convert all your rune essence into runes—ideally ones which will grant runes to speed along Lord Raddallin's unification?"

"Of course," Endel said. Then to Lord Raddallin, he added, "There are some... vagaries in the records. Each altar attunes a specific elemental energy into the runes. I am confident in the locations of some of these, while others will be a gamble. And some will be unreachable until we can make diplomatic arrangements."

"I find fire is convincing to an obstinate enemy," Lord Raddallin said. "Do you have that one?"

Master Endel gave Raddallin the same pinched smile he'd given the jarl when he'd asked after his weapons. "Of course, my lord. Although there are a great many other options besides fire."

"You have the floor, wizard," Raddallin said, gesturing expansively at the room. "Regale us."

Here at least, Master Endel was on firmer ground. He described runes of air and earth and ice, of body and mind, law and chaos, and more. He enumerated spells that could be crafted out of their combinations—blasts of fire, yes, but also spells to befuddle foes or sap their energy. Spells to make short work of building outposts and new fortresses. A world where almost anything was possible.

"Is the mine secure?" Adolar asked. "What happens when the Fremennik decide they want to reclaim access to the essence?"

"They won't," Endel said firmly. "They are well paid, and they aren't interested in magic. The jarl has his mind on his own unification schemes and there are many other clans to pursue."

"For the moment," Raddallin said. "But that's nothing we can't manage. Especially if we have the runes to work with."

Valzin eyed Endel speculatively. "Is it possible that Moranna of the Narvra has rune magic we don't know about?"

Endel frowned. "If she has, she's not used it."

"Would you know?"

"What are you getting at, Sana?" Raddallin demanded.

"A mere notion," Valzin said, with a shrug. "It sounds as if it can do almost anything. And we do find Moranna ahead at every turn."

"Not every turn," Raddallin said.

"My apologies," she said. "She's still a thorn in your backside that no one can pull. You can't deny that. So how is she managing it?"

No one answered—no one knew. Of all the warlords of the Asgarn, Moranna of the Narvra Tribe seemed the most insurmountable obstacle to Raddallin's rule. They called her the Ghost of the Eastern Reaches—what she lacked in valuable territory, she made up for with an uncanny ability to be everywhere at once, whispering in every Marshal's ears, driving back every ally Raddallin made.

Ilme dipped her quill in the inkpot, slow and thoughtful, her stomach in knots.

You are observant and obedient, her aunt had said. *And very easy to overlook—no one thinks much of a girl your age. This is how you will earn my protection. Lord Raddallin is trying to destroy everything we stand for—and if you want to live, you will help me see to it that the Narvra aren't crushed under his ambition.*

She will want to hear about the rune essence mine soon, Ilme thought, adding another line to the record. She recalled Zorya's great glowing eyes and the tear of Guthix, and his warning: *Humanity has been like the tadpole in the mud, but now it must grow its legs and take to the new world… or it will perish.* No hint of what the right path would be for Ilme herself. No sense of how she would weather this.

She glanced up at Raddallin. Moranna might be the stronger warlord—the Narvra might be more intimidating, perhaps even more skilled as warriors, but she had come to think only Raddallin could be a monarch. Moranna reacted—not acted. In the absence of this foe, she would not dare anything so great as unifying the tribes. She would pretend it was in their nature to stay, small and fighting. Moranna was incapable of imagining a united Asgarnia.

But Moranna would never admit it, and Ilme would never speak it—that would only lead to her destruction. She studied the rune essence laid before Lord Raddallin, the strange tug of it quieter now that she'd gotten used to it. She imagined how different things would be with the powers Master Endel had described in her hands… She could make Moranna forget her, make herself invincible, burn down her aunt's war room…

Endel rapped his knuckles against the stone table, startling Ilme. "If we access the runes, we can ferret out her sources. That much I can promise."

"Or simply lay waste to her armies with fire and ice," Valzin said cheerfully. "As you said, easy as breathing." She grinned at Ilme, her blue eyes dancing. "Make sure you write that down."

✦ ✦ ✦

Ilme reviewed her notes with Master Endel in the war room once the others had left, adding a few matters that had occurred to him.

She finished and looked up to verify that she could go. Master Endel was studying her, a thoughtful expression on his face.

"There's another matter we should discuss, I think," he said. "You can feel the magic in the rune essence?"

She'd already admitted as much when she described the essence mine, so there was no point in lying to him just to get away quicker. "Yes, Master Endel."

"What exactly do you notice?"

"A… It's a sort of… pulling? Like someone has a hook in me? In the core of me? But it doesn't hurt."

He winced at her clumsy explanation. "Azris tells me she caught you several times onboard the ship, standing beside the crates. She was rather sure you were stealing it."

Ilme flushed. "No, master, I just… I was curious."

"Curiosity is an excellent attribute," he said. "I wonder if it's more."

"I don't know what you mean," Ilme said, feeling her cheeks burn. There was nothing about standing near the essence just to feel that deep-down pull that would lead Endel's back to Moranna and her connection to Ilme—was there?

"I think," he said, kindly now, "that you find yourself *drawn* to it. That perhaps you have an inborn knack. Have you considered studying to be a wizard? If all goes well, Lord Raddallin will be pressing me to expand our ranks. And quickly."

Ilme startled. "Oh."

Endel frowned. "That's not a yes."

It wasn't. How could she agree to study with him if they were already aware Moranna had a spy inside Falador? She might want very much to be a wizard, she might have felt the draw of the rune essence. But if she studied with Master Endel she would no longer be invisible.

And if she said outright that she didn't want to learn, he would know she was lying.

"It's a great honour," Ilme said. "I... May I think about it?"

"Of course," Master Endel said. His gaze flicked over her once more. "You ought to come with us when we hunt the rune altars, anyway. I need to recruit a colleague or two, and I have no confidence at the moment in Eritona's stomach or Azris's temper. You at least reliably present well."

"Thank you," Ilme said, wanting to be anywhere else at all. "I'll... I'll take these notes and copy them over now."

She needed to send a message to her cousin, to meet him in the usual place and figure out what she ought to do. She hurried up to her quarters, a little room tucked behind the one Azris and Eritona shared, to copy her notes and write a letter.

When she passed the other room, the door was ajar, and Azris's voice slipped through the crack.

"Honestly, you should have seen her: swanning around like she was some sort of emissary from Varrock."

"Ilme?" Eritona's high, sweet voice was nothing but puzzlement. Ilme could imagine her, dark hair in braids, pretty face in a frown. "She's so quiet. I can't imagine."

"Oh, she was anything but quiet," Azris went on. "Acting like she was Master Endel's favourite new apprentice and sweet-talking the jarl's son."

Eritona coughed, her illness still lingering. "Be fair. She was *supposed* to be acting as if she was Master Endel's apprentice."

Ilme shouldn't have stood outside the door listening. There was nothing to discover here—even if she twisted and prodded at it, the most useful thing she could find was that she'd annoyed Azris enough to notice her. And since Master Endel was already noticing her, this was a much smaller problem.

"No one *asked* her to be all smug about it," Azris snapped. "Gods at the barrier, if Master Endel brings her along..."

They just don't like you, Ilme thought. *And that's fine. You're not their friend either.* She pressed on to her own rooms. She had letters to write.

✦ ✦ ✦

Ilme waited a few days before taking her secret stockpile of notes and slipping from the settlement, the chaos of knights preparing to ride a cover for her own departure. The White Knights of Saradomin would ride the border of Raddallin's territory: Falador and the holdings of warlords now pledged to him or replaced by his favourites. The Kinshra, the Black Knights of Zamorak, would be sent to rout the monsters in the mountains to fulfil a promise to Raddallin's allies there.

Ilme asked the least frazzled stablehand she could find to saddle her a horse, and waited outside, watching the divided knights prepare for travel, throwing sneers at each other when they thought they wouldn't be seen.

She thought of the Fremennik, of how she'd seen only that stone dedicated to Guthix, the first god, and their strange worship of it—and the hints of demons in their art and manners. By comparison, Falador teemed with gods, even gods whose worship opposed each other. People went to multiple shrines for multiple problems, but even if they only revered one god among many, they had to accept the field was crowded.

The Kinshra, for example, followed Zamorak, and praised him as a god of change and improvement, while the White Knights worshiped Saradomin, whom they held as a god of order and wisdom, and called Zamorak a god of evil. The Kinshra disagreed and considered Saradomin a god of control and punishment.

That both served Raddallin so faithfully was a testament to the warlord's force of personality and skill.

Perhaps it will be enough to stop Moranna, she thought.

But then what? Ilme took out the notes she'd tucked in her bag and considered them. She could leave them here. She could destroy them. She could refuse to help Moranna any longer. She could go back to Master Endel and tell him she would love to become a wizard, and sit beside Eritona and Azris as an equal—

Except she would be confessing to treachery, and it wouldn't just be Moranna she had to worry about, it would be Lord Raddallin. And every time she imagined what the great man would do if he knew, it only got more fearsome. She was trapped.

She remembered Zorya's words again: *After centuries of upheaval the world is in balance. Great changes are upon you! Humanity has been like the tadpole in the mud, but now it must grow its legs and take to the new world.*

And one sixteen-year-old girl would be ground to dust by such changes.

No, she thought sliding the papers back into the bag. Maybe it made her a villain, but she couldn't confess and stay safe. She had to convince Moranna to let her come home before anyone figured out who she was.

The stablehand brought her a horse, a dappled grey gelding, and she climbed into the saddle, heading toward the western gate in the palisade around the settlement.

Instead she found Grand Master Adolar, frowning at her from the centre of the path. Her pulse climbed up her throat as he caught her horse's bridle and pulled her to a stop.

"Yes, sir?" she said.

"Ilme, is it?" he said. "Where are you going? It's dangerous to ride alone."

"To the druid's grove, west of here, sir," she said. She lifted the green flag that hung on the horse's reins. "I have pilgrim flags. I've never been bothered when I ride with them."

"You are Guthixian?" he asked. "There's a chapel in the fortress.

Why not go there?"

"I find I'm out of balance," Ilme said, not even a lie, "after the trip north. And while the chapel is a lovely place for contemplation, it isn't the same. I would grow dizzy walking the path around the sanctuary the way I do the druids' grove."

Adolar did not move. "Doesn't it trouble you that you worship a god who asked not to be worshipped?"

Ilme bit her tongue. *Doesn't it trouble you to worship a god who only wants you for your obedience?* Regardless, this wasn't the trap Adolar thought it was—she didn't worship Guthix in the same way Adolar worshipped Saradomin, prayers and offerings and asking for things. She would have said no one worshipped Guthix that way, but for the Fremennik of the Wolf Clan and their calls for blessings on their weapons.

"Master Endel has given me permission, sir," she said instead. "Excuse me, if I don't leave now, I won't be back before sunset. Unless you require a scribe?"

Grand Master Adolar only eyed her suspiciously. Ilme did not monitor her expression—it would look the same if she were anxious about him knowing where she was going or if she were anxious about being kept back. But he didn't dismiss her, and until he dismissed her—

"Adolar!" Valzin called, striding out of the palisade exit, ignoring the stares of the White Knights. "Messenger just came in saying there's trolls on the border with the Kareivis tribe. That's your path but our task—shall we make it a race? Whoever takes the most trolls before the threat is routed wins?"

Adolar turned to her, any suspicion he had for Ilme washed away by irritation at Valzin. "You'll do no such thing!" he burst out. "Take your Kinshra to the mountain frontier where you've been sent and stay out of the White Knights' way!" He started toward his own horse, shouting orders to his lieutenants. Ilme nudged her horse forward, but cast a glance back at Valzin, who offered her a jaunty salute.

As if we were comrades, Ilme thought, and wasn't sure what that meant. She imagined Valzin knowing she was Moranna's spy and keeping her secret—for a price. Imagined her handing Ilme gladly to Raddallin. Imagined her never noticing, Ilme was so far beneath the Marshal. Any of these were possible—Valzin was a riddle.

She rode for a few hours, before the forest grew thick and she turned onto a narrow path through the trees, slowing as she neared the grove. She tied the horse to a post in a clearing meant for such visits, before continuing on foot.

The druid's grove parted the woods around a circle of standing stones, a large craggy stone decorated with the tears of Guthix at their centre. She nodded to the druids standing near the entrance to the circle, and they regarded her without speaking. There was an uncanny stillness in this place, a preternatural quiet that seeped into Ilme and settled her anxious energy. The rune essence, Endel's offer, Valzin's curious gaze, Adolar's chastisement, and even the reason she had come here in the first place, all washed through her. If there was magic in this place, it didn't pull at her the way the essence did—as Adolar said, Guthix had no presence. The god slept and left his followers to their own fates, free to use the gifts and tools and wisdom he had left behind.

For good or ill, she thought, walking a circuit of the stones, letting her concerns settle and fall away as she walked. The druids paid her no mind as she did. They were simply sharing this same quiet space.

Ilme had circled the grove three times when she saw the man she'd come to meet standing in the trees—her cousin, Martyn. Only a little taller than her, his brown hair and beard reddish in the dying light. He wore a peaked hood and a quiver at his hip. As she passed him, he fell into step beside her, arrows rattling as he walked.

"What news, cousin?" he asked in a low voice. "You've been gone a long time. We could have used the information the Kinshra would coerce the Massama tribe to Raddallin's side."

"I told you before," she said back, just as softly. "Master Endel required me to travel north with him. I was in the Fremennik lands."

"Looking for runes," Martyn said. "Did you find them? Did you bring them here?" He reached up and tugged the strap of her scribe's kit.

All the pages waited in her bag, all the secrets she'd uncovered— the lie Master Endel had told the jarl, what things the Fremennik believed. The tensions in Lord Raddallin's court and the battles won and lost and predicted to continue. Everything she owed Moranna.

She yanked the bag back. "Of course not. And we didn't find runes, we—"

Her cousin sighed. "What a waste of time."

Ilme almost told him, no, they'd found something better—a mine of rune essence, a guardian deep under the earth—and stopped herself. What would Moranna do if she knew about a newly discovered guardian?

The temptation to withhold information from her aunt rose again in her, and with it, a righteousness: she was protecting something greater.

Maybe you don't have to tell Martyn everything, Ilme thought.

But she would have to tell him *something.* "Endel wants to keep looking for more sites that might be key to rediscovering rune magic. He'll have knights with him when he goes, but it isn't settled when or how many."

"Might be a good chance to attack," Martyn mused. "Mother's looking for a way to hit him on Falador's southern border. Take out some of those weaker allies. What else?"

She shook her head. "That's all I know."

Martyn grabbed her arm, hard. "We both know that's not true. You're a nosy little crow, always picking out treasures. And you owe this family. You wouldn't want to anger Mother, would you?"

Ilme had been twelve when her father had died in one of Moranna's battles, the younger brother who'd served his warlord eagerly and capably. Her mother had been no warrior to step into her husband's place. She had instead warned Ilme of the dangers of the Narvra chieftain's household and taught her to be wary and circumspect. That hadn't saved her mother from a fever, and suddenly, Moranna's court became all the more dangerous to an orphaned Ilme. Martyn and his siblings had made a sport of cornering Ilme with his friends, twisting her arm, pinching her skin, laying threats around her like traps. *If you don't... If you do...*

So she'd gotten very good at moving quickly and quietly, at knowing what people wanted and needed.

It became the way she survived within the court of the Narvra Tribe. She played her cousins off each other, making herself the least interesting target. She knew how to ply adults to her side and how to be where she couldn't be hurt. She cultivated a self that was quiet and obedient and said all the right things. And it worked.

Until Moranna noticed her.

"*You* will be my spy," she'd said. "You will be the key to stopping Raddallin's mad plans. Or," she added, "you will die."

And now Martyn could corner her even here in the grove of Guthix where she would normally expect to be seeking peace and steadiness.

Ilme drew a deep breath. "The Kinshra have punished Lord Keerdan. I expect they will force him to step down and be replaced by Lord Raddallin's niece and loyal retainers. He has also noticed my aunt being alert to all his actions. Marshal Valzin has already suggested there's a spy." She glanced back at him. "It's only a matter of time before they realise it's me. Tell Moranna I need to come home."

"Is that all you're worried about?" Martyn chuckled, releasing her. "Valzin is a troublemaker. No one with sense listens to her. Give me what you have, and I'll give you something to protect you."

Ilme rubbed her arm, fishing through the papers with her body blocking the bag. She deftly separated the pages from the Fremennik expedition from the others—Moranna wouldn't know where the mine was or what was within it—and handed these to Martyn as they came around the central stone, hiding them from the druids.

He rolled them into a tube and slid them into the quiver, then pulled out a necklace with a huge orange gem hanging from the braided leather strap. "Here."

Ilme took it. The gem shone with an eerie iridescence. "What is it?"

"Protection," he answered. "If you get caught and they try to drag you off, you trigger it and you won't be such a little mouse for at least a little bit. Don't lose it. And don't set it off unless it's an emergency. It's some God Wars artefact. You're very lucky she's loaning it to you."

Moranna wasn't going to let her come home.

"And keep it under your shirt," Martyn added, as he turned to go. "If you're going to be tagging along on Master Endel's hunt for rune altars soon, you need to make certain they don't catch you."

THREE

◄◆►

Master Endel's expedition didn't get underway until after winter had passed. Long months of strikes and retreats among the knights, of Azris and Eritona poring over maps and ancient texts, of huddling in the dark, waiting for the weather to turn again. Long months of Ilme riding out to the druid's grove, sometimes to meet Martyn and sometimes to sit with her guilt.

Ilme thought of Gunnar and the Fremennik, of how cold winter must be when their summer still had such a bite to it. She thought of Zorya and wondered if the frog guardian slept beneath a mud of rune essence while snow piled on the mine's entrance.

Some days, she went into the room where the rune essence was stored, waiting for the altars that would shape it into runes, and simply sat with the feeling of magic pulling on her soul. It had stopped feeling dangerous at some point in the dark, snowy winter, and begun to feel right and comfortable. She let herself imagine a future where she was not bound to flee back to Moranna, death on her heels. Where she could be Master Endel's third apprentice and craft runes like wizards had done in ancient times. She wouldn't worry about how a changing world might chew her up if she could wield runes—she indulged perhaps too long in that fantasy.

There had also been the arguments about who would accompany Master Endel on his expedition. He'd enlisted another wizard, a Saradominist called Unaia, who was an accomplished summoner in addition to studying theories of runecraft. She brought a pair of apprentices, a young man and a woman. Azris would come of course, and Eritona, and Ilme—which gave Master Endel the advantage on apprentices, in appearance at least.

For protection, they would need soldiers. Sanafin Valzin had volunteered to go along, leading a faction of her Black Knights.

"I find myself intrigued," she'd said. "And can't a knight also wield magic? Maybe I'll take to it like a second sword."

"Just what we need," Adolar said dryly. "Zamorakian spellcasters."

"You should get used to the idea, Sir Adolar," Master Endel said. "To my knowledge, runes don't have a creed requirement. We shall soon have Zamorakian spellcasters, and Saradominist spellcasters, Guthixian spellcasters, Armadylean—and Lord Raddallin will find a use for every one we can."

Gritting his teeth, Adolar agreed, but Valzin had only smiled. "Maybe you can debate the matter while we find out if it's possible."

Adolar could not ride with them if Valzin was gone—one of them needed to remain with Raddallin, he argued—but he could send a detachment of White Knights, to keep the wizards safe... and to be sure that the Zamorakians didn't gain any particular benefit from being there first.

The knight who led the detachment out of Falador was a lieutenant named Perior, a broad-shouldered man with dark skin and a close-cut beard. He eyed Valzin and the Kinshra with particular mistrust, but kept his knights in tight formation and was polite, even friendly, to the wizards in his charge.

Neither Azris nor Eritona seemed to enjoy travelling. Azris complained often about the insects, and how they ought to have sent the knights out to find the rune altars first, and then sent the wizards to fix them once that was done. Eritona fretted over the many people in their party and their discontent with each other. She settled for checking on Ilme so incessantly that Azris finally told her to give it rest and stop annoying the scribe.

Unaia's apprentices, Zanmaron and Chloris, did not introduce themselves to Ilme, nor deign to speak to her, but she was glad of them all the same. It was much easier to slide out of notice with the apprentices jockeying for position with each other.

"Perhaps we should divide our forces," Unaia suggested when they had made the long trek around Misthalin to the frontier beyond the town of Varrock. She was a striking woman, with thick reddish hair, a pointed chin, and a Saradominist's desire for hierarchy.

"I wouldn't, Master Unaia," Valzin cautioned. "There are things hunting in the wilds that you could waste a great many runes on, and still die in the process."

"And we don't know what's required," Endel added. "The old ways needed circles. Great rituals of wizards acting in—"

"Very well, Master Endel," Unaia said, briskly. "You are in charge of this expedition. Lead on."

✦ ✦ ✦

In the nights beside the campfire, while Master Endel, Eritona and Azris sorted through the runes they'd brought and what ancient talismans might help, Ilme secretly recorded the budding tensions between the wizards and the full flower of dislike between the Black and White Knights.

The world is in upheaval, she wrote. *Great changes are upon us.*

In ages past, the priests of Guthix said. the upheaval had been the God Wars. *While Guthix slept*, the hymns all went, *jealous gods came to Gielinor and walked its surface, demanding fealty from the humans and primacy from their fellows*. It had ended only when Guthix had woken and put a stop to the fighting, banishing all gods beyond the edicts, before reminding humanity he would not save them again. Therefore, the priests said, they must solve their own problems. They did not mention the possibility of someone like Zorya, Ilme noted.

Watching the Saradominists and the Zamorakians divide into their own little encampments, Ilme wondered if the gods were content, now, to fight by proxy through their worshippers. She wondered if that left the followers of Guthix to stand up and stop them. She didn't think that was possible.

But there was Sanafin Valzin, yet again, striding through the camp as though there weren't a single thing stopping her, saluting her knights and Perior's alike with a jaunty insouciance.

She's up to something. Find out what, Martyn had said, the last time Ilme had met with him, when she'd told him Valzin herself was coming along. *Everyone knows she came down out of Misthalin to raise up a king in Asgarnia. Probably chose Raddallin because he's easiest to manipulate.*

That was the simple answer—the answer one drew from the situation as if looking at a chessboard. But a knight on a gameboard could only take a predetermined path and it moved with only one purpose. You could predict a gameboard.

Ilme mentally listed what she knew about Marshal Valzin as they rode. She had come from Misthalin, the second child of a duke. She worshipped Zamorak, which Ilme suspected her family had disagreed with, as full of Saradominists as Misthalin was. She fought with a sword. The Kinshra obeyed her eagerly. Ilme had never seen her lose her temper.

She *had* seen her make a lot of other people lose theirs. Valzin had a way of dancing around a debate that made it seem as if she had no firm opinion except a desire to prove others wrong—

No, Ilme thought, returning to the argument about the rune altars. It was as if she was testing each of them. Making them shore up their arguments. Baiting them into... what?

Had Valzin gotten what she wanted here? Ilme couldn't say, and it rattled her.

Perhaps, she thought, all Valzin wanted was to help realise Raddallin's goals—a united Asgarnia, a kingdom where no god was ascendant.

◆ ◆ ◆

In the long-slanting light of late afternoon, the party of wizards, apprentices, Black Knights and White Knights came to a river, deep in the lands of the Asgarnian Tribes. The waters were swift with spring melt, but the bed was wide and shallow. On the other side lay a dark forest.

"We should make camp," Unaia called. "Wait until daylight. Who knows what's in those woods?"

"The rune altar should be very close to here," Endel said, scanning the thick trees on the other side.

"And it will still be there come morning—" Unaia began.

Valzin cut her off. "What are we looking for?" she asked Endel.

"A ruin," Endel said. "It might be no more than a pile of rocks. But once it would have been a stone circle." He pulled out the map, scrawled with notes. "The river has moved its course since the altar was established—it's been eight thousand years, so it won't be on the banks as it once was. But there should be remains. It isn't *just* stone."

"Then how are you *sure* it's there?" Valzin asked.

"I'm not," Endel said, simply. "But if it isn't, then we ought to turn back because all my maps will be suspect, and I'd rather know that as soon as we can."

"This is preposterous," Unaia said.

"Then it will feel a great deal more preposterous once we've forded the river and your pretty robes are wet," Valzin said, brightly. "So I hope you find a way to make your peace." She directed the Kinshra down to the water to test the fording, and once a few experienced riders had made the passage, the others led the wizards' horses into the water. The White Knights and Unaia had little choice but to follow, and then they were in the wild edges of Misthalin.

The forest closed around them, green and shadowed. The call of birds, hidden in the thick canopy, rose and fell as they passed through, the path narrowing as the trees crept closer. The party narrowed with it, a line of knights ahead and the three apprentices behind. As the light faded further with the approaching dusk, Ilmic scanned the woods as she led her horse, searching for signs of the rune altar—or riders from any of the tribes opposing Raddallin.

"Do we know if the Kareivis Tribe has scouts here?" Eritona whispered, as they came up to a clearing where Master Endel was conferring with Master Unaia and Sir Perior. "What do we do if they've been tracking us?"

"We don't get caught," Valzin whispered back, appearing as if from nowhere behind them. All three green-cloaked girls jumped. "Hand your reins to Helmut there—your master wishes to go hunting."

"I *hate* when she does that," Azris muttered, handing over the reins. "How does she *creep* like that in armour?"

While a handful of knights set to picketing the horses and setting a camp, Master Endel led the wizards and the bulk of each force into the dark woods. Ilme walked close beside Azris and Eritona, wishing she had stayed behind as the setting sun set long shadows reaching through the wood.

But then... she felt it.

Azris did too—Ilme saw the girl turn to the left, just as she felt the pulse of magic, a lure pulling against her soul, beckoning her off the path. Ilme grabbed Azris's arm, and the other young woman whispered, "What is that?"

"What is what?" Eritona whispered, edging up close behind them, peering into the dense ferns. Something low to the ground moved away from them, sending a shiver through the plants.

"What is *that*?" Eritona repeated, grabbing Azris as well.

Ilme stepped forward, watching the movement, feeling the strange pull beyond it, as if the thing in the ferns were being tugged along as well. "I think... I think it's the rune altar," she said.

"Rune altars can't move," Eritona said, almost a squeak now.

"Guthix wake and save us," Azris swore. "She means the... the *pulling*... thing. Not the rabbit or whatever it is." She raised her voice. "Master Endel! I think it's over here!"

The ferns ahead of Ilme stopped trembling. She took another step, and whatever it was came toward her now, weaving back and forth. She bent, trying to peer through the underbrush.

"What is it?" Master Endel demanded, coming up beside her. "Is it *here*?"

Whatever was in the ferns suddenly sprinted away... racing in the same direction she'd felt the faint tug from. "I think it's that way," she said, pointing after the trembling ferns.

Master Endel began wading through the undergrowth. "Come on, girls. It's not going to come to us."

If Ilme had not known what the pull of magic on her soul felt like, she would have passed the fallen rune altar by. In a clearing surrounded by towering elms, the tumble of huge stones, their surfaces obscured by shaggy moss and layers of dirt, might have been nothing more than a perch for wolves, a hollow for a badger, a dark nest for creeping insects.

But it wasn't.

Master Endel broke through the underbrush, striding up to the stones. He pulled away the moss from one facet, revealing a broad flat surface, split by a ragged crack. Weathered marks of words in an unfamiliar language had been carved deep into the surface.

"This is the altar," Master Endel murmured. His hands smoothed the stone surface of the table, running down the edges of the crack. "Something's badly damaged it, but if we can… If it's possible…" Unaia came to stand beside him, peering at the carvings.

Azris peered over his shoulder. "Do we have the runes to repair it?"

"Here," Master Endel said, thrusting the bag of runes he carried into her hands. "Let me read this and you can make a tally."

Ilme's tongue stuck in her mouth. A vortex of magic flowed into the fracture, only instead of feeling like rune essence did—an insistent dragging on her soul—this felt more like the world was narrowing into a passage that she wanted more than anything to race down. The *table* was broken, yes, the altar damaged, but the power was still here.

"It's not broken," she managed, almost panting.

Master Endel frowned at her. "What was that?"

"We could try sealing the cracks with rune essence?" Azris went on, running her hands over the crack in the stone.

"The markings," Unaia began.

"Air," Ilme whispered, her thoughts overflowing with the answer, like a great wind sweeping everything else away. "It makes air, it wants air."

Master Unaia looked at her, eyes narrowed. "How did you—"

She broke off with a sharp cry, her eyes widening at Ilme's feet. Ilme looked down and saw a small, purplish creature sniffing at her boot. It looked like a dragon out of one of Master Endel's history books, only it was the size of a cat.

"What in the shattered planes is that?" Perior said, drawing his sword.

"Leave it!" Master Unaia said.

"Ilme," Master Endel said sternly. "You need to back away very slowly."

The little creature looked up at her and made a chirruping sound, its wings unfolding and tilting expressively. Ilme took the directed step back, but then crouched to offer her hand to the little dragon to sniff. Its forked tongue shot out and grazed her knuckle roughly. The wings tilted again, and it made another little gurgle.

Abruptly it became still, its neck extending as it searched the forest. It scrambled up the ruins of the rune altar and sprang into the air, flapping up into the canopy of the trees.

Behind Ilme, Valzin let out a sharp hiss, gesturing for silence. In the shadows, something clattered, reminding Ilme of Martyn's arrows rattling in their quiver as he kept pace with her. The sound echoed from the opposite side of the clearing: a signal and response. Ilme backed into the altar, searching the trees.

"Get it working," Valzin said. "We're about to have company." She pulled her helmet down, obscuring her face and gestured first to her lieutenant, and then the leader of the White Knights. Perior hesitated, but hearing the strange rattle again, and then the unmistakable crunch of leaf-fall deep in the brush, he nodded once, and made the same silent gestures to his knights. Black and White, they formed a circle around the trio at the rune altar, swords ready.

"Do we have air runes?" Azris asked.

"Be quiet," Master Endel said, eyes still on Ilme. "I'm thinking."

"The carvings say the same," Unaia said. "This is the air rune altar. Whatever your scribe is talking about, she's got that much right."

A spider dropped from the high branches, as large as a carthorse, its legs sharply pointed around an abdomen marked with blazes of red. It rattled its mandibles, and the sound echoed again, not just from the farther side, but all around, the spiders circling their prey. Azris screamed, grabbing onto Ilme's arm. Her other hand shot into the bag of runes, grasping wildly.

The knights' gazes turned upward, tracking the spiders as they dipped lower, and so the wolves creeping from the forest verge came terrifyingly close before a Kinshra knight spotted them and sounded the alarm. One moment, everyone was tense, preparing—the next came the chaos of battle, the clash of metal, and the screams of beasts and humans alike.

Unaia shoved her apprentices to one side, pulling a scroll from her belt. She shouted strange words and the air split, a praying mantis the size of one of the wolves tearing free of empty space. The summoned mantis hooked a spider out of the air with scythe-like legs.

"Make a circle," Unaia snapped, pointing at the apprentices. "You, you—on my left. You—" her finger moved from Azris, hesitating for a moment, before indicating Ilme, "—and you, on my right. Endel—"

"Flip them," he said, over the shouts and snarls. "Azris to her left, boy, you come over here. Guthixian, Saradominist, Guthixian, Saradominist. Ilme, get out of the way." He snapped at Azris. "How many air runes do we have left?"

The clatter of a chitinous body made Ilme spin around. One of the terrible spiders had dropped down behind the knights. It seized the praying mantis in its jaws and snapped its head.

Two sharp legs struck the Saradominist apprentice's shoulders, their hairy tips snagging in his cloak as the spider slammed him down. Zanmaron thrashed, trying to kick at its high, arching abdomen and Ilme could only stare, a scream caught in her throat.

The necklace, she thought desperately. Moranna's amulet would keep her safe—but could she trigger it to save him?

A sword broke through the spider's head with a crunch and a splatter of ichor. Its legs pulled in, as if clutching its heart, and the apprentice's blue cloak ripped with the sudden movement. Valzin stood over him, shining sword dripping gore.

"Get it working!" she bellowed at Endel and Unaia.

Endel yanked the young man to his feet, shoving a gleaming white stone the size of a coin into his hand. "Stand here, don't move."

Wolves charged the wall of knights. Another spider dropped swiftly from the trees, sinking poisonous fangs into a Black Knight distracted by a snapping wolf. Every wizard and apprentice, Ilme besides, took one of the air runes, made a circle around the ruined altar. The vortex of magic kept spinning, the altar's ragged magic still hungry, and nothing changed. Hot panic washed over Ilme.

Endel threw something to her, and she caught the gleaming weight from the air. It was a talisman, etched with curling lines, a blessing of air. "Hold that!" he shouted. "Azris, we need something to repair it!" Endel barked. "A rune of law or a rune of the astral."

"There's only one law rune!" Azris cried back.

"Dig in the bottom!" Eritona wailed. "There's at least three."

Another spider dropped—this one larger, dripping poison, right onto the altar, right into Unaia's reach. The master brought her rune up and with a grunt of effort, it crumbled in her hand. The stone became a swirl of light, hazy as fine wool wrapping around her hand, and then it burst out with a gust of wind strong enough to blow the giant spider back, crashing down between Ilme and Unaia's male apprentice.

It twitched, starting to turn over, one scythe-like leg stabbing down beside Ilme. She raised her own runestone, but with no training, no sense of how to access the magic bound inside, it was only a gleaming rock, the talisman a pretty weight.

But a weight would do: she smashed the talisman into the spider's leg, snapping it at the joint.

"There's a girl!" Perior crowed, as he and another of the White Knights descended on the beast.

"Ilme, pay attention!" Endel snapped. "Azris, give me the law rune, and hold my staff. We're trying again!"

A howl echoed through the woods, something deep and terrible, far beyond the beasts that prowled the grove and harried the knights. Something animal deep within Ilme locked her joints, told her to freeze, to hope that the howling beast didn't see her.

From the shadowy woods burst a wolf like a siege engine, powerful muscles bunching under moon-silver fur, teeth to rival the swords of the knights of both orders. A thing out of children's stories, of nightmares—*don't go into the wood alone, or else you'll be devoured and no one will ever find your bones...*

It had heard the noise of the attack, the shouts of the humans, and known there was prey to seize.

"Cut it off!" she heard Valzin shout, and saw the White Knights nock arrows in response. "Don't let it reach the altar!"

The wolf didn't so much as flinch as a dozen arrows peppered its side, seizing Unaia's female apprentice by the head as it bounded past, snapping her neck and tossing her into the scramble of the smaller wolves and spiders. A Kinshra knight struck it across the face with his sword, and the great wolf responded by slamming its head against the knight, sending him sprawling. It wheeled around, turning back toward the altar, its huge yellow eyes on Ilme.

An air rune in her left hand, the talisman in her right, Ilme dimly realised that even if she could force the rune to work for her, it wouldn't be enough to stop the monster now surging toward her—no, right on top of her—

A burst of light and heat and an invisible rush of magic screamed around her like a whirlwind. A weight yanked against her neck—and the wolf yelped as if hit by a weapon she had no hands to carry, cringed, pulled free of her. Knights sprang forward, black and white, putting a wall between her and the suddenly weakened creature.

The air rune slipped from her fingers as Ilme reached up and touched the necklace, now hanging free of her blouse and burning to the touch. *That's what it does,* she thought numbly.

"Ilme!" Master Endel roared. She turned back to the circle, scooping up the dropped air rune and stepping back into place. The others thrust their runes forward and Ilme matched them, shoving both the talisman and the rune into the broken stone.

Ilme felt the vortex *stop.*

The magic began to spin in the other direction—but to speak of *direction* or *spin* felt insufficient. It was as if the axis of some invisible world had shifted inexorably. A gust of wind swept around the circle of them, from nowhere blowing nowhere, and every hair on Ilme's skin stood on end, a brightness searing out of the weathered carvings of the altar—

Ilme blinked and the chaos of the battle was gone. The circle was gone. The forest and the ruins and the wolves were gone.

She stood high on a flat-topped hill overlooking an endless forest on a warm, moonless night. The stars glittered overhead, peeking through the last glow of a setting sun. There was no river, no city in the distance, no monsters and no knights. Before them stood the altar, or perhaps its undamaged double, the carvings clear and sharp, stones erect and neatly balanced—an altar surrounded by menhirs. The vortex of the altar wheeled like a falcon in the summer sky, a slow winding in that felt as if it must take a century to trace the path from edge to centre. Like the circuit of Guthix's sacred grove, her soul longed to follow it.

"Where are we?" she breathed. She looked around, but only saw Azris, clutching Master Endel's staff and staring at her with eyes wide as coins. "Where is everyone else?"

Azris swallowed, searching the strange and silent forest beyond the hill. "You had the talisman," she said. "I had the staff. Hopefully they'll still be alive when we return." She turned back toward Ilme, and asked, "Where did you get that necklace?"

Ilme's breath caught and she reached up to cover the amulet. "I… It was just a gift."

"A gift? I've never *seen* an amulet do something like that. It has to be ancient. Who would give you that?" She narrowed her eyes. "Did you steal it?"

"No!" Ilme burst out. "It's… My aunt gave it to me."

"Your aunt," Azris repeated, stepping toward her. "You told me you were an orphan."

"I am."

"But you have a mysterious aunt giving you amulets that stun monsters?" She tilted her head. "Master Endel doesn't know you have that. He would have wanted to examine it. Which means I don't think you've had it very long. But you don't *go* anywhere except the grove…"

Ilme grappled for a lie that would appease her sudden suspicions, seize the truths of Azris and bend them away from her secret. "I…" she faltered. "I have a lover. Nobody can know."

Azris snorted. "A lover who meets you in the druids' grove and gives you priceless artefacts? You'd have to be courting Raddallin himself for a gift like that. Or another warlord…" She trailed off, eyebrows raised. "Or," she said, eyes growing sharp, "another *warlord*. And maybe you weren't lying. Maybe your aunt gave you that because *you're* the spy Moranna of the Narvra sent."

In all Ilme's fears and imaginings, Azris had never been the one she expected to discover her. The terror came as if from nowhere, a crashing wave to sweep her from her feet.

"That's ridiculous," Ilme said, scrabbling for something else. "Master Endel's right about you. You're so afraid of anyone—"

"Maybe we'll just *ask* Master Endel," Azris interrupted. "I'll bet if anyone knows the provenance of that necklace it's him. Or maybe Master Unaia. Or Marshal Valzin."

Ilme raised her hands, the talisman still clutched in one. "Please. It's not like it seems."

"Is that what Lord Raddallin would say?" Azris asked, her sureness, her cruelty growing. "Because I think he'd be *very* disappointed in you."

She licked her lips, thinking, and nodded toward the altar. "You had a strong reaction to the rune essence. And you were the one who noticed the ruins first, who knew they were bound to air." She held out the bag of rune essence. "Take this. See what happens."

Ilme folded the bag against her chest. "Are... Are you..."

"Do it," Azris said. "We're going to bring Master Endel back his runes."

Ilme turned, shaking and set the bag between her feet. "I don't know."

"No one knows," Azris said scathingly. "But you've been happy to pipe up with your *feelings* all through this, happy to stick your nose into Falador's business and pass it along to your warlord aunt."

"I didn't..." Ilme began. *I didn't want to. I didn't tell her everything. I hid the rune essence mine, especially.* But there was nothing she could say now that mattered. She reached into the bag with both hands, cupping a double-palmful of the rune essence, pale grey and already pulling toward the slow vortex of the air rune altar. She drew a slow deep breath and blew it out, trying to quell the shaking, trying to dispel images of exploding magic or rifts that spilled demons.

She shut her eyes and concentrated on the current of magic, pushing aside the terror building in her. She thought again of Zorya, and the guardian's warnings... but also the reassurance: this was the goal, after all, the reason the rune mine had appeared. They were *supposed* to seize this magic again.

For long moments, she just stood, her hands full of rune essence gravel, her mind trying to grasp hold of the power emanating from the altar. She had no training, no sense of what she was supposed to do—and yet Azris knew her secret. How could Ilme deny her anything?

That frantic need, that *want* searing through her soul suddenly overtook all her thoughts—and it was as if something in her shifted, aligned to the spiralling power of the altar, and poured through her palms into the rune essence she clutched there, sucking all her breath with it.

And then it faded.

Ilme gasped, unable for a moment to fill her lungs or unclench her fists. The rune essence pressed painfully into her hands. Azris stepped up beside her and unpeeled her fingers.

It wasn't rune essence she held any longer: in each palm lay three shining rune stones, the bright nested arcs that marked them as air runes shimmering in the strange ambient light.

Azris gave a short, barking laugh and picked one up, holding it gently as a songbird's egg. She grinned and for a moment, Ilme felt light as if they'd managed something together—they'd done it. They'd achieved the extraordinary. They'd made runes again.

Then she stumbled, dizzy.

"Runecrafting," Azris said, primly, "is difficult to do well. Theorists say it takes a little of your soul when you do it."

"Is that what it is?" Ilme said, her voice shaking.

"Maybe," Azris said, still admiring the runes. "As I said, just theories. But you'll recover." She turned the rune over in his hand with one thumb. "I think Lord Raddallin doesn't need to know anything just yet. So long as you keep taking care of this for me."

"This?" Ilme asked.

"You make the runes," she said. "And I'll take the credit. I'm the apprentice after all. It's not my fault you seem to be born with an aptitude."

Ilme swallowed. "And if I do this, you won't tell about Moranna?"

"We'll see." Azris nodded at the altar again. "Finish the rest of that bag. We have a long way to go to find all the altars."

FOUR

THE EIGHTH YEAR OF THE REIGN OF LORD RADDALLIN
OF THE DONBLAS TRIBE
THE THIRTEENTH DAY OF THE MONTH OF FENTUARY
THE ASGARNIAN FRONTIER, THE ROAD TO FALADOR

Ilme knew two things as they continued their expedition to find the rune altars. The first was that she was exceptionally lucky if the price Azris charged for keeping her secret was runecrafting. She'd been correct that Ilme recovered quickly enough—more so the more she did it. The sacrifice of runes, the circle of wizards—the techniques that had repaired and re-established the Altar of the Air had served to reawaken the altars of air and earth, fire and water. Master Endel was easily persuaded that they match the first success and put the talismans in Ilme's hands, the staff in Azris's.

In the strange space of the rune altars, Ilme could pretend none of the outer world mattered. There was only the rune essence, the pattern of magic flowing into the altars, and the quiet sacrifice of her core self to make something so full of power and possibility—she could imagine not wanting anything else. She stood in these strange pocket-worlds—an archipelago in a limitless sea, an island on an ocean of lava, a cavern of folded stone—and let herself forget everything that threatened her.

But it always ended: she would hand the runes over to Azris, and they'd return to Gielinor for Azris to proudly present 'her' hard work to Master Endel.

And this was the second thing Ilme knew: the price for Azris's silence would not *stay* runecrafting.

"I've been thinking," Azris said, as they stopped for the night on the road to Falador, having left the mind altar and its cracked entrance a few days before. "That necklace you showed me? I think I should have one like it."

"What necklace?" Eritona asked. "Did you bring it with you? Can I see?"

Ilme swallowed, terribly aware of how many people were in earshot—Master Endel and Master Unaia going over the maps, Unaia's apprentice and Valzin beside the fire. Perior and a handful of White Knights sorting supplies. "The... um—"

"Her aunt gave it to her," Azris said, cheerfully, her dark eyes glittering. "It's lovely. You can get one for me, surely, can't you, Ilme?"

"I... I don't know."

"Oh, Ilme. I believe in you." Azris gave her a winning smile. "Set up the tents, would you?" And she swept past to go talk to Master Unaia's remaining apprentice.

Eritona turned to Ilme. "I don't like saying it, but she can be absolutely beyond the Edicts. Is your aunt a gem cutter or something?"

"It's complicated," Ilme said, which would only pique Eritona's interest, so she dropped her voice and nodded after the other apprentice. "Is Azris romancing Unaia's apprentice?"

"Zanmaron?" Eritona followed Ilme's gaze to where Azris was possibly flirting with the Saradominist apprentice. "I don't know.

Do you know? She *has* been talking to him an awful lot."

Ilme shrugged. "Strange place to be starting something up."

"I don't know about that," Eritona said. "My cousin's village was attacked by giants and she came out of it engaged. Not to a giant," she added. "To the girl she was hiding in the cellar with. Fear makes you impulsive, I think. And Zanmaron's not bad looking. Although I don't like his beard."

Something in the branches chirped overhead, and both of them looked up. "Huh," Eritona said, peering into the bobbing branches. "It's your little friend again."

Sure enough, the little purple dragon creature dropped down out of the tree, gliding around the two young women to land on a rock on the side of the road where the woods began. It cocked its head at Ilme and chirped once more.

Valzin came up beside them. "What is it you're doing that has that little beast following us for miles and miles?"

"Nothing," Ilme said. Then, "Nothing I know of." But the little dragon had appeared each time they found another altar perching in the snags around the water altar, hiding in the grass beside the earth altar, squeaking at her from the palm trees as they dug down to the fire altar.

"I think you have a pet then," Eritona said.

Ilme walked toward the little dragon, hand out to let it sniff, the way she would approach a dog. But when she came within a foot of the creature, it launched itself up into the nearest tree and sat chattering at her as if scolding her for having the nerve.

"I *don't* have a pet," Ilme said.

"Well if it follows you all the way back to Falador," Valzin said, "it's either your pet or we'll have to do something about it. It bit one of my knights." She smiled at Ilme. "A moment of your time, scribe?"

Ilme cursed to herself. She snatched the folded canvas from the supply pile. "I have to put up Master Endel and Master Unaia's tents."

"I can do it," Eritona said, scooping the fabric from Ilme's arms. She grinned at Ilme. "I'll get Azris to help and I'll see what I can find out about her secret." She winked and turned away.

"There you are," Valzin said. "Walk with me?"

Ilme's heart was in her throat and it was all she could do not to seize the amulet hanging under her blouse. "I have other chores—"

"There comes a point," Valzin said, "where I cannot in good conscience let you continue as you have been. It's becoming…" She sighed, as if Ilme had disappointed her. "…a bit embarrassing."

"I don't know what you mean," Ilme lied.

Valzin put an arm around her shoulders, steering her toward the path that led through the woods, down to the stream. "It means I'm going to give you some advice. The good word of Zamorak, if you like."

"No thank you," Ilme said. "I follow Guthix. I don't need an ev—" She bit off the word *evil,* knowing it was imprudent. "Another god."

But Valzin laughed. "Who told you 'evil'? Adolar? Unaia? Would you rather follow a god for whom the many shades of the world can be distilled into black and white?" She dropped her voice as they walked into the woods. "I always thought it was a bit of a broadside target, calling the knightly orders White and Black—as though we are the opposite of them. I prefer 'the Kinshra.' It means 'the ones that spark the fire'."

Soon the quieter sounds of the camp faded, the burbling of the stream filling in the space between the shouts of knights. Ilme kept searching the trees, all her nerves expecting an ambush.

"Zamorak is a god of change," Valzin said as they walked, as if Ilme had asked. "When you really look at the world, what truth is there beyond the inevitability of change? When we cling to stability, to satisfaction, all we are cultivating is disappointment because nothing ever stays as it is. Kingdoms crumble, gods fall. Lords rise—or fall. Magic… reveals itself."

Ilme kept her eyes fixed on the trees, something in her chest knotting into itself, as if the energy of her soul were trying to swallow its own tail. "The world is in upheaval," she recited. "Great changes are upon us."

Valzin laughed. "Your guardian. Here's the secret: great changes are always upon us."

"Is that… Is that why you left Misthalin?" Ilme glanced sidelong at the Marshal and found the other woman watching her with a smirk.

"Great changes?"

"That… I've heard the Church of Saradomin is the more common faith in Misthalin," Ilme said carefully. "And it seems like change would mean disrupting the order they… prize."

"They like things just exactly as they are," Valzin agreed. "Stay in your role, excel where you're placed, don't make trouble. *That* is why Lord Raddallin has my support, if you're wondering."

Ilme frowned. "Because Misthalin told you not to make trouble?"

"Because change is constant, ambition is the only way to guide that change. And Lord Raddallin's ambition reaches far," Valzin added, conversationally, "much farther than someone such as, say, Moranna of the Narvra."

At her aunt's name, Ilme felt her pulse surge, the weight of the amulet hanging against the bony centre of her chest too heavy to ignore. Maybe she wouldn't have time to worry about Azris's demands.

But Valzin continued, no longer looking at Ilme, "Asgarnia—a united Asgarnia—feels like a demon's promise, all steam and illusion. The warlords will never unite, not without a great ambition and a greater effort. Raddallin has the vision and the wherewithal, and now the allies to do just that. To move his lands from fractious tribes into a glorious and powerful kingdom. Why wouldn't Zamorak bless that? Why wouldn't Saradomin, come to that— order among chaos. It's right out of his prayerbook."

Ilme said nothing. Valzin's words felt like a winding trap impossible to shake. She was young, but she was not such a fool that she couldn't spot the tripwires. They stopped at a short drop where the path slid, overlooking a steep embankment and the stream below. From here, one could scramble down the crumbling dirt to the water... or fall hard enough to break a bone.

She made herself look at Valzin, who watched her as if waiting for something. "He's fortunate to have your support," Ilme said.

"And yours. Every person counts. Any ally might be the stone that turns the enemy's charge," Valzin said, holding Ilme's gaze with her cold blue eyes. "Azris has been keeping you awfully close lately."

"I'm... We're friends."

The Marshal nodded as if this were something wise indeed. "I've been rattling on about my faith. Maybe you should do me the same turn. Tell me," she said, "what does Guthix teach about treachery?"

Cold panic poured over Ilme. There was no hoping for safety—Valzin *knew*. She made fists of her hands, waiting—the amulet had triggered itself last time, would it do so again?

"I... I believe Guthix wishes mortals to find their own path," she said. "To... seek peace and balance. He would probably suggest forgiveness and recompense, if necessary." She swallowed. "Is that what you mean?"

"In a way. Let us say," Valzin went on, nodding at the drop, "that you are... trapped. Pinned, perhaps, against a steep cliff. A dark pit. Your enemy stands before you, threatening to push you in unless you do as she says. What then is the wisdom of Guthix?"

"I… That you should… should perhaps negotiate?" She thought of the Fremennik, their warlike worship. "Maybe you should use the weapons at hand to free yourself."

Valzin laughed, loud and brash, and Ilme felt her cheeks burn. "Is that not what Zamorak would advise?" Ilme asked.

"I don't think he'd find it an insult." Valzin smiled at Ilme, laughing, mocking. "Though it lacks vigour. But Zamorak's not here. Do you want to know what I would do? I would jump off the cliff."

Ilme was suddenly, terribly aware of the drop into the stream. "What?"

"I would jump off the cliff," Valzin repeated carefully. "You are trapped, unmoving. Nothing can change. You are prevented from escape, from fighting. This is intolerable—to be denied the chance for change to be forced to sit in your fear. Fear causes hesitation, and hesitation will cause your worst fears to come true. So what can you do?

"You can jump," she said. "See what it is you're afraid of. Take away that which they are holding over you."

Tell Raddallin you are spying for Moranna, Valzin did not say. *Azris cannot blackmail you if you take that away.*

But Ilme couldn't imagine anything so terrifying. How could Lord Raddallin forgive that treachery? What would happen if Moranna found out? If she held very still, moved very carefully, she could weather this, surely.

Valzin's mocking smile said, *You can tell yourself that.*

Below, the stream burbled over rocks and roots and the hard, hard ground. She could not hear a single person in the camp beyond, and now not even the birds filled the quiet forest.

"It doesn't concern you," Ilme said forcing herself to sound calm, eyes on the drop again, "in this example that the bottom of the cliff might be covered in... sharp rocks, or full of vicious wolves, or just be very, very far away. It could go poorly. And the... enemy might change her mind. Or weaken."

"Or she might push you in because she also finds her position intolerable," Valzin said. "I don't like leaving the reins of my life in another's hands. And I think here our gods would agree. You are the master of your own fate, the arbiter of your soul's yearning. To let anyone tell you otherwise is to spit in the gods' eyes." She patted Ilme, very gently on the shoulder, and Ilme tensed, digging her heels against the mud as she braced.

But Valzin only said, "Let's consider another puzzle. See how our gods align: a spy is sent into an enemy camp. She might be a threat to that camp, a blade to cut that army's hamstrings. But Zamorak would argue she is a blade with two edges. She knows a great deal about who sent her. She gets to choose which way she cuts.

"I wonder what would Guthix say?" she added.

For a moment, Ilme said nothing, did not even breathe. "I suppose he would say it is her choice. That she should do what is best for the good of all. That she shouldn't leave valuable tools to rust." She swallowed. "If such a person existed."

Valzin nodded as if satisfied. "Very wise. Blade or tool, you bear the responsibility for who wields you. I think we can agree on that much." She looked up at the trees. "You ought to trap that little dragon. If nothing else, you could probably sell it." And without another word, she returned to the camp, leaving Ilme in the quiet woods, standing beside the drop into the stream.

Ilme stood a minute, watching her go, not sure if she'd just been threatened or warned or invited into a conspiracy. Not sure if Valzin had just unburdened herself or spun a grand lie.

Not sure, really, what she was going to do next.

✦ ✦ ✦

Ilme rode back to Falador with a lump in her throat the size of a rune. Valzin's words turned over and over in her thoughts, waking her in the night, spilling out of her daydreams.

It was the only answer. It was madness to even consider.

She was trapped. She was the only one trapping herself.

When they'd left the camp by the forest stream, Master Endel had given her a few runes to carry in a pouch around her neck. "Just to see how you respond to them," he'd said, a little giddy. It was like being asked to transport jewels, rare as they were, but this, apparently, was how it had been done in ancient days and the opportunity to "start a wizard from the seeds of magic" was too exciting to pass up.

"I don't think you should waste this on me," she'd said.

"Nonsense," Master Endel had told her, closing her hand around the runestones. "Nothing's being wasted. If nothing comes to you before Falador, you can just hand them back. Just see what happens first."

She took a few runes out of the pouch as she rode, clicking them against each other as she rubbed a thumb over their smooth, faintly dusty surfaces. The rune markings shimmered, as if they'd been grown into the rock like crystals, but for all they felt in her hands like polished stones, the very centre of her *thrummed* with the knowledge they were nothing less than condensed power.

Ilme clicked an air rune against an earth rune—that should make a blast of energy and scouring sand if she somehow combined them. She nudged them apart again—she wasn't going to be a wizard.

Something dropped into her lap, startling her. She clenched a fist around the runes and yanked the reins back with the other hand. Claws sank into her legs. The horse shied and whinnied, and

Ilme dropped the reins to push aside… the little purple dragon creature. Trying to sniff the runes in her closed hand.

"Easy, easy," she heard Sir Perior soothe the horse. He'd dismounted and caught her mount's bridle quickly. "Are you all right?" he asked her.

"Yes," she said. "Fine."

The little dragon seemed unperturbed by the uneasy horse. It hooked one claw delicately over her wrist and pulled her hand down level with its muzzle, staring at her closed fingers. Ilme unfolded them slowly, so it could see the runes, gleaming like eggs in the nest of her palm. It nudged each with its nose, then sat back on its haunches and looked up at her.

"Rue," it said. Then it curled up on her lap, hooking its claws carefully into the fabric of her cloak, tucked its nose under one translucent blue wing, and went to sleep.

At a loss, Ilme looked at Sir Perior, still holding the horse's bridle. "What do I do?" she said.

"I think you have a pet," he said amused. "Maybe your master will know what it eats."

"He's not her master." Azris's voice came from behind her, sharp and superior. Her chestnut horse waited, switching its tail irritably. "She's just a scribe." But her narrowed eyes weren't watching Ilme, but the little dragon curled on her lap, and Ilme knew what Azris's next demand would be.

In that moment she made up her mind.

✦ ✦ ✦

When the walls of Falador appeared on the horizon, she had a plan brewing. It took four days before she was ready, but on that morning she strode into Raddallin's war room—not slipping around the edges, not making herself invisible. She thought of the unassuming essence, changed into gleaming runes and held that in her mind as she approached the table, chin held high, the little dragon she'd taken to calling Rue, perched on her shoulder.

"Lord Raddallin?" she said. He did not hear her, still bent over his maps. "Lord Raddallin!" she all but shouted.

He looked up—everyone looked up. Grand Master Adolar and all the White Knights against the far wall. Marshal Valzin and the twin Kinshra by Raddallin's chair. Master Endel and Master Unaia bickering beside the window, Azris and Eritona and Zanmaron, standing against the wall. Azris frowned, eyeing Ilme in confusion.

"Yes?" Raddallin said. "Ilme, isn't it?"

"I have lied to you," Ilme said, still too loud but not stopping, not trusting she could begin again if she faltered. "I was sent here by my aunt, Moranna of the Narvra, to gather information and to report your army's movements."

She had no more than said her aunt's name when Grand Master Adolar stiffened, gesturing sharply at the White Knights arrayed against the opposite wall. They swept in, a clattering of armour, to surround her. Rue hissed at them like a cornered cat, and Ilme reached up to squeeze his foot.

Ilme found Valzin on the other side of Raddallin, her blue eyes inscrutable. No ally there. Not yet.

"I was not willing," Ilme said, more loudly. "She is my guardian and I have no one else on Gielinor. I thought I had no choice. I didn't fight her—until now. Yesterday, I told her son, my cousin, that your army means to ride for Misthalin, to attack the city of Varrock in a show of force. That none of the other warlords know because you fear a traitor, but this show of force is meant to cow them."

She had sent the message to arrange a meeting with Martyn by bird the moment they returned, told Azris she was going to the grove to ask for another amulet and asked her to cover for her absence. Azris had agreed, covetous as ever, and Martyn had snatched up Ilme's frantic report with the same kind of greed. He didn't even ask her how she'd found it out.

"Perfect," he'd said. "This is exactly the opportunity Mother's been waiting for." And Ilme rode back ready to leap over the cliff.

In Raddallin's war room, Ilme held still as the knights drew their weapons, surrounding her. Raddallin frowned at her, his thick auburn brows furrowed together, but he gestured at the White Knights to hold.

"We have no such plans," he said.

"I know that," Ilme said. "But she doesn't. She has been waiting for the right moment to attack your southern holdings, and this would be it. If it were true. She wants this opening so badly, and her son wants to provide the answer even more. They won't question it. You could fall upon the Narvra while she rides, and eliminate Moranna."

Blade or tool, Valzin had said, *you bear the responsibility for who wields you.* Ilme had accepted her choices were narrow and narrowing by the day—sacrificing Moranna was inevitable, and the more she thought about her aunt's easy cruelty, the less conflicted she'd felt about the betrayal.

"This is the most transparent trap I've ever heard of," Adolar said. "You may be clever, but Lord Raddallin will not entertain such nonsense."

"It's not very clever if you can spot it so fast, Adolar," Valzin mused, still watching Ilme.

"You decide what to do with the information, my lord," Ilme said to Raddallin. "Ambush the Narvra, guard your southern flank, march on Misthalin, or simply stay in Falador and watch what she does. I have come to your war late, and I have been your blade as best I could, but I'm not a strategist."

"And you've been Moranna's blade for a great deal longer!" Adolar interjected. "You cannot entertain this—"

"Why do this?" Raddallin asked. "Why tell me now?"

Ilme thought of what lies would appease him—that she was swayed by his great rulership? That she was entranced by the dream of united Asgarnia? That she was awestruck and fearful of the promise of runes in his and his allies' hands?

But she knew none of these would be right, only the truth.

Or most of it.

Ilme nudged Rue onto the back of a chair, so she could remove her amulet. "Moranna gave me this as protection. It triggered on our journey and someone noticed," she said, carefully not looking at Azris. "I was likely to be blackmailed or turned in and I realised that, considering everything, Moranna hasn't earned my sacrifice. I don't want to sit and be fearful and wait for something to change, when I know in my heart what needs to be done."

Adolar leaned around Lord Raddallin to scowl through his moustache at Valzin. She shrugged. "You can't be disappointed if I gain a convert. It's a very compelling religion."

"She cannot be trusted, my Lord," Adolar said in a low voice. "She's a traitor—first to you and then to Moranna."

"By that argument," Valzin said, "you're a traitor to Misthalin. Really, we all are. And I can't imagine Lord Raddallin holding that against any of us."

Adolar spun on her, furious. "Are you behind this?"

"Behind what?" Valzin scoffed. "Setting Moranna up to fall? I wish. I'm surprised you don't wish it for yourself."

"My lord," Endel piped up, furious, "I had absolutely no idea of any of this."

"He didn't," Ilme confirmed.

"One wonders *why* you did not notice, Endel," Raddallin said.

"Because, my lord, I am a good scribe and a good reader of people," Ilme said boldly. "And though I am not trained, I'm a skilled runecrafter: I made most of the runes we brought back. You can ask Azris."

"Azris?" Raddallin asked. "Is this true?"

Azris looked as if she'd swallowed a toad, but she managed one stiff nod—she could do nothing else. Ilme wasn't lying and Ilme could easily tell Lord Raddallin she had been the one to blackmail Ilme.

Endel stared at her, astonished, calculations of how much rune essence, how many runes she must have crafted, seeming to drift over his face.

"Master Endel has suggested I study with him," Ilme dared. "That I would make a good wizard—I think he's right. If you would keep me. I don't wish to return to the Narvra. Especially now I've told you what Moranna's done. She would execute me, most certainly."

Raddallin considered the map spread before him, the markings of the armies, the fortresses, the paths they might take. "If you are going to make such a confession, my dear," he said at last, "then it will be complete. You will tell me everything you have passed to Moranna. You will tell me what she knows and what she doesn't."

Ilme nodded. "Of course. What my cousin has let slip, and what I know that she wants." She swallowed. "I could get him for you. Her son Martyn. He'd still meet me again if I asked."

Raddallin narrowed his eyes, a different set of calculations crossing his face. "You're very willing to betray your family."

"If they didn't want me to betray them, they had ample opportunity to kindle better warmth in me," Ilme said, her cheeks hot. "As it stands… this court has shown me more kindness and given me more to hope for than Moranna ever could." She sucked in a breath and before she could think better of it, offered her last bargaining chip. She tossed the amulet onto the map.

"There, my lord. You can lock me up," she said. "While you look into it. I won't fight. I can't," she added, a little ruefully. "Not without that."

Raddallin stared at the amulet. All his advisors around the table waited, unwilling to interrupt.

He sighed. "I will say this: you are very thorough. An attribute I appreciate in my allies." He nodded to Adolar and Valzin. "Put her in the chapel. Guard the doors."

"What about the dragon?" Adolar asked.

"Stay," Rue hissed, the word undeniable.

"Let her keep it," Valzin said. "This is going to take some time, after all. And all it does is nip."

White Knights and Black marched Ilme through the hold, into the wooden-walled chapel of Guthix tucked into its heart. Ilme went without protest, without revealing the vortex of fear and shame and dizzy exhilaration tearing her apart inside.

Fear causes hesitation, Valzin had said, *and hesitation lets your worst fears come to claim you.*

Ilme scratched Rue's scaly head. She had not hesitated. She had not dared, not for four days straight. Now she could only answer their questions, and wait.

FIVE

◆◆◆

It was meant to be a kindness, keeping her in the chapel under guard instead of in one of the damp and dirt-floored cells that prisoners were kept in, but it was still a prison. Light poured in through the stained-glass windows set into the wood-panelled walls, but she could not see out of them. The packed earth was oiled smooth, but there were no reeds softening its surface. Food came twice a day and she was allowed to walk the path that wound around the chapel's walls—there was nothing much else to do, except huddle up to sleep on one of the hard benches beside the doors. Rue mostly slept or tried to sneak past the guards, who always shooed him back into the chapel.

She thought of the god, slumbering deep below the earth, protecting Gielinor from interlopers and wishing only for the survival and strength of humanity. Did he count on them setting themselves against each other? Was she pursuing that peace choosing herself over Moranna, the Donblas over the Narvra—or was she making everything worse?

Valzin hadn't been wrong: things kept changing, whether you were just a person trying to figure out where to stand, or a god striding over the planet. New people claimed power. New threats arose. New opportunities unveiled themselves…

Unless Raddallin decides to execute you, she thought, staring up at the teardrops painted in a circle on the ceiling as she lay on the cold ground. That was still a definite possibility. Still a great change, she thought numbly. For her anyway.

Ilme had told the knights everything she could remember, what she'd kept from Moranna and what she'd shared. What Martyn had pressed her for and what he'd let slip. It was hours of talking that first night—a week? Two weeks ago? She'd lost count. The food came, the guards changed, she slept on the floor or the benches, and then she woke and she walked.

Moranna of the Narvra filled her thoughts—her fierce owl-eyed gaze, her shining armour and her steel-grey hair. The angles of Ilme's father's face softened in his eldest sister's scowl. Try as she might, Ilme couldn't imagine the warlord bending the knee to Raddallin. This wouldn't end in surrender.

I am fighting for our very way of life, Moranna had said fiercely, that night she'd declared Ilme would go to the Donblas tribe as a scribe. *Raddallin would sweep every tribe under his banner, crush our history beneath the heels of his heretical knights. He only gathers the followers of the interloper gods to erase us.*

Ilme thought of the White Knights and their prayers to Saradomin, Grand Master Adolar and his sneering attempts to proselytise. She thought of the little chapel to the desert gods tucked up against the mountain, miles from their homeland, and the odd little shrine on the forest verge, where people left offerings to a carving of a sacred plant. She thought of Valzin saying, "When you really look at the world, what truth is there beyond the inevitability of change? When we cling to stability, to satisfaction, all we are cultivating is disappointment because nothing ever stays as it is."

Nothing ever stays as it is, Ilme thought, walking the circle. That was true, and that was not counter to the belief that Guthix had brought people to the world in order to cultivate peace and balance. And she had to admit, Adolar wasn't wrong—they were stronger when they had order and expectations and listened to their histories.

Great changes are upon us, Zorya had said, the mouthpiece of sleeping Guthix. *Humanity has been like the tadpole in the mud, but now it must grow its legs and take to the new world... or it will perish.*

That made her think of Gunnar and the jarl, and the lie she'd help tell. She wondered if she told him the truth, spread out everything that had happened, whether he'd have the same urge to make something change, to break out of the shackles of his father's and his clan's expectations.

Ilme walked and slept and ate and prayed. She found herself inventing little prayers to all these gods—Guthix and Zamorak and Saradomin and even the odd harvest god down by the verge that she knew nothing about. The priests of the grove taught that none of them were here and now, not since the God Wars, but if she listened only to her footsteps, fell into the rhythm of the circuit, she found it didn't matter: *Please let there be a balance. Please let it change for the better. Please let there be peace after this. Please don't let me die.*

✦ ✦ ✦

One morning, she awoke to voices at the door: Azris arguing with the knights.

"First of all," she said, "you can't keep me from my devotions— that's just *cruel*. Second, I'm to bring her this, otherwise I'll be in trouble with Master Endel."

"Do your devotions in the courtyard," the White Knight said, holding out a hand. "Give me the book. I'll pass it along."

Through the doorway, Ilme could see Azris clutching a heavy book to her chest, a haughty sneer on her face. "Oh? Are you going to explain which chapters she needs to read based on how her studies were going on the road? Do you even *know* what she was studying? Just let me in!"

"She's a spy," the Black Knight began.

"And I'm *not*," Azris said, shifting the book under one arm so she could count off on her fingers. "I was born in the Donblas tribe, I hate politics, I don't ever leave Falador if I don't have to, and Master Endel told me to give her this book and those instructions. Let me in!"

The knights searched the book and, finding nothing, grudgingly agreed to let Azris see her. The other girl came in and took Ilme by the arm, marching her back to the far wall under the large stained-glass window and its circle of teardrops.

"Eritona won't shut up about who figured you out," she whispered. "She's asking everyone and no one's saying. Did you tell them it was me?"

"No," Ilme said. "Of course not."

Azris searched her face, as if Ilme were hiding something, as if she were Valzin nesting truths inside lies. "What do you want?"

Rue leapt up onto Ilme's shoulder. "I want not to be executed," Ilme said. "I want my own bed back."

Azris frowned. "I can't... I don't have anything to do with that."

"I wasn't asking you to. I'm not going to tell anyone you were blackmailing me, if that's the reason you came—what good would it do?"

This only flustered Azris worse. "But you *could*. Why wouldn't you? What do you want?"

Ilme sighed. "I have bigger problems than getting some kind of short-sighted revenge. Like being executed."

Azris waved this off, irritably. "No one's executing you. They've absolutely routed your aunt's army. Spent piles of runes throwing magic at them—there's about a thousand missives waiting for Lord Raddallin from all the tribes *and* Misthalin's dukes wanting to talk accords. The Narvra are done for."

"And... Moranna?" Ilme asked.

"I have no idea," Azris said. "They'll be back in a few days, I guess you'll find out. Mind," she added, "I *don't* think you're integral in all this—they would have done it without you. But it'll look bad." She shoved the book at her. "Here. Master Endel will want you to read this, so if he asked, I brought it to you so you could get started."

Ilme took it: *The Rune Mysteries Uncovered.* "What is it?"

"History of runecrafting and early spells," Azris said. "I can't give you a spellbook—the knights would throw *me* in here if I tried—but you won't look quite so stupid if you read that first."

✦ ✦ ✦

Three days later, she had read the book cover to cover, and at last the doors opened to admit Sanafin Valzin, filthy and bloodstained and grinning.

"Your aunt's dead," Valzin said. "I don't mean to sound heartless but... well done. When you decide to cut both ways, you really deliver."

Ilme stood, searching for the grief she ought to feel like testing for a broken tooth. But there was no sore gap, no jagged place where Moranna had lived in her, cold and distant and calculating. Nor was there relief at her absence, only a kind of emptiness, as if she were a vessel poured clean.

"Good," she said finally. "That means the balance has reasserted itself."

Valzin chuckled. "You're adorable, you know that?"

Ilme wasn't sure if that was a compliment or an insult. "What happens now?"

"Now," Valzin said, "we see about putting your actual skills to use."

"I can study with Master Endel?" she asked, hardly hoping.

"Of course," Valzin said. "And you can assist Lord Raddallin—King Raddallin, soon enough—in other ways. Your aunt wasn't wrong about you, I think. People don't tend to notice you're watching them. Maybe you just watch them while you study."

Cold poured over Ilme. "You want me to keep spying?"

"*I* don't," Valzin said. "Raddallin does."

"On Master Endel?"

"No, no. Endel's fine. But he has plans to recruit more wizards. We'll need to form treaties to let you all pass safely through Misthalin, Al Kharid, the waiting gods know where else. So, be friendly and watchful and… tell us what the others miss, before we have another situation." She smiled. "You've already made inroads with the jarl's son up by the mine, from the sound of things. That's what we want."

"What happened to *blade or tool, you bear the responsibility for who wields you*?"

Valzin blinked at her, no smugness, no triumph in her. "Yes," she agreed. "You chose. You chose Raddallin—I thought we were all clear on that much."

"What if I don't want to be anybody's tool?"

Valzin set a hand on her shoulder, guiding her out of the chapel. "Then I suggest you set yourself to studying those runes and gaining the sort of power that makes you the one holding the tools. So long as you are young and unskilled, you'll have to choose *who*, not *if*."

✦ ✦ ✦

By the time Ilme returned to the Wolf Clan's summer encampment the following summer, she felt as though someone new—someone better—had grown inside her skin.

"It's so *cold*," Eritona said as they looked out from the ship's railing, clearly a little giddy. "And this is summer?"

"It's warmer than it was last year," Ilme told her. "And it's warm inside the buildings. They're very smart about it."

The Wolf Clan's summer encampment spread down to the pebbly beach, great racks smoking fish for the winter all along the edge of the settlement. She did not bother pretending to be polished or superior or distant, and grinned as she hiked up the beach, following Master Endel, Azris, Eritona and the others, who would unearth the next shipment of rune essence. She knew now not to wait for the jarl's leave, and merely left Eritona to Azris to find Gunnar standing off to the side, watching Endel and Unaia intently as they approached the jarl and his two older sons. Ilme slipped up beside him.

"Hey. Do you want to see something?" she whispered.

Gunnar startled. A year later, he had grown an inch or so and his face was starting to narrow, but he was still caught in the slow climb of adolescence where nothing seemed to happen. At least this time he didn't scowl at her.

"You came back," he said dumbfounded. He looked at Rue, perched on her shoulder. "What is that?"

"Rue," the little dragon said, smugly.

"I met him while we were exploring." She took an air rune from her pocket, silvery and light, and Rue scaled down her arm to sniff at it. "He likes runes."

Gunnar stared at the little dragon and the rune it hunched over. "To *eat*?"

Ilme laughed. "No, he eats just about everything else. He's just interested in runes. I really want to see what he makes of the mine and Zorya. Can we go show him?"

Gunnar glanced back at his father, the jarl, all iron and bear energy, still holding forth with Master Endel and Master Unaia. When Gunnar turned back, a scowl had lowered itself over his face again.

"We should go now," he said. "Before anyone gets ideas. I think Zorya missed you. And you can tell me what's—I cannot *believe* a Moon Clan mage has travelled more of the world than me."

Ilme kept her smile rigid. As much as she wanted to tell him *everything*, Master Endel had reiterated the importance of maintaining the lie about being from the Moon Clan.

"There is no wisdom in risking our access to the rune essence mine right now," he had said. "'The Moon Clan' are better off than we would be trying to make new allies—that much was clear from my discussions with the jarl, and I'm sure this visit will only reaffirm matters."

"What happens if the actual Moon Clan come to speak with them?" Ilme asked. Endel waved this away.

"They haven't left their island in generations. They won't bother. And we will make certain the Wolf Clan are well rewarded for their assistance."

As they climbed the cliff to where the mine lay, Rue flying back and forth between them, Gunnar called back, "So, are you a mage now or something? A wizard?"

Or something, she thought. She pushed that aside. No one asked her to report on Gunnar anyway.

"My aunt... died," she said. "So I don't have to be a scribe anymore. I can learn to... I can take the tests to be a mage." She still hadn't figured out what initiates did to become mages, but Gunnar seemed unbothered.

"Leashed demons, you're weird," he said, reaching down to pull her up over the last rocks. "I don't know what your aunt has to do with you not learning magic, but I'm glad you don't have to do what you hate. Too bad you didn't get rid of the other initiate. Can you do any magic?"

"I only know a few little spells," Ilme admitted. "Do you want to see?"

"Show me when we get to Zorya." He stopped and turned to her. "Also you have to promise you won't turn into a self-important kind of wizard."

"I 'have to'?" she teased. "Who's self-important now?"

Gunnar made a face. "What about this: promise me you'll make What's-her-name, the other initiate, look stupid at least?"

Down into the mine they climbed, into the eerie light and the close, humid air. Rue tracked along all the walls, flying up to the edges of the ceiling, chirping excitedly to himself. Ilme drew a deep satisfied breath and felt… not her soul tugged in a thousand directions, but an aligning of herself—all of this could become magic. She could make all of this become magic.

"Well, who comes now, down into my burrow?" Zorya's deep voice rumbled out of the gloom. Ilme broke into a grin as she saw his great glowing eyes. "Ah, the little fire-starter!" he said with utter delight. "You've come back!"

Valzin's saying echoed in Ilme's thoughts, *I prefer 'the Kinshra'. It means 'the ones that spark the fire'.*

"Why did you call me that?" she asked, but Gunnar spoke over her, saying, "She's a wizard now, like you wanted. She has runes."

"And a little friend," Zorya said, lowering his head to peer at Rue. The dragon looked from Ilme to the guardian and back again, as if looking for confirmation of what it was seeing.

"You shouldn't tell the jarl," Gunnar added suddenly. "About being a wizard-seer-whatever. He doesn't trust your master and he'll probably not trust you, and then you won't be able to come visit. If anyone asks, just say you're a scribe."

The urgency in his voice surprised her. "I won't," she promised.

"I won't get self-important, and I won't tell the jarl." *And I won't start any fires,* she thought. *Leave that to the servants of the god of change.*

Gunnar grinned at her. "Are you going to show the spell now?"

"Yes! Let me see," Zorya said. "I have waited a very long time for this."

Ilme took out the air rune again, small and shining in the palm of her hand. Something fundamental in the core of her turned toward it, like the needle of a compass. She glanced at Gunnar, leaning too close, and suppressed a grin.

"Can you take the book out of my bag?" she asked. "Hold it out on your hand over on the other side of the cavern there." Gunnar did so, eyeing her mistrustfully. When he'd stood away from her about twenty feet, she nodded and he held the book up, balanced on his palm.

A shift of that deep power and the rune collapsed into a swath of shimmering energy that twined around her fist as she clenched it, before following the sweep of her hand toward the book and gusting outward... missing the book and knocking Gunnar onto his backside.

Zorya chortled, but Ilme cried out and ran over to the boy. "Are you all right" she asked, pulling him up. "I'm sorry! I was aiming for the book, I swear."

He scowled at her. "I'm fine. Now you have to hold the book, but I'm going to go get my bow." She startled, and his scowl broke into a snort of laughter. "You thought I meant it! You should see your face!"

"A very good start," Zorya declared. "You will be able to build much with these. And you have others—you've been repairing the altars."

Ilme climbed up onto a shelf of rock in the cave wall, close to the massive frog's head, while Gunnar settled down on the ground.

"We've repaired five rune altars," Ilme told Zorya, digging in her bag to fish out more runes. "*I* made these." The runes shone in the hazy light of the essence mine—brilliant fire, shimmering water, bright air, and pulsing mind. "I'm still learning how to use them, but the wizards who already have been studying are doing amazing things. They've actually started creating *buildings* with it."

"What are they building?" Zorya asked, indulgent as a grandfather. "I assume you're not all tipping over Fremennik warriors."

"The fortress," Ilme gushed. "Falador is becoming a city—like something from a fairy tale. We only just found the old law altar, and that's actually important for making the walls go up. It's so interesting—like choosing the right words, almost." She smiled. "But they've built the central tower and it goes right into the mountain and then right up to the sky. I wish you could see it."

"Where's Falador?" Gunnar asked, wrinkling his nose.

Ilme flushed. She was still supposed to be from the Moon Clan. "That's… That's the name they're calling my home town. It's also some… old city on the continent. From a long time ago."

Gunnar made a face, but it was no different than the other faces he made when she said she did something different than him. Zorya's great eye was watching her, but there was no discerning what the guardian was thinking. Did he know she was lying? Did he care?

Suddenly, she felt as if not all that much had changed after all.

"Master Endel brought his colleague this time: Master Unaia," Ilme went on. "She's very interested in creating more spells to build with. You might like to talk to her."

"I wish to talk to everyone who will make their way to me!" Zorya declared. "I am very interested in humans! Especially if they bring an… offering?"

"Oh right!" Ilme reached into her bag and took out the cloth-wrapped slice of cake she'd made sure to take from the ship's table the night before. She clambered down and set it on the ground before the guardian, whose tongue shot out and swept it from the stone.

"Delicious," he said. "I am so fond of dwellberries." He sighed and looked down at her again with his great glowing eyes. "You have stepped onto a path now, Ilme. You cannot fathom the reach of it. It will carry you far and into strange lands, and I only hope that you will find yourself on it, not lose yourself."

He sounded oddly grim, and worry stirred in Ilme. She glanced back at Gunnar who was frowning with the same worry. "Can I not just leave it? I will. If it's dangerous."

Zorya settled into the crouch of his low-slung body. "It's too late for that, child. What will be, will be. Change comes, and we can only guide it, not stop it. Be humbled and not dizzied by it."

It sounded so much like what Valzin had told her. "Fear causes hesitation," she said, "and hesitation will cause your worst fears to come true."

Zorya's throat swelled, the booming creak echoing in the cavern as he released it, making the stones around them ring. "Fear causes hesitation," the frog guardian corrected. "Hesitation gains one time to *think*."

"Unless it freezes us," Ilme said. "Is that not worse?"

"You tell me, child," the guardian said, as if she had said something wise and not asked a question whose answer she could not fathom. "You tell me."

But Ilme found she could not make sense of the guardian that evening, high up in the foothills beyond the Wolf Clan's summer encampment. It would take a very long time—thirty years, nearly—for Zorya's meaning to come clear, and the true reach of the path she'd chosen to be revealed.

PART II

THE WAR

Protect your self, protect your friends. Mine is the glory
  that never ends. This is Saradomin's wisdom.
A fight begun, when the cause is just, will prevail over
  all others. This is Saradomin's wisdom.
The currency of goodness is honour; It retains its value
  through scarcity. This is Saradomin's wisdom.

—EXCERPTS FROM SARADOMIN'S
BOOK OF WISDOM

SIX

THE FORTY-SECOND YEAR OF THE REIGN OF KING RADDALLIN OF ASGARNIA

THE SIXTH DAY OF THE MONTH OF PENTEMBER

FREMENNIK PROVINCE

A boy could grow from a babe in cloths to a warrior dead in the time that had passed since the rune essence mine had cracked the earth wide. Some things had not changed: the Moon Clan sent their miners and their tribute in turn. The Wolf Clan still made their summer camp on the shores of the Northern Sea where the fish were plentiful, and their winter camp inland where the storms were milder. Jarl Viljar still ruled them, an iron-fisted man no one dared depose.

A blessing and a curse in one breath, Gunnar Viljarsson thought, tying the last of the skins taut to make the wall of the longhouse.

"Do we hang all of them?" another warrior, a woman called Fronya, asked. Gunnar didn't have to ask what she meant: the shields of the subjugated clans went up next, and for the third summer they had no tribute from the Seal, the Salmon, or the Bear Clans. Gunnar suspected the Falcon Clan were next—their promised warriors had not arrived in the camp yet. Viljar's steel grip was slipping and he would not admit to it.

Gunnar eyed the Salmon Clan's shield—his heart twisted with grief, and he buried it quickly down.

"Put them all up," he said. "If it's not settled. We'll be at war soon enough."

"You've built it off true." Gunnar looked back to see Viljar striding down the longhouse, eyes on the green Stone of Guthix at the far end, the throne in the clutches of Guthix himself, mouth wide and horns broad.

The years had bleached Viljar's dark hair white, a rakish scar cutting diagonally across his face, but there was no stoop to the jarl, no slowness. He might have been like the mages, so full of magic that their ageing seemed to stop.

Gunnar thought for a moment of Ilme, of the last time she'd been here, looking more like his daughter than his agemate. Grey streaked Gunnar's beard, the corners of his eyes crinkled into rills, but Ilme, once his elder by a handful of years, was as smooth and trim as if she were barely thirty. It was eerie.

"The hill's eroded since last year, jarl," Gunnar told his father. "The posts are more secure here."

"It's off centre," Viljar said, gesturing at the stone.

Gunnar waited, irritated. *Let the old man ask. Let him say the whole building needs to be moved. Let him find fault where there is only sense.*

The fates in their cavern kept on spinning out life for Viljar, and so he kept his control over the Wolf Clan, continuing on as though he would never die, never need to name an heir. Reigo had been dead a decade in an ill-planned battle against dissidents from the Bear Clan. Ott had been executed last summer for trying to depose Viljar—just as Ilme had seen. And Gunnar—a grown man, a father, a widower, a warrior with too many victories to count, a patient leader of his people—had stayed where he was, to be treated as if he were still tripping over his own axe.

"Of course, jarl," he said. Because what else could he say?

Viljar only huffed a noise of disgust. "The god already knows you are imperfect," he said, turning away. "Let your works remind him."

Someday you will be dead, jarl, Gunnar thought viciously. He would be the jarl after Viljar and there was nothing his father could do about it.

Well. Almost nothing. For a moment, he imagined Jarl Viljar taking a war club, swinging for his skull, and with the raising of that imagined weapon, freeing all the tightly wrapped anger in Gunnar. He could kill his father. He could succeed where others had failed—

No, he told himself. *Be patient.*

A call rose outside. Gunnar gestured at Fronya to hang the shields, and went out to see what it was.

Night was falling with the lazy turning of summer, the sun rolling around the arch of the sky in a long spiral. A cluster of his kinsmen and women were scattered along the beach, where they'd been collecting driftwood and seaweed while the tide was low. But they were all turned to the water, to the ships coming in.

To the sails, emblazoned with the crescent of the Moon Clan.

For a moment, Gunnar was again the boy Viljar still saw him as, tripping on his axe, elated his odd friend had come to visit. He had not seen Ilme for several years now, but when she came, she stayed for weeks, visiting with Zorya and Gunnar too. She told him of her wizard studies, for all the sense they made, and of the world beyond where she was allowed to travel, and he told her of the Wolf Clan's ranging, of his family, of the things he had battled in the Wilderness they braved as they roamed.

"An ice giant?" she'd cackled, one far-off evening when they had still looked the same age. "If I didn't know how stubborn you are, I'd never believe you."

"All right," he'd allowed, good-natured, "I may have had help from a warrior or three."

"Or ten," she'd said. "You should have taken some runes the last time. If you put three fire runes together, you could knock one over, toes over nose."

He should tell the longhouse-tenders to get the fires going, to make sure there was food aplenty and the hospitality rites were prepared... but Gunnar's feet led him to the beach, to where the boat, waving its green flag of peace, landed with a crunch of pebbles and the green-cloaked wizards were climbing out, to where his father stood at the crest of the beach, waiting with his warriors flanking him, all posturing grimness. Gunnar ignored them and searched for a brown-haired woman with a crooked smile.

He stopped.

Ilme was not in the boat.

Three women stepped onto the shore, their hooded cloaks a green as deep and rich as the shadows of pine branches. The brooches they wore, the crescent moons, were radiant nacre, not the polished silver Ilme wore. Their eyes though—these reflected silver as the moon, and just as cold. The first woman, her face lined, her hair a pale cottony white held beneath a circlet of more pearl and silver, came forward, leaning heavily on a spiralling crozier that cradled an ice-blue teardrop, her gaze locked on Viljar. The other two women followed, a perfect triangle, seeming to glide up the sliding stones of the beach.

"Jarl Viljar," the old woman pronounced, "you have been deceived."

Gunnar shivered, and made a sign to avert evil, flicking his fingers down and away, but Viljar only sneered, axe in hand as if he might challenge the old woman. "Who are you to make such a declaration?"

"I am Saldis of the Moon Clan," she intoned. "I have seen the travels of the Wolf Clan and the long reign of Viljar Olefsson. I have seen you kill the mountain lion bare-handed and watched you weep over your dead wife. I have seen your death, Jarl Viljar, but I will not speak it. And I have seen you have been deceived."

More people made the sign of aversion. Viljar's mouth twitched. "Who would dare?"

"You will take me to the rune essence mine," Saldis said.

A chill ran up Gunnar's spine.

"I will not," Viljar said. "You may be a queen among your people, but you have no claim here."

"No," she said. "Fate has the claim. The will of Guthix has the claim." She tapped her crozier against Viljar's chest. "Thirty years ago, you received guests from the Lunar Isle. You gave them hospitality, secrets, and access to the cavern of rune essence."

"What of it?" Viljar demanded. "We have no use for such things."

"They were *not* of the Moon Clan," Saldis said.

"What?" Gunnar spoke before he could stop himself, and one of the Moon Clan mages turned her eerie silver eyes on him in admonishment.

"They were charlatans," Saldis went on. "Seekers of power they do not deserve. They came here to scrape the blessings of the god from the earth and take them back to their king in the south, so he might lord over his rivals with the magic that humanity has been denied. Now there are runes in Gielinor again."

"There have always been runes," Viljar said dismissively. "What do we care?"

"You may not care. You may rely on your axe and your clan. But giving such power to humans destroys the balance. We have seen it again and again; it has proven true, again and again; and it will happen once more."

Gunnar's thoughts were reeling. None of this made sense—he tried to remember what Ilme had said of her home, of her peers. He didn't know how big the Lunar Isle was, only that it was smaller than the range of the Wolf Clan. Perhaps Ilme and the mages they'd dealt with were from the other end of the island. He tried to remember the name of her village.

"Have you seen this destruction?" Viljar said sceptically. "Has it come to you in your dreams? Tell me where its ships sail from, where its armies march?"

Saldis stared at him a moment. "Terrible destruction."

"How convenient, O Mage," Viljar sneered. "Now I have heard your visions, hear mine: these false Moon Clan mages cause no trouble. They visit the mine, they take stones we don't want, they leave offerings to the guardian, and pay us for the privilege. They have lied to me, and I will demand retribution for that dishonour, but I fail to see how it's the Wolf Clan's trouble if some fractious southerners fight each other with spells instead of swords."

Gunnar thought of Ilme's description of the spells she'd learned—blasts of air and ice and fire, spells to addle an enemy or strengthen an ally. He imagined her people deciding they would rather keep the mine for themselves, and throw away any agreements with the Wolf Clan. How bloody would that battle be? How strong would the Wolf Clan stand if they couldn't even hold onto the Salmon and the Falcon?

Three fire runes together and you could knock an ice giant toes over nose.

A schism. A miscommunication. *Zorya,* he thought. *The guardian will know.*

"Heed me," Saldis said. "Or trouble will come for you soon enough, Jarl Viljar."

The jarl didn't break his gaze, didn't lower his axe. "I'm bound by tradition to offer you hospitality," Viljar said. "But not to listen to any more of this. I've enriched my clan, I've kept them safe and spread our territory and our glory—I'll not have outsiders telling me my business. Even your purported betrayers didn't insult me thus."

He turned his back on the Moon Clan and strode back up the beach. Warriors trailed him, making warding gestures, then the hearth-workers, the fire-tenders, glancing back at their visitors. But a third of the clan still lingered on the beach, eyeing the Moon Clan.

Eyeing Gunnar.

Gunnar stepped forward to meet Saldis, who still watched his father with a sour expression. "Mage," he said. "I am Gunnar Viljarsson. I may… I may have been in your visions of before. I'm the one who found the mine as a boy." She turned a sharp eye on him, but said nothing, so he continued, more firmly. "There's been some misunderstanding. But once you've done the rites, I can take you to the mine. I can take you to the Guardian of Guthix there. He'll be able to explain everything."

Saldis drew a deep breath, closing her eyes, and Gunnar wondered for a moment if she had dipped into the dreaming world and glimpsed their future.

"This is wise," she declared. "Once your father is satisfied, you will take us to the cursed mine."

Gunnar led the three mages to the longhouse where the meal was nearly ready, sorting through all the ways this mistake could have been made. But as he imagined rivalries and misunderstandings, vague dreams and small rebellions, he could not help but notice that Saldis and the other two mages moved through the rites without prompting or error.

+ ✦ +

Getting Saldis up to the mine took some ingenuity and muscle, but that night they descended into the earth, surrounded by the hazy glow of rune essence. Gunnar eyed the mages, noting the way they tensed all over, the same way Ilme did when she had first come into the mines. When he was young, he'd thought she looked like a fool who'd jumped into an ice-cold tarn, all shocked muscle and panic, but he knew now it was the recognition of the magic all around them. Something Gunnar had never been able to feel.

"It's this way," Gunnar offered, pointing down the passage. When the Moon Clan mages didn't move, he led the way. Surely there was an error. Surely Zorya would know what was going on.

The great frog was hunkered down in the back of the damp cave, humming to himself, a sound that seemed to fill the cave. As they entered, Zorya opened his eyes, half-lidded to regard them.

"Young Gunnar," he croaked. "And guests. Is Ilme with them? Has she brought cake?"

Gunnar bowed politely. "They aren't… They have disturbing news."

"Your father?" Zorya guessed. He blinked at Gunnar, then licked his own eye. "It was bound to come soon."

"Are you the Guardian of Guthix?" Saldis demanded.

"I am," Zorya said. "You are… Saldis? Welcome to the rune essence mine, the gift of Guthix."

"You are the guardian," Saldis said, "and yet you allowed yourself to be *deceived* by the Asgarnians. They have overtaken your mine and stolen its gifts."

"They think Ilme has been lying," Gunnar explained. "They think the miners who come here have nothing to do with the Moon Clan. Could you explain the truth?"

Zorya chuckled. "Ah, I see. You're angry they have been play-acting. If it eases your pride, I did not think they were from the Moon Clan. Like children in costumes, it has been very amusing. And they were not rude about it."

The blood seemed to leave Gunnar's head. "What?" he said.

Zorya tilted his head, so one great eye focused on him. "They are from the south. As she said, they are from Asgarnia."

"Why... Why didn't you tell me?" He felt dizzy, as if his soul weren't quite tethered to his body. "Why would she lie?"

"They didn't think themselves worthy on their own merits, but that's their own foolishness." Zorya asked. "It seemed important to them to pretend, and not at all important to me that they were pretending. It's not as if they were Bandos and his goblins coming in to raid the place—believe me, I've sent them fleeing a time or two!"

Hot shame boiled in Gunnar's chest. Ilme had lied and Zorya had helped her, and he'd been in the middle, stupid and deluded. This must have been part of the plan. Make friends with the jarl's son, keep him busy, keep him distracted. Feed him enough to help to keep him in line for the leadership, because then you'd have a jarl you could manipulate. What an idiot he'd been. His father was right.

He glanced at the Moon Clan, and found they were paying him no mind at all.

"Great Guardian," Saldis said, sternly. "We have come from the Lunar Isle to see for ourselves the lies of the Asgarnians. And now we see exactly how our visions connect to what has happened here. *You* have let the Asgarnians steal the god's gifts, and because of that error, great destruction will follow!"

Zorya blinked at Saldis. "A gift cannot be stolen when it is freely given. The rune essence is for all of humanity's use. To learn again the magic Guthix granted this world. I am the guardian and my task is to determine who is right to claim this essence—I have done so."

"That magic is flawed, great one," Saldis said sternly, as if she lectured a rival not a demigod. "We don't want it. Guthix did not want it *for* us! It has only brought destruction."

"*You* don't want it," Zorya corrected. "You have your own rune essence mine. But no guardian." He blinked ponderously at the mages. "Why is that?" he asked, a slight edge to the question.

"There has never been a guardian on the Lunar Isle," Saldis said stiffly.

"Is that what they say?" Zorya turned, his great legs clawing the stone. "Young Gunnar, tell them this: the Asgarnians are no threat. You are friends with Ilme. She comes here and tells me of the world beyond," he added to Saldis, like a fond uncle speaking of his rambunctious niece and nephew. "It's one of my small joys."

Gunnar couldn't speak, those same stories wheeling through his thoughts. When so much of what Ilme had said had been a lie... how could he believe in any of it? His shame curdled in his chest, hardening into anger. How could he believe they were friends, when she had gone to such efforts to deceive him? How could he believe Zorya?

"Why didn't you tell *me*?" he burst out. Zorya blinked at him.

"Did it matter?" the guardian repeated. "You were not friends because of where she came from or what cloak she wears. You are friends because you are alike. You suffer under the same strictness, you laugh at the same jokes. You yearn to see the world and she delights in telling you of it. No one has ever sought your joy, Young Gunnar—that seemed more important to me."

The Moon Clan were staring at Gunnar with their bright silver eyes. Deep inside, his soul felt molten, seething, something burnt and bubbling and ready to burst.

"You should call Ilme back," Zorya said, gently. "It's been too long since we spoke."

Gunnar turned from the guardian. "If she comes back here," he said, "I will make her sorry she ever lied."

SEVEN

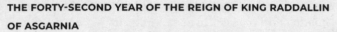

Ilme sat at the far end of the meeting table, rubbing the tense spot between her brows and remembering a far-off summer where a freckled boy had sneered at her and told her wizards were all self-important and rude. She looked down the length of the table at her colleagues and knew she couldn't argue otherwise.

"I can write another treatise if you like," Azris drawled, both hands clutching the arms of her chair as if she perched in a throne. "It doesn't change the answer."

Zanmaron stood behind his own chair, antsy and trying to loom over the others, his red robes embroidered all over with a quilted pattern of feathers. "What part of 'A pity we can't teleport to the rune essence mine' sounded like 'Azris, please spout off'?" he demanded. "I have read your treatises, I understand the limitations, and I don't think I'm the only one who feels they could be experimented on further—if only because it would solve a great many problems if you were wrong!"

Eritona leaned toward Ilme, a slight movement perfected in foreign courts and councils. "Have they parted again?" she whispered. "Has anyone told you?"

"I have no idea," Ilme whispered back. Azris and Zanmaron's tempestuous cycle of courtship and collapse felt like the one true alignment of Zanmaron's former and current gods: it was perpetual as Saradomin and as ever-changing as the goals of Zamorak. If they weren't fighting because they'd called it off, they were fighting because they were about to. Or because they were annoyed that they were on the verge of giving into their mutual feelings.

"We should have come back a week later," Eritona murmured. "Maybe they'd have worked it out."

"And skipped this meeting," Ilme added.

Eritona sighed. "We need to be there for the dwarves. The council will absolutely want to promise them runes we can't deliver, and that will make *this* look like a friendly chat if someone doesn't take a firm hand."

Ilme scratched Rue's shoulders as he dozed in her lap. Summer was fading, the cool of autumn coming on as the month crept forward. Outside the windows, a bank of grey clouds bunched up along the horizon, threatening rain. Ilme found herself powerfully homesick for the signs of the seasons' changing that she knew best: the smell of grasses drying in the fields and blackberries fat on their canes, the flames of turning oak leaves, the chatter and whistle of redwings in the brush.

All Ilme wanted was to go home to the Wizards' Tower, to sleep in a bed she knew every lump of for at least a full day, talk to no one at all, read not a word of the correspondence that had no doubt piled up in her absence. She had been gone for months, traveling with Eritona from court to court, as she reaffirmed and negotiated the treaties that let the wizards of Asgarnia—and now

Misthalin—travel through other lands to use the rune altars anchored there.

This was her life now—a season or two studying, experimenting with the runes. And then following Eritona, the diplomat, as she balanced the wishes of King Raddallin's allies against Asgarnia and the Wizards' Tower's wants. *This ruler wants more runes and that one wants weapons. This one wants good Varrockian mithril and to get that we'll need to offer Misthalin more wizards to shape magic for them.*

While Eritona listened and calculated and worked her easy charm, weaving promises together like threads on a loom, Ilme listened and watched and asked the right questions. *This one is afraid his neighbour will gain a better deal. This one doesn't fear your army but fears your influence over others. This one thinks she can get special treatment and if she does, she'll stay your ally.*

So many years on—thirty? So much more skilled, and doing exactly the same work as when she was a girl. Worse, it bored her more than it bothered her. She'd rather try and test Azris's findings than peel back the motives of another warlord or queen or council member.

Although, if it was going to be like *this* when she met with her colleagues…

"Just admit you didn't read it!" Azris snapped.

"I checked your calculations!" Zanmaron shouted. "Of course, I read it!"

Falador was the last stop before she could go home, unload all those notes and treatics and *rest*—and she was spending it listening to her colleagues argue about how nice it would be if they didn't have to travel to the rune essence mine.

"It is wise to retest hypotheses?" offered Master Temrin, the grey-robed, grey-bearded master, who seemed to speak everything as a question. "But wiser to find a new direction of inquiry?"

"If you are both *finished*," Master Endel said curtly. "Zanmaron, Master Strekalis isn't here, so I will speak for him: this is a poor use of your time. Azris, let your work speak for itself and stop taking the bait."

Perhaps they were all tired and longing for home. Endel too had grey in his hair now, but not so much as he ought to have. *By all rights*, Ilme thought, *he should be dead*.

The rune magic had seeped into all of them, prolonging their days. If Ilme kept crafting runes, kept casting spells, she would easily live another forty-six years—and possibly never notice.

Except when she travelled: those rulers and chieftains and monarchs all seemed to wither and drop like spring flowers. She set it out of her mind when she could—she knew the other wizards did, they hardly spoke to anyone outside the tower—but there were moments when time's passage seized her irrevocably and pierced her heart.

She thought of Gunnar again and sighed.

"Master Unaia," Eritona called down the table, "how many more fire runes is the delegation from Camdozaal asking for? I'm afraid I missed the answer when you said it earlier, and given the tally from the council in Karamja, I need to know what we're looking at before we join the Council of Falador."

Master Unaia held the high seat today, looking as if she had grown into the thronelike chair at the end of the table by Saradomin's ancient blessings. "They wish their allotment tripled."

"I still fail to see how we can meet that need," Zanmaron said. "We'll have to increase the number of mining expeditions, and too many of our number just don't have the aptitude for gathering rune essence of sufficient purity."

"The Imcando say they have samples of their work that will be very convincing," Master Unaia said, refusing to look at Zanmaron.

He flushed. "I think that's motivation enough. And the council knows what is best for Asgarnia."

"Does that shorten the path from the Fremennik province?" Zanmaron asked, acidly. "Does it solve Azris's absurd equations?"

"My equations—" Azris began, nostrils flaring.

"Enough!" Master Endel barked. "The council will be here any moment with the dwarves, and I for one have no interest in giving them the impression we are fractious and petty. Sit down and wait and stop being a terrible example for the apprentices."

Ilme glanced over at the wall at the apprentices in question, who sat mute and upright, afraid to misstep. Green-robed and red, blue-robed and grey—and all of them absorbing every word spoken as if it were the secret to their future success instead of the sniping of people too passionate about their work to separate themselves from it. They looked so young, so hopeful—had she looked so young and hopeful? Had she ever pictured *this* for herself? A not-quite-diplomat performing magic for foreign courts and running herself ragged!

A spy, still.

Beyond the apprentices, a figure appeared in the side door that led out to the courtyard: High Marshal Valzin, her riding armour shed for a trim red jacket and crisp shirt, her shining black hair now curling to her collar. She surveyed the table of wizards with narrowed eyes before her gaze fell on Ilme. She held up a letter.

Ilme frowned at her.

"High Marshal," Unaia said cautiously. She sat stiffly, her regal posture now more that of a hunted animal's. "Did you need something? We have an agenda."

"Oh, don't mind me," Valzin said "I came to find Wizard Zanmaron and then Wizard Ilme. But they're occupied. I'll wait."

Unaia's mouth tightened. "I see. Well, when they are finished, I'll send them to find you. You can go."

Valzin tilted her head. "Do you send them places? I was under the impression you all served different orders now. Ah well, not everything can have the precision and care of a military, even under Saradomin's grace."

Now it was Unaia's turn to flush—Zanmaron had begun his studies as a Saradominist, only to convert to the teachings of Zamorak some years later. She wasn't his superior any longer. Moreover, everyone knew Unaia blamed Valzin for the loss of her apprentice—given she had shouted it at the top of her lungs.

"I'll wait here," Valzin went on, sliding in beside the apprentices, who watched her wide-eyed. "I find it very educational, and my studies of magic can always improve."

True to her teasing promise, Valzin had learned to cast spells with runes as well—mostly of the sort that made combat quicker and more deadly. This in turn had drawn the promised Zamorakian spellcasters into the fold, for if Sanafin Valzin was doing it, then there was a fashion in certain circles.

Which had also influenced King Raddallin to pick it up—he didn't use runes frequently enough to stop the grey streaking his beard, but Ilme knew that those in other lands murmured at the king's continued strength.

Far gone were the days where Falador was merely a holding of a minor tribe—now the city was a spectacular fortress, a symbol of humanity's strength. With the defeat of Moranna of the Narvra, the remaining tribes had quickly fallen in behind Raddallin, even those who had first pledged themselves to Misthalin. A series of skirmishes secured Asgarnia's border and sent Misthalin back to its halls to consider what came next. The wizards built their tower there on the pushed-back border, a reminder of the power they wielded for Raddallin and a beacon to wizards of Misthalin—*this is the centre of magic, this is the birthplace of the new age.*

The doors to the chamber opened, admitting first the council of Falador: a dozen well-dressed men and women with their retainers. Ilme tracked them as they entered, marking new faces and old—the council seemed to be in constant flux these days, so much that it hardly seemed worth remembering their individual names.

But as she scanned she marked a shift: there were three more Saradominists than last time. She frowned, and glanced at Valzin. Was this the reason she was watching?

The council filed in along the opposite end of the long table, talking among themselves. Their leader, a dark-bearded, pale-skinned man, clapped his hands together once. "Well. I hope you wizards had a pleasant journey. Everything to your liking? Anything you need before we get started?"

A harmony of breaths, of voices beginning to speak, sounded around Ilme, but before any more complaints could be spoken, the doors opened again to a quartet of muscular, bald dwarves, resplendent in gilded armour and leather skirting and trim.

Three wore forked beards, dark hair split with more gilded beads, and the last, a woman, had tattooed lines worked along her jaw that matched the fine tooling of the leather. Each of them carried a case, the woman's nearly twice her own length and perched on her broad shoulders. All of them wore Saradomin's four-pointed star prominently on the chest pieces of their armour.

The Imcando of the great hall of Camdozaal were fabled smiths, great workers of metal and ore. Their creations littered tales of ancient heroes, their own heroics as warriors under Saradomin's command in the God Wars the stuff of legends. While they generally shared the faith of Misthalin, Asgarnia was the one offering them runes.

The foremost dwarf, the only one not carrying a box of some kind, came to the end of the table and brought his hand up level with his chest, his thumb pointed out, straight at Master Unaia.

"Generous council, wise wizards: the Imcando greet you, our sisters and brothers in Saradomin's grace."

"Demons in the pits," Master Endel muttered.

Unaia at the head of the table had the good grace to look annoyed. It was one thing to be in discord when the doors were closed, and another to do so in front of outsiders.

"I bid you welcome," Unaia said, primly, "for all the orders of the Wizards' Tower."

"May your skill rise to meet your ambition."

"Zanmaron," Unaia snapped. "Sit."

The dwarf frowned at Zanmaron as he took his seat, before continuing to Unaia. "I am Seppan of the Imcando. These are Ramarno, Temur, and Solonis. We would like to present you with some examples of what your gift of runes has allowed us to craft."

On firmer footing, Seppan gestured to the dwarf behind him, who stepped forward, offering up a long weapon case. Seppan opened it and withdrew a warhammer, its metal head and spike shining red as hot coals. The haft was blackened wood, inlaid with twisting lines of silver that put Ilme in mind of flames blazing up the length of it.

"Orikalkum," Seppan announced, holding the warhammer up to the light. "Smelted of orichalcite ore and the dragonbreath stone. Incredibly strong and lightweight." He tossed it to Master Temrin, who caught it out of the air as if it were nothing more than a bound-up scroll. "We haven't smelted it since the God Wars. It took dragonfire to heat, but with the rune combinations, we can replicate the intensity of the flames."

Across the room, Valzin tapped her cheek with the letter.

Ilme scanned the room and calculated a path around the Imcando over to the door beside Valzin that wouldn't draw too much attention, scooped Rue up with one arm, then murmured a quiet, "Your pardon—my dragon," before quickly making her way there. Valzin stood, suddenly no longer interested in the proceedings.

"Please tell me," Ilme said when they stepped outside, "that this isn't about going to Varrock."

"This? No, what's wrong with Varrock?" Valzin asked, all innocence.

Ilme gave her a dark look. "What's in the letter?"

"It's *your* letter." Valzin handed it over. "Not that it matters, but I probably agree with you about what's wrong with Varrock. I didn't leave because I loved it."

Ilme sighed. "What's wrong with Varrock is that I want to go home, not traipse out to Misthalin to argue about selling runes to merchants that cross the border."

Soon after Raddallin's kingdom had been founded, Misthalin began making overtures, and Ilme and Eritona were sent along with Sanafin Valzin—still a hereditary Peer of Misthalin, second child of the Duke of Varrock—to negotiate the treaties. Misthalin made Ilme think of the Fremennik and their Guthix-stone, of the things she took for granted as immutable features of life, only to be swiftly disabused of such notions. For a long time, she'd assumed they were the same, but in a hundred tiny ways, Misthalin asserted its differences.

"Do you ever miss it?" Ilme asked Valzin once.

"It's not for me," Valzin had said. "That was made very clear—stay where you're set down, follow the rules, all glory to Saradomin and so forth. But all the same? I will never not be the second born of the Duke of Varrock and the dukes will never not feel they owe something to their kin, so why not use it to our advantage sometimes?"

In the courtyard outside the council room, Valzin raked a hand through her hair. "A Misthalanian queen seemed like such a tidy idea when we started. Then she had to go and die, leave a bunch of entitled in-laws to Raddallin, and rile everyone up about finding him a new one. Absolutely no one knows what to make of the fact Raddallin's not ageing normally and we have spent entirely too many meetings discussing the likelihood of 'issue' and who gets Asgarnia if Raddallin dies first."

Ilme frowned. "Has he *still* not declared a successor?"

"Of course not," Valzin said wryly. "He's never going to die." She sighed. "I keep suggesting knights he ought to adopt—they don't have to be the *perfect* choice, he's allowed to take it back— but he always changes the subject: 'I don't need to worry about this now, Sana!' His throne is secure, his magic is sound, and his kingdom at peace. But how long will that last?"

"He ought to just adopt you," Ilme said.

Valzin waved her away. "That would go over *terribly* well with our blue-and-white friends, I'm sure. What's in your letter?"

"Nosy," Ilme said. But she turned it over and broke the seal. The envelope held a second enclosure, bark paper folded around a piece of scraped parchment. "Oh! It's from Gunnar."

"Please tell me the Fremennik have a bride to offer."

I KNOW YOU LIED.

Ilme's breath caught in her throat.

That was the only legible line on the page. He'd started several times, scratched them out, tried to put words to paper and failed again and again. Only those four words, stark as blood in the snow, remained: *I know you lied.*

How many times had Ilme told Master Endel they couldn't keep lying to the Wolf Clan? How many times had she laid out the risks, the problems they were courting?

How many times had she then let Master Endel convince her that this was the most peaceful path? How many times had she admitted it would be easier to wait until Jarl Viljar died, when Ilme could smooth over matters with Gunnar, the new jarl? She had believed it, imagined the conversation—they would fight, surely, but he would understand. They were friends, after all, and she was making great things happen.

But in all those imaginings, she was the one who told Gunnar. She did not leave it to a stranger, who would only wound his pride and leave him humbled and humiliated.

There would be no smoothing things over now.

"Oh dear," Valzin said. "Bad news from your barbarian epistoler?"

Ilme swallowed and looked up, but for all her teasing, Valzin looked grim, a knight ready for orders.

"They know," Ilme said. "They know we're not the Moon Clan."

"By the empty helmet," Valzin swore. She took the letter and frowned. "What if he means something else?"

"What else could he mean?" Ilme demanded. "I knew this would hap—I have to go." If she left today, if she could find a ship, if the winds were with them—

No, not a ship. She didn't need a ship because the ship was only to seal the lie, to make sure it seemed they came from over the Northern Sea.

"Hold on," Valzin said. "We need to wait, we don't—"

"*I* need to go," Ilme said. "I need to make things right with my friend before I lose him."

Valzin grabbed her arm. "We don't know what the Fremennik are planning. We don't know what this means for Asgarnia—it's not about your *friend*, it's about someone we considered a tenuous ally having a reason to go to war, and a resource we can't afford to lose! How many of those treaties fall apart if we don't have the runes to offer?" She nodded at the room behind them. "What happens when the Imcando can't make these weapons Raddallin's so excited to get?"

Ilme yanked her arm free. "If there's no war, he doesn't need them. I'm going. If you're afraid we've already lost the Fremennik, then draft up new treaties or find me an army or come yourself. But I am leaving as soon as I have the horse to travel on."

There was that light in Valzin's eyes, that dancing spark of the challenge Ilme had set her, the debate she would pursue like a hunting hound. But Ilme wasn't a sixteen-year-old girl anymore, dizzied by the deft words of Sanafin Valzin.

"You're charging into danger," Valzin warned. "Nothing less."

"I am refusing to be pinned in place," Ilme returned. "Didn't you teach me that once? If there's a chance at war, I'm the one who stands a chance of stopping it. You've all said that, since the beginning. You can't pretend I'm too helpless to be of use now."

For a moment, Valzin only regarded her—inscrutable as ever, impossible to pin down—and Ilme nearly left, already well aware that High Marshal Valzin had no true authority over her. If she wasn't going to be a partner in this, then Ilme didn't need her.

But Valzin's gaze dropped and she sighed, sounding more tired than Ilme had ever known her to be. "You're right," she said. "You're right. But let me explain to Raddallin first. Do me that favour before we go."

EIGHT

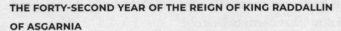

Jarl Viljar refused to budge his stance all through the spring and summer months: the deal he'd made with the Asgarnian wizards would stand, the mine was his to permit or refuse entry to, and he had no interest in listening to the Moon Clan's concerns. Still Saldis and her attendants stayed with the Wolf Clan through the season, testing Jarl Viljar's hospitality as Saldis made her nightly appeals to the jarl's sense of honour, decency, and righteousness.

"Guthix made this error once before, so we are disrespectful to compound it," she said. "The rune magic brought us to ruin. We shamed him and destroyed the world."

"The gods did the destroying," Viljar said. "And it was your lot who brought the runes forth—the Wolf Clan doesn't exist to perform your penances, mage. You are testing the bounds of my hospitality."

Over and over, Viljar stubbornly refused to acknowledge his error. Over and over again, the Moon Clan dared his temper.

Gunnar didn't return to the rune essence mine the whole season, unable to face Zorya and the lie the guardian had known all along. He'd sent the letter he'd promised Zorya he would write to Ilme, but the fury that seethed up inside him had made it impossible to find the words—how betrayed he felt, how confused. How he didn't know what would come next. That turbulence built and built in him, like waves on the sea building into winter storms of catastrophic tides and surges.

"Your father is risking the stability of the world," Saldis told him, as he pinned fish to the smoking racks along the seashore. "You know what needs to be done."

Gunnar looked up, the stirring anger in him sucked down into panic. "Are you… Are you saying you've had a vision of me killing him?"

The old woman paused. "I don't need to have a vision to know what needs to happen," she intoned. She ground her crozier into the sliding stones of the beach. "He's not leading you as a jarl should."

The traditions were clear: a son succeeded the jarl upon his death. But tradition was only a plan—history was littered with jarls whose death had been helped along.

And sons who snatched too quickly for their birthright, only to be struck down. He thought of Ott kneeling for the axe, of Reigo sent against the Wolf too hastily and without enough warriors.

Gunnar turned to the broken surface of the sea, the salty wind stirring his hair. "Viljar is still strong," he said. "Guthix doesn't call him back to the earth yet."

Saldis scoffed. "The tools are in your hands, Gunnar Viljarsson. Don't blame this madness on the Sleeping God."

Before the season turned and the storms drove the Wolf Clan from the shore, the ship from the Lunar Isle returned. Viljar saw the Moon Clan off, as befitted a jarl with departing guests. But the parting felt more like a bear chasing off a wolf that had strayed too close to its den.

"May you return safely home," the jarl declared, biting each word off, "and carry only praises of the Wolf Clan with you."

Saldis scowled at him. "May you find the fortune you seek. And reconsider your foolish choices."

"May your island be your resting place," he snapped back. "And soon."

The Wolf Clan would need to depart for their inland settlement soon, lest the winter storms that battered the shore wash their works away. The Fremennik had grown restless in the presence of the true Moon Clan. At least the wizards who had pretended to be Moon Clan had been polite, if distant, and were only the faintest mimics of the eerie silver-eyed mages who stared and proclaimed doom and would not leave.

"I don't know that I prefer them," Gunnar overheard Fronya say, as they watched the mages leave. "Think I'd rather have none of them, to be honest."

"At least they didn't lie to us," Gunnar muttered.

The warrior snorted. "They're all lying, every magic user. Steel and iron are honest at least."

"Shame Viljar's willing to let them laugh up their sleeves at us," Ivo Brokentooth said, watching the jarl giving directions to the fire-tenders. "A real jarl would hunt those wizards down. Make them wish they'd never lied."

"Your axe came from those wizards," Fronya pointed out.

Ivo sneered. "We can make our own weapons. We're not soft-handed foreigners. Or we *weren't*." He spat on the ground. "Ott wouldn't be sitting on his axe handle."

Gunnar watched Ivo, Ilme's distant warning coming back to him *Just a... mage's sense, I guess. He seems to want the throne worst. I suppose if you wanted to slip away before Ott did anything, he probably wouldn't chase you.*

She was never from the Moon Clan, he reminded himself. *She was no sort of seer. She made that up, too.* Over and over he turned through those memories, searching for the lies, all the evasions.

"We're also not the trained mercenaries of the Lunar Isle," Fronya said. "They don't tell us who our enemies are."

"You're young," Ivo said dismissively. "You don't remember what we were before." He was still watching Viljar. "If I were jarl, I would clean up this clan."

"But you won't be," Gunnar spoke up.

Ivo looked back at him, eyes narrowed. "What was that?"

"You're not going to be jarl," Gunnar said. "So it doesn't matter what you think."

Ivo chuckled, coming to his feet. "You're not gonna be jarl. A jarl's got to have command. Vision. A man has to be afraid of disappointing his jarl, and we've all watched you disappoint Viljar from the day you were born. You couldn't even stand up to Viljar when he married off your girl, cast your heirs to other clans. No one fears you, Gunnar. You ought to go find that smug little seer whose been making a fool of you, go see if the soft-handed foreigners would like a pissant jarl for their troubles."

The storm inside Gunnar swelled to a fury, a tide that washed up the shores of his self. He lunged at Ivo axe-first, all instinct and anger, the demand for a trial by combat chasing the urge to bury his axe in Ivo's broken-toothed sneer.

Ivo's own axe came up, blocking Gunnar's swing, but Gunnar forced it down, all that anger in his muscles now, and fear washed over Ivo's face as Gunnar kicked his heel into the soft point behind his knee and shoved into his shoulder, knocking Ivo out flat—

"Gunnar!" Viljar roared. "What in the name of the dark witches of the wood are you doing? Stop it!"

Gunnar leapt back, again all instinct, but this time it was a cowardly boy, the disappointment of the jarl, who reacted. The fear vanished from Ivo's face, and he smirked around his jagged smile.

"Ivo insulted him!" Fronya called, eager and watchful. "He was about to call—"

Suddenly Viljar was on Gunnar, yanking away the axe. "Don't you dare call for a trial on one of my warriors," he hissed. "Ivo, get up, you lump of puke."

You know what needs to be done—the Moon Clan mage's words burned across Gunnar's mind. In that moment, tossed on the storms of his humiliation, he wanted nothing more than to cut Viljar down.

But... Saldis hadn't *seen* it. She hadn't seen him defeat his father, she hadn't seen him become jarl. He pulled the axe closer to his chest.

"That's what I thought," Viljar spat. "All of you get to work—the storms are coming early—I can feel it. We leave at first light."

Gunnar didn't follow them back to the settlement—no one seemed to care if he did. He watched Viljar walk away, sparing him no thought at all, and unbidden he remembered a long-off summer, when he was still a young man, his beard soft, his axe unblooded.

Ilme had arrived, and his father had finally noticed Gunnar was spending a lot of time with the odd wizard girl. He'd warned him not to get ideas about a Moon Clan wife in various insulting and threatening terms. Right in front of Ilme.

"Your father is..." Ilme had begun, letting the sentence dangle.

"A monster?" Gunnar had suggested. "I don't want to marry you. A mage wife sounds awful. Don't even think it."

"I wasn't thinking it. I don't want to marry *anybody*," Ilme said. "Let alone some jarl's son." She watched Viljar stride off. "I think he's afraid," she said, softer. "I think he's afraid somebody will find out he's not iron through and through. I think he's very afraid it's going to be you, someday. But that's all a terrible excuse for treating you like a burden and a problem. I hope he regrets it someday."

Gunnar had snorted. "The jarl doesn't regret things."

"Then I hope he lets you go," she'd said. "You shouldn't have to wait around on him when you'd rather see the world and he only makes you stay to be unpleasant."

It had made him want to squirm away, that truth laid bare, and he'd covered it back up with all the things he owed the Wolf Clan, all the promises his birthright made him. He would be his brother's warrior—one or the other of them—and that was that.

She was trying to drive you apart from them, he told himself, that anger churning up again. *She was trying to break your resolve.* Grief tried to poke its head above the waves of his anger, but he shoved it down. Ilme had known exactly what she was doing.

And so did Viljar—Ivo wasn't wrong. Viljar had poisoned everyone against Gunnar and now he was leading the clan to ruin, all for some weapons and his pride. What happened if he stood by his father? What happened if he brought him down?

Something had to be done. Someone had to take steps.

Up on the mountain, deep in the mine, Zorya waited. If Ilme wouldn't answer for her lies, if Viljar wouldn't take charge of the situation, then Gunnar would begin with the guardian.

NINE

---◄◆►---

The approach to the Wolf Clan's summer encampment by land led the Asgarnians beyond the deep Wilderness and up through the passes over the mountains. Autumn had settled over the hills like a red blanket, but up in the crossings snow was beginning to fall. Ilme found herself grateful for the detachment of Kinshra who rode with her, along with Master Endel, Master Unaia, and Zanmaron. If she'd come alone, she wasn't sure she'd have made it.

Not alone, she amended. Rue had come, of course, the little dragon always at her side was tucked up under her cloak as the snow began to fall again. He poked his nose out. "Cold."

"I can't do anything about that," Ilme said.

"Go home," he said, burrowing under her arm.

"You didn't have to come," she reminded him. But she bundled him into the folds of her robes.

Zanmaron stomped up to her, bundled nearly as tightly as Rue. "They really don't have *any* wizards? There's nothing to prepare against?"

Ilme shook her head. "Just warriors. Very skilled warriors. But we shouldn't go in assuming we're going to fight—no one's said we're blocked from the essence mine. As far as we know the agreement is still in place."

Zanmaron gave her a sceptical look. "They brought me and not Eritona. They're expecting a fight."

Ilme returned the look. "You don't think that had more to do with the fact you can't be in the same room as Azris without screaming at each other? Gunnar is… hurt. It might be complicated. I don't think we're looking at a battle."

"Azris and I are *fine,* thank you: we simply know each other too well." Zanmaron sniffed. "Unlike you and the jarl-to-be—a few dozen visits, a few dozen letters. And all that time you were playing a role. How can you possibly know him?"

Ilme shook her head. "It doesn't matter. By the time we get there, they should have moved on to their winter camp. We may only be dealing with the guardian."

A part of her hoped that would be the case. She dreaded seeing Gunnar again as much as she hoped he would be there waiting for her.

I know you lied.

✦ ✦ ✦

The first time she'd almost told him the truth, they'd been twenty-eight and twenty-five, an age where the gap between them had vanished and the nature of their friendship settled and deep-rooted. His father had found him a wife the year before, a young woman from the Salmon Clan called Fiera, who was pleasant and quick-witted, and built a fine house each summer. And if she treated Ilme a bit like she was an odd dog that had followed Gunnar in, she was kind at least and never made the sort of fuss Viljar did.

"Take your friend up the mountain," Fiera would say when Ilme visited. "Talk to the guardian, and be back for supper in one piece, please."

The summer after they'd wed, they'd had a baby, a little girl with Fiera's pointed chin and Gunnar's pale hair, called Thyra. Gunnar put her in a sling, Fiera checked the knots a half dozen times before letting them leave, and Thyra had gone up the mountain to see Zorya with them.

"I'm going to tell you something," Gunnar said to Ilme when the camp was out of sight at last, "and you can't laugh."

"I can laugh if I want."

"I wanted to call her Ilme."

She'd stopped short. "The baby? Why?"

"Because you're important to me, dummy." He looked down at the baby, prodding her to grab his finger. "Nobody else ever stopped to notice me, alright? Nobody ever cared what I had to say—not before I proved I could take on a giant on my own."

"I still have yet to see that."

He scowled at her. "Shut up, this is important. Fiera pointed out it wouldn't... It wouldn't go over well. My father... Well, anyway she's Thyra, and she can't be your namesake but I hope you'll still treat her like she is."

All over again, she had been sixteen, trapped in a lie that squeezed more tightly around her by the moment. She'd thought of Valzin's admonitions, the advice to leap into the void rather than be caught. *You don't know me,* she wanted to say.

But then... that was a deeper sort of lie. She told all the truths that mattered to Gunnar. She took the little baby's hand. "I would be honoured."

The second time she'd nearly told him was fifteen years later, the summer after Fiera had died of a sudden fever, leaving Gunnar and their daughter. Thyra, at fifteen, was budding into a bright and sturdy young woman, quick-witted as her mother and observant as her father.

A valuable bride, Viljar had declared, to shore up their ties to the Salmon Clan.

"She didn't want to go," Gunnar said dully. "Of course she didn't. But there was no stopping my father. They took her away in the night. I failed her and now I might never see her again."

"They're her mother's people," Ilme offered. "They won't harm her, surely."

Gunnar grew silent again, choked by grief. "I already think of leaving all the time," he confessed. "She was my only anchor and Viljar's sunk her in a far away harbour. If I chase my daughter, I will exile myself and she won't be allowed to receive me without risking Viljar's wrath." He shook his head. "I wonder some nights if I could run off and become a mage like you. Hide away on the Lunar Isle. Search the visions for a way to undo this. Somehow." He blinked up at her. "Maybe you could *see* for me."

And again, it wasn't right—none of this was right—but she could only think that unburdening herself gave him more to carry, and his back was close to breaking.

"She will come back," she said instead. "You're closer to her than I am to you—it just hurts right now."

There was never a time the lie wouldn't hurt, there was never a time she could explain herself. She kept saying *not now, later* and later never came. He was going to be angry and he was going to hate her, but she had to remember this was all so much bigger than her and Gunnar. Asgarnia had too much to lose.

✦ ✦ ✦

When they reached the road that led down to the settlement, Valzin called a halt. "I want to scout ahead," she said.

"If you scout ahead," Master Endel replied, "they'll see your armoured knights and assume we're here for war. Let me come with you—the jarl… Well, we're not old friends, but he knows my face."

"That comes next," Valzin said. She looked at Ilme, gauging. "We'll just ride a little ahead and see if the settlement's occupied, if they look like they're preparing for a fight. You stay here—"

"We're not made of glass," Zanmaron spat.

"No, you're my emergency artillery," Valzin said, patiently. "Stay here and if you hear fighting, make some fire." She gestured to the knights and they set off down the trail.

Zanmaron slid off his horse and sat beside the road, working at the laces of a boot. "Where do you lay the odds on them needing this magical artillery?"

Master Unaia shifted in her saddle. "Must we use the High Marshal's… unpleasant nicknames?"

Master Endel took a palmful of runes from his pouch. "Be ready to cast and be ready to close your mouth and look thoughtful while you eat stewed fish—it could go either way."

Ilme looked up the mountain again, toward the mine. "We ought to see if there's anyone up there," she said. "We ought to… Someone should check on Zorya."

Master Endel cast a sidelong look up the mountain. "You probably should stay close… But the guardian might have a better sense how the Fremennik's temper is."

"I can be quick," Ilme said.

Master Endel slipped the runes back into their pouch. "I didn't see you go," he said significantly.

The snow clung to her boots as she made her way to the rift in the rock. Other feet had walked this path, churning up the mud beneath the falling snow, but she couldn't tell how many or who. The rope they'd used in those early days had long since frayed away, a series of ladders and platforms now making a path down into the rock. Ilme picked her way down into the mine.

"Zorya!" she shouted. "Zorya, are you awake!"

"Empty," Rue warned her. "Turn around."

"No," Ilme said, continuing down and down. "Zorya can't leave. He must be in the deep parts."

"Dangerous," Rue said.

The rune essence mine had expanded greatly in the last three decades. The narrow tunnel she had followed that freckled boy down was now a path as wide as Zorya, and winding passages spiralled out like the tentacles of some deep-sea squid, deep chasms gaping beyond the walkways. The faint glow of rune essence hung around them, almost a cloud. Rue began to circle over the walls, his usual path tasting the rune essence, but he was fidgety, looping back to twine around her ankles.

"Zorya!" Her voice bounced back from uncountable directions.

And then, in the distance, she heard voices. She froze. Gunnar and Zorya. Shouting.

She started running.

Where the passage levelled out, a huge cavern opened wide. Ilme remembered when they'd broken into this place, how they had pushed through the stone and found a void like Falador's great hall, deep beneath the earth. How she'd been eager to find Zorya, to lead him here where he would have so much more space to move.

The guardian had squeezed down the still-tight passage at her urging, always indulgent. But when he'd seen the vast cavern, the curved dome of the ceiling sparkling with crystal and pockets of rune essence, he'd let out a deep, booming croak Ilme could only call elated.

"This is wonderful," he'd said. "I had no idea this lay down here! I—who have been here beyond memory! Isn't that something?"

He'd even managed to hop across it, his powerful legs launching him over the cave's puddle-filled floor.

Now, Zorya crouched halfway across the room, his throat sac pulsing in an agitated way. Gunnar stood before him, axe in hand.

"There *is* no path forward!" Gunnar shouted. "There's no future for me—do you not see what you've done?"

"Put the axe down," Zorya said. "You're upset, this is not the time—"

"I asked for your *help*! I asked for you to stand up for what's right—how can you claim to come from Guthix and not be willing to tell the false Asgarnians they've wronged us?" He didn't drop the axe. "How could you lie to *me* like that? You're *nothing* like I thought."

I could kill it—he'd told her flat out that first day. He could, he knew how—hadn't he bragged about taking down giants?

"Gunnar!" Ilme shouted. "Stop!"

Gunnar turned at the sound of her voice and for a moment, there was so much hurt in his face, Ilme knew she should have flouted Master Endel and King Raddallin and told him from the start.

But then his expression hardened into a hatred that cut her to the core—he was never going to forgive the lie. She hadn't known him as well as she'd thought.

"Ilme," Zorya said. "Please—the lies have made him angry. But you all lie so often—"

"Put the axe down," Ilme said, "and we can talk."

"I don't have anything to say to you," Gunnar said.

Rue flew loops between them. "Stop, stop, stop!"

Ilme snatched him out of the air, clutched him to her chest. "I'm sorry," she said, walking toward Gunnar. "I wanted to tell you—"

"Did you? Or were you all laughing about how you duped the savages?"

"Nobody duped anyone," Ilme said. "We made an agreement—"

"You lied," Gunnar said advancing on her. "You knew the jarl wouldn't trust you if you weren't from the Moon Clan—"

"Your father?" Ilme said. "Your father didn't care who we were. He cared we took charge of the mine and gave him weapons for the trouble."

"And now he looks like a fool!" Gunnar shouted. "Now *I* look like a fool!"

"If they think you are a fool, then they are fools," Zorya declared. "If they won't make you jarl when your father dies, then you should go—"

"Are you trying to make me kill him too?" Gunnar said.

"Stop!" Ilme cried. "*Who* is saying you should kill your father?"

"— go and see what the world is full of," Zorya went on. "You are not limited—"

"Enough!" Gunnar howled. "Enough! You can't—" But they were all shouting over one another and Ilme couldn't make out the rest of what he said as he lowered the axe, reached across his belt—

Something behind Ilme sizzled. She turned and a creature stepped through a rift in the air, all muscle and horn and vicious teeth.

A demon, Ilme realised. A summoning rift.

Azris's whispered voice sliced through her memories. *Maybe the Moon Clan don't worship demons, but the Fremennik do. Everyone knows that.* They didn't, they couldn't.

You have raised mountains and leashed demons, Jarl Viljar bellowed to the Sleeping God. And here and now, when Gunnar had reached for the innocuous-looking pouch at his belt, a demon had appeared, as if drawn by a leash.

"What have you done?" she cried.

But Gunnar only stared at the demon, axe clutched in a determined grip.

The creature spread batlike wings, blocking the exit and roared, loud enough to shake the cavern. Ridged horns curled from its skull, its red skin rippling with muscles as it hefted a wicked-looking sword. The air burned in Ilme's nose and eyes and she backed away, one hand reaching for her rune pouch, one hand pulling Rue away, pushing him toward the back of the cavern,

"Demon," Zorya intoned. The creature hissed around terrible fangs and uttered a string of guttural language, heavy with disdain. Zorya returned with a booming so deep it rattled the chains draped over the demon's arms.

Then the great frog lunged forward, jaws parted, slamming into the demon, as if he were trying to swallow it whole. The wicked blade came up, slashing Zorya's slick skin, and the guardian pulled back.

Ilme clicked air runes together in her hand. Fear and force of will collapsed them together as she thrust her hands forward and gusts of wind with them. The demon threw Zorya aside, the spell narrowly missing the giant frog as they tumbled, scoring the demon's back and leaving dark lines of ichor running from it.

The demon howled. It turned and backhanded Ilme, flinging her across the wet cavern floor. Her head bounced against the stone, sending stars across her vision, and she heard the tinkling sound of runestones bouncing over the floor.

Rue landed on her chest. "Up, up, up!"

Her skull pounded, pulsing with a rhythm that felt like it was shaking the very earth. She let her head fall to the side… and saw the demon's cloven feet stamping closer.

Ilme rolled out of the way, scrambling to her feet. Her head swam, her runes were all over the floor. She fumbled for the pouch she wore around her neck, trying to conjure a blast of earth this time. The demon lunged for her, claws snatching at the stones near her feet. Zorya slammed into the demon again, driving it from her.

It reached up and sank its terrible claws into the guardian's dappled back. A white foam bubbled up from Zorya's slick skin and the smell of burning flesh flooded the air. The demon screamed, a sound that threatened to crack Ilme's skull, as the poison left black and boiling tracks across its skin.

Ilme searched the cavern for the summoner—but there was only Gunnar, circling the demon and Zorya, looking for an angle to attack.

I could kill it…

How can you possibly know him? Zanmaron had asked. She felt as if the world were slipping underneath her.

"Get away from him!" she shouted. But Gunnar was already moving, blade aimed—

Rue flew straight into her stomach, runes clutched in all four claws. "Here! Here!" He let them fall, clinking to the ground. Ilme swept them up, years of study and practice letting her sort them by touch—earth, water, blood, nature—

She collapsed the last, willing vines to erupt from the stone to bind the demon. But the creature, burned by Zorya's poison, thrashed and twisted from the grip of the frog's jaws and the spell missed, gnarled roots clinging to only Zorya's foreclaw.

The demon broke free, launching itself skyward. Dripping ichor, one wing torn, it looked as if it were trying to escape. And then it dropped, straight down on Zorya, who sat bleeding, battered, bound to the floor.

In that moment, too many things happened. Ilme closed her fist around the remaining runes, choosing the first spell that came to mind. Fear and rage burned through her—so hot and bright she might have crushed the stones physically in her grip. But the magic unlocked between her fingers, freed by need and will, and she threw a wave of scouring earth toward the falling demon.

At the same moment, Gunnar struck, leaping forward, axe high. He would hit the path of the spell—the demon would die but he would die too, and she couldn't call it back.

But Zorya pulled himself up, lunging toward the demon, as if to knock Gunnar aside—

And then the demon vanished, a rip in the air swallowing it once more.

The spell she'd cast swept over Zorya instead as the great frog sprang up. A horrible cry of pain burst out of him, the sweep of wind and sand tearing his flesh—

His cry broke off as Gunnar's axe came down in the guardian's skull.

For a moment, time froze, and Ilme couldn't hold the idea of Zorya being anything but ferociously alive in her head. In the next breath, he would rise. In the next breath, he would laugh with relief. He would praise her quick spells and Gunnar's caution and...

Rue settled on the bulk of the guardian, on his torn and bloody shoulder. His wings fluttered, agitated as he hopped down the great frog toward the axe. The immutable axe.

"Runes!" he said. "Runes! Fix it!"

Ilme reached into her rune pouch. As if there were any runes in all the worlds of gods and elves and humans that would bring him back. She felt a strange emptiness, that gap in her self that had opened when Moranna had died, but this time when she prodded at it, the pain and grief rushed in.

She clapped hands to her mouth, her heart ripping in half as if a whole other axe cleaved it.

"Fix it!" Rue said. "Runes! Runes!"

"No," Ilme said. She couldn't. No one could. "Rue, come away please."

Gunnar stared at her over Zorya's still body, over the puddles of blood that slicked the cave floor, his face a mask of horror. "He's dead."

Ilme squeezed her eyes shut. They should... what? Bury him? Burn him? Gods beyond, she wanted to scream. "He... He was so kind..." Her throat closed. Nothing she could say would be enough.

"He's dead," Gunnar said again. He looked down at his buried axe, then up at her. "You killed him."

Ilme blinked, tears breaking over her cheeks. "What?"

"You made all of this happen—"

Her grief froze in her, hardening into anger. "Are you... Are you *mad?*" she said. "He's dead. Because you... *You—*"

"What did I do?" he shouted, sounding as if his mind *was* breaking. "I trusted you, both of you. You have no care, no thought for what you've *ruined*, and it was your spell—"

"Don't you dare!" she shouted back. He was bigger than her, he was stronger than her, he'd fought a score or more terrible monsters and she'd barely begun, but in that moment she thought her rage and grief might be able to tear runes straight from the essence int the walls of the mine, might form a wave of flames and glass and sharp edges. "You have absolutely no right to lay this on me. I lied, yes, I lied and I'm sorry for it but I didn't have a choice and when you get down to it, it didn't matter to you one bit! None of this had to happen! It's your axe in his skull..." Her voice broke.

Gunnar took a step back from her. He pulled his axe free of the great frog's skull with a hideous crack of bone. He looked haunted. The way he'd looked when his daughter had been taken.

"This ends here," he said grimly.

"Are you going to kill me too?" Ilme snarled back. She scooped the runes she'd let fall from the ground. The power of them surged into her hands, sprayed forth in a stream of water, Gunnar dodged around it though, coming at her with the axe bared.

Frantic, she cast again, the same spell she'd tried to bind the demon with, and this time the vines caught Gunnar, tangling his legs and trapping him in place. He swung anyway, the axe falling short, the anger and disgust in his eyes injury enough.

"You will pay," Gunnar panted, ripping at the vines, straining at their grasp "You will all pay—you think you are safe in your 'Asgarnia' but we are coming. We will have revenge on your misdeeds!"

Moranna would have killed him there. Valzin would have too—Adolar, Raddallin, even Endel, she thought, would have heard the threat and ended it while Gunnar was trapped and injured and at her mercy. But in her grief and her panic she could hardly hear it—he had been her friend, he had been Zorya's friend, and now, and now—

One of the thick vines snapped. Rue circled her. "Go!" he said. "Go! Go! Up!"

This time, she did not argue—she had been wrong about Gunnar, as wrong as she could be, and she was wrong about what came next. With Rue chasing her up the scaffolding, she fled out into the snow and down the road where the wizards and the Kinshra waited. Valzin met her. "There you are! By the empty helmet, why would you run off like that? The Fremennik have left and—"

"We have to go!" Ilme gasped. "We shouldn't be here."

Zanmaron, trying to wrestle his boot back on, scowled up at her. "What? What happened?"

"The guardian's dead," Ilme said. "And the Fremennik are riding for war."

TEN

——◆▶——

Gunnar broke free of the bindings and chased after Ilme,
following her footprints down the mountain's slope to
where they disappeared in a churn of hoofmarks and strange
boot prints. Fleeing. Back to the kingdom they'd built on stolen
rune essence.

What would you do if you'd caught her? he asked himself.
Standing over Zorya's body, he'd been angry enough to kill her, if
only in vengeance for the guardian. That she'd lied, that Zorya
had helped her, had shattered him. That she'd summoned a
monster to kill the guardian, that she'd cast her foul spells to hurt
Zorya. That she'd taken the demon back when he was inches
from ending it, and let his blade fall—

The judder that had shook his arms as his axe split the guardian's
skull ghosted up his limbs again, and Gunnar shut his eyes. No.
Zorya had already been dead. It had been another cruel trick.

But he knew too that if he had caught Ilme running down the
mountain, if he had cornered her without her runes in hand…

he wouldn't have killed her. Not first, anyway—he would have asked her to explain. Nothing made sense, and if it would only make sense…

He gripped the axe. *Nothing makes sense,* he admonished himself, *because you have been a fool.*

The Wolf Clan had left with no thought for where Gunnar was. He raided the stores of wood they left behind, stacked for next year in the higher hills, and brought them to the cave. He built a pyre around Zorya, and stayed until the smoke started to pool in the cave's ceiling, thinking of all the things he had lost.

✦ ✦ ✦

In the morning, he was a different man.

The path to the winter camp of the Fremennik led down the slope of the mountain, away from the storm-tossed sea, where the earth stayed warm from the deep springs below, and they could build their settlements into the caves that lined the mountain slopes, fishing in the ice lakes and hunting on their shores, living off the stores they'd built all summer. Gunnar reached his people a day and a half after leaving the mine, and came up to the cave hall entrance, axe in hand. A structure like the end of a longhouse protruded from the slope of the earth, the great doors lit by dancing torches.

Two warriors stood outside the doors—Ivo and Fronya. She looked startled when she recognised him; Ivo, cruelly amused. He stepped forward to block Gunnar's progress, to issue the challenge Gunnar had been prevented from giving, to declare him exiled, to just stab him and leave him bleeding on the frosty ground— Gunnar didn't care. Ivo didn't matter.

As the other man came into reach, Gunnar hit him upside the head with the flat of his axe, never slowing his stride. He heard Ivo hit the ground as Fronya moved out of his way, letting him into the winter cave hall.

Inside, the structure carved its way into the hillside. It was warm and dark under the blanket of earth, the fires burning under the chimneys carved up through the mountain. All eyes watched him as he approached Jarl Viljar, seated at the high place at the back of the cave hall.

"There you are," his father said. "Where have you been? Chasing monsters again?"

He's your father, Gunnar told himself. *He's your jarl. You will give him this one chance.*

"The Guardian of Guthix is dead," Gunnar announced, his voice catching horribly on his grief. He cleared his throat and continued, "We must prepare for war."

The Fremennik turned slowly to regard Jarl Viljar, who scowled at his son. "You're not the jarl," he said. "You don't declare war."

"The guardian is *dead*," Gunnar said again. "Those Asgarnians and their wizards did it. They only ever cared about their rune essence—the Moon Clan tried to tell you and you didn't listen. You wanted luxuries and trade and coin, and now Zorya is dead." He threw the axe down.

Jarl Viljar came to his feet, iron and bear, looking down on his only son with disgust. "I lead this clan," he said. "I sail its warships. I bring the bounty of Guthix to us. And now we have only your word that the wizards have killed the guardian—in winter, no less. They are soft and they are weak—"

"They are not, no matter how many times you say it!" Gunnar said. "It's the Wolf Clan that's soft and weak—you've let us falter!" *You've let me falter,* his thoughts spat. *I should never have trusted her, I should never have called her friend.* "Salmon and Seal and Ox thumb their noses at us and nothing happens! Falcon is laughing in their beards! And now what should be soft-handed foreigners are making the Wolf into fools! I have listened to you for all my days and what do I have to show for it? The gift of Guthix plundered for mere weapons. My heirs and yours scattered to the storms! And now I have seen the great guardian of our god slain in cold blood—all because you were so easily duped—"

Viljar stepped down and hit Gunnar across the face.

Ears ringing, head spinning, Gunnar didn't think—he struck back, punching his father hard across the cheekbone.

It happened so quickly. There was no stopping it. Gunnar saw the moment his fist hit Viljar, the slight widening of his eyes—Ilme had been right, he'd been dreading this all his days and had convinced himself it wouldn't happen. His face collapsed, and Viljar was falling, hard and fast. He stopped as his head struck the green stone of Guthix, the twin of the one beside the sea. There was a dull, hollow crack and a splash of blood.

And Jarl Viljar lay still and very dead.

Gunnar wanted to scream. Wanted to run from the cave. First Zorya, now his father. And he couldn't take it back.

He *wouldn't* take it back, he realised. For all he wanted to scream, to run, to bring Viljar back—if he somehow had his wish and he could stop his father's death, he would not apologise for striking him. Viljar had pushed him one to many times and now the world was changing, and Gunnar was the one who would steer his path.

Steer all their paths.

He bundled that grief, that panic, under the sureness of anger, and turned to face the Wolf Clan. His clan.

They stared at him, the warriors with hands on weapons, the fire-tenders wary and distrustful. Other jarls had come into the title this way, but not in recent memory.

Gunnar stepped over and set his hand upon the stone. "What Guthix has granted us is always temporary," he said. "We are frail, after all, even our strongest. My father knew this. I am glad he died a warrior, though I mourn that Guthix would take him this way." He clutched the pointed tip of the stone, felt his father's sticky blood along the side where his head had struck. "I mourn that he died before he could see reason. I mourn he died before he could see our great victory."

There were times before—times that Gunnar would soon bury in his memory and never think of again—when he would listen to Ilme describing what it was like making runes, how the magic felt flowing through her, carrying part of her soul with it. In this moment, Gunnar felt something similar, something flowing through him, carried like a ship on a wave too great for it. As if the voice of a jarl of the Wolf Clan were filling him like a spirit that wandered from father to son upon death. He didn't look on those warriors with fear—they would follow him. They had to. He was the jarl, and the jarl called not just for war, but for a holy retribution.

"We will not be frail any longer," he declared. "We will retake our clans and we will sail to war."

"Against who?" someone asked.

"Asgarnia," he said. "The Moon Clan warned us. They have already struck first. One of their wizards killed the guardian in the mine." He pointed at Viljar, dead on the floor. "And when the jarl denied our duty, Guthix struck him down."

Murmuring ran through the hall. Someone came forward with a cloak to cover Viljar, but Gunnar stopped them. "No. Gaze upon him. This is what comes of disregarding Guthix. We were never to have magic. We knew this. And we pretended it didn't matter so long as the Wolf Clan chose steel. We were *wrong*. This is why the other clans deserted us. This is why the tribute has ceased.

"When the spring comes, we will pacify the other clans. We will avenge the death of the guardian and the plunder Jarl Viljar allowed. We are not pawns of lesser gods, and we know the teachings. Humans were not meant to have runes. Humans are not strong or wise enough to cast magic. The Asgarnians have flouted the sacred teachings of Guthix and for this, we must wipe their works from Gielinor."

ELEVEN

————◆▸————

Ilme stood before King Raddallin, feeling like nothing so much as a scraped-out skin, as she finished her report of what had happened at the Wolf Clan's settlement. He looked down at her, his brows heavy with concern.

"Why would he kill the guardian?" Raddallin asked.

"I don't know," she said truthfully. She had been turning it over and over in her mind—there were so many parts of that horrible fight in the cavern that made no sense. Why would Gunnar kill Zorya? How did Gunnar summon a demon?

There is no path forward! There's no future for me—do you not see what you've done? She swallowed. "He was angry. Desperate. I think... I think he had lost face with his clan because he was friendly with us." *With me*, she thought. *I made this happen.*

"Your Majesty," Master Endel said from beside her, "we have hopes that Jarl Viljar will listen to reason... and a generous offer to enhance his coffers and armoury."

"We are to arm the enemies that seek to… what did he say?" Raddallin turned to Ilme. "'Make you all pay'."

You will all pay—you think you are safe in your 'Asgarnia', but we are coming. She hadn't made him so vicious, so violent. That had been in him… somehow. And she hadn't seen it.

"That was the son," Endel pointed out. "The father has been very reasonable. And we cannot lose the rune essence mine."

"No," Raddallin agreed. "To my knowledge, most of our treaties have the payment of runestones woven into every exchange. Not only would we be stymied in our own defences and capabilities, every agreement we've set would collapse." He leaned over to where Valzin stood to the right of his throne, dressed in a trim purple gown with a high collar and a divided skirt for riding. "Any word from Perior?"

Old Grand Master Adolar had died several years prior, refusing to handle the runes. Perior had taken his place as Grand Master of the White Knights, much to Valzin's benefit. The camaraderie of the rune altar exploration and that one brutal fight had thawed the old split between Black and White Knights.

Valzin winced. "Any day, Your Majesty. But…" She bit off her words. "Never mind."

"Speak, Sana," Raddallin said. "Everything in the open please."

Valzin met Ilme's eyes, and a thrill of panic went through her. "The boy sounds like a fanatic, to be perfectly honest. The best use of our time and resources right now would be to claim all of the treaties which require mutual protection and mobilise. Assume we are at war."

"Against the Fremennik?" Endel said incredulously. "They don't have two runes to stack together."

"But they have your essence mine," Valzin countered. "We will have a shortage soon enough if we don't do something. And they will continue to gather more warriors."

"Rubbish," Master Endel declared. "I have spent time with the Wolf Clan. Jarl Viljar is a man concerned only with what lies on his own oxhide, so to speak. He's not waging war across half the continent even if he is ready to take my head off."

"But Gunnar might," Ilme said. She didn't want to say these words, didn't want to admit how wrong she'd been. Didn't want to doom her friend. But she owed King Raddallin an answer.

"Gunnar is the next jarl," she said. "Our plan was always to admit to the deception when he took over, to hope that the connections we had fostered would keep him and the Wolf Clan friendly and let Jarl Viljar take on any shame from the grave.

"But... that isn't going to work. He's furious. He's angry I lied, and he was angry that the guardian knew, and... if he was angry enough to kill the guardian, then I assume he will make good on his threats. I agree with the High Marshal. Sooner or later, the Fremennik will be a problem."

"Even so," Master Endel said, "we have runes and rune essence to last us for years if we don't mind a little austerity. Gunnar's not an old man, but he's not a young one anymore. We could start over with his successor, whoever that is. Moreover, he's not jarl yet. I still know a thing or two about managing Viljar."

The doors to the chamber broke open, one of the White Knights' pages running down the length of the hall, her cropped hair sticking up in all directions with sweat. She dropped into a kneeling bow, before bursting out, "Sir Perior's scouts reached the winter city. The old jarl is murdered and his son has seized control. The Fremennik chased them off—they say they will wipe the scourge of rune magic from the world!"

Ilme swallowed against the sudden lump in her throat. She thought, dizzily, of Zorya, of the guardian saying, *You have stepped onto a path now, Ilme. You cannot fathom the reach of it.* They had all made their choices.

Endel cleared his throat. "That…That does change things. But let's not ignore Gunnar Viljarsson doesn't have an army to match Asgarnia's. They only know how to raid coastal settlements. And if things have continued as they were the last time I visited, the Wolf Clan has lost more than a little of the control they'd gained with our weapons. He simply doesn't have the numbers."

"And what if he gets them?" Valzin asked.

"Then that is a problem for the day it occurs," Endel said. He turned to Raddallin, "Going to war right now against the Fremennik is a waste of time. All freshly crowned rulers sit on a precarious throne—you know that as well as anyone, sire. If you sweep in with your knights, you will anger all the other clans."

"Or, do it now and stop them getting ideas," Valzin added.

Raddallin sighed heavily. "If we ride to war, what do we say to our allies?"

"That we won't be pushed around?" Valzin suggested.

"That we are weakened without the agreement," Ilme said. "Perhaps… Perhaps Master Endel is right. If you go to war against the Wolf Clan you're telling everyone our treaties are precarious."

Valzin clucked her tongue. "Not a lie."

"We can go to war with the Wolf Clan," Endel pointed out. "We can't go to war with Misthalin and Ardougne and who knows where else." He turned to Raddallin. "I should apprise Unaia and Strekalis of the situation. If I may, Your Majesty."

"Go," Raddallin said. He nodded to the page, waiting quiet at the foot of the dais. "You too, girl. Get cleaned up and go to the kitchens." He frowned, troubled, as they both left the room. "I want an accounting of how much rune essence we do have. How many runes. Who we need to watch if this doesn't blow over the way Endel is suggesting. Where is Eritona? Is she in Falador?"

"I… I'll find her, Your Majesty," Ilme said, bowing, and hurrying from the room.

✦ ✦ ✦

Eritona was in the library, running a stiff copper brush over Rue's scales. When Ilme walked in they both looked up. "Any word?" Eritona asked.

Ilme started to tell her King Raddallin needed her, that they were on the brink of war, that there were carefully phrased letters to draft and send, that Jarl Viljar was dead and Gunnar had seized the clan. But suddenly she felt as if someone had dropped a huge weight on her, and all she could think of was the demon, plummeting straight down at Zorya. Tears flooded her eyes and she pressed a hand to her mouth.

"Oh, sit!" Eritona cried, pushing Rue off her lap and guiding Ilme to a chair. "When is the last time you slept?"

Ilme shook her head, not trusting herself to speak. Did it count as sleeping if you woke a half dozen times through the night, your head full of death and your throat aching to scream or vomit?

Rue crawled up into her lap. "Your friend... bad."

He was trying to talk more, the words clumsy in his mouth. She scratched under his chin and clamped her teeth around the sobs shaking her. She should have known. She should have stopped this. Eritona sat down and tucked an arm around her.

Azris came into the library, a bounce in her step. "You're back," she said. "Sorry, I was busy."

"Not now," Eritona said.

Azris frowned. "What's wrong with her?"

"Azris!" Eritona said. "You were just with Zanmaron, did he not tell you—"

"We were *busy*," Azris said. "Spare me your moralising, and tell me what's going on?"

"The guardian *died*," Eritona said. "The one in the mine.

And…" She mouthed the next words as if Ilme couldn't hear the faint whisper of her words. "The jarl's son did it."

"I don't know if he did," Ilme admitted, swallowing down the grief. "It was… chaotic and… I can't believe he would have killed Zorya."

"I told you they worship demons," Azris said.

"Do they do summoning?" Eritona asked. "I thought they hated magic."

"It's the runes they have the issue with," Azris said. "And you've seen that great monster they tell everyone is the face of Guthix in their longhouse—this was always likely."

"We never talked about summoning," Ilme said. "He never mentioned it."

"And you never mentioned being Asgarnian," Azris said. "Who else was in that cavern?"

Ilme hesitated. "Me. Rue. Zorya."

"And did *you* summon a demon? Did Rue?"

"Bad friend," Rue grumbled.

"Exactly," Azris said. "Look, I know you're friends—er, you *were* friends with him. But I knew him too—"

"As a child," Ilme said. "You haven't been to the essence mine in thirty years."

"Yes, well, he was a horrible kid—it's not a wonder he turned out to be a horrible man."

"Azris!" Eritona cried.

"You were a horrible kid too," Ilme shot back. "Or have you forgotten?" She wanted a fight, she wanted someone she could scream at, hurl spells at, so that all this could go *somewhere* that wasn't the knot of sorrow in her chest.

Azris regarded her, stone-faced. "No," she said. "I haven't forgotten. And I haven't forgotten either that you were a traitor once—"

Ilme shot to her feet, hand reaching for the pouch of runes faster than a thought. Eritona seized her wrist, yanking her back down. "Stop!"

"You were a traitor *once*." Azris repeated, more loudly. "And I know you're not going to do it again. Especially when it doesn't do you any good." She sat down at last, her gaze level with Ilme. "You still think nobody is watching you, but I know you gave up everything to be right here. You have worked as hard as anyone—maybe not on the most impressive developments, we can't all be brilliant—"

"Writing the same treatise three times isn't brilliant," Ilme said hotly.

Azris waved this aside. "The point is you are sad, you can be sad. You can be angry. But you are going to have to remember that you are, and have been for as long as it matters, a wizard of Asgarnia, and if that spindly jarl's son is hurt that you have a higher calling, then he can go rot out beyond the Edicts!"

Ilme shook her head. "That's not it." She couldn't help thinking of all the choices she'd made, all the assumptions that had set them tripping down long paths they could never have seen the end of.

Azris threw up her hands. "Well, I tried. He doesn't deserve your guilt though. Only one of you responded to a silly lie with murder."

"You can't remake an air rune into a blood rune." Eritona said, a little primly.

"No," Azris said with a long sigh. "Master Unaia set some of her wizards to that experiment, and all they got was wasted runes."

"I mean, you can't make the jarl's son into someone he's not."

"I just… I don't understand *how* he could have killed Zorya," Ilme said, sadly.

Azris patted her knee. "I have some books you can read. Summoning's not really that complicated. I'm sure you'll work it out."

"Watching gods, Azris," Eritona said. "Do you listen to yourself?"

"I have to go," Ilme said, untangling herself from both women. If she stayed here another moment, she was either going to start weeping or strike Azris. "Eritona, King Raddallin wants to discuss the state of our treaties with you. I'm going to start checking our essence stores."

Rue landed on her shoulder as she left the library, following the curving staircase down the tower to the vaults in the deep levels of the fortress. "Your friend bad," he said again.

"Azris is Azris," she said. "She's an ordinary sort of bad."

Wasn't she? Ilme suddenly didn't know—she'd prided herself on her ability to read people, to know what they wanted and what they might do. And then she'd been so very mistaken. She'd known Gunnar was proud, that telling him the truth would be hard—she'd known if he found out on his own it wouldn't go well. He was hurt, he was humiliated, he was trying to protect himself from feeling like a fool. But she'd imagined he'd want to be reassured, want to be helped back to feeling settled.

She could never have imagined him killing Zorya. Not if he'd threatened to do it a hundred times.

But she couldn't see another answer. There had only been the four of them in the cavern—her and Zorya and Gunnar and Rue. She hadn't summoned the demon and Rue couldn't have. Zorya certainly hadn't done it and that only left Gunnar, reaching for his pouch and shouting—

She shut her eyes. That was it: she had gotten him wrong. That was the only real answer.

Valzin was already in the primary essence vault when she arrived, scrutinising the crates and piles of unformed rune magic. The vault itself was as large as the Wolf Clan's longhouse: even without having made a trip to the rune essence mine that year, it was nearly full.

Valzin nodded at Ilme as she entered. "Any chance Endel's collection of books includes the ledgers for some old war's quartermaster? Would be nice to have a sense of how fast we're going to run through this."

"Isn't that why we have the knights?" Ilme asked. "His Majesty pulled this kingdom most of the way into existence before we ever had runes."

"Mm, but war makes people restless," she said. "What happens when Karamja or Misthalin or the Imcando find out Asgarnia's got an enemy? We don't know how many fronts this war will have."

"None at the moment."

"At the moment."

Ilme frowned. "You sound excited."

"Excited's the wrong word," Valzin said, a crooked smile pulling at her mouth. "I have my uses in Raddallin's new court—ferrying messages to Misthalin and making placating noises at his allies. But the Kinshra and I are a lot more useful on the battlefield. I think Raddallin would do well to remind everyone he hasn't lost the fire that made him king in the first place." She turned to Ilme, something wild in her blue eyes that Ilme hadn't seen in a long time. "It's how the world works. Great changes are always upon us."

"Maybe it will all settle down quickly," Ilme said. "Maybe someone will talk sense into Gunnar. Maybe we'll get the essence mine back without a lot of trouble."

But even as she thought it, she knew that Gunnar wouldn't let his guard down among the Fremennik. She had been the only one he'd have confessed his anger to, the only one he would have listened to when she said *let it settle*—and now there was no chance of that ever happening again.

TWELVE

THE FIFTY-SECOND YEAR OF THE REIGN OF KING RADDALLIN
OF ASGARNIA

**THE FIFTY-SECOND YEAR OF THE REIGN OF KING RADDALLIN
OF ASGARNIA**
THE ELEVENTH DAY OF THE MONTH OF PENTEMBER
THE SALMON CLAN'S MAIN SETTLEMENT

The Salmon Clan had no winter camp. Built along a river seeking its way inland on the far northern island, they dug their longhouses into the earth and built stone into their walls. The waters they built alongside were wide and freezing along the shoreline, as Gunnar's warriors rowed him against the current toward the buildings ahead. He eyed the people gathering along the shore, looking for a pale-haired woman of thirty years. Would he even recognise Thyra? What would happen if he didn't? What would happen if she turned from him?

Gunnar squashed down those thoughts. Of course, he would recognise her. Of course, she would be glad to see him—glad as she could be, since the Salmon Clan must be brought to heel, but he would give them a chance to accept the word of Guthix, and the rule of Gunnar Viljarsson.

They were the last of the clan he would bring under the Wolf's control. It had been easy to get to this place, one final clan and so much sureness in his goals that he did not hesitate. That first winter, the Wolf Clan had been agitated, their preparations for the thaw full of whispered anxieties and fractious arguments. When they had returned to their longships, the Falcon Clan was waiting, having seized their chance to strike at the clan weakening under an ageing jarl's rule.

It had been more of a battle than Gunnar had expected. But his would be the long path, and with the memory of Zorya's death and the knowledge of Guthix's blessings, his clan had crushed their attackers and sailed on to attack the Falcons' settlement further south along the sea. If he were Ott he would have killed them all. If he were Reigo, he would have left the settlement to think about what it had done.

But Gunnar Viljarsson had to be a different sort of jarl—a jarl bearing the truth of Guthix. He would need every warrior he could muster. So when the Wolf Clan had made evident that the Falcons were not going to triumph that day, Gunnar had brought their jarl onto his ship and laid out his plans.

The world was in danger. Rune magic had to be eradicated. Asgarnia had to be stopped. And if the Falcon Clan did not see the necessity of this course of action, then the Wolf Clan would make certain they could not stand in their way.

Gunnar needed every warrior he could get—but he could not risk treachery again.

The clans that had once been bent to Viljar's rule—the Seal, the Falcon, the Mammoth—these had been his first task. Bring them back under Wolf's rule, and add their warriors to his tally. It had taken more than a few years, but now the jarls who ruled them were dedicated to his cause, their warriors eager for the coming war. They had been at his side as they sailed down on the other clans of the Fremennik—the Ox, the Larch, the Sturgeon, and all the smaller clans whose emblems blurred together. They were all the Wolf. They were all the army of Gunnar Viljarsson.

And now, the Salmon—fat and settled and unburdened by their promises to the Wolf, thirteen years neglected. The winter storms had been fiercer and stranger the last few years, disrupting fishing grounds and swamping fields. The small clans flocked to his banner, eager for solutions, eager for answers. But the Salmon waited inland, silent and sullen, for him to come to them.

This part was all ritual—the rival chieftain requesting hospitality, the receiving tribe declaring their strength and lineage. Words that meant *don't underestimate us, don't test the bonds of hospitality.* But even as they brought him into their longhouse, into the heart of their power, with Gunnar's longships, his warriors, his ever-growing clan, they were only words. The Salmon jarl, a man called Orvar Sigurdsson, beckoned his warriors to dedicate their weapons on the green Guthix stone at the centre. Gunnar watched and waited in much the fashion he'd waited for a tiny Thyra to finish a recitation of which berries were her favourites.

This was the simple part, he thought, noticing how Orvar never met his eyes. But Gunnar was very ready for the difficult part.

His own warriors laid their weapons on the stone, acknowledgement of the truce now in place and a pledge to defend their hosts for the duration of the hospitality agreement. Gunnar rose last, knees a little stiff, and approached with his axe in hand.

His father's face as his fist connects… the hollow crack as it hits the stone…

Gunnar fought the urge to flinch from the memory as fresh as that autumn day so long ago. He set the axe against the stone and looked up to find Orvar watching him warily.

Good, Gunnar thought.

"Will our daughter be joining us, jarl?" he said, all politeness for Thyra's father-in-law. It was the least he could do.

Orvar's nostrils flared. "Thyra is among the fire-tenders. I'm sure she'll be happy to see you, jarl, when her tasks are complete."

"Great Jarl," Gunnar corrected, all mildness. "I am Great Jarl of the Fremennik now, Orvar."

Orvar's eyes darted away again. "Of course. Word of your campaign has spread over the sea. The gift of Guthix, the necessity of crushing the runecrafters. But this is talk for after we've eaten. Please, sit."

As Orvar turned, Gunnar grabbed his sleeve. Orvar bristled at the affrontery. "Would you have my daughter bring over my plate? I would speak with her."

He sat again, looking over the warriors of the Salmon Clan. They seemed hale and keen-eyed men and women—valuable additions to his army. He searched among them for hints of his late wife—Fiera's tilted nose, Fiera's curling hair. Had Thyra thrived among them?

If she hadn't, he could easily forgo these warriors and leave the Salmon Clan in their grave when he sailed away.

"Great Jarl," a woman said. A plate slid into view, and he looked up into the face of a woman with a pale blond braid and a pursed mouth—and his daughter's bright, bright eyes.

"Thyra." The word gusted from him like a sigh of relief. "I'm so glad to see you."

"The Salmon Clan is grateful to offer you hospitality," she said back.

He beckoned her around the long table. "Fronya, move down. Thyra, come here, please. I want to hear how you've been. I want to know everything."

Thyra's cheeks reddened, and she glanced backwards, first at the fire, then at the table of the Salmon jarl. "I'm sorry, I have duties to attend to—"

"Nonsense," he said. "I'm sure Orvar would rather we have a chance to talk. Sit."

Thyra drew a deep breath, then came around the table and

climbed over the bench to take Fronya's vacated seat. "It's been a long time," she said at last.

Fifteen years. Life's whetstone had sharpened the girl Viljar had bargained away, but Gunnar could still see his curious, sometimes serious little girl within her.

"Are you happy?" he asked. "Which one is your husband?"

"Alvis," she said, nodding toward the jarl's table, and the wiry, dark-haired man beside him.

"A good husband?" he asked.

"It's not as if I could trade him in," she said a little wryly. "He's the jarl's son."

Gunnar frowned. "You're the daughter of the Great Jarl," he said. "He should make himself a little more worthy. Children?"

"Three," she said. "Two boys, and a girl." She hesitated. "You never wrote."

"Viljar—"

"Has been dead a decade. They say you killed him."

His father's face as his fist connects... the hollow crack as it hits the stone...

He forced those memories down. "Guthix killed Jarl Viljar," Gunnar corrected. "Any who stand against His will should be prepared to have their heads dashed against the stones."

Thyra studied him a moment, and he was startled to see not himself, not Fiera, but a glimmer of his father in that frank, appraising gaze. "Do you intend to dash Orvar against the stones? We've heard the fate of the Seal and Elk jarls."

"No," Gunnar said, firmly, as if he were sure, as if by *being* sure, he could make it so. "No, no, no—I come with offers of unity and friendship. I come to share my vision with my daughter's adopted clan. I'm sure Jarl Orvar will be glad to dedicate his weapons to Guthix's cause."

Thyra said nothing a moment too long.

"You think not?" he asked.

"I don't know," she admitted, eyes on the jarl's table. "There are questions. People talk. They say your only plans are to make all Fremennik subject to your rule. That victory over the southern lands is a fool's aim. That you are chasing satisfaction for a personal slight, and a man who would burn the world because a woman made him look stupid is a poor leader indeed, and the Salmon Clan would be better off sailing into the ice."

Gunnar's temper flared. "Who says these things?" he demanded.

She met his gaze. "Are they true?" she asked. And when he didn't answer, she added, "It's Aunt Ilme, isn't it?"

Ilme flashed in his mind, laughing on some summer evening, Thyra on her knee, the sun low and the sky lavender, telling him stories while they watched nighthawks loop over the meadows below: of worlds beyond broken altars, endless fires and circling stars and swamps that flowed from beyond time itself.

"Don't speak her name," he said. Ilme was nothing—a spark that lit the tinder. "Don't think about her—this is so much more than the lies of the Asgarnians. Do you see that? Does the jarl see that? All the clans are behind me—except Salmon."

Thyra considered the table. "He wonders why you haven't come. He wonders why isolate the Salmon Clan."

"Because, I, unlike some people, do not make promises I don't intend to keep," he said, fully in mind of the Salmon Clan's betrayal of Viljar. "I come here certain of my word that the Fremennik will destroy Asgarnia and all its allies."

She regarded him, her face a mask. "They say you're still defending the mine."

Gunnar gritted his teeth. The rune essence mine—the grave of the Guardian of Guthix—was a sore point. He had collapsed it that first winter, made it a monument to Zorya. And still Ilme's

Asgarnians crept in like ants seeking crumbs. Some summers they did not appear. Some summers Gunnar could not spare the warriors and when they returned to it, there were wizards crawling over the mine, breaking through the rubble.

"What is worth doing is worth doing *right*," Gunnar said, biting back his temper. "I have the army. I have the vision. I have the blessings of the god." He leaned in slightly. "I have three hundred longships, and nearly ten thousand warriors. Let them excavate a collapsed mine: I am coming for something far more precious. And I would rather the Salmon Clan be by my side, than working against me." He drew back, added more softly. "I would rather have my daughter by my side."

It had been a long time, and there had been so many other people guiding her, changing her, whispering in her ears—how could he think he knew Thyra, after all, when Ilme had devastated him so completely—

"Great Jarl," she said, "I have three small children. I am no warrior. I am no asset in the battle you describe." She frowned. "Unless... you mean to settle in the southern lands?"

She had always been a clever child, always a quick learner. He smiled, his anger fractured, crumbling under pride. "I do," he said. "Eventually. Will the Salmon jarl join me?"

"That is a lot to ask," she said. "But maybe less so with ten thousand warriors."

"Will *you* help me?" he pressed.

She hesitated. "Of course, Great Jarl. But... you don't mean to attack the southern lands now? With winter approaching?"

"To begin with," he said, "I intend to remind the settlements along the Northern Sea's shores that they are in the realm of the Fremennik. After that, when they think they have the measure of us, I intend to show them that the realm of the Fremennik is the realm of Guthix and none are safe."

"What does that mean?"

Ilme in the summer, Thyra on her knee.... worlds of endless fires and circling stars and swamps that flowed from beyond time itself...

"Simply," he said, "we destroy their rune altars."

THIRTEEN

◄◆►

THE FIFTY-FIFTH YEAR OF THE REIGN OF KING RADDALLIN OF ASGARNIA

THE TWENTIETH DAY OF THE MONTH OF SEPTOBER

ARDOUGNE, KANDARIN

Ardougne made Ilme appreciate the artistry of Falador. Old bones of the former city, shattered by war and rebellion, held up the newer sections, all wooden and gleaming. The scent of pine baking in the summer air hung thick around her as she dismounted in the stableyard. Between the old stone was so much wood: wooden palisades, wooden walls, even logs corrugating the mud into a wooden road through the gates.

"What *are* they doing with all those runes we sent them?" Azris asked, staring up at the timber-framed manor that seemed to be Ardougne's palace. A star of Saradomin hung bright and burning gold where the lowering sun struck it high on the wall. "I thought they were meant for rebuilding. Why would you not rebuild with stone?"

"They had their hands full battling the mahjarrat," Sir Perior of the White Knights said. His dark skin glistened with sweat, but still he wore his full riding armour. "It would have taken all those runes to destroy him."

"Which, we do not need Eritona to remind us, was not in the treaty," Zanmaron pointed out, moving to help elderly Master Strekalis down from his horse.

"Not explicitly," Perior admitted.

Ardougne and its larger kingdom, Kandarin, had been ruled for many years by Hazeel, a mahjarrat, one of the immortal lieutenants of Zamorak. Not a god, but far more powerful than a mere human. Rebels had sought aid from Asgarnia and the Wizards' Tower, and the now Saradominist government had begun rebuilding the walled city on the edge of the elven Wilderness. Asgarnia had not *explicitly* overthrown the neighbouring kingdom, Ilme knew. What the wizards of Kandarin did with the runes was their own business. But there was no ignoring the timing. Or the star of Saradomin shining over the town.

"Surely," Perior went on, "you don't think it would be better for the mahjarrat to still rule? He was a tyrant. A violent creature."

"And how fortunate your siblings-in-faith have taken over," Zanmaron said darkly. "One wonders what they do with other Zamorakians."

Master Strekalis huffed, as he beat the dust from his red robes. "Nonsense. 'To each to the extent of their own abilities, for the price of their own sacrifices,'" he quoted. "You and I are not Hazeel—we could not be Hazeel in a thousand lifetimes. Why should we worry about suffering for his crimes or his weaknesses?" He took his walking stick down from the saddle, and patted the horse's neck with one gnarled hand. "Zamorak approves of their ambition, their survival, I'm very sure."

"Bored," Rue complained, curled in the sling Ilme had made for him. She scratched his jaw. "Tired."

Master Strekalis peered at the little dragon from beneath prodigious eyebrows. "You're a grumpy baby today!"

Rue huffed. "Not baby."

"Calm down," Ilme said affectionately. She searched the yard, busy with White Knights and grooms. They were losing light, and she wanted to get moving.

A man strode toward them from the manor, trailed by a wizard in blue and white robes. He was middle-aged, plain and serious-looking, with a close-trimmed beard of reddish brown over pale skin. She was darker-complected, black hair bound up in a topknot that displayed her long neck and tasselled earrings.

"Welcome to Ardougne," the man said. "I'm Nevan Carnillean. This is Master Jana. Come this way, we'll show you to your rooms before dinner."

He'd turned to walk away when Ilme interrupted. "I would like to see the excavations first."

Nevan Carnillean looked back over his shoulder, frowning. "Tomorrow."

"Today," she said. "Now, if you please."

"Ilme," Azris said under her breath.

Nevan Carnillean had been among the handful who had led the rebellion against Hazeel—Ilme knew that much. He was used to holding his ground against stubborn forces.

But, she suspected, he knew when to retreat, when to yield. You did not overthrow a near-god tyrant in one swift move.

"I am here for one purpose, my lord," she said. "Your letter said that you were close to discovering the site of the death altar, and I want to see what exactly it is that you've found. That altar is critical to the defence of Asgarnia, and by extension the defence of Kandarin—and all of the agreements between our two countries. The sun is up. I am well. Either find me someone who can take me to the excavation, or I will find it myself." She turned to Master Jana. "Is it you?"

Jana paused. "I'm... involved in the search for the lost temple, yes."

"Perfect," Ilme said. "Then I'll go with you."

Jana looked askance at Carnillean, who sighed and opted to yield. "Fine. Dinner will be served at sunset." He gestured at the others. "Which of you would rather refresh yourselves than dig in the dirt?"

Rue growled and hooked his little claws over the edge of the sling. "Tired!"

A silent conference passed between Zanmaron and Azris, and Ilme was on the verge of declaring she would go alone, thank you very much, when Master Strekalis hobbled forward. "Give me the baby, Ilme. You, Zanmaron and Azris go see to the rune altar."

Rue curled tight against Ilme and reflexively she cradled him. "Not baby." Then, "Tired."

"I don't know if you ought to be alone, master," Zanmaron began.

Strekalis waved him off. "I'm hardly alone with Perior and fifty White Knights roaming the manor. Besides I am *laden* with runes. Go search the site. Rue, come here!"

Ilme scooped Rue from the sling and held him out to the older man. Rue climbed onto Master Strekalis's shoulders, stretching around the back of his neck like a scarf. "Protect," he growled.

"Yes, yes," Strekalis said fondly. "You're a very fierce little baby."

Jana led them from the manor to the western side of the city. "It's a bit of a walk," she apologised. "But I assume you'd rather walk than ride after your travels." Then she added, "Lord Carnillean's letter wouldn't have mentioned it, but we've actually broken through into a void. A room beyond. They were spending today shoring up the dig site, but we might have found the temple itself."

Hope flared in Ilme. The death altar was one of the few they had not been able to find, its runes described as powerful components in combat spells.

A memory rose up, unbidden—herself, so much younger, sitting under a tree with a map spread out, her finger circling the kingdom that was becoming Kandarin. "Here, there's supposed to be an altar that makes death runes."

"You wouldn't *use* those, would you?" Gunnar asked, sounding worried. "What do they do? Wake the dead and things?"

She'd hesitated. *Yes, yes, a hundred times yes.* "It's not exactly like that," she'd said. "It… amplifies things."

Ilme huffed out a breath to exorcise the memory. "Can you see the altar?" she asked. "Where you've broken through?"

Jana shook her head. "Our records suggest the temple is very large—"

"I know," Ilme interrupted. "I was hoping the orientation would… Well. Progress is its own blessing."

"A very Guthixian proverb," Jana said, with a smile. She cast a quick look at Zanmaron. "Were you troubled on your travels? I don't know how far north your path brought you, but we hear about the Fremennik raids. It's… well, it's what Lord Carnillean wants to discuss most."

Ilme flushed hot. "The Fremennik have always raided the coasts," she said, mechanically repeating Master Endel's words. "They've had bad storms the last year or so. They're just chasing resources."

"Perhaps," Jana said, doubtfully. "Rumour has it they have a grudge and a 'Great Jarl' this time." Then she added, "They were the ones giving you access to the rune essence mine, weren't they?"

An entire decade had passed, and still the panic of that moment—of Zorya dying, of Gunnar turning on her, of the demon ready to kill her and Zorya both—would sometimes crash over her, fresh as the day. She felt as if ice were spreading out from her core and she drew in a deep breath, trying to press it all back in.

This was why they needed the death altar. *This* was why she could not wait.

At first, she had tried to fix what was broken between her and Gunnar. She had sent letters and asked for hospitality in the ritual ways and even fought to go along when the knights would try to secure the mine. She had told Eritona everything she knew—about Gunnar, about the Fremennik—and nothing worked.

Eventually, she had to forget it, forget him. She stopped chasing stories of the Wolf Clan's exploits. That was King Raddallin and his advisors' job. She was meant to do research, to spy, to go where she was told.

And then the raids began.

Master Endel wasn't wrong—the Fremennik raided the coasts and isles when resources grew thin or jarls became agitated. But for the last few years it had been sustained and uncompromising—villages wiped away. Outposts bristling with longships replacing fishing camps. Raddallin sent knights to support the battered settlements, but more often than not they arrived too late, chasing the Fremennik down the shore. Their outposts would vanish onto the longships before any army could reach them, only to reappear in a different spot.

"Eventually," Valzin had said before Ilme and her party had left, "we will need to accept that Master Endel's plan of 'let them tire themselves out' is ineffective."

"They're bound by the Northern Sea," Perior pointed out. "They're mostly attacking their own. He might still be right."

"I think Kandarin would have opinions about your use of 'mostly,'" Valzin returned. "And whatever we've done for them thus far, they know we want their rune altar."

Jana's question still hung over them, the suffering and damages to Kandarin's northern settlements heavy in her words. Ilme cleared her throat. "We are handling the situation."

Jana's gaze flicked over her. "Lord Carnillean will be very glad to hear exactly how that is being accomplished."

They wound their way through the city, out to the western gate. Beyond, the ground had been cleared right down to the river that wound down from the forests, the thick trees that had given Ardougne its shining wooden repairs watching warily from a distance. Several cart lengths' from the gate, a pit the size of a small house disturbed the ground, ringed by wattle fence on three sides. Dirt had been piled in hills to either side.

Ilme glanced back at the gate, trying to match the maps she'd found to the location of the city. The death altar had been lost even before the other altars had fallen into disrepair, a holy relic of an ancient elven site. The maps all placed it outside Ardougne—but with the city rebuilt after the destruction wrought by the mahjarrat and his forces, it was harder to say if they were far enough outside or too close.

Jana climbed down the ladder first. Ilme moved to follow.

"Wait," Zanmaron said in a low voice. Azris stood beside him, arms folded, the two of them a united front. "What's your plan here?"

Ilme frowned. "Go down and see if they've found anything. If they haven't, we need to find other sites."

"You are *not* digging in the dirt," Azris declared.

"Why not? We need that altar—"

"Because you don't know the first thing about it and you're likely to bury yourself under a ton of stone!"

"You know they don't have the altar," Zanmaron said. "What are you going to do when you see that for yourself?"

Ilme looked from one to the other. "Climb back up and go have dinner."

Azris and Zanmaron exchanged a look. "Do you *promise*?" Azris asked.

"Of course, I… What's this about?" Ilme demanded. "You're acting like I'm being unreasonable."

"Not unreasonable," Zanmaron said.

"*Obsessed*," Azris said. "The word is obsessed. We should have been here in another two days, but you wouldn't stop."

"We made good time," Ilme protested. "That's a bad thing?"

"Look," Zanmaron said. "You obviously still feel a lot of… responsibility—"

"Not that you should," Azris chimed in.

"—for the business with the Fremennik. And you're right, the death altar would be very valuable. But not so necessary you need to destroy yourself finding it."

"We don't have enough rune essence stored to waste time with weaker spells," Ilme said sharply.

"Do you actually think the Fremennik are going to march all the way to Falador and attack us?" Azris asked. "They've only managed to be a nuisance and it's taken them ten years to do that."

"We need the mine back," Ilme said, moving toward the ladder. "And Gunnar isn't just going to hand it over to us. If it's not here, I'll make a note and we'll go back."

She climbed down before either of them could argue. Jana was waiting with a pair of lit oil lamps at the bottom. Tunnels radiated off the sides of the pit on three walls, and Jana indicated the one that headed to the south. "After you."

Darkness folded around her, the lamp too dim to press more than a foot or so from her. The walls of the tunnel squeezed so close in places that earth crumbled from them as she passed, scraped free by her shoulders. Ilme felt as if she were slowly exploding, over and over—*he promised to destroy us, he promised vengeance, he is coming, and I have to be ready*. But here, everything narrowed down to a point. There was only moving forward, only looking ahead that one or two feet. Hoping what was at the end was worth it.

Down and down they went, down more ladders, winding their way into the earth. Exploratory tunnels bent off the main one, and Ilme could only follow Jana as she took each turning—roughly west, Ilme thought, if she still had her bearings. The passage widened slightly as one wall gave way to rough-hewn stone, still dusty with the yellowish dirt of the tunnels behind.

In the middle of the wall, a dark hole gaped like a hungry mouth.

"Here we are," Jana said. She held her lamp up to the hole, and the mouth widened into a gullet that stretched on beyond the lamp's dim light. Ilme put her own lamp through the hole, followed by one shoulder and then her head. With the lamp held as far as she could reach, she could see the dark shadows of intercepting passages. She rose up on her tiptoes—

"No," Azris said, and her arms went around Ilme's ribs, pulling her back through the rough-edged hole.

"I wouldn't advise that," Jana said. "The excavation team tells me they're planning to map out the location from the surface and try to dig a ventilation shaft in the next few days. Right now we don't know if the air is good."

"Right now you don't know if it's full of giant spiders and shadow beasts," Zanmaron said. "You didn't see the altar in there, right?"

"No," Ilme said, still considering the hole.

"Then we go."

"Just a moment." She handed Zanmaron her lamp, pulled out her notebook from her satchel, and flipped through to where she'd copied the map of the lost temple. She studied the paths, the bends in around the many columns. She peered back into the hole, and felt disappointment flood her.

"This isn't it," she said. She poked at the stonework—very rough, not remotely elven. She reached around, trying to dislodge the piece to get a better look.

"Stop!" Jana said. "You might bring the wall down!"

The stone broke in half and the wall didn't come down. Ilme turned it in her hand, studying the chisel marks—worked, but not well. Seated very tightly.

"Ilme," Azris said in warning tones.

"Just a *moment*," Ilme said again. She sat down on the dirt floor, opening the notebook to sketch out the shape. What else would be here if not the temple? Something that connected to the temple? Something that later scholars might have mistaken for the temple?

"It's getting late," Jana said. "Perhaps we should return for dinner?"

Ilme didn't even answer this time. She flipped backward through her notes—secret tunnels the mahjarrat had built? The ancient ruins of what had come before Ardougne? A sunken elven city?

"Ilme, you can do this back in the palace," Azris began.

"No, I can't," Ilme said. If she could place these tunnels she could decide whether they needed to mount their own expedition, because if they didn't have the death altar, they wouldn't have the spells necessary to defeat Gunnar's army when he came.

You have to fix this, she told herself.

Azris and Zanmaron murmured over her: *How do you want to* and *You go* and *Save me some* and *You'd best find me later.* She heard them kiss, heard Azris talking to Jana as she led the other wizard away. Zanmaron crouched down beside Ilme.

"I won't ask you to promise me you won't go through that hole," he said. "But I *will* promise *you*, that if you try, I am going to haul you out of here."

Ilme looked up at him. "This is important."

"I didn't say it wasn't," he said. "I said 'don't climb in the hole full of the-gods-only-know-what-monsters.' Also, I *implied* that you're a liar who said she wasn't going to do exactly what she's doing right now."

Ilme pulled another book from the satchel. "Would you have kept arguing with me if I told you I would do what I damn well liked down here?"

Zanmaron sighed. "Probably. What can I do to help make this faster?"

Ilme hesitated—*nothing*, she wanted to say. This was her problem, her solution. The others had been ordered along by King Raddallin—under advice from, she suspected, the High Marshal.

"Here," she said, handing him her notebook and a charcoal stick. "You don't trust me to look in the hole, you try and sketch what you see. There are multiple passages in there. I want to try and match it to something."

Zanmaron set his lamp on the edge of the hole and went to work, while she pored over the texts she had by the meagre light of her own lamp. If she let her mind drift, she could almost pretend the rest of the world didn't exist—there was only this narrow passage, deep under the ground, nothing beyond the reach of her lamp mattering.

"If you find it," Zanmaron asked idly, "are you going to suddenly specialise in devastating combat spells?"

"Are you trying to convert me?" Ilme asked, in the same tone.

"Listen, I can't help it if the Red Order has the best combat spells. You all should keep up." Zanmaron crouched back down beside her, holding out the notebook. "If you want to do this, I'm your friend—I'll help. But there is no amount of preparing that will make anyone ready for war."

Ilme snorted. "You start a lot of wars, then?"

"No," he said. "I'm just not an idiot. We were children when Raddallin conquered the other tribes of the Asgarn. We both saw how difficult that was—he clearly doesn't want another war. He's learned better."

Ilme regarded Zanmaron soberly as she took the notebook. "I'm worried Valzin is right. I'm worried he won't have a choice."

The tunnels matched nothing about the reports of the lost temple, but in the notes the apprentices had gathered for her, Ilme found a reference to haunted passages that led into the elf lands. *Visions of human armies, wasted by some unseen hand.* Ilme shuddered. Well, she'd promised not to go in.

But if these were those tunnels... if they abutted the lost temple... it would have to go...

"I think the entrance is actually inside the city wall," she muttered. She looked up toward the hole. "But these would have to connect, if I'm picturing it right. We could get to the altar through those tunnels."

"Wonderful," Zanmaron said. "Does that mean you'll get off the floor now? Because if your dragon hasn't bitten Master Strekalis by now, then Master Strekalis has fed him so many sweets he's likely to be sick."

She let him help her up and picked her lamp back up, following him back out through the passages, making plans. If Gunnar found out they had the death runes, maybe he'd leave them alone. "Tomorrow I want to—"

Zanmaron held up a hand to stop her. A distant, insistent horn echoed down the tunnels, again and again. "What is that?" he whispered.

"A signal?" Ilme said.

They rushed through the tunnels, the close earth impeding Ilme's movement, as if it meant to drag her back. The horns echoed again and again, and her thoughts filled with armies, with the mahjarrat returned, with longships appearing in the field between the city and the forest. She broke free into the air, to Zanmaron scaling the ladder, to the chaotic roar of hundreds and hundreds of voices.

Night had fallen, the purple edge of sunset still peeking above the dark and foreboding forest. Only now the silent trees poured forth warriors armed with swords and axes, armoured with horned helmets and shields with ferocious demonic faces. Fiery arrows struck the palisade. One shot high, over the wall, igniting a thatched roof within the city. Here and there above the wave of warriors, great creatures burst into being—wolves and mammoths and icy behemoths—summoned to battle.

For a brief, bizarre moment, as she climbed free of the pit. Ilme thought of the ghosts haunting the passages below, the tormented soldiers returned to life. For a moment, it made more sense than what she was seeing: the Fremennik didn't attack inland, everyone knew that. She had time to prepare, she had time to choose the battlefield.

But Gunnar had changed the rules.

"The gate!" Zanmaron shouted and broke into a run. Steel grating clattered down over the open gate, and the guards there called back to halt it, shouted at Zanmaron and Ilme to run.

Ilme sprinted after them. An arrow zipped past her, slicing a path across her back that burned with pain and forced a cry from her. Another and another hit the ground before her. She gauged the distance to the approaching Fremennik, the time she had—

And saw a contingent of the fierce warriors racing straight for the excavation pit.

For less than a breath, she tried to make sense of it—but all too quickly she thought of maps and legends, and stories meant to tempt her friend away from the life he didn't love. The splinter of a memory: her finger circling what was rapidly becoming Kandarin.

Gunnar knew the death altar was here. Because Ilme had told him.

Ilme turned without thinking, pulling runes from her pouch. They collapsed together into a wave of magic, an arc of earth that swept toward the approaching attackers, knocking them off their feet. She couldn't let them get to the excavation. If they destroyed it, the death altar might be lost altogether, those powerful spells cut off when Asgarnia needed them most.

But there were so many more Fremennik coming.

She heard Zanmaron scream her name. A blaze of flames ignited alongside her, the Fremennik warrior caught in it howling. Ilme turned and this time crushed air runes in the fist of her left hand, willing wind to sweep along the now-burning grasses, carrying a wave of fire toward the next set of warriors. Arrows rained around her.

Zanmaron thundered up beside her. "Come on, come on!"

"They're going after the altar!"

"Let them, you fool!" He grabbed her arm, pulling her away. "The gate's shut, the city's on fire—we have to find another way in."

"There isn't another way in!" she shouted as they retreated. She threw another gust of wind, this one a howling gale that skirled through the whipped-up flames and threw shields and warriors alike aside.

"There is going to be another way in because Azris is in there!" he roared. "I don't give a damn about that altar if it means she stays trapped in there!"

The moment froze around her—the Fremennik would destroy the excavation, she was sure of that, and Azris was formidable, not to mention Master Strekalis... but Rue... she'd left Rue behind. Maybe Azris would save him, maybe Strekalis would carry him out, but if Ilme stayed here she could not say she had done everything to protect him.

Another rain of arrows sang through the air, and Zanmaron

crushed runes into a shield that sizzled as the missiles shattered against it.

"Keep them back," Ilme said, "and follow me."

She sprinted away from the excavation pit, away from the approaching Fremennik, toward the corner of the wall. Behind her came the crackle of flames, the boom of lightning. She searched the length of the wall ahead and heard Zanmaron curse. "They're in armour! How are they so fast?"

"Here!" Ilme shouted, coming to a halt where the wooden wall had been built around an older stone section, and the ground was soft with moisture. Away from the wall, imagining the angles of the spell, Ilme sprinted and then turned. She glanced once at the approaching Fremennik coming around the corner of the city, starlight glinting on their armour.

Zanmaron cursed again, clutching his arm where an arrow had scored a cut along his biceps, but instead of pulling runes he yanked a different pouch from his belt, and hissed a deep sibilant word. The air shivered, split, and a great beast of metal stepped free of the summoning portal.

The sound of the portal and its smell—like hair burning and honey cakes—swept another wave of old panic over her. But the steel defender stormed forward, sweeping an arm like a column through the attacking soldiers, heedless of the axes and swords that battered it.

Ilme squashed the panic down and plucked another set of runes from her dwindling supply. Her pulse threatened to burst from her chest. She crouched low and cast the wave of earth right against the surface of the ground, so that it swept up the crumbling mud and slammed all of it against the wall. A slope of earth built halfway up the wall.

Another portal opened, another creature, this one a man of fire that howled like the winds Ilme had thrown across the field as it joined its steel comrade. "Faster!" Zanmaron shouted. "I don't have another!"

Ilme threw a second wave of earth up the first, building the slope into a ramp that reached most of the way up the stone part of the wall. "Go!" she shouted at Zanmaron. "Up the wall! You'll have to pull me up behind!"

"Are you insane?"

"Go or I'll push you up with another air spell!"

"By the empty helmet!" she heard him spit as he bolted toward the wall. He leapt to catch awkwardly at the edge. He pulled himself up, turned, and beckoned to Ilme, before his attention jerked to the fight. The steel creature suddenly let out a keening cry and dissolved into magic. The Fremennik broke past the fiery summon, and Ilme raced for the wall. She jumped, arrows zipping through the air, and Zanmaron caught her wrists, hauled her up, and immediately swept another shield around them. Her torn back screamed and fresh blood rolled over her skin.

Ilme leaned over the edge of the stone wall section and cast the biggest air spell she could directly into the makeshift ramp. Dirt sprayed everywhere, carried on the tornado of her spell, and she flinched back, pelted by the burst of it. A rock caught her cheek, gouging it deeply, but the ramp was gone. She dropped back behind the edge of the wall.

Above her, Zanmaron swore. "Azris, you lunatic."

Puzzled, Ilme followed his gaze. The palace rose above the clustered buildings of Ardougne. At the peak of its roof, she saw a mote of bright blue light gleam, and then a stream of magic, bright with the powers of the water altar, streaked down to smash into a roof below, smothering the fire but sending timbers flying— undeniably Azris. A second mote gleamed red, a torrent of flames erupting toward the army beyond. A second wizard perched on the roof.

Ilme hoped it was Master Jana and banished the image of frail Master Strekalis balanced on the thatch of the roof. She peered and peered at the flashing motes, but there was no way to see if a small purple dragon was up there too.

One after the other, she and Zanmaron scrambled down the wall. Ilme had no idea where she was. They were somewhere on the southern side of the city, on the western end…

And between them and the palace there was fire and screaming and night.

"How many runes do you have?" Ilme asked. "I'm down to a handful."

"Only a dozen or so," Zanmaron said. "I burned through a lot."

An explosion rang above the din, echoing through the warm air, and Ilme and Zanmaron jumped against the wall as a second smaller boom shook the sky.

"I thought they didn't have runes!" he hissed.

"They don't," Ilme said, trying to piece together what would do that, what Gunnar would have—*you have no idea, you have no way to find out.* "We have to go. Rue—"

"Right—stay along the wall. If they breach—"

"When," Ilme said grimly.

"It'll be the other side of the city." He nodded to her. "Stay close."

The fire inside the city spread quickly, rooftop to rooftop, and twice they took a turn only to find a hastily assembled barrier across the road blocking their way. Ilme's lungs screamed, the smoke and the endless race across the city sending sharp needles of pain between her ribs. Citizens burst out of the darkness, some running ahead of her, carrying their belongings, some taking up arms and running toward the wall.

More explosions—the breach of the wall came with a roar of triumph that swept over the city like a roll of thunder. Ilme checked the runes in her pouch again. Not prepared, not nearly prepared enough.

Soldiers kept trying to force them south, with the other refugees, as the sounds of battle grew louder, nearer. They evaded the first few, aiming back toward the palace, back toward their friends. The smoke grew thicker, Ilme's eyes and nose streaming with it, ash tracking black lines down Zanmaron's face. At one point they found themselves trapped in a narrow alley facing approaching Fremennik, and Zanmaron spent the last of his fire runes filling the gap with a towering cyclone of flames, which caught the roofs on either side.

"It's already on fire!" he shouted as they retreated.

As was the palace—smoke obscured its gleaming Star of Saradomin, and the roof where Azris had stood casting blasts of water below was lost in flames.

There was no sign of Rue or Azris or the others. The trickle of refugees became a frantic flood—Ilme could hear the soldiers shouting orders now, the roar of the Fremennik. The White Knights organised around the refugees trying to get them out the southern gate.

"Where's Sir Perior?" Ilme shouted.

"Went back for the mad wizards on the roof!" a White Knight shouted back. "The palace is on fire. You need to go!"

"They're still inside?" Ilme cried.

"You need to go!"

"*You* can go rot beyond the Edicts!" Zanmaron snarled. He dodged around the knight, tearing off toward the burning building. The White Knight put his hand up to stop Ilme, but she was quick on Zanmaron's heels.

Into the smoke, into the darkness, Ilme strained to keep her eyes on Zanmaron's red robes ahead of her. One hand holding her sleeve to her face, she clicked runes together in her palm, finding a pair of air runes to clear the smoke from in front of them. Ilme felt as if she were sliding out of her own body, a spirit coming untethered.

She shouted for Rue, picturing him trapped behind the fire, picturing him struggling at a window, picturing worse. The smoke began to thicken again, and she imagined him gasping.

A surge of magic rippled through the air—above them and to the left. She grabbed Zanmaron's robes and pulled him toward it. The palace was a maze, dark as the underground passages and as full of death. In the darkness she heard beams groan, the far-off collapse of the ceiling.

Water suddenly soaked her shoes. She heard coughing, heard voices. Zanmaron shoved past her, and ahead she saw the glow of a light orb she recognised as Master Strekalis's and green robes around a body crouched low on the floor.

"Azris!" Zanmaron shouted.

Azris looked up, fearful, frantic. She was soaked through, as was the wood around her—a haystack of splintered beams and boards, a spill of cracked stone. The ceiling had come down here, part of a stairwell—

Azris blinked at them, dazed and coughing. "I can't get them out," she said weakly.

Ilme searched the jumble of broken building for signs of Rue and the others, and saw Sir Perior, pinned down by a huge beam, grey with pain and shock. There was no sign of Strekalis or Rue.

Zanmaron went to her, tearing part of his robes to make a mask. Ilme dropped to her knees beside Perior—his arm disappeared under the beam, one leg pinned.

"Zanmaron, summon another—"

"I don't have more pouches!" He dropped beside her and cursed.

"Gotta come off," Perior managed through clenched teeth. "Crushed."

Crushed and the building was filling up with smoke, the fire creeping closer. Ilme took off her belt, shoving the nearly spent rune pouch into a pocket. She wrapped it around Perior's arm just above the elbow, pulling tight and tighter, eyeing the heavy length of the beam.

She swung back to Zanmaron. "Find some sort of lever. Three of them."

"I tried that," Azris said. "It didn't budge."

"There's three of us now," Ilme said, tossing aside rubble until she found a length of iron, some piece of the ceiling. Her lungs burned, her back screamed, but she fitted it under the beam near Perior's shoulder, wedged a rock under it. Zanmaron fitted a smaller joist beside it. Azris grabbed Perior's sword from the floor where it had fallen. On the count of three they all heaved.

"It's absurd we don't have a spell for this," Zanmaron grunted.

Perior pushed with his good arm, wriggling out from under the beam. His arm was a bloody, broken mess. Zanmaron helped him up and Azris ripped part of her skirts off to wrap his arm. But they weren't finished.

"Azris, get him out," Ilme said, scrambling up the rubble that had shifted with Perior's escape. "Rue! Strekalis!" She heard another room collapse behind her. "Rue!"

"Here." The Red Order Master's voice came distant and reedy. Ilme threw aside stone and splintered wood, trying to find the source—

Strekalis's bony fingers reached through, a foot from where she had been digging. "Ilme?"

She tore her fingernails pulling aside more plaster and splintery rubble, opening the space. Another rafter had come down, buried in the rest of the ceiling. Master Strekalis peered out from under it, panting. Blood streamed from his nostrils, a black and purple bruise darkening his face along one side. He smiled, crookedly at her.

"We were afraid…" he gasped, "you might have… been caught… Is Zanmaron…?"

"Here," Zanmaron said, leaning close to the hole. "Master, are you hurt?"

"I'm dying," the old man said, with a rough laugh. "Each to… extent of his abilities… for the price… his sacrifices." He flinched, shifting slightly, and brought Rue out, curled tight and shivering. He pushed the little dragon through the rubble. "Take him. Go."

Ilme bundled Rue to her chest and he burrowed into her, shaking and unspeaking. "It's all right, it's all right," she crooned, feeling his fluttery little pulse against her.

Zanmaron yanked on the beam that blocked the passage. "I'll make a shield, push it out, make some space." He looked back at Ilme. "Tell me you have soul runes!"

She shook her head, hating the answer, hating she wasn't *ready*. "None."

Strekalis reached through, grabbed Zanmaron's wrist in one shaking hand. "You'll *go*, boy. I did my utmost and… here I end."

Another explosion. Another crash of collapse. The smoke was pouring in thicker.

"No," Zanmaron said. "Ilme, get a lever." But the beam was buried, they'd be lifting half the building to budge it.

"Guide the order…" Strekalis broke off coughing. "Can't punish those… Fremennik… if you both die."

"He's right, Zanmaron, we have to go." She yanked on his arm, but he fought her. "What are you going to make me tell Azris?"

That stopped him.

"Clever… girl…" Strekalis panted.

Zanmaron hesitated, tears brimming in his smoke-reddened eyes. "Goodbye, Master Strekalis," he managed. "Thank you for everything."

Strekalis smiled weakly. "May this change... drive you..."

They fled, back the way they came, through the ruined palace, into the stableyard and out through the gates into the night, not looking back at the city in flames, the Fremennik warriors and their summoned fighters rampaging through the streets. They fled into the forests, with Azris and Perior and the White Knights who had made it out. Back to Falador, with news no one wanted to hear.

She had assumed—they all had—that Gunnar would merely be a copy of his father. A jarl who would bluster and threaten and make trouble if they tried to enter the Fremennik lands. Ilme should have known—should have realised he'd listened all the times she talked about the rune altars. That even if it took another decade, Gunnar would keep his promise.

But in the forest, in sight of the burning city, wounded and grieving, Ilme realised she had forgotten one very important thing: she might not be ready, her friends might not be ready, but they were none of them alone.

FOURTEEN

————◆▶————

What Ilme remembered most about the law altar on the island of Entrana was the view of the water, the Unquiet Ocean surprisingly still, the sun glittering on the waves. The tang of salt, and the bright freshness of spring had made it feel like everything was brimming over with potential. In all their journeys to find and repair the rune altars, it had been one of her favourites.

Regrettably, she'd told Gunnar as much.

"The law altar is gone," Perior said grimly. "They say the entrance to the rune altar has been obliterated—they can't even find all the pieces."

King Raddallin, the council of Falador, the king's advisors, and representatives of the four orders of wizardry had assembled to discuss that summer's offensive against the Fremennik's Ardougne outpost—hopefully the last of such meetings, since within Asgarnia a growing chorus of voices decried Raddallin's slowness in quashing Gunnar's forces.

But with Perior's report, the map of Kandarin lay forgotten on the table.

"How did the Fremennik reach Entrana?" Lady Geniven, one of the councilmembers of Falador demanded. "We have them nearly surrounded at the Ardougne outpost."

"We have *some* of them surrounded," Valzin corrected from her seat beside Raddallin's throne. "The rest, one assumes, put their longships to work. At which point anything coastal is easily taken."

"Everyone knows they don't attack in winter," another member added. He was new, a man with a forked beard—*Lord Keerdan?* Ilme thought. She was having the worst time keeping the new councilmembers straight. "What are they doing?"

"Making us look foolish?" Valzin suggested. "The Great Jarl has made it very clear that relying on what we know to be true of the Fremennik in the past is hardly better than telling ourselves bedtime stories."

Perior gave her a dark look. His armour was dulled, scuffed and dented from recent battle. His left arm, amputated at the elbow after the attack on Ardougne, now terminated in an iron replacement. "The High Marshal is correct. One presumes they sailed around the Western Sea. Longships are mentioned in the reports."

"It's an odd altar to target," Zanmaron said. He sat between Ilme and Master Temrin, wearing the ornate robes of the Red Order Master. "The uses we've found for law runes are limited and largely rely on Master Endel's cache of astral runes from the Lunar Isle."

Ilme wanted to protest the Fremennik couldn't know that—but what did Gunnar know? What had she said, telling him tales of their travels, their successes with rune magic?

"It is a *holy* site," Lady Geniven said in clipped tones. Long, long ago, the Saradominists held, their god had first set foot on Gielinor on the island of Entrana. "Clearly," she went on, "the Great Jarl seeks to spread his demon-worship as aggressively as possible. And clearly the orders have not found the true purpose of the runes most blessed by the Lord of Light—"

"Ilme," King Raddallin asked, "when is Master Endel due to return? We need to know how to rebuild the law altar."

"He's gone to Ardougne, Your Majesty," Ilme said. She hesitated. "But I don't think you'll like his answer."

"If the Green Order are incapable—"

"That's quite a leap, Lady Geniven," Valzin interrupted, mildly. "Much like assuming that Jarl Gunnar's target was Saradomin. Entrana is on the path to most of the rune altars—water, nature, fire, even chaos if he dares head into the Wilderness. If the Fremennik are looking to completely destroy the rune altars, then it's worth knowing not just how to repair them, but remake them."

"The only texts we have about the creation of the rune altars are ancient and not a lot of help," Ilme said. "They're fragmented and missing context. Some of it is fully allegorical. We figured out how to repair them, how to seat them on their nexuses of power—it's possible we can work backwards from what we know, but the complexity will increase. The Moon Clan claims their founding seer is the one who created them. Their records might be better, might be even more mythologised—but they're also unlikely to want to help us given... everything. However, Master Endel is the expert so he ought to weigh in." She met the councilwoman's gaze. "I would no more ask Master Unaia about rebuilding rune altars than I would ask Master Endel about improving summoning pouches."

"How is our rune supply?" Raddallin asked. "Specifically, the ones the High Marshal mentioned?"

The Blue Order wizard, an affable young man with a blond beard called Pharas, looked up from his notes, flustered. Ilme didn't blame him—Raddallin didn't always understand the pure numbers in relation to the use of the runes, and the council *never* did. Moreover, Valzin had named nearly every altar. "We mostly… We might need to consider a hiatus on disbursements to our allies. At least until we know how long it will take to repair an altar."

Ilme turned, startled. "It might take *years*. Are you suggesting we break our treaties?"

"I'm suggesting," he said carefully, "that we might need to renegotiate some of these—particularly the elementals—if we want to make certain we have enough to stop the Great Jarl."

"Which we were told was likely to happen this summer," another man on the council said. "At what point do we accept that Kandarin's woes are not Asgarnia's?"

"They need support," Sir Perior said. "So does Entrana."

"We don't have a defence treaty with Entrana," Valzin pointed out.

Perior had never been good at disguising his emotions, and the hurt and anger on his face as he turned to Valzin were bare as an open wound. "It's a holy site."

"It's also a sovereign power that rejected offers of mutual defence when presented with them," Valzin said. "We haven't retaken Ardougne and the Fremennik have already moved again."

"Entrana is in ruins." Perior turned to Raddallin. "Do not make me choose my duty, sire."

"You chose your duty—" Valzin began.

Raddallin held up a hand to stop her. "Has the Great Jarl established another outpost on Entrana?"

"No, sire," Perior said. "We're scouting for other possible outposts around the Unquiet Sea, but this was very much a raid. Strike and run."

"So we know he has forces in Ardougne, but we also know he's taking the next steps—I suspect that means he knows he's about to lose Ardougne." He turned to Ilme. "Where will he go next?"

Ilme looked down at the table, imagining the world stretching beyond the borders. If he'd gone for the death altar because he feared it, and then to the law altar because she'd loved it... would he destroy air next or nature, because she'd humiliated him with those? Soul because it was so precious? Chaos because it too sounded dangerous?

"We should reinforce all of them," Ilme said. "He means to destroy all of them."

"If we try to reinforce all of the rune altars," Grand Master Perior said, "we won't have the forces to defend Asgarnia. Falador could fall while we're dawdling in the desert."

"It's not our responsibility," young Lord Keerdan began.

"If his longships are in the Unquiet Sea," Valzin said, "then he's closest to Southern Asgarnia and Karamja. The mountains make going north unlikely. Karamja has no defences. We should leave it—deal with it later. Have the White Knights who aren't in Ardougne reinforce the water altar. The Kinshra continue directing the assault on Ardougne as planned."

"Agreed," King Raddallin said. "And we'll send word to the other nations that they should secure their altars."

"And Entrana?" Perior asked.

Raddallin hesitated. "You have four days to see to Entrana. Bring Asgarnia's prayers to the church and make certain they're secure, and then I expect the White Knights to be in Lumbridge." He gestured to the wizards along the opposite side of the great table. "I leave the masters of the orders to determine who should accompany them."

"I'll go," Ilme said.

"No," Raddallin said. "You will start the work of figuring out how to rebuild a rune altar. Once we reclaim the mine, we'll have no time to waste. If Master Endel returns from Ardougne and takes over, you can join reinforcements."

Zanmaron folded his arms. "Since Temrin and I are the only masters here, grey and red it is."

Temrin stood. "I will muster my own, I suppose?"

"Thank you, Your Majesty," Perior said fervently.

The meeting rapidly shifted to discussing logistics, supply chains and why exactly Asgarnia did not have a navy to combat the longships. To Ilme it became only noise—her thoughts were full of sources of stone and methods of alignment and which books she ought to be searching, back in the Wizards' Tower.

But too quickly her focus fell apart and she was soon imagining the ways Gunnar might choose his targets, the friends who might be caught when he did. Ardougne sat in her mind, always, the fire and the terror and Master Strekalis's last words.

The meeting ended, the council milling around, muttering to each other—Ilme didn't need to hear what they were saying to guess the gist. They were tired of defending Ardougne, tired of the sentiment rising in Kandarin and elsewhere that Asgarnia had provoked the Fremennik. Tired of Raddallin not *ending* it all.

Beginning to ask if perhaps Raddallin were still the right king to lead them.

Beside her Zanmaron sighed heavily. "I cannot tell you how little I look forward to going to Entrana. I didn't like it when I was a Saradominist, I can only imagine how I will loathe it now."

"You can send someone else."

He sniffed. "I can give Perior four days of my time. He's earned it." He stood. "Although I suspect the High Marshal will want a report. How long have they been at each other's throats?"

"It's new," Ilme said, glancing back at Valzin, still seated at the table, drumming her fingers against the arm of her chair.

She and Zanmaron passed through the door and into the hall beyond.

"Well, knowing you, I'm sure you'll have dug out the root of it before I get to Entrana. I'll send back some shards from the law altar with my reports." He sighed again. "Letters—if I leave a letter for Azris, will you make sure she gets it as soon as she's back?"

"Of course." She dragged a hand over her face. "Oh, I need to send a letter to Master Endel about the rune altars. I have to catch Valzin before she rides back out."

"Better hurry," Zanmaron said. "That woman knows how to vanish like she's cracked Azris's teleportation problem."

She went back into the meeting room. Raddallin and Valzin were stood near the window, him looking out, her watching him. Ilme started to speak, but before she could, Raddallin sighed.

"Go ahead and say it."

"I don't know what you mean," Valzin said briskly. "Your Majesty doesn't need my approval to send the White Knights where you think they're needed."

"Sana. We're not friends because you're careful with my feelings. Out with it."

Ilme stood, trying to decide whether she should leave or announce herself. She eased back toward the door. Valzin flicked a gaze toward her, still seething irritation. Ilme froze in place.

"Fine," Valzin said, holding Ilme's gaze now. "You're making the same mistakes Misthalin did. Coddling the Saradominists. Giving in to their claims of divided loyalty—when a White Knight can't choose his king with his full voice, how long before he can't countenance a king who doesn't serve the same god? How long until he insists he can only ride beside his fellow Saradominists?"

Raddallin turned. Ilme stepped forward, trying to interrupt, not wanting to surprise him.

But Raddallin spoke over her. "You're getting ahead of yourself. The Saradominists are useful—they are disciplined."

"We are in the middle of an invasion, Raddallin. Mark my words, this won't end soon. Already your council is half Saradominists. Already your Grand Master is pursuing his own concerns. And if you cannot rely on the Grand Master, then I question how you can rely on his knights. And if you can't rely on the White Knights, then Asgarnia is hamstrung. They have made themselves too integral to this kingdom, while never bending to its goals—"

"Enough," Raddallin said wearily. "I hear you. While I am king, I swear the Kinshra will have equal footing with the White Knights. Meanwhile, it behoves us to secure Entrana. A small kindness to an ally."

For a moment, Ilme was sure Valzin would argue with Raddallin—here she was, his greatest ally, the one who told him what others wouldn't, the one who perhaps knew better than most what risks they were running, and what did he do but ignore her? For a moment, Valzin looked vicious.

But then she smothered it, tucked it behind a cool mask of unconcern. "Very well," she said. "If you are still taking suggestions, I would press Perior to take additional wizards with him." She turned toward Ilme, pinning her with a sharp blue gaze. "Ilme, is there anyone among the green order who's particularly adept with the water altar? We might as well build up our stores."

"I… will get you a list," Ilme said.

"Wonderful," she said, smiling. "If you'll excuse me, Your Majesty, I have preparations to make." She strode away, down toward where their ships were docked, never looking back.

Raddallin watched her go. "If you are going to tell me not to trust Sanafin," he said, not looking at Ilme, "then I expect you to have extraordinary reasons."

"Your Majesty, I wouldn't… I'm not…" she started, so flustered the words wouldn't form correctly.

"She doesn't look at things the way other people do," Raddallin said. "And without that, I wouldn't be here."

"I think… I think she has a point, Your Majesty," Ilme said. "About the Saradominists."

"And they have a point about the Zamorakians. Asgarnia's strength is that we keep all these philosophies in balance. That was the vision, that was the plan. But Sana…" He paused. "Old wounds heal slow. She should have been the Duchess of Varrock, you know."

"I thought she was the second-born."

"Oh, her brother died. An apoplexy. Quite young, too, and the title should have gone to Sanafin. But she's not wrong: the Saradominists have a firm hold on Misthalin and when your daughter is caught dabbling in Zamorakianism, well… Misthalin is not Asgarnia. They have appearances to uphold. And Sanafin is not someone who bends because she's told to." He sighed. "It's a shame—for Varrock. What they see as devious is actually quite inventive, quite tenacious. I would have lived out my days as chieftain of the Donblas and nothing more without Sanafin Valzin. Even this—" he gestured expansively at the map of Ardougne, "—Perior is a superlative knight, but Sana has been warning me of something like this for a long time. Well," he amended, "she assumed it would be Misthalin in the early days, not the Fremennik. I don't think anyone expected the Fremennik."

Ilme looked away, uncertain of what to say to him. After spending so many years in the court of Falador, Valzin didn't unnerve her the same way she once had. If Ilme found her hard to read, at least she found her less unpredictable—and she, too, had seen the value in those Zamorakian virtues. To see a problem as a challenge, to ask if things were really the best they could be.

To be ruthless, in some measure, when what was at stake was too great to risk.

"She's a valuable ally," Ilme said. Then, hesitantly, thinking of the council half-filled with Saradominists, "Is someone telling you not to trust the High Marshal, sire?"

Raddallin did not answer her right away. "No one with sense. Old wounds heal slow. And there's no sense in fracturing Asgarnia when our enemy is proving wilier than expected. Forget I said anything. Valzin has my trust and... my sympathy."

"Of course," she said. "If you'll excuse me, Your Majesty, I'll... I'll go find those names for the High Marshal, and start working on the rune altar research."

Ilme walked back to her rooms, fretting over Raddallin's revelation. The great strength of Asgarnia was that there were many wisdoms working together toward the same vision. But what happened if that vision began to fracture?

FIFTEEN

To the eyes of Asgarnia and the fretful world, the Fremennik horde seemed to vanish—the people of Ardougne reclaimed their city from too-few warriors, the nature altar and the water altar both stood, untouched; the White Knights and their wizards left behind guards and rushed back to Falador, uncertain of where they stood.

But high on the slopes of White Wolf Mountain, the Fremennik did what they did best and hunkered down for the winter. Where lesser peoples feared the elements, they had stores and livestock from raiding settlements, and a growing supply of dried fish and meat. They knew how to find caves, to dig shelters into the slopes, even if the timbers were strange and the animals they skinned unfamiliar. And best of all, the southerners did not come up its slopes.

The outpost near Ardougne had fallen at last, its two great purposes fulfilled. The Asgarnians wouldn't find the death altar in even their unnatural lifetimes, and all their attention had been on Ardougne when Gunnar had sent the longships around the continent to destroy the law altar. Those warriors had been instructed to build a settlement inland on the eastern side of that sea, a harbour for half their navy, while the other half sailed around the farther side, scouting for a way westward come summer. The rest Gunnar had brought up the rivers and then to here, to the mountain they called the White Wolf.

"Fitting, don't you think?" Gunnar asked Thyra.

Her gaze flicked to Alvis, her husband, before she said, "Fitting. But cold."

"Cold is in our blood," Gunnar said. He too eyed Alvis. "Wolf blood."

"No doubt you have many masterful plans that turn on this place, jarl," Alvis said.

"Great Jarl," Gunnar corrected. "And yes."

"Many spoiled cities to plunder," Sundri, the jarl of the Mammoth Clan said. "Makes that island look like a fish hut. Can't wait. How long do their storms last?"

"Long enough to plan," Gunnar said.

"How many more altars are there?" Sundri asked.

Nearly a dozen—at least that Gunnar could remember. He imagined the rune essence, leaving as he had, spreading out across the map of the continent. He knew the edges of the Northern Sea, the paths of the troll-plagued mountains. But the world was so much wider and wilder than he had grasped—it might take years to destroy all the rune altars. Would he even remember why he'd begun this quest by then?

He thought of Zorya, of the shame that curdled around his heart when he realised he'd been tricked. No—he wouldn't forget.

"Have you ever seen a goblin?" Ilme had asked him once. They had been twenty-two and nineteen, the summer he should have sailed his first raiding party but had been made to stay home.

"No," he'd said. "They're like... green dwarves, right?"

She gave him a funny look. "Huh. I mean, they're both short. Some of them live underground." She paused. "I wonder if dwarves think goblins are like green humans." She'd set a pair of stones on the ground, perched in the blue blossoms of creeping thyme. "This is the Ice Mountain, and this is White Wolf Mountain, and here where the goblins rule."

"What are *their* hospitality rites like?" he asked.

"Yelling," she said, simply. "And Master Endel had to wrestle one of their champions. It was... Well, fortunately they want you to lose. Now when we go to the altar, they let us pass." She'd rocked the stone that was meant to be the Ice Mountain. "It's funny. The God Wars were so long ago, but to them it's like it just happened. They're still waiting on their war god."

"That's all the heathens," he'd said, stubbornly. "Pretending the Edicts will fall."

When spring came, they would pour down the mountain, and the altar beyond that goblin village would only be the next step of his plans.

"We have a long path ahead of us," he said to Sundri. "But many rewards."

"When will you return to the Wolf Clan?" Alvis asked, as if he were merely curious. Thyra started to interrupt, but Alvis shot her a look and she fell quiet.

"Why would I return to the Wolf Clan?" Gunnar asked. "I have a purpose. A destiny."

"Indeed, we all share in your vision, Great Jarl," Alvis said. "But that's what I mean: you have capable jarls serving you, endless armies. And this destiny will take years."

"Then let it take years."

"Perhaps it need *not* take years," Alvis said, voice like a glass-smooth sea. "Perhaps you should let some others into your confidences?"

"Alvis, we talked—" Thyra began again.

"Hush," Alvis said, as if he were being fond, as if he were being kind. "I'm asking the Great Jarl a question."

Gunnar held his son-in-law's dark gaze. Of all Viljar's crimes and cruelties, this was the one Gunnar held against him still: he had sent Thyra away and married her, too young, to this eel of a man. He had watched Alvis since she had been returned to him, and found him again and again to be wanting. He did not raise a hand to Thyra, he was not cruel to her in obvious ways—but Alvis Orvarsson was the sort of man who only cared what his own net caught, and he clearly had his eyes on Gunnar's power. Whispers threaded through the cave-houses now that Gunnar might be mad, that Gunnar might be too old, that someone ought to step in—and he had no doubt where they started.

I am the one Guthix dreamed victory for, Gunnar thought, watching him. *I am the Great Jarl and not you.*

"Come spring, we will resume our campaign," he said to the table at large. "This is our home until then, may Guthix dream pleasantly of it. Alvis," he added, "Thyra, walk with me."

Alvis stiffened at the request, his hand reaching for his sword by instinct, but Gunnar ducked out the exit and into the snowy evening without concern.

The air was crisp and sharp after the warmth of the cave-house, the moon a bright eye looking down from the clear sky. Thyra caught up to him first. "What troubles you?" she whispered.

"What troubles us both," he said grimly. "He needs to be punished."

"He…" She hesitated, searching his face. "Of course, Great Jarl."

Gunnar pulled her close, kissed her forehead. "You can stay, or go. It's not—"

She shook her head. "I should stay."

Alvis trudged up to meet them, stopping beyond the reach of a weapon, tense and alert. Thyra crunched back to his side in the snow.

Gunnar watched the moon. "Hati hunts tonight," he said. "The wolf that craves the moon. The seers say he's due to catch it soon." He looked over at Alvis. "Do you know what happens then?"

Alvis frowned, puzzled. "The moon escapes. The moon always escapes and the fool wolf licks his wounds and tries again."

"And yet Hati always chases." Gunnar took a step toward Alvis. "You've been circling me for a while. Like you think you're on the hunt. But, like the moon, I am no prey for you."

"I don't challenge you, Great Jarl—"

Gunnar shook his head. "Exactly There is no challenge. I won. I'm the Great Jarl and your plots will fall to nothing. Your jaws can't hold the moon."

Alvis narrowed his eyes. "If someone told you I was plotting—"

"Don't lie to me, Alvis. I already know." Gunnar took another step closer, saw the fear shining in Alvis's eyes. "We have three paths before us. The first, you leave us. You don't want to sail under my flag or pledge your axe on my Guthix stone, then I cut you free. Your marriage is dissolved, your allegiances forgiven. You can leave and don't come back."

Alvis glanced at Thyra behind him. "You can't—"

"The second path," Gunnar went on. "You stay. You swear a blood oath to Guthix that you support me, and my cause. You put these Hati-dreams behind you, and become my obedient dog."

Alvis's expression flickered as if he tallied odds in his thoughts. Before he could respond, Gunnar continued, "Now that could be the best course for both of us, except for one thing: I don't trust you, Alvis. You treat my daughter like less than the great lady she is, and you scheme against me. You could swear on every drop of blood in your veins, and I would still be waiting for the day you betrayed me."

A dagger was not a proud weapon, not the sort of weapon you brought to a trial by combat, but it did the work. The blade flashed in the moonlight before Gunnar buried it in Alvis's ribs up to the hilt.

"The third path is I get rid of you," Gunnar hissed in his ear, "the way I should have long ago."

Alvis gasped, tried to grab for his sword. But he only managed to pull it a few inches free of the scabbard before his strength failed. Thyra screamed and caught her husband under the arms as he staggered.

Gunnar yanked the dagger free, spilling a gout of dark blood onto the snow, and Alvis toppled to the ground, bringing Thyra to her knees.

The moon watched, cold and still.

"Why?" Thyra gasped. "Why?"

"I'm sorry," Gunnar said. "I'm so sorry. I should never have let Jarl Viljar give you away. But you're free now."

"I... I..." Her voice caught, and she howled again. "I did not ask for this!" she managed.

"No," Gunnar agreed. He crouched down beside her, beside Alvis's corpse. "You didn't have to. And perhaps... perhaps I shouldn't have let you watch. But you know now, I will never let anyone treat you poorly. Just as I will not stand for treachery." He considered her a moment. "You didn't know he was talking about overthrowing me, did you?"

Thyra looked up, horrified. "No. No, of course not."

"Of course not," Gunnar agreed. "You would never. My dear girl. But if you know who else he was talking to, you should tell me." He helped her up, away from her husband's body. Blood stained her kirtle and her furs. "Now, you were witness. He could have defended himself. I didn't take his weapon."

Thyra nodded, eyes on his face. "He insulted you," she said. "You reclaimed your honour."

"That's right," Gunnar said. "My honour, the Wolf Clan's honour, and the honour of Guthix. Your honour. This is how we redeem ourselves, our family."

Another memory sifted up out of his thoughts, as if washed up on a tide from the future.

I don't know what your aunt has to do with you not learning magic, but I'm glad you don't have to do what you hate. The flotsam of other confessions—a picture coming together with the truths he now knew.

He smiled. "How we redeem our family." He laughed once. "That's going to be what makes all the difference."

Thyra knotted her hands together. "As you say, jarl. As you say."

"No one is here. You can call me 'father'," Gunnar said. He sheathed the dagger again. "It's cold. We should go in. We've earned a rest." And they would need to descend the mountain sooner than he'd planned.

SIXTEEN

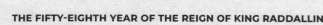

Ilme stood over the remains of the mind altar, one hand on the hilt of a staff, one hand kept close to her rune pouch. The altar's remains had been swept into two great heaps; the new stone ready just beyond the circle of rune essence that marked the original's position. Wind shushed through the pine forest around them, and the Kinshra encircling the site shifted, armour creaking as they watched for the goblins that lived nearby, or a Fremennik ambush.

"Any time now, Master Endel," Valzin said, standing on the edge of the circle with Ilme.

Master Endel knelt behind one of the four amulets positioned around the circle of rune essence, eyeing the level of the ground. "In good time, High Marshal," he said. "We don't want to rush this. Ilme, move that amulet a thumb's width to the left—don't scatter the rune essence."

Ilme started to kneel, but as she did, she tilted the staff and the blue crystals wired at the top sparked angrily. She straightened and Master Endel pursed his mouth. "I told you not to bring it."

"It works fine," Ilme said. "It just has some temperamentalities."

"If it explodes—"

"It's not going to explode."

"I have seen your tests, Ilme, and I will be *very* proud when the prototype is stable. But I don't think it is yet." Beside Master Endel, the young blue wizard Pharas and Geloydra, one of Zanmaron's newer apprentices, eyed the staff with deep suspicion.

Ilme did not know where Gunnar would send his warriors. She did not know where to send Asgarnia's troops and which of its fabled Knights should lead them. She could not renegotiate a treaty nor find a new rune essence mine nor bring the guardian back to life. She could not solve Azris's teleportation puzzle nor carry the rune altar stones to where Master Endel directed. She could not stop this war.

Instead Ilme had bent her research toward a different end: a source of rune magic that didn't require individual runes. The result was the prototype staff she carried.

"These equations are ludicrous," Zanmaron had said, when she showed him the work she'd done to plan the staff. "You're implying the energies are unlimited. They can't be unlimited. Everything eventually degrades."

"I understand that, but it only balances if they're unlimited. And it's making equivalent energy." Ilme hesitated. "When it doesn't explode."

"So where is it coming from?"

But that would be a problem for a different time, a different wizard. For now, it worked.

"Here." Ilme held the staff out to Valzin. "Could you? Don't jostle it."

Valzin chuckled. "Are you going to ask me not to blast anyone with it?"

"If you see something worth blasting, do your best."

"No! No," Endel said. "Don't make it explode."

Ilme crouched down and adjusted the amulet, lowering her eye to match Master Endel's. The energies had to be in close to perfect balance if they were going to lock the altar into place. She shifted so she could see the amulet to her right. "That one needs to be rotated maybe two degrees now. Geloydra, could you—"

Geloydra was busy hissing something at Pharas, who'd turned red and furious under his blond beard. "Geloydra!" Ilme said sharply. "What's going on?"

The Red Order wizard shrugged, all innocence. "He said he was afraid."

"I said this place is eerie," Pharas said stiffly. "Ripe for an ambush."

"And I told Little Boy Blue not to worry, there are wizards here with actual battle skills."

"*No*," Ilme said, as sharply as she would to Rue when she caught him trying to dig runes from her pouch. Geloydra startled, and for a moment looked so young, so guilty. "We don't do that here," Ilme said standing up. "You ride together, you fight together. I don't want to hear anything about red and blue. You're Asgarnian. *Act* like it."

"Yes, Master Ilme," they both murmured, and fell silent.

Valzin chuckled as she reclaimed the staff. "You've got them scared."

"I don't want them scared, I want them focused," Ilme said, scanning the trees. "Pharas isn't wrong."

"All the more reason to speed it up," Valzin said.

After the attack on Entrana, the Asgarnian forces had spread out trying to secure the rune altars that seemed most vulnerable to attack, trying to find where the Great Jarl's horde had disappeared. They reached the water altar too late to save it, sent scouts that found the nature altar shattered too. Reports flowed in of

Fremennik ships sailing the coasts of Menaphos and Fremennik settlers in the Wilderness to the north and the coasts of the River Salve. Worse, they seemed to know where the Asgarnians could not easily go—where their supplies and armies could not safely reach. So Raddallin moved armies to guard the borders, the White Knights pressed toward the Fremennik outposts, and the wizards went to work trying to rebuild the altars.

This was the first of their attempts. Master Endel directed two Kinshra and two wizards of the Grey order to manoeuvre the great blocks of granite into place according to the charts he'd devised. The stone, Ilme knew, didn't matter, but the shape, the cuts, the placement did.

"Finished?" Valzin demanded when the last one was in place, four more Kinshra abandoning their posts to shift the great altar's surface into alignment.

"Hardly," Endel said, standing up and dusting off the knees of his robes. "Make a circle."

Ilme remembered the first time they'd repaired an altar, that day in the forest when the monstrous beasts poured out. She found herself glancing up at the trees, looking for dark many-legged shadows, as Endel directed them—*stand here, switch spots, hold this, Ilme, watch the stuff!*—trying to bend channels of magic back into this spot.

Suddenly, the magic caught on something—a thin whine reverberated in the space between the bones of Ilme's face, and she winced. A point above the stone altar began to glow with a faint blue light.

"Pharas, take another step in," Endel said, eyes locked on the glowing spot. "Don't break the circle."

Valzin paced around the outside of the circle, watching with keen interest. Endel stepped forward, hand clutching a fistful of mind runes. His hand shook as he reached toward the glowing point, as if he were pushing against something physical. He crushed the runes against each other, and a glittering stream of light flowed through his fingertips.

On the other side of the circle, Valzin eyed the ribbons of rune magic with a puzzled frown. Her blue gaze flicked up to Ilme's, brows arching as if to say *could he make it any slower?*

Then an arrow struck the side of her head.

Valzin dropped like a dead limb, the Kinshra all shouting orders, blowing horns to bring them all to alert. More arrows hissed through the air. Pharas whipped around, runes in his palm and flung a shield up to cover himself and Geloydra.

"For the Narvra!" a voice bellowed, too close, too ferocious.

Ilme's focus shrank down to a point, fear scaling her throat—*no, no, no.* Moranna was dead, the Narvra were disbanded, and Valzin couldn't die. Unthinking, she threw a shield over Master Endel and started toward Valzin, feeling the connections of the spell strain against her—

"Stay where you are!" Master Endel shouted over the Kinshra and the chaos. Ilme froze "Don't break the circle! If you break it, the whole spell collapses and the backlash will kill us!"

The Kinshra moved like a hive of insects, directed by unspoken signals—some swarmed Valzin, making a shield wall around her; others slid into formation, pushing outward toward the sources of the attack. Still others formed shield walls for the wizards—but there were not enough. More arrows peppered the grove from other angles, the clash of weapons close enough to make all Ilme's nerves scream at her to *move.*

Instead, Ilme gripped the staff and raised one hand, pulling on the magic she'd tapped within the crystal. A blast of air streaked from her palm—but it veered off, nearly striking a Black Knight and smashing a branch from a tree. Ilme swore.

"Ilme!" Endel shouted. "Stop—"

"I *have* it!" she cried back. She lowered the staff—the crystal had jostled loose, breaking free from the cage of wire she'd carefully woven around it. Ilme jammed it down, pinched the broken wire over itself. The staff sparked, biting her fingers and she swore again.

Beyond Geloydra, a group of attackers in dark leathers sprinted through a gap in the Kinshra's defences. Ilme slammed her staff into the ground, one hand holding the crystals in place, and a tunnel of wind, cold and fast, speared the centre of them. The encroaching soldiers burst outward like leaves scattered before a gale.

The rune altar ritual anchored her feet to the ground, pulled against her as if the threads of her nerves tied her to every other wizard there. She thought of Ardougne. She thought of the fearful people in the streets. She thought of Master Strekalis, dying in the rubble. Whispering, *Each to the extent of his abilities, for the price of his sacrifices.*

But no hero, she was sure Zamorak was wrong. To the extent of their abilities, yes, but together for something greater. *Protect yourself, protect your friends,* the Saradominists' wisdom went. Master Strekalis's sacrifices held back the Fremennik while the people of Ardougne fled, protected Rue, shielded Azris and Perior.

Rune magic kept seething from Master Endel's fists. The wizards held the circle. Shields shattered. The staff sparked, her mouth full of the coppery taste of electricity as the elemental magic made a conduit of her, a tornado of power. It shot threads of lightning through her spells, the howl of a gale drowning out the cries of soldiers and Narvra rebels alike. She shoved her other hand into her pouch and pulled out runes of fire and water.

I gave up everything for this, she thought as she wove another spell between the staff and the runes. *You will not take it from me, or me from it.*

Another defensive shield shattered. Another rain of arrows fell on them—Ilme threw up her arms to protect herself and one grazed her arm, leaving a trail of blood and searing pain. Reflexively, she let loose a firestorm that smashed into a pine tree and snapped it in half.

She heard Geloydra cry out—turned, expecting the girl to be injured.

Master Endel sagged against the altar, two arrows buried in his back, eyes shining with pain and grief.

"No," Ilme breathed.

But he held his fistful of runes close to the glowing light, hand shaking, breath hitching. "Don't... break... the circle," he managed.

"No one move!" she shouted, hating how her voice cracked. Hating that she could only stand there, an object in this ritual, a conduit for this magic. Hating that she knew there were spells that could heal him, runes that could do the work—but they had so few, and no way to replenish their stores.

Each to the extent of his abilities for the price of his sacrifices, she thought, as the ritual turned to razor wires along her nerves. She wanted to scream, to weep, but the battle kept coming, the cries of "For the Narvra!" still echoing, and so instead she cast and cast and cast.

The last fragments of magic slid between Master Endel's shaking fingers. The spell snapped closed like a trap closing, and the mind altar shone briefly, whole and complete, before settling, ready to be accessed.

Master Endel slid from the altar to the ground, with one final, gusty sigh.

Ilme, Geloydra and Pharas rushed to him. "Don't pull out the arrows!" Geloydra said, voice shaking. "They say that's the worst thing you can do."

But Ilme saw at once it would not matter. Master Endel was dead. He had held the spell so none of them would be harmed, and in doing so, sacrificed his life.

Later, Ilme knew, she would weep. She would weep until she couldn't wring another tear from herself, and then she would find there were more. His was not the first loss she'd endured. But it struck the closest. He had seen in her what seeds might grow if she tended them. He had not been as kind as Master Strekalis, perhaps, but he had believed there was something in her greater than a ragged little spy.

She realised she had not, after all, given up everything. The war had found more to steal away.

For now, she swallowed. "It worked," she told him, brushing the hair from his slack face. "You did it. And my staff didn't explode. Two successful tests."

The Kinshra chased down the last of the ambushers and dragged back a few survivors. Ilme hovered over them, looking for familiar faces, family members who'd survived—but she knew none of them. She did however, recognise the Fremennik-style swords, thick and etched with ravens, piled at their feet.

"They're working with the Great Jarl?" she asked one of the Kinshra lieutenants.

"News to me," he said. "But we'll certainly find out."

She went to Valzin last, expecting the worst and knowing she would be of no help if she was wrong, and she might shatter if she was right. But to her surprise, the High Marshal was awake, her shining cap of hair sticky with blood that ran down her neck and over her face. She lay in the lap of another Black Knight, a young man with a needle and thread, stitching shut the wound.

"It lodged in the bone," the man said. "Lot of blood, but it didn't break through. It's fortune itself that it didn't hit your neck or your eye, High Marshal."

"Thick-skulled," Valzin said, her words slurring just a bit. "Heard it all my life. Any of yours dead?"

"Master Endel," Ilme said grimly. "But the ritual finished. He did it."

Valzin sighed. "I'm sorry. He was a clever man. That his enemies outflanked him is not a measure on his soul."

Ilme bit her tongue and the Zamorakian blessing, not wanting to think about whether Master Endel, who had begun the lie that set Gunnar off, earned or did not earn his death. He had meant well, but he had not seen the paths. "They said they attacked for the Narvra," she said instead. "But they have Fremennik weapons."

Valzin laughed, almost manic, despite the man stitching up her head. "Finally. I... almost gave up."

Ilme frowned. "What?"

"The beauty of war," Valzin said. "Your enemies flush themselves out. Can't help it. Always happens eventually. Can't wait to tell Rad."

They needed to pack things up, wrap Master Endel's corpse, see to injuries. They had to get back to Falador, as quickly as they safely could, and Ilme realised she was the most senior able member of the expedition. "You need to rest," Ilme said, to Valzin. "You had a head injury."

"I need to plan," Valzin murmured. "Someone decided to make a very stupid mistake today. You have to make the most of that sort of thing."

SEVENTEEN

———◀◆▶———

THE FIFTY-EIGHTH YEAR OF THE REIGN OF KING RADDALLIN
OF ASGARNIA
THE THIRTY-FOURTH DAY OF THE MONTH OF RAKTUBER
FREMENNIK OUTPOST, EDGE OF THE WILDERNESS

Gunnar knelt before the Guthix stone, the rough shape of his god's fearsome face poised behind his throne, the letter crushed in one hand, its words seared into his mind as he tried to master his temper and realign himself with the goals of his god. But his thoughts kept returning to the letter, to the *gall* of the man writing it, to the way his plans were fraying apart as if they were not the destiny laid out by the sleeping god, but only fragile mortal intentions.

I need warriors, not weapons. At least a hundred. Raddallin's Zamorakian hound survives.

Tymon of the Narvra, as the letter writer styled himself, epitomised everything Gunnar loathed about the Asgarnians: self-important, narrow-minded, convinced the world was built around him and for the benefit of him. Even begging the Great Jarl's assistance, haughtiness bled out of his words. Did the man think Fremennik sprung whole from the ice?

If they did, Gunnar's forces would be in even greater trouble.

There remained an outpost on White Wolf Mountain, but the rest were spread throughout Gielinor to better strike the rune altars and keep the Asgarnians moving. The world believed the Fremennik were stuck in their ways, knew only the ice and the sea and the beasts of the north. But as they travelled and built and won over those people who Asgarnia's ambitions had left behind, they saw the Fremennik's true great advantage: they were survivors. They would last long beyond this. They would succeed.

Raddallin's Zamorakian hound survives.

One task. One *simple* task: assassinate the High Marshal. Gunnar gave them the location, the expected numbers of Black Knights, the means to buy the goblins' inattention. And what?

The Green Order Master is dead.

That Master Endel had been killed was a poor consolation. The man had been the source of the lie that had compromised Viljar and played the Wolf Clan as fools—but he was an old man, and if his death elevated Ilme, then it had come out of its proper place and time.

It was a beginning, he reminded himself. A sickness that would eat Asgarnia from the inside out. The Narvra weren't the only ones resentful of their king's unnatural rule—rebellions brewed in all corners of the country, only one had to take hold.

We have reports one of the green wizards now wields a terrible weapon. A staff that casts spells of wind without the use of runes.

Ilme. He felt certain it was her with the staff, her making him look foolish. Some ancient part of Gunnar remembered wanting this for her, wanting her to be able to protect herself. That small, decaying part lit up, glad she was alive.

But the greater part of him simply wished her *gone,* and whatever light remained, it only ignited his anger. Endel may have created the lie, but Ilme had made it personal. Ilme had colluded with Zorya, and then *killed* Zorya with her foul magic.

Gunnar had achieved something no mere jarl could have dreamed of—and yet for all their successes, his people craved a season of rest. His goal was too enormous for them to hold within their own thoughts. And if he sent them out to be nothing more than mercenaries for the Narvra and their fellow malcontents, then he could only blame himself when he found more Alvises muttering about his downfall.

And there were more traitors—he was certain of that. More Fremennik wondering when they would return home, when they would go back to the sea and the ice. More bands of warriors that seemed to vanish, even as he brought replacements from the clans in their homelands. What did any of the Fremennik care about Asgarnian politics? About Zamorak and Saradomin? About which treaties were weak and which were symbolic?

Gunnar had spent the last winter trying to root out the sources of these doubts. It led in circles, no one admitting to hearing anything, no one admitting to repeating it. He needed his warriors, his people, his *horde*. He needed their loyalty. If the doubts grew, if they became prone to war fatigue and disbelief, then his great goal of destroying rune magic would fail.

They have repaired the mind altar you said was permanently destroyed, the letter read. *You should guard the other ruins if you wish them to remain that way.*

Gunnar did not have the warriors to guard every shattered altar, every destroyed passage. He had his wits, and his understanding of the web that linked these fractious southern nations together. He could topple Asgarnia if he pulled the right strings, he was sure.

So long as no one toppled him first.

Guthix, Gunnar prayed, *when you stir, gods tremble; where you walked, bounty blooms! You have raised mountains and leashed demons. You have shown me the error of our ways, and the path to salvation. Do not abandon me in this place, at this time.*

Only silence answered, as befit the Sleeping God.

For the first time in a long time, he wished Fiera were here—she would have listened, would have soothed his worries—

But no, what he needed was someone to help solve his problem, to point to the weak part he couldn't see. And that hadn't been Fiera's strength; it had been Ilme's. And that had all been a lie.

You don't need anyone, he told himself. *The Great Jarl stands alone.*

Footsteps approached. "Great Jarl?"

Gunnar straightened at the interruption, but did not turn. "I'm busy, Fronya."

"You said…" she began. "You said to tell you if we found anyone trying to leave. Anyone spreading rumours or… dissatisfaction with your cause."

Gunnar looked back. Fronya had streaks of grey in her braids now, deep lines in her cheeks, but she was as loyal a retainer as he could have asked for and a fierce warrior still. She looked afraid. Beside her, Jesper, a younger warrior with a reddish beard, looked as though he might run.

"What's happened?" Gunnar demanded.

"You're not going to like it," Fronya said.

He stood. "What's *happened?*"

"Your daughter, Great Jarl," Jesper said, all in a rush. And for a moment, Gunnar panicked, imagining Thyra hurt, Thyra dead.

But then Fronya said, "She stole supplies. She had letters from the other outposts. We think she was heading to Rellekka, but she won't tell us anything." She hesitated. "We took the children back to the longhouse, but she's locked in the smokehouse."

"We kept it quiet," Jesper said. "What do you want to do?"

A sickness that eats from the inside out, Gunnar thought. *A dozen tiny rebellions.* But no—every part of him turned against the thought. They were wrong. Thyra wouldn't hurt him this way.

"Who sent her out of the settlement?" he demanded.

"She won't talk to us," Fronya said.

Fine, Gunnar thought. Thyra would talk to him. He would sort all of this out.

Thyra sat in the centre of the cold smokehouse, her legs folded under her, her hands tied behind her back. The smell of fires baked into the walls after only a season hung dense and greasy on the air. A bright bruise marred her left cheekbone and her pale braid was coming loose. She looked up at him, only exhaustion in her eyes, and in that moment she seemed so small, and all his rage was for her captors.

"Who hit her?" he demanded.

Jesper held up his hands. "It was an accident, Great Jarl."

"She didn't want to come with us," Fronya said.

"Of course she didn't," Gunnar said. "She's done nothing wrong. I gave you a task of the utmost importance, and you bring me *my daughter?* How could you think she was fleeing? How could you think—"

"Because I was."

Thyra's quiet voice stopped him like an axe to the chest. Fronya and Jesper looked away, as he turned to face her. "No, you weren't," he said firmly. "We're not discussing you going for a walk beyond the outpost, they think you were—"

"Leaving," Thyra said, her pointed chin raised. "Leaving for Rellekka. Leaving to find a ship to the Salmon Clan."

Gunnar stared at her. "What has Orvar been telling—"

"Jarl Orvar hasn't sent a word to me since we left," Thyra said, as if she weren't tied up, as if she weren't his daughter. "I don't want to be here. I don't want to watch you burn the world. I don't want to see what happens when everything crashes down on us. And… I'm not alone in that, Father."

She'd always been stubborn, even as a little girl. How many times had she gone tromping out into the meadows to pick flowers when there was work to be done? How many times had she tested his patience refusing to come when called? But these were minor flaws, not betrayals.

"This is the will of Guthix," Gunnar began, off-balance.

"This is the will of *Gunnar*," she said. "You're hurt and you're angry and you want to make something of that. But this has gone too far. How many people have died? How many people are going to die?"

"As many as it takes!" Gunnar shouted. "This isn't about you or me—this is about the safety of the world, the will of Guthix, everything Zorya warned about!"

"Do you think Zorya would have wanted this?" she shouted back. "Do you think any of this is what he meant?"

Zorya, laughing, avuncular, delighted at all their stumbling steps into the future. Zorya, admitting to the lie, uncaring about the lie. Zorya, dead, with Gunnar's axe buried in his skull—

"I was willing to hear you," Thyra went on. "I was willing to believe you were still a good man, a good jarl. You talked of settling and colonies. And then you abandoned the outpost at Ardougne. We are not settlers. We are an army marching to our deaths, pretending at a future."

"When did you turn on me?" he murmured. "When Alvis died?"

Thyra looked up at him, grimly. "When you *killed* him? Alvis wasn't the one questioning your methods, he only envied your power. *I* was the one asking how to best turn your destiny."

"No one will turn my destiny!" Gunnar snarled. "I will destroy the rune altars and then I will crush Falador and take back all the rune essence they stole."

She set her jaw. "They're repairing them. They're catching up. Would Guthix allow that?"

Strike her, kill her, make her pay—he turned away, shocked at the urge to harm Thyra. For a moment, Gunnar could only think of Ott's execution, of his brother bound and on his knees waiting for the axe, of Viljar standing there just watching. Had his father grieved? Had he seen in Ott the little boy who once trailed after his father?

I am not my father, Gunnar thought. *I am the Great Jarl.*

"Then I will break open their city and destroy their rune essence first. They will watch with ashes in their mouths as I wipe rune magic from Gielinor," he said coldly.

"Untie her," he said to Fronya.

Fronya and Jesper exchanged a look, but the older warrior went and removed the bonds. She pulled Thyra to her feet, and Gunnar forced himself to face his daughter. He was the Great Jarl, after all. He could be more generous than Jarl Viljar.

But he could not brook betrayal.

"You are no daughter of mine," he said roughly. "You will leave this place as you are right now, you will never return. If any of the Wolf Clan or any of the clans that give me fealty meet you, they will be sworn to shun you and if you speak a word against them or me, they will kill you on sight."

Thyra blinked at him. "We are in the Wilderness," she said. "You have to give me a weapon."

"You will leave this place," he repeated. "You will never return. You will thank me for my mercy."

"My children—"

"My *heirs*," he corrected, "remain here."

Here at last he seemed to wound her. "You can't."

"I am the Great Jarl," he said. "I do as I wish."

"No," she said, finally frantic, finally afraid. "*No!*"

He nodded to Fronya. "Escort her out the gate and make clear to all she is no longer Fremennik."

"Father!"

Gunnar ignored her, wrapping his heart in ice. "I want a list of her conspirators: those who wrote these letters from the other outposts. When we march on Falador, there will be no doubters in my ranks." Those, he thought, as he left the smokehouse and Thyra's screams, he did not need to be so generous with.

EIGHTEEN

THE SIXTY-FIRST YEAR OF THE REIGN OF KING RADDALLIN

OF ASGARNIA

THE FIRST DAY OF THE MONTH OF RINTRA

FALADOR

Master Unaia frowned at the staff laid out on Ilme's worktable. "It's not very… royal-looking," she said finally. "Shouldn't you fix that before you lock down the design?"

"I haven't locked anything down," Ilme said as she swabbed salve over the burns splotching her left thumb and the girdle of her hand. "I'm still calibrating it though. It's more temperamental than the air one."

"Of course," Unaia said. She looked around Ilme's makeshift workshop—they had much better tools, much better resources in the Wizards' Tower, but Ilme saved herself days of travel by staying in Falador between deployments. The room was cramped with her belongings as well as borrowed tools and books and bowls of carefully separated runes. Rue had tucked himself into a helmet, hung upside-down from a nail in the wall, and eyed Unaia with the same sort of trepidation that she eyed the room.

"Does your master think this is the best use of your time?"

"Azris?" Ilme said. "Azris wants to know what I need to make a hundred of these."

Master Endel's funeral had been too quick, too brief—the necessity of war. They shrouded him in green and buried him in the grave ring around the druid's grove with a guard of Knights. Azris, Eritona, Ilme and the other Green Order wizards held a short vigil in turns, along with Zanmaron—who held Azris's hand through her part, and only spoke softly to her—Pharas and Geloydra, and Master Temrin.

"He was a good man," Temrin said. "A proud seeker of knowledge. He never sat in his ignorance, which is the greatest thing I can say of a person."

Grief and anger still swept up on Ilme months later. Master Endel had in some ways been the cause of the Fremennik invasion, but he had been a man of vision, a man who wanted better for the world. They would be building on his beginnings for a long time yet.

And he would always be the man who had chosen to save a ring of frightened young apprentices at the expense of his own life.

"I still question if Azris was the right choice to succeed Master Endel," Master Unaia began. "Especially since Zanmaron—"

"Master Endel was very clear about his wishes," Ilme said, tying the bandage off. "I need to re-seat these crystals. Did you have something specific you need help with?"

Unaia pursed her mouth. "I've been speaking with Pharas, and he's expressed an interest in working under you, on these elemental staves. Naturally I wondered if you'd done anything to encourage him."

Ilme frowned. "Encourage him?"

"He belongs to the Blue Order," Unaia began.

"Can the Blue Order not work on elemental staves?" Ilme heard the arch tone in her own voice, and tried to temper it. "I am not trying to steal your apprentice, Master Unaia. I don't particularly want an apprentice."

Unaia blinked at her. "Whyever not?"

Ilme considered the staff, her mind full of all the people this war had taken from her, all the people it could still take. Endel. Strekalis. Zorya.

Gunnar.

"I think it's best we all keep ourselves flexible for deployment," Ilme said, quietly. "I couldn't teach an apprentice reliably and be available to the king."

"I suppose," Unaia said. "Though I imagine for appearances' sake, your help is not in high demand at the moment."

"Rude," Rue grumbled, almost too soft to make out.

The attack at the mind altar had only been the beginning of Asgarnia's internal struggles. While Ilme led the expedition back to Falador, the White Knights were in Karamja, trying to secure the nature altar and drive the Fremennik back to their longships. Meanwhile, Gunnar's army appeared outside Varrock where the earth altar was located. King Raddallin had taken forces to Misthalin, honouring their treaty, and spent seven days pushing back the Great Jarl's horde. For a moment, it seemed possible they could crush the Fremennik on both fronts.

It was dangerous, but with the growing whispers that the Great Jarl's ability to run Asgarnia in circles meant the kingdom was weak, its vision flawed, its king already beyond his strength. Kinshra, White Knights, wizards—all sides had agreed they needed to seize the opportunity and end this now.

Then the Narvra returned. A riot broke out in Falador, beneath the banner of the disbanded Kareivis tribe and spurred by discontented nobles. Port Sarim in the south declared itself independent, under the protection of the Massama, suddenly revived after their long ago defeat by Raddallin.

"What insurrectionists do under ancient banners and dead names," Ilme said slowly, "has nothing do with me."

Except it did—Gunnar's fingerprints were on all of these. Worse, the unrest meant Asgarnia could only focus on its own borders. When the Fremennik attacked Kharidia, destroying their mage arena and the fire altar besides, Kharidia's call for aid went unanswered—Raddallin could not divide his forces any further.

Menaphos, the site of the soul altar, the source of precious runes, went silent, refusing Asgarnian contacts. No one could make the trek to re-establish the nature altar. Misthalin filled with the same rumblings that presaged the rebellions in Asgarnia.

"The Narvra will fall again," Unaia reassured her, mistaking Ilme's mood. "We will prevail. And you've done so much." She paused. "I wonder, if the Green Order still suits you. If I recall correctly, you joined largely because Master Endel is the one who made overtures."

"I'm Guthixian," Ilme said.

Unaia shrugged. "Things change. I think you'd be quite the asset to the Blue Order. And a credit to Saradomin's teachings besides. Your god, after all, doesn't want worship."

Ilme grit her teeth, knowing it was futile to argue with Master Unaia. She made herself count to ten, untwisting the wires that held the red crystals in place, choosing her words carefully.

Rue grunted in his helmet. "Bad friend."

Ilme shot him a disapproving look. "Manners."

"Here you are." Valzin stood in the doorway, her cheeks flushed, her blue eyes dancing. She nodded at Unaia. "Ah, Master Unaia. How are you? Do you mind if I steal Ilme for a moment?"

Unaia stiffened. "High Marshal."

"We were just finishing," Ilme said. Rue leapt from his nest to perch on her shoulder. "Thank you for your concern, Master Unaia, I'll... keep it in mind." She stepped around Unaia, and followed Valzin out into the hall. "What's happened? Another attack? Where?"

"Downstairs," Valzin said, striding away from the little room Ilme had commandeered. "Not an attack. I have something *interesting* you need to see."

Ilme frowned, following her. "What is it? Did you recover their naphtha barrels? Or... some sort of summoning pouch?"

"Better," Valzin said. "We have a spy. And she's asking for you."

Ilme frowned. "One of the Narvra."

"One of the *Fremennik*," Valzin said as she turned down a staircase. "Thyra Gunnarsdottir."

Ilme knew not to expect the fawn-legged girl with the pointed chin she remembered from the summer before she'd been sent off to marry. But when she saw the gaunt woman with the mud-stained clothes, for a moment, Ilme was certain Valzin had been tricked.

But then Thyra looked up at her—those same berry-bright eyes, Fiera's chin, Gunnar's nose, sharp and a little long. Then Thyra said, hesitantly, "Aunt Ilme."

A pair of knights—one Black, one White—stood guard in the cold little room, the smell of old straw and damp crawling on the air. It was cramped and cruel, and Ilme imagined what stories Thyra must have heard of the Asgarnian monsters. How much this place must have fed into those stories, and Ilme, standing there—ageless, unscarred.

All over again, Ilme wished she could wind back the years; if she'd only told the truth, if she'd only helped Gunnar leave—

But she caught herself—she could not pretend she was the only one whose choices mattered. She could not hold the whole war on her shoulders.

"Is it her?" Valzin asked, one hand perched on the pommel of her sword.

"Yes. Thyra," Ilme said, moving to sit beside the other woman, "what are you doing here?"

Thyra regarded her solemnly, hands folded in the lap of her tattered skirt. "I've been exiled," she said. "I need safety."

"And you came to *Falador*?" Ilme asked incredulous. "Thyra… we're at war."

"I'm well aware," Thyra said. "Where do you think I've *been* all this time?"

"Which returns us to the question," Valzin said, "why are you *here*?"

Thyra drew herself up. "My father is going too far. I wanted him to stop. I was going to Rellekka to the lawspeakers and the other jarls. But they caught me. I was exiled." She swallowed. "He has my children. I want my children back. That's what I want from you—safety and my children."

Ilme shook her head. "I don't… I don't know…"

"What do you have that can pay for those things?" Valzin interrupted. "Your father's not exactly circumspect about his goals. We know what he's doing."

"Yes," Thyra agreed. "But his plans are changeable. Fickle at times."

Valzin eyed her. "And you know something worth how many children's lives?"

"Three," she said. "And yes."

Valzin sighed, when Thyra didn't continue. "I see we're at an impasse. Very well. You can remain here in this room, safe from your father, regardless of what you tell me. If you give me valuable information, I will see your quarters improved. And we will discuss how to rescue your children. Fair?"

Thyra looked to Ilme, sitting beside her. "Can she promise this?"

"She's…" Ilme thought of how best to explain Valzin to Thyra. "…she's like the king's sister. He will listen to her."

Thyra said nothing for several moments. At last, she turned to Ilme again. "Why did you do it?"

Ilme sighed. "My master began the lie thinking Jarl Viljar—"

"No. Why did you kill Zorya?"

"What?" Ilme asked, startled.

"You loved him," Thyra said. "I know you did. My father thinks you lied about this too, but… it's never made sense to me. You loved the guardian. Even if you deceived my father, I don't understand why you'd kill Zorya. I may not have many options, but before I go any further, I want the answer to this. Why?"

"I… I didn't," Ilme said, too flustered for careful words. "Gunnar told you *I* killed Zorya? *He* killed Zorya."

Thyra blinked at her a moment. "No," she said. "He wouldn't."

"He *did*." Ilme caught herself, tried again. "I think… I think he meant to kill me. He summoned a monster and Zorya… Zorya got in between us. I tried to help." She paused. "I did hurt him. I was trying to hit the demon, but the spell caught Zorya. I didn't mean to but… I wasn't as careful as I should have been." She shut her eyes. "Maybe your father didn't mean to either. But it was his axe in Zorya's skull. And his demon that he summoned."

Thyra tilted her head, frowning. "My father is a summoner?"

"Your father is a madman with an army seeking to eradicate rune magic," Valzin said. "Are you going to help us, or help him?"

Thyra studied her another long moment, as if asking without words whether she could trust Ilme too, but there was no way around it—she was exiled, alone, trapped in this tiny, dank room.

She folded her hands and looked down at her knuckles. "He's angry you've figured out how to rebuild the rune altars he destroyed. His goals were always to finish that, then destroy this city and take the rune essence back. But since you keep rebuilding them, he intends to strike Falador instead. That is his next goal."

Valzin snorted. "Let him try."

"He has allies you don't know about," Thyra went on. "Small enemies he's made great. He'll break your city open and destroy the rune essence—that was always his plan."

Ilme frowned. "The rune essence?"

"And so we should shelter you, here in this city you expect your father to destroy?" Valzin said. "Pardon me if I think your payment is a little short."

"It's information you didn't have," Thyra demanded.

But Ilme's thoughts were racing, her memories full of the mine and the silky grains of rune essence running through her fingers. *People think,* she'd told Gunnar, like she was sharing a secret, *that we have so much essence in the tower where the vault is, but they can't even imagine what the mine holds.*

And Gunnar scoffing, *You should just build your city on the mine. Then you don't have to go away every autumn.*

The tower's not in the city, she'd told him. *Which means it's much easier to move to a mountain up north, at least.*

"Thyra, give us a moment." Ilme grabbed Valzin's arm and pulled her outside the cell. "We don't keep the rune essence in Falador," she whispered.

Valzin frowned at her. "No, we don't. Why does that matter?"

"If Gunnar plans to attack the city and steal the rune essence," Ilme said, "then those are two separate attacks."

"Does he know that?"

"He *does,*" Ilme said. "I told him about the tower. About the vault. Thyra *doesn't*—clearly, she thinks it's just part of harming Falador. But he said he's going to destroy the rune essence."

"Maybe he forgot where we keep it."

"No," Ilme said. "All this time, he hasn't forgotten. He hasn't forgotten a word. He's known how to get to every altar, he's known all the obstacles, all the places we've struggled, because I was the idiot who told him. He didn't forget where the rune essence vault is. The attack on Falador is a feint."

"Destroying the Jewel of Asgarnia is a 'feint'?"

"Would you pay the slightest attention to the Wizards' Tower if you knew he was attacking Falador?" Ilme demanded. "Of course not. If he attacks Falador, that's where all our resources need to be. He knows that too." She hesitated. "And I know him. He won't leave the rune essence behind. The rune essence is the point."

Valzin frowned, considering. "We don't know when he's going to attack."

"No," Ilme agreed. "But we know what he's looking for, we know what makes him angry."

"You want to convince the Great Jarl to attack Falador?" Valzin said, a slow, almost-devious smile curving her mouth.

"I want to convince the Great Jarl to walk into the Wizards' Tower," Ilme said. "Where I can deal with him myself."

NINETEEN

◄◆►

THE SIXTY-SECOND YEAR OF THE REIGN OF KING RADDALLIN OF ASGARNIA

THE THIRTY-EIGHTH DAY OF THE MONTH OF PENTEMBER

IN SIGHT OF FALADOR

Falador shone in the early morning light, a jewel aflame on the dark velvet of the hillside. Its guard towers as high as the oaks the Fremennik felled to build their longships, its staggered walls and palisades like cliffs overlooking the vast sea of Asgarnia's fields. The seat of Raddallin's power. The birthplace of a new age, the font of rune magic. At a distance, it seemed so solid, as if it had always stood, it would always stand—how could such a marvel be anything less than permanent?

But nothing in the world is permanent, and even the greatest fortresses rot away in time. Falador, the Jewel of Asgarnia, faced an army darkening the horizon like a blotch of mould.

✦ ✦ ✦

Gunnar rode out on a bay gelding, heavy with armour and ready to end this. Years and years of striving, and now his goals were in reach. When this was finished, he could rest. Falador would crack like an egg, shattered on the might of the Fremennik and their gathered, imperfect allies. All the non-combatants, his settlers and hearth tenders, had been sent north to Ice Mountain, to prepare a new outpost for the army once Falador had fallen.

He closed his eyes and savoured this moment. Already he could picture it: the summoned beasts and siege engines tearing down the curtain walls. The disciplined White Knights unprepared for the sheer volume of the Fremennik horde. His people knew by now how to break a city. That Falador was larger, sturdier, made no difference.

The Asgarnians would find too many of their wizards and Black Knights had been sent away—too focused on rebuilding the rune altars. Gunnar had waited for this, biding his time, biting back his temper. Let them think they're winning.

"Gate's coming up," Jesper said beside him, and Gunnar opened his eyes.

The Wizards' Tower stretched like a flame before him, bright with the dawn. Gunnar adjusted the stolen White Knight's helmet so he could count the windows, assess how many storeys it rose. He checked the satchel he carried over one shoulder, and the sword in its scabbard.

Everything was coming together just fine.

✦ ✦ ✦

War lay in the city's bones, the conflicts of warlords writing scars across its infant self. There were still those who remember the bold attacks of the Narvra in the early days, the Kareivis, the Massama. In the stained-glass windows, the stories of Raddallin, a hero on the battlefield, wreathed in flames of magic and followed by knights of every creed, shone bright and cheerful when what they depicted was violence.

What they depicted was defence, kingdom and nation.

As the army of the Fremennik horde flowed over the fields—banners of fallen tribes, towering monsters, siege weapons of far-off enemies—archers lined the walls, reminded of kingdom and nation. Wizards stood ready, runes clicking in their hands. The White Knights, prepared behind the gates, armour bright, swords ready. Their grand master, calm and certain. Their king, mounted like a warlord again, sword and fire staff in hand.

A howl like the restless dead skirled over the field—Fremennik war horns—chilling the marrow of every Asgarnian.

✦ ✦ ✦

No one made a fuss as the squadron of White Knights rode into the Wizards' Tower. If there was one thing Gunnar knew by now about Asgarnians it was this: they were too convinced of their own mastery, too sure they couldn't be used or tricked. Certainly not by mere barbarians.

There were four of them—Gunnar, Fronya, Jesper, and a young Wolf warrior called Bragi—who entered the tower. The others encircled the building waiting for the right time to strike.

Soon, he thought, feeling the simmer of his nerves. *It will be over soon.*

The tower inside was bright with white stone, strangely airy for a building made of rock. He didn't know where the vault of rune essence would be, except it wasn't below him. He found stairs on the opposite side of the vast entry hall and made toward them, all confidence, all sureness.

But when he made his way up the first half flight, a knight in black armour appeared to block his path. And then another.

"Gunnar Viljarsson, I presume," a voice said behind him. He looked back and saw a woman in the same black armour, her dark hair cut short like a shining cap, her eyes blue as a summer sky. Sanafin Valzin. Raddallin's Zamorakian hound. Gunnar drew his sword.

"You do presume, Zamorakian," he said. "Do you want to die today?"

"Your daughter let us know you'd be visiting," she said, unfazed by the threat. "We've been waiting."

Grief and fury stabbed through Gunnar's heart. "Where is Thyra?"

"Safe."

"You'll forgive me for not taking the word of an Asgarnian."

"You'll forgive me for assuming you don't ask in good faith," the woman shot back. "You can come with us, or you can make it difficult."

Gunnar turned fully to face her. Below him Fronya, Jesper and Bragi stood ready to fight. They could hold off the Black Knights in the entry way—there weren't all that many, he didn't need them to hold off all that long. Which left the two ahead of him, and whatever lay upstairs.

Through the doorway, he gauged the light of the rising sun, the lengthening of its rays. *Asgarnians,* he thought. *Always too convinced of their own mastery. Always certain they could not be bested by mere barbarians.*

"I think," he said, "I will be difficult."

Just before the barrels of explosives outside shattered every window and shook the whole tower.

＊ ◆ ＊

Fire devoured the roofs of Falador as arrows rained down on the shields of the armies below. On the wall, the song of bowstrings slapping, runes crackling into magic, the grunt of the dying—all made a symphony of war.

Fire turned the Fremennik lines. The White Knights, in strict formation, split a trebuchet from its tenders like wolves laming a deer. It burned like a beacon, as its twin smashed another hole in the curtain wall, and the Fremennik poured through.

✦ ✦ ✦

Gunnar had the pleasure of seeing Sanafin Valzin startle. The Black Knights, unprepared for the sudden explosion, all leapt, turning, expecting more trouble. Gunnar did not wait to see if they regained their focus. He turned back up the stairs, met the two knights in three quick strides. The first he merely seized by the arm and wrenched down the stairs in a clatter of armour. The second, recovering, drew her sword, but Gunnar came in fast, smashing his own blade into the side of her head, bouncing the helmet off the stone wall.

He hurried past, aiming for swiftness, for confusion—the explosions set off chaos in the tower. Wizards in robes of red and blue and green and grey hurried back and forth, demanded he tell them what was happening. Gunnar ignored them, eyeing the rooms as he passed. One had to be the vault.

Up another staircase—he heard shouting down below now, the Black Knights recovering, and he hoped his warriors would earn the trust he'd placed in them. People streamed past; it didn't matter. He only needed the vault. He only needed to end this.

What he had imagined, Gunnar couldn't say. It was a small room—so much smaller than the mines, as Ilme had said. Long and narrow, the floor shining patterns of black and yellow stone that peeked out from beneath boxes and heaps of glittering rune essence. He let out a breath, half sigh, half laugh. This was it. He'd found it. Even if he failed at everything else—even if they rebuilt a hundred altars—he would succeed *here* and no one could say he had let rune magic survive. He hauled the door shut, dropped the bar across it.

"Gunnar," a voice said. "Stop."

✦ ✦ ✦

To fully capture the battle for Falador in song or stained glass would be an act of greatest fiction, each moment too sharp, too jagged to fit neatly together: the smell of the burning roofs. The echo of screaming horses. A young wizard collapsing on the battlements, an arrow speared through her jaw. The king, a comet carving through his enemies with fire and sword. Howling wolves and snarling bears, shimmering with spirit energy, knocking aside soldiers. The White Knights fighting mightily to block the breach in the city walls. The banner of the Narvra collapsing into the seethe of its army.

To capture the battle in song or stained glass would mean admitting that neither the jewel of Asgarnia and the Great Horde of the Fremennik was winning. War is ugly, and kingdom has its costs.

✦ ✦ ✦

For half of a lifetime, he'd imagined seeing Ilme again, had prepared for what he would say, what he would do, and so the alien flush of delight that hit him startled him. She was his friend—on some unshakeable level, his soul was so sure it was a good thing to see her again.

"I know what you're doing," she said, so calmly. "I won't let you take it."

This is your enemy, he told himself, his nerves a buzz beneath his sureness. *She killed Zorya.* He wondered how he looked to her—if she recognised him or if she thought him a stranger. *He* hadn't used rune magic to pervert the flow of time.

"You misunderstand," he told her. "I don't want to take the rune essence."

That stopped her, puzzled her. "Why are you here then?"

From the bag he carried, he drew out the flasks. Two glass bottles full of lurid liquids, taken from Kharidian alchemists. Together, they burned hot enough to crack stone. Add a third solution, the barrels of naphtha that had destroyed the tower's windows would look like popping logs in a fire. Gunnar's back clinked, heavy with the bottles.

"I'm here to destroy it," he explained. "To make certain the essence is mingled irrevocably with the ashes of your tower."

Her frown deepened. "That will kill you too."

Fate was like a warship, its oarsmen tireless—but all sailings had their limits. Gunnar tilted the bottles held between his fingers so the liquid clung in sheets to the curved sides.

"That's the plan," Gunnar said. "That was always the plan."

TWENTY

Ilme stared at the bottles in Gunnar's hand, frozen. This wasn't in their plans. They had prepared for a frontal assault on the tower, they had prepared for him to infiltrate, she had been prepared for the possibility she might have to kill him—but their plans had rested on the assumption that Gunnar was trying to steal back the rune essence. That he expected to remain alive.

All he had to do was smash those bottles.

If she killed him, there was a good chance they'd smash anyway.

"You can't do this," she started.

"I am the Great Jarl now," he said. "I do what I want."

All through the war, she had fought with herself, struggled to remember this was bigger than her mistakes, greater than her sacrifices alone could solve. It wasn't about her fight with her friend.

But here and now, it was only her and Gunnar and a feeling of grief welling up in her chest.

"Why would you kill yourself?" she asked. "Is it because of Zorya?"

"Don't talk to me about Zorya!" he snarled. "Don't you dare. You lied, you flouted his bargain, desecrated his gifts—"

"He gave them freely."

"He didn't know you were making weapons of them!"

"Yes, he did!" Ilme stormed forward, but Gunnar held the bottles high, ready to smash them and she stopped. "Gunnar, I didn't lie about what spells we made. I showed you both—"

"Oh yes you did," he said. "You killed him with them."

"And your axe?"

Gunnar flinched. "He was already dead. Your demon made sure of that."

Ilme flushed, furious, all her grief boiling away. Just as Thyra had said, he was pretending she'd done it. "How many times have you told that lie? You know you're the one who called the demon. You know it went wrong. Just admit you were trying to kill me, and accept Zorya died because of it."

"Why are you still lying?" Gunnar demanded. "I was there. You summoned the demon."

"I don't know how to summon things," Ilme said. "I've never learned."

"Your dragon—"

"Rue found me. I didn't call him." She hesitated. "Everyone says you worship demons and your brother was a summoner—"

"I'm not my brother. And I can't believe you still think we worship demons."

There had only been four of them in the mine—Gunnar, Ilme, Zorya, and Rue. Zorya had not brought the demon forth. Rue couldn't have. Ilme knew she hadn't done it.

And Gunnar persisted in saying it wasn't him.

"If it wasn't you," Ilme said, "and it wasn't me... someone

else was in that mine. Someone else killed Zorya. Someone else started this."

Gunnar stared at her a long moment, as if she were the one holding explosive flasks in one hand, and in his expression Ilme saw her own heart mirrored: someone else had broken them. Someone else had made their friendship unfixable.

"There must be someone in the Wolf Clan who was angry," she sped on, trying to call up faces, names. "Not your father, he would have just killed Zorya. Maybe—"

"No," Gunnar interrupted. "No. No—you aren't tricking me again."

"I'm serious," Ilme said. "If they're still out there, they might be manipulating you—"

"The only person manipulating me is you, Ilme." He shook his head. "For a moment, I almost believed you. After all this time, all this work, every gift of Guthix, sacrifice I've made, I still nearly believed you when you said it was all for nothing."

He threw the two bottles in his hand against the floor, their oily contents splashing over the tiles, igniting where they mixed into white hot flames.

◆ ◆ ◆

When people spoke of the Fremennik, they spoke of their relentlessness, their tenacity. If they retreated, you did not celebrate, you feared the fiercer attack it presaged. One warrior fell, two more took his place. A summoned creature shattered, a greater one appeared. People spoke of the prowess of the White Knights, the unity of Asgarnia, but the Fremennik were endless—and in the presence of an unending pressure, all things fall apart.

◆ ◆ ◆

Flames leapt from the floor as eagerly as if they'd caught on dry grass. Gunnar drew another flask from his satchel and Ilme didn't think, only swept her staff toward him, aiming the spear of air at the flask in his hand. The tunnel of wind snapped his arm back, throwing the flask behind him to smash against the wall.

The room was thick with fumes and heat. Ilme pulled runes from her pouch, water to complement the air, crushed them together and loosed a bolt of icy water over the flames.

The water didn't quench the fire. The conflagration spread over the mound of rune essence behind, carried on the water like oil on vinegar.

Ilme cursed, coughing as the vapours scalded her throat. Gunnar yanked another flask free of his satchel and pulled back an arm to throw it into the spreading flames.

The earth runes nearly slipped through her fingers as she seized them, collapsed them with her hand still half in the pouch. The wave of soil cut between the flames and Gunnar as he hurled the flask, blocking and smothering the fire.

"Gunnar! Stop!" she shouted. "I don't want to kill you!"

Someone banged on the barricaded door, too far to reach, to solid to easily destroy. Gunnar smashed two more flasks, flames bursting into life between them, and met her eyes over the fire.

✦ ✦ ✦

People described the Fremennik as endless, but anything that pushes for an end will find its limits. A warrior sent to war for twenty years will tire. A child grown in conflict will want conflict's end. The White Knights swept their lines like ghosts. Their trebuchets fell one by one, until the last, only able to aim at the inner walls, was left flinging the carcasses of horses. But they had been told to stay. To hold. To fight.

In the north, on the slopes of Ice Mountain, their families gathered, prepared to start again—another outpost, another home, another attempt to gain a foothold. If this was Guthix's will, who were they to argue? They argued anyway, in quiet voices over fires, in the forest's depths, by the rivers where they washed.

On the Ice Mountain's slope there was a cavern, a perfect place to settle the Fremennik, to wait and see if at last the Great Jarl's vision was complete. A hall beyond any they could build.

A hall already inhabited—Camdozaal, the home of the Imcando dwarves.

The Imcando saw the Fremennik approaching, knew the stories of their tenacity, their endlessness. The Imcando, who made their own storied weapons, told their own tales of hall and creator, of safety and defence.

This cavern was not for the Fremennik, but in their fear, the Imcando made certain it was for no one.

+ ✦ +

Another wave of earth, another fire smothered. Gunnar leapt back out of the way of her spell, reaching for more flasks.

How foolish could he be? But he'd already told her—he'd planned to die here. He'd planned to reclaim his honour by any means necessary. *Each to the extent of his own abilities, for the price of his own sacrifices.*

Another time, it would have made her sad, but a rage boiled up in Ilme instead. "You *idiot!*" she shouted at Gunnar, fumes burning her throat, her eyes, her nose. "Someone else started this—if it's about Zorya then killing both of us isn't going to change anything!"

"Destroying the rune essence and you will change plenty!" Gunnar retorted, pulling out another flask.

"I don't want to kill you!" Ilme shouted. "Gunnar, I *don't*. But if you don't stop, I'll have no choice! There are people in this tow—" She broke off coughing.

Something shattered at her feet—a flask, the third flask, the catalyst first this time. The noxious liquid splashed up her hem, staining her green robes black. She met Gunnar's eyes and saw only hurt there. In each hand was their destruction, the components that made the oily flames.

She didn't want to kill Gunnar.

Panic swallowed Ilme. She grabbed at her runes, all instinct, the stones bulging between her fingers. Gunnar threw the flasks and she crushed together the errant stones slipping from her grasp. Her mouth tasted metallic, sparks biting her tongue as the air staff's magic swept through her.

A wave of water flowed out from her, a torrent like a waterfall crashing sideways. White foam coiled at the spell's terminus, where it crashed into the flasks, shattering the glass. The fluids mixed, the flames erupted.

And as before, the water carried a fire so hot it could crack stones along like ship sailing over the waves.

Before crashing over the Great Jarl, Gunnar Viljarsson, and engulfing him in flames.

✦ ✦ ✦

The battle stretched, an indrawn breath, a rising tension. No quarter given, no retreat called. The city, nearly broken, the White Knights holding its inner wall. The Fremennik exhausted, their resources dwindling as quickly as the Asgarnians.

✦ ✦ ✦

Ilme realised she was screaming: what she took for Gunnar's howls of pain was the tearing of her own throat. He was strangely silent, mouth agape, his shape only shadows between the searing bright flames as he stumbled, an uncertain body.

Ilme drew runes, hands shaking, thoughts reeling—earth smothered the fire, that's what she needed. But at the same time, some animal urge told her to go, grab him, pull him away.

You are covered in that oil, she thought numbly. *He can't touch the explosive oil. We'll all die if he touches you.*

She drew together the earth spell—too big, too much, but she just wanted to stop the burning. It swept over him, bearing him away from the stain on the wall where the first flask had shattered and smashing him to the floor. The flames vanished under the wave of magically-generated soil, and so did Gunnar.

Ilme ran to him, wary of more fire, but as the spell faded, the earth dissolving into magic, she saw she'd managed: all the fire was out.

But Gunnar Viljarsson lay dead, his features ravaged by the fire, his chest crushed by the earth. His vision incomplete, his destructions still enough to damage the world. His dearest friend, once, feeling as though she had done everything wrong.

"Oh, Gunnar," she managed, a lump rising in her throat.

The banging on the door had grown rhythmic, the strike of a weight trying to smash through. The bar bent, the hinge snapped, and the door fell in, letting a handful of Kinshra through, Valzin pushed past them, eyes wild, sword out. She took in Ilme, Gunnar's corpse, the mess of the vault.

"What did he do?" she asked. "What did he tell you?"

Ilme shook her head. "He meant to destroy it. He meant to die—" Her voice broke, the tears she'd been swallowing down for too long spilling over. "He was going to kill me," she said, between sobs. "He was going to kill everyone here. I tried… I tried…"

Valzin knelt down beside her, a firm hand on Ilme's arm. "You succeeded."

"Not at what I meant to do."

Valzin sighed. "You're too hard on yourself." And to Ilme's surprise, the other woman hugged her, her armour pressing painfully into Ilme's shoulder. "Come on," Valzin said quietly. "Come away. You did your best. It's almost over. Now we have places to be."

✦ ✦ ✦

A shadow crested the hills beyond Falador, a darkness that had no place in the high sun of midday. It formed a block, a wall, and on rattling hooves bore down on Falador, pinned down and nearly broken.

On the wall, for a moment, the young archer watching caught his breath—another army, another enemy. But the shadow did not falter, and soon enough he saw the banner of the Kinshra, called away at the worst of times, arriving when needed most, much to the despair of the Fremennik.

TWENTY-ONE

———◄◆►———

The heat of summer came early that year, and the itch of sweat beading down Ilme's back stirred up a phantom panic in her. After so many years, warm weather meant imminent orders to battle.

But that day, there was to be no battles—only celebration of heroism and peace at last. All the city seemed crowded in the great courtyard, ignoring the clammy air to see the White Knights gleaming in the sun like winged icyene arrayed before the Lord of Light. Anticipation buzzed through the crowd, the memories of the battle already changing to tales and legends.

The memories sat heavy in Ilme's heart. She thought of Thyra, the last time she'd seen her, after Gunnar had died, after they'd shrouded and wrapped his burned corpse. The remainder of the Fremennik horde, in the absence of their leader, had retreated to the River Lum. Raddallin agreed to let Thyra, escorted by a handful of Knights, return there with Gunnar's body to either settle or reclaim her children.

"I don't know how they will take it," Thyra said to Ilme, as they considered the box that held her father. Then she added, "I don't know how I am taking it."

"He was a complicated man," Ilme said. "It's fair to have complicated feelings."

"If the rest of the Fremennik feel complicated about it, that means your war isn't over."

"Maybe they'll change their minds. A season to lick their wounds. King Raddallin's agreed to leave them where they are."

But Thyra only shook her head. "I don't forgive you," she said. Then, "I don't forgive him either."

That Ilme could not argue with—she had failed Thyra, several times over, but when she thought about that last day, there was nothing she could have done differently. She hated herself for not knowing how to reach him, for choosing to keep lying, because lying was the easy choice. She hated Gunnar for what he'd done, for the people whose deaths he'd caused, for refusing to listen to her.

She turned to Thyra. "Do you know of anyone in the Wolf Clan who might have been willing to kill Zorya?"

Thyra had frowned, puzzled. "No. No one. We didn't trust the mine but… everyone loved the guardian. Even Jarl Viljar wouldn't have killed him."

You don't always know people as well as you believe, Ilme thought, leaning out from a low window near to the dais at the back of the courtyard. Rue lay hot and lazy at her feet, and the cheers of the crowd echoed off the buildings as King Raddallin ascended the dais.

Ilme was tense all over. There was nothing untoward about celebrating the heroism shown during the attack on Falador. There was nothing inappropriate about the Council of Falador wanting a ceremony to bestow honours on those who had saved the city.

"We have been too long, a nation imperilled," King Raddallin's voice carried over the crowd. "But through it all, through enemies far and near, Asgarnia has persisted. I, your king, have persisted. Because of the dedication, the determination, the sacrifice of so many, *we* remain sovereign and whole."

The gleaming knights below, in white and steel and blue, stood rapt and silent. Beside King Raddallin, Grand Master Perior, a half-cape slung over his missing arm, beamed, proud and glistening with sweat.

"In our direst hour, at the moment of our greatest need," King Raddallin went on, "the White Knights did not waver. They defended this city with everything they had and drove the Fremennik from our gates."

Ilme searched the crowd on the dais. Unaia beamed, proud and delighted. Azris looked annoyed. Zanmaron looked as though he were going to explode. And beside King Raddallin, Sanafin Valzin stood statue-still, her face a mask of stone.

It was not a celebration of all the Knights of Asgarnia.

"Therefore the Council of Falador has declared today one of distinction for the White Knights, who have ever been an integral part of Asgarnia's strength and have truly proven that once more for all to see," King Raddallin went on. "Furthermore, the Council bestows upon Sir Perior this blade of honour, in recognition of all he did to save the city."

Perior stepped forward, shining as the sun, to take the sword, gleaming runite and steel, from one of the councillors, a thickset man wearing the star of Saradomin.

Ilme watched Valzin raise an eyebrow as Raddallin gestured Perior toward the crowd. Ilme leaned forward, remembering that night at the air altar, that time when Perior and his knights had fought beside the Kinshra and Valzin like brothers- and sisters-in-arms, dedicants to the same cause.

Perior looked out over the crowd, grateful and satisfied. "There are no words that can truly encompass the pride I feel for the White Knights nor the love I bear for this kingdom. We serve because we are called, and I cannot imagine any man or woman in our order refusing the call." He turned the blade so that it flashed in the light. "But there is one I would be remiss if I did not thank."

Ilme glanced again to Valzin, but strangely her face had gone hard and still again.

"And that is Lord Saradomin, the great arbiter of goodness, the architect of peace. If not for his teachings, we would be nothing."

Valzin nodded slightly, as if to herself, then turned and left the dais. Ilme cursed and turned from the window, hurrying down the stairs. If she was fast, if she didn't run into anyone, she might catch her leaving—

As the stairs descended into the gallery beside the throne room, Ilme saw Valzin enter below her, head down, mouth tight. Ilme started to call out to her, but then the king appeared chasing after his friend.

"Sana, wait!"

Ilme stepped back, away from the banister.

Valzin stopped, not looking back. "What does my king require?" she said, no warmth at all.

"Sana," King Raddallin began, a chiding note in his voice. "Don't tell me you're jealous."

She smiled, a small bitter smile. "You never listen, Raddallin."

"You can't deny Perior deserved a commendation—"

Valzin turned, eyes sharp. "What? What did he do? What did Perior do that I did not? What did the White Knights do that the Kinshra did not meet or best? Because we were not *here* when the attack began? Because I was hunting your great enemy for you? Because we were *only* able to flank them and stop them burning the city to the ground?"

Raddallin held up a hand in a calming gesture. "The council—"

"Of course. 'The council'. You know perfectly well that the council will bend itself into knots to deny the Kinshra have ever been anything of value to them, when we have stood by you always. Before even the White Knights saw sense."

"Yes!" Raddallin said. "The Kinshra *are* Asgarnia's—they are the equals of the White Knights and always have been. They deserve the same recognition. They will have the same recognition, I swear it."

"Then why this?" she gestured behind him. "Why separate us, if we both equals?"

"The council—"

"The council. Exactly. The council that teems with Saradominists. This," she said calmly, "is what I warned you about. The Saradominists will sit in their satisfaction and pat each other on the heads and say how wonderful they are. They will erase all the rest, first by words and then by deed, and that includes you, Raddallin, if they get the chance."

Raddallin looked down. "You are very seldom wrong in my experience," he said, his voice slow as if to counter her galloping argument. "But what I need right now, what Asgarnia needs *right now*, is a steady course and a boat that is not in danger of being tossed over in the waves. Asgarnia has succeeded despite all odds, *because* of its many faiths. I need the discipline of the Saradominists, the caution of the Guthixians, the ingenuity of the Zamorakians—all these equally. But you aren't wrong: I find myself trapped by the fact that the Saradominists dislike being one among many. They want to be reassured they are the wisest, the greatest—but that is *their* weakness. Can you not see that?"

Ilme peered past the banister at Valzin's pale face, turned up toward her king, her friend. The stone mask was back, but something strange and soft shone in her eyes.

"What I see," she said, her voice firm but quiet, "is what I have already seen played out before. The trap is not new. You believe you are different than the kings of Misthalin. I know that you are. But I fear that the Saradominists are exactly the same." She shook her head. "The things I have done for you."

"Are what a subject owes her king," Raddallin said, a flash of anger finally. "I have promised you, Sana: the Kinshra will be rewarded as well. And if the council complains, I am the king. It will be done."

"You are the king," she echoed. She wet her mouth. "I think we're finished. May I have your leave?"

Raddallin frowned. "Sana—"

"May I have your leave?" she said, biting off each word. "Your Majesty."

He hesitated. "You are my dearest friend, Sanafin. You know that."

"And your loyal servant." She sketched a bow, and taking this as leave, turned and strode from the gallery. Raddallin watched her, and all signs of the anger that had burst from him fled. He seemed tired, and very alone.

Ilme eased her way up the stairs, silent as a shadow, leaving the king to his thoughts and worrying once again, that their differences might be greater than their unity.

PART III

THE TOWER

Battles are not lost and won; They simply remove the weak from the equation.

—ZAMORAK'S BOOK OF CHAOS

TWENTY-TWO

Eight years later, Azris of the Green considered herself in the looking glass, the prototype earth tiara carefully positioned around the coils of her dark hair. The gold band sat low on her pale forehead, making her brows look heavier, and at the crown of her head, a curl of metal arced upward—purportedly to balance the energies that were meant to make this a stronger version of the earlier runecrafting tiaras. She made a face, turning her head to one side then the other.

"Does this look ridiculous?" she asked.

In the mirror, she regarded Zanmaron. He was still in bed, half under the tangle of blankets, his hair a mess. He held a book by its covers, pages hanging down, and was studying the binding intensely. At her question, his eyes flicked toward her.

"Yes," he said, and returned to his study of the book.

She turned, reaching up to untangle the crown. "You're supposed to say I look gorgeous and commanding."

"You look gorgeous and commanding," he murmured, flexing

247

the binding. "And also like a very flashy scorpion is perched on your head."

Azris ripped the tiara off and resisted the urge to throw it at him. He'd only demand to know why she'd asked a question she didn't want an answer to. "What are you *doing*?"

"I'm *thinking*."

She dropped the tiara on the cabinet below the looking glass, with a *Clang* that was not nearly as satisfying as if she'd thrown it, and tried to fix her hair. "Get up," she said. "Get dressed and *go*. I have about a thousand things to do, and I don't need to add Unaia seeing you skulk out of here after I've left and deciding to eel her way into my day to suggest I'm *affiliating* with you."

Zanmaron set the book down in his lap and frowned at her. "If we're not 'affiliating', what do you call this?"

"I mean, she thinks you're using me to make the Green Order prop up the Red and I am *sick* of the implication that I'm so starry-eyed about you that you're actually leading my order. Get *up*!"

He closed the book and set it on the nightstand. "Has she *met* you? I'd be better off sucking up to Temrin like she does and taking over the Grey than tell you to do anything."

Azris turned and collected her papers from her dresser, checking that the letter was with them twice and biting back her annoyance. *You are stubborn* was not the same thing as *You are good at leading your order,* and even if he meant well, she wasn't in the mood to interpret the extra steps.

"She's still angry I left her tutelage," he went on. "It's not about you."

"Yes. Well, it's been fifty years, and you have to work together now, so sort it out, because I don't much like being in the middle of it."

Azris did not think of the war with the Fremennik fondly—who would?—but it had to be said, everything worked much more smoothly when the orders all had the same goals, the same focus: survive and protect Asgarnia. Now? Now they fragmented, chasing their own goals, noticing their own differences. They began to seem more like the White and Black Knights Azris remembered in her youth, the days of Valzin making Grand Master Adolar red-faced and spluttering.

The Knights were a different problem. She unfolded the letter. *Though it has been a long time since I've visited, I think it best for me to reacquaint myself immediately—*

Zanmaron came up behind her and put his arms around her. She crumpled the letter in surprise. "Ignore Unaia. And Ilme's ridiculous crown." He kissed her behind the ear. "What have you got to do that's so urgent?"

He was mussing her hair, but she leaned back into him. "To start with, I have to drag Ilme down to the library and make her choose an apprentice, so Unaia gets off my back about *that too.* She's convinced Ilme's stealing all the Blue Order apprentices. That Pharas boy took Green Robes last summer and every time Ilme borrows another apprentice because they're curious about staves, it's as though she's spat upon Saradomin in the flesh."

"Someday Unaia will test her hypotheses more thoroughly and realise that the only thing driving apprentices out of the order is her steel grip on them." He kissed her neck. "Here's my hypothesis: Ilme *could* wait."

Reluctantly, Azris peeled his arm off. "Counterpoint: I have to make sure everything is ready for tonight, and that specifically means making sure Ilme's going to keep it together."

He pulled her back. "Make Eritona do it."

"Eritona has her own problems. Not all of us have so much free time we can spend the whole day dawdling over hypothetical research problems."

He sighed. "Oh fine." His arms stayed around her though. "Speaking of research, I think I might have an answer to Ilme's rune altar problem. Will you tell her to come find me when she's done with apprentices."

Azris frowned. "What's she doing with rune altars? She didn't tell me about that."

He hesitated. "It's about the staves. It's just related to altars. Maybe. I'll tell you if it ends up being worth the trouble."

She eyed him a moment, but his mouth was set in that way that said he was going to be as stubborn as she was, and she *did* have a thousand things to do. "I won't forget."

He kissed her. "It's one of your more infuriating attributes."

"Get *dressed*," she said, going to the door with her papers in hand. "And if Unaia sees you coming out of here, *you* have to deal with her."

In the hall beyond, Azris straightened her emerald robes and picked a stray thread out of the gold and black embroidery, checked her earrings hadn't come loose, and walked purposefully toward the stairs that led up to Ilme's workroom.

Master Endel had left her too much to live up to. He had founded the Green Order, discovered the rune essence mine, repaired the rune altars, and then figured out how to rebuild them. That he'd left Azris the leadership of the Green Order and not, for example, Eritona with her skills in diplomacy and order, meant he had seen something in her. But since she'd taken the robes of leadership all Azris had managed to do was hold the order together by her fingernails while the Blue and the Red and the Grey pulled at it, and prove for the fourth time that she couldn't make teleportation work.

The Fremennik who'd stayed in the north had effectively made reaching the rune essence mine impossible. Without launching a new campaign of war, they had no reliable way to reach it. She spent less time in research and more time arguing with quarry workers over the dimensions and quality of stone for the rune altar rebuilding projects, plotting caravan routes and treaty acknowledgements to transport the stone and wizards to their final locations, or explaining to the high-born parents of Asgarnian and Misthalanian apprentices that they could not simply be given wizard status as a matter of entry.

Which did not include meeting with the other heads of the four orders and dealing with Unaia without giving into the very un-leaderlike urge to tell her where to shove it.

Endel the Green would be a wizard of renown. Azris the Green would be a footnote, a no one. Sometimes she eyed the apprentices wondering which one would supplant her, and whether everyone would cheer at it.

Azris found Ilme sitting at her worktable, frowning at a tablet covered with scratched notes and fiddling with the end of her brown braid. She didn't *look* like someone who'd gotten upsetting news, which boded well.

Rue sat on the table batting a sharp-pointed awl toward the edge. Ilme reached out and caught it as it fell. "I told you to stop."

"I don't like it," he said.

"You don't like anything." She looked up and saw Azris. "Good morning. Everything all right?"

"More or less," Azris began.

"I do like things," Rue said, stubbornly. The little dragon, after years of being taciturn, had slowly built up a substantial vocabulary. "I like runes. I like books. I like spiders. Crunchy," Rue said. He blinked at Azris. "Have you eaten? Them?"

"You may have all the ones you find," Ilme told him. "In fact, why don't you go find some now?" She sighed, turning to Azris like a woman facing sentencing. "I was hoping you'd forgotten." She frowned. "Where's the earth tiara?"

Azris sat down on the stool opposite her. "It didn't fit," she lied. "But I had to push back rebuilding the earth altar another month anyway, so don't worry about that now." She glanced at Ilme's worktable. "Any luck with the non-elemental staves?"

"Still in progress," Ilme said, slowly. "I got a law prototype to stabilise. Trying to figure out the anchors for a nature one. I suspect chaos will be for some other wizard to figure out. Why are you asking about my staves? I thought you were going to drag me down to choose an apprentice."

"I am," Azris said. "It's ridiculous you don't have any. But before we go…" She shuffled the papers she'd brought with her. "The High Marshal is arriving tonight."

"And there's a banquet," Ilme added. "Which I will be on time for."

Azris hesitated. "And you're all right?"

"Why wouldn't I be?"

Azris gestured vaguely at Ilme, as if she could stir up the words that made this conversation end easily. But she only managed to come up with, "You get *peculiar* when the end of the war comes up. Valzin's been gone a long time. She was there when… when you…"

Ilme stared back, blank-faced, as if she were not thinking at all of the gruesome death of Gunnar Viljarsson. "That's true," she said, in too-even tones. "But it's been a long time. Valzin and I have written to each other. Everything seems to be fine now. Why wouldn't I be happy to go back to normal?"

Azris made a face. "It's not really *normal*. The king gave her a truly ludicrous sword—I hear it's as tall as a horse, as good steel as the Imcando used to make—but that's entirely made up for the blunder with Perior and the council?"

"You don't think so?"

"I think assuming that Sanafin Valzin doesn't hold a grudge against you is a dangerous choice. And I don't think it was ever about the sword. Although I hear Perior's in a snit now because his sword's not as fine."

Ilme made a face. "You know he regrets what happened as much as the king. I wonder if he and Valzin have made up too."

Azris shrugged. "Pick yourself an apprentice fresh from Falador, and they'll know better than I do. Assuming you're ready to go?"

Rue pounced on something near Azris's feet and peered under his claws to see empty floor. "Is it possible we could just skip this?" Ilme asked. "I'm happy to advise all of them, but—"

"Yes, I'm well aware," Azris said. Rue sniffed her hems and she nudged him firmly away with one foot. "You can't keep borrowing the other order's apprentices. Master Unaia is furious, which means it's a matter of time before Master Temrin is too."

Ilme shrugged. "They come to me. And I don't *need* an apprentice."

Azris bit back a scream. Sometimes, she missed being young and foolish and a little terrible, and being able to scream at people when they were infuriating without it having too many lasting effects.

"Fine," Azris said. "*You* don't need to. But the *order* needs you to. I have limited options for trained wizards for apprentices to study under, absent a sudden ability to communicate with the dead from the war. I am making apprentices teach younger apprentices just to keep them. We don't have the luxury of you being too good for an apprentice."

Ilme's cheeks reddened. "That's not it," she said tightly.

Azris cursed to herself. "What's your concern here? They're just students, not trolls. Give them some books to read and keep working on your staff project." She shook her head. "Or the altar problem—what is that? Zanmaron said he had something to run by you."

"I don't have an altar prob… Oh. He means the energy limits."

"What does that have to do with rune altars?" *And why,* she thought, *did he not tell me?*

"He had the notion that the staves are somehow tapping the energy nexuses the rune altars exist in. Sort of like the elemental plumes Master Endel used to seek out."

Azris frowned. "You can't though. They only connect through the altars."

"That's what I said," Ilme agreed. "He's a little obsessed. I suppose he'll figure it out eventually. Like you and teleportation. We've all the time in the world."

Now Azris felt her cheeks burn, but before she could retort, Ilme raised her gaze to the planks of the ceiling and sighed. "Do you ever wonder how long this lasts?"

"How long what lasts? Zanmaron trying to prove me wrong?"

"Us," she said. "Life. I don't even remember how old I am anymore. Gunnar was a child when we met and he died an old man, and here I am, plucking my first grey hairs. How long does it go on?" She swallowed. "How long to we have to live with… everything that happened?"

Azris cursed—this was what she'd feared, this was what she came to Ilme to stop. She grabbed Ilme's hand, and for a moment, she felt the weight of her authority settle on her. "Don't," she said. "Don't dig into that pit. There's nothing valuable buried in there."

"Sometimes we should dig up the ugly things," Ilme said.

"Fine," Azris said, squeezing her hand. "Dig: would you give everything up?"

"What? Runecrafting?"

"Yes. Because that's the alternative: give it up, this art you've spent all your life honing, this skill you were willing to defy your evil aunt to claim—this skill that your precious Gunnar wanted to strip away from you so badly he burned half the continent down!

Honestly, Ilme, look me in the eye and tell me after all that, after everything we sacrificed, that you want to give it up." She couldn't. She wouldn't even if there had been no sacrifices already made, no tithes laid on the altar of the world. And Ilme wouldn't either—Azris was sure.

Ilme sighed, a lump building in her throat. "No. I love this. I think it makes the world a better place. Even if… even if it causes problems too."

Azris held onto that feeling. "You want to avoid an apprentice because you don't think they ought to follow your path, fine. I understand. But I'm going to tell you that much like you yourself, most of them are going to do it anyway. They are what they are. Make sure they don't go astray. Warn them of the dangers of befriending genocidal maniacs."

Ilme glowered at her, and Azris figured that was better than sighing at the ceiling. Besides there were times she needed to be a friend and times she needed to be the leader of her order. And in both cases, she'd let Ilme falter too long.

"Come on. Let's go." She took Ilme by the arm and hauled her off the stool. She stepped backward and nearly trod on Rue, who flew up and landed on Ilme's shoulder with a hiss.

"You were the one playing by her feet," Ilme chided. He curled up sulkily behind her neck.

"Your bad friend should go away."

Azris scowled. "I think I liked you better when you talked less. Come on," she said to Ilme. She led her from the room, down the winding stair of the tower to where the apprentices of the Green Order loitered.

The Wizards' Tower still housed a sizeable number of apprentices, even after the losses from the attack on Falador nearly a decade before. They were not all young, they were not all terribly skilled, but they were eager to help keep the new-found art of runecrafting alive. *A fortunate problem to have,* Azris reminded herself. Master Endel had run the three of them—her, Eritona, and Ilme—in circles trying to keep his experiments going.

And if another war broke out, they would need as many wizards as they could train.

Azris pushed those dark thoughts aside and clapped her hands as they entered, and the apprentices all turned toward her.

"Wizard Ilme has agreed to take one of you on," she said. "Isn't that wonderful? Why don't *you* sit here"—she pressed Ilme down behind a writing desk—"and they can come up one at a time to be interviewed?" She bent low beside Ilme's ear. "That black-haired boy is the son of the Duke of Lumbridge, pick him."

"You pick him," Ilme said, as Rue perched on the back of her chair to peer over her shoulder. He sniffed at Azris's papers, flicking his little black tongue out like a serpent.

"Bad friend," he said again.

Azris pulled her papers away. "Fine, don't come to me when you need more coin for tools." She swept from the library—if she hurried, she might be able to get to her own workrooms, to pull out her last treatise. Something about what Zanmaron has said was nagging at her—

"Ah, Azris!" a voice called as she started up the stairs. Azris flinched. She turned and found Unaia striding toward her, her blue and silver robes swishing in elaborate layers, her dark hair fixed beneath a winged tiara. Two apprentices, a dark-haired young man, and a whip-thin blond youth followed behind.

"I'm so glad I found you," she said, saccharine sweet. "I need more workrooms for the Blue Order's apprentices, and I was hoping to get your help figuring out which spaces could be repurposed. It seems the Red Order is nearly taking over the Tower sometimes."

Azris grit her teeth, banishing any daydreams of research. It would keep, while Unaia would only cause more problems.

TWENTY-THREE

A pale-haired young woman sat down across from Ilme, chin high. "Well met, Wizard Ilme. I'm Cordelia. I'm very interested in your work on air runes."

"Thank you," Ilme said, and lapsed into an awkward silence.

Truth be told, she'd thought Azris had been bluffing. She had no idea how to interview apprentices, and she'd been sure she could keep avoiding it. What had Master Endel asked her?

Let us say that you are trapped. Pinned, perhaps, against a steep cliff.

She flinched. "What... makes you want to study runecrafting?"

Why did Azris assume I wouldn't handle Valzin returning well? she thought, only half-hearing Cordelia's answer. *What if she's right?*

She realised Cordelia had finished, and was waiting on her, a pinch of worry forming between her almost invisible eyebrows. "Sorry," Ilme said. "I'm somewhere else. What are you interested in studying now?"

She thought of Gunnar's death, and the bitter scent of burning flesh flooded her nose. She made herself breathe while Cordelia rattled off half the projects the wizards of the tower were engaged in. She thought of the face he made, the moment she'd realised he really hadn't killed Zorya, and neither had she. Like he might, after all this time, still trust her.

And then: the moment after when he refused to hear a word.

The thought that Zorya's murderer might still be out there in the world haunted her whenever she let it rise to the surface. Even if she could reach the Wolf Clan, by now they were probably dead or so old she wouldn't recognise their face. She would carry that guilt forever.

Who do you trust? she thought, studying Cordelia. *How far will you trust them?* She couldn't be the one they trusted—she'd given Gunnar everything he needed to destroy the world. She couldn't ignore them—Azris was right. The Order needed wizards.

There had been something about the war that felt as if everything would end when it did. When Gunnar fell, there seemed as if there would be nothing beyond that loss. She was ended. But the world kept going. Ilme kept going, and years and years later she found herself startled by that simple truth: there is always more to come. There is always more you can give up.

Not this time, she told herself, and concentrated on apprentices.

More apprentices took Cordelia's place, all of them painfully young. *What's your name? What have you learned? What would you like most to study?*

What would you sacrifice to study it? she thought. The boy before her—the black-haired son of the Duke of Lumbridge—could not answer that question. None of them could. What did any one of them know of sacrifice?

What spells have you learned? What runes have you handled? What books have you read?

When the day comes, how will you choose: this order, this nation, your friends, your self? she thought, as a boy from Al Kharid, freckles sprinkling his tan skin, looked hopefully up at her.

Maybe Azris was right. Maybe she needed to get out of her gloomy thoughts. She searched the cluster of apprentices—what would she even ask them to do?

"Rue," she said, "will you go find Zanmaron for me? If he can't come here, find out where he is and I'll go to him."

Ilme rubbed her forehead, too aware of the crowd of young apprentices watching her. She stood and crossed the library to where some of the older apprentices were arguing over a book, but there was more space for her to breathe, to clear her thoughts.

It was a wonder, Ilme thought, that these apprentices spent so much of their time in the libraries of the Wizards' Tower. At their age, she was travelling Gielinor hunting rune altars and crafting runes—she'd had to research as she went, battered copies of Master Endel's ancient translations, loose papers of other wizards' treatises only just copied down.

"No, this is the one you need, I promise!" the blond girl was saying. "Ozzikan is entirely too basic." Ilme remembered the girl, one of Temrin's protégés, trembling and white-faced, when Ilme returned to Falador after the attack. She had been on the wall, she'd said in halting tones.

But in the library Mei bloomed, hungry for truth and discovery. All the best virtues the Grey Order prized.

"Master Zanmaron was very clear about what he wanted," the boy in the red robes was saying. "And he's been very obstinate about who helps with this problem." Kelavan was a young man with a strong face and a mild demeanour that hid a passionate substance and made him almost incapable of standing up to Zanmaron.

Mei pressed the book toward Kelavan. "Just tell him it was your idea!"

"Excuse me?" Ilme said, and both apprentices jumped. She smiled to herself. "I find myself in need of some sort of apprentice test. What are your masters giving you to work on?"

Mei grinned at her. "Good morning, Wizard Ilme. Master Temrin's given me free rein of the library actually. I don't have much in the way of exercises. He says I ought to build a foundation myself." She held out a book. "This one's interesting."

Kelavan blinked at her a moment, as if he weren't sure how to answer. Ilme offered him a reassuring smile. "I can ask Zanmaron myself as soon as I track him down if you can't think of anything. Rue went to fetch him."

"No, I…" Kelavan looked at the stack of books he was still holding. "Do you want me to write them down?"

Ilme waved this away. "Just a summary."

"He has me checking his calculations," Kelavan said. "And in between, he sets me proofs which have been deemed impossible. 'To hone my ability to question and test'—and in case they are wrong." He listed a few: a proof for evading shields, a proof for bending the line of an attack, and a proof for reversing the directionality of a spell.

This was not what Ilme was looking for—she did not see the benefit in training apprentices to throw themselves against well-established brick walls and they seemed too young to fling them at the vastness of the library. But then what did she know? She had no apprentices.

A thought occurred to her: "He's not given you Master Azris's teleportation treatises, has he?"

Kelavan frowned. "No. Should he have?"

"He should *not*," Ilme said. "Unless you somehow discover something that actually warrants revisiting the problem, it will be entirely about tweaking Azris's nose and you shouldn't get in the middle of that." She looked between the apprentices. "Don't get in the middle of any of your masters' spats. But especially not *that* one."

The boy blushed. "Right."

"I can fetch you some of the early exercises Master Temrin gave me," Mei offered.

"Thank you, that would be a great help," Ilme said.

Mei turned back to the shelves, and Kclavan regarded Ilme awkwardly a moment, before asking, "Have you heard the High Marshal is coming this evening? I've never met her."

Ilme made herself smile, even as her thoughts overflowed with the memories of Valzin being struck by that arrow, Valzin breaking down the door to the rune essence vault, Valzin furious after the sword ceremony, like she could break the whole world. "She is a force of nature," Ilme said. "I'm glad she's back."

Rue flew into the library, circling over Ilme's head as the apprentices all made little shrieks of delight. Ilme reached for him. "Come on. Stop showing off."

Rue settled on the table. "Your grumpy friend says you come there."

"'Grumpy friend'?" Mci said. Then clapped a hand to her mouth to stem the flood of giggles. "Oh! Master Zanmaron?" Kelavan looked uncomfortable.

Ilme sighed. She took the first book Mei had offered, flipped to a page and went back to the waiting apprentices. "You, you, and you," she said, selecting Cordelia, the would-be Duke of Lumbridge, and the freckled Kharidian boy. "Here is the beginning of the proof outlining the escalation rate for combining elemental runes of the same type. I want you to finish it, find the point it breaks down, and tell me why. How you do your work is more important to me than your results. I will come back in an hour and see how you're progressing."

"Your bad friend," Rue said, clinging to her shoulder with needle-sharp claws as Ilme left the library, heading for Zanmaron's study. "Is it coming?"

"'Are *you* coming?'" Ilme gently corrected. "And I am. You can go tell Zanmaron if it's such a rush."

"No," Rue said stubbornly. "I like to stay with you. You're thinking. Thinking sad things. You're making the face."

"Just old memories," Ilme said. "Old puzzles I can't solve."

✦ ✦ ✦

Zanmaron's study always looked as if a whirlwind had blown through it. Today, he had pushed all the papers to the sides of his great, slate-topped worktable. Chalk figures and diagrams covered the surface, and he'd rolled up the dusty sleeves of his work robe past the elbows. He didn't look up as Ilme came in.

"When we summon a creature," he said, "where does it come from?"

"This again?" Ilme said. Rue leaped from her shoulder and grabbed Zanmaron's discarded cloak and dragged it under the table to make a nest. "You can't reverse a summoning and produce teleportation—I think that's Azris's third treatise, which as I recall you definitely read."

He glowered up at her, his hair sticking up on end from where he'd dragged a hand through it. "I'm not asking about reversing it. I'm saying when we cast a summoning, we're pulling a creature from *somewhere*. Say you were to summon a wolf—you're taking it from the spirit world, so far as we can tell. Or a demon—you pull it from the infernal dimensions. Each thing has its place, and that place is not *here*."

A creature stepping through a rift in the air, all muscle and horn and vicious teeth. Ilme felt cold. "What? Why would you say that?"

But Zanmaron forged on. "Unaia had me practice summoning

before we relearned runecrafting—she pretends she never did, but we all know that was her specialty. Anyway, yes, you're summoning it from somewhere—let's assume that's right—but if you do those calculations, they come out as flawed as your calculations about reaching the rune altars."

The creature blocking the exit, batlike wings spread, roaring to shake the stones.

"I don't…" Ilme said, trying to keep her thoughts on Zanmaron. "I'm not following."

Zanmaron pulled a fistful of parchment from the piles around his worktable. "When you tried to work the calculations that assumed your staves drew power directly from the rune altars, the calculations didn't work. And when we hypothesised that the staves might be breaching the barriers to the rune altars with hitherto undiscovered teleportation spells, they didn't work. And Azris was furious for a month."

Zorya's great voice, booming 'Demon'. It was only her, Gunnar and the guardian in the cavern. But beyond the cavern…

If it wasn't you and it wasn't me… someone else was in that mine. Someone else killed Zorya. Someone else started this.

She'd assumed it was one of the Fremennik. She'd assumed it so easily.

"I need to sit down," Ilme said.

"Right?" Zanmaron said, eyes blazing. "It's exciting!"

Her thoughts were scrambling, trying to follow the path he was leading her down, while also remembering…

Zanmaron…

Zanmaron had been there the day Zorya died.

He could have followed her. He could have stood just beyond the cavern's entrance and worked the summoning. He'd said it himself—once, long ago, Zanmaron of the Blue had been trained at summoning.

He could have been the one to deceive her and Gunnar both.

"It's exciting," he said, "because I worked it backwards, and I think there's another plane involved."

"Another... Another plane?"

"Yes like... like..." He held his hands up, pressed almost together. "A binding. Or really glue. There's something between holding all the parts together. We can't call it the 'glue plane' though, we'll have to find something else. Watch it be one of those forgotten discoveries your old master loved so. Your staff equations fall in line when we add this glue-layer. If we are in fact pulling wolves or demons—or what have you, it doesn't matter, I don't think we need to get out summoning tools for this—but if that's correct, then I think it works as well."

There weren't only two of us and Zorya in the cavern, she thought. *Was it you?*

He frowned at her. "What are you staring at?"

"I'm thinking," she said slowly.

Zanmaron eyed her, all suspicion. "You're *not* telling Azris about this. Not yet. I don't want a flurry of 'I already dealt with teleportation' nonsense before we figure out what this means. If we help her solve—"

"No," Ilme said. Her nerves were sizzling, a rising anger filling her. But she had to be sure. "Do you remember the day we went to the rune essence mine to try and persuade the jarl not to break our alliance? Why did you come?"

He stared at her as if she were posing a puzzle he couldn't work out. "Because we were concerned your friend might choose to be a violent madman?"

"Why *you*?"

"Why not me?" But he frowned, deep in thought. "I think... I feel like Azris and I were fighting? Which doesn't narrow much... Oh wait, no. That was the one and only trip I wore those horrible boots I got in Lumbridge and had blisters on my feet for *weeks*. Awful. And Azris did not care and I was very in my feelings about it. So I think it was the fighting."

"You..." Ilme stopped, the memory coming back to her, bright and clear: when she left the others, Zanmaron was down on the ground, taking off his boots. And when she came back he was just relacing them. It was odd how that stood out, in the memory of rushing down the mountain side—seeing Zanmaron, his knobbly red sock, bright as blood, before it slid into the boot.

She tried to imagine the cycle of removing and replacing the boots that would have had to have happened and could not—it was comical. It would have drawn notice. It could not have been Zanmaron.

"Are you all right?" Zanmaron demanded. "You look ill."

"You didn't kill Zorya," Ilme said, hardly more than a whisper.

Zanmaron stared at her. "Are you having some kind of mental break? I'm getting Azris—"

"*Not* your grumpy friend," Rue interrupted from his nest on the floor. "Your bad friend. Your bad friend killed the frog friend."

Ilme dropped down on the ground to peer under the table. Rue regarded her with his bright yellow eyes. "Rue?" Ilme asked. "What do you mean?"

"Your bad friend," he said.

Zanmaron dropped down beside her. "Who is your bad friend?"

Ilme sighed. "No, Rue, it wasn't Gunnar."

Rue sat up, tail wrapped around himself in an affronted sort of way. "*Not* your cold friend. Your *bad* friend."

"Azris?"

"You cannot possibly think Azris—" Zanmaron started.

"Not your bossy friend, your *bad* friend!" Rue said, growing annoyed. "Your *bad* friend!"

"Do you mean—"

"One by one through all the people of your acquaintance cannot possibly be the best way to narrow this down," Zanmaron said. "Who was there that day?"

Ilme sat back on her heels. "Master Endel. Unaia. The Kinshra. I don't think there were others." She looked up. "Can Unaia summon a demon?"

"She *wouldn't*," Zanmaron said. "It's against *the rules*. Setting aside whether it's right or wrong, it's not *done*. How could she look down her nose at the rest of us if she'd *killed a Guardian of Guthix?*" He shook his head. "She's not your friend either."

"Master Endel wouldn't have. I don't think."

"Who among the Kinshra can make a summoning pouch?"

Ilme shook her head. "I don't know. Valzin's coming tonight. I could ask." And how much chaos would that create, asking which Kinshra had set off the war that nearly broke the world and set runecrafting back twenty years.

But at this, Rue streaked into her lap, digging his little claws into the front of her robes. "That one. Your bad friend! Your bad friend! The Vaaall-zin. The Valzin killed the frog friend. Zorya. Valzin."

TWENTY-FOUR

Ilme froze, pieces coming together. Not a wizard who wanted everything to keep growing. Not a Fremennik who respected the guardian. Valzin had gone ahead while Ilme had gone to the essence mine. She'd had time to get there, to wait. To watch.

Valzin in the ambush of the mind altar, bleeding from the head saying, *The beauty of war.* Saying, *Finally. I... almost gave up.*

"She... she planned it," Ilme said, reflexively folding her arms around Rue. "She did it to start the war." Suddenly she couldn't catch her breath. "She lied."

"You don't know that," Zanmaron cautioned. "It was almost thirty years ago. Rue might remember wrong."

"Not wrong," Rue protested.

"It's... Maybe," Ilme said. But so many things were suddenly making sense: Valzin's insistence the war was coming before it started, Valzin's glee when Gunnar declared he'd see them destroyed, Valzin's steadfast insistence that the Fremennik would come soon enough.

Valzin in the hall below, saying to Raddallin, *The things I've done for you.*

"Can she make summoning pouches? Does she know how to do that?" Ilme asked.

Zanmaron went still and silent, his mouth clamped around the words he wouldn't speak. "Don't," Ilme said. "Don't you tell me you don't remember. What did she show you?"

"Nothing exactly." He hesitated. "You know I left Unaia's tutelage. That was a reason. She had a strict system for what I could learn and when, rules about how my work belonged to her until she deemed me a full wizard—I hated it. That wasn't a secret. But Valzin's the one who noticed I should have been summoning greater things. More difficult entities."

"Like *demons*?" Ilme demanded.

"No one ever said demons! But she told me there were books in Falador, so I looked into it myself, and that did include demons, although to be clear, aside from the difficulty, there's nothing wrong with—"

"Nothing wrong until you kill a guardian and start a war that nearly destroys the world!"

"Put your head down. I'm finding Azris," Zanmaron said, coming to his feet. "You need to rest."

"I need to find Valzin," Ilme said standing as well. What would she say? Maybe she ought to go straight to the king—

Zanmaron turned, blocking her. "No. No. Don't. Don't poke at this."

"She started the war!"

Ilme felt the world tilting, her sense of everything reorienting around this simple fact. The war was not the natural outcome of Endel's lie and Gunnar's deep-rooted pain. Valzin had made it happen—somehow—and if she had done that, the war became almost a prelude, a promise of future deceptions.

"Fine," Zanmaron said. "Let's take that as fact. She started the war. But the war is over. Valzin won. Do you want to be on the wrong side of a woman capable of killing a Guardian of Guthix? And returning to the initial hypothesis, why would Sanafin Valzin, arguably the second most powerful person in Asgarnia, pick a fight with a bunch of ice-crusted barbarians?"

"What an interesting thought experiment," a voice said behind them.

Ilme turned. Sanafin Valzin stood in the doorway, scarlet coat draped over one arm. She'd cropped her hair again, the gleaming threads of silver just beginning to show themselves as her use of runes had dropped off. She grinned, blue eyes bright. "I do hope this hypothetical is related to some new weapon design."

"High Marshal," Zanmaron said, smoothly. "Welcome. Yes… we… Well, the Blue Order is working on some weapon designs they think you'll appreciate. But Wizard Ilme and I… disagree about their immediate usefulness. We're not starting another war anytime soon. What do you need with these things?" He paused. "The past puts everyone in a bad mood."

Valzin made a little moue. "One hopes it remains in the past. I suppose that depends on if we resecure the path to the essence mine." She smiled at Ilme. "I was coming to ask if you wanted to play king's table before dinner. The gods beyond the Edicts know I could use some quiet conversation—and a sense of what's lying in wait for me. Do you think that would settle you, or make it worse?"

Ilme couldn't speak. For all of Zanmaron's logic, she felt sure she had it right. Only Valzin could have done it. How could she have missed this? For a moment, she felt as unmoored and uncertain as that fateful day in the cavern.

You can jump, Valzin's voice slipped through her thoughts. *See what it is you're afraid of.*

"Let's play," Ilme said. "We can use my study." She looked back at Zanmaron. "Will you take care of Rue for a bit? Let him eat your spiders."

Zanmaron stared at her, as if he could remake his argument via significant looks alone, but he took the little dragon, who went reluctantly.

Valzin gestured at Zanmaron's face. "Maybe wash up, Master Zanmaron. You look like you've been literally wrestling with your equations." He rubbed a self-conscious hand over his chalky face and shot Ilme another look laden with meaning as she left.

"I'm very curious how the new masters of the orders are handling things," Valzin said as they walked. "Who would have thought spoiled Azris and sullen Zanmaron would become the pillars of their disciplines? I suppose that's one of the downsides of living this long. People change so much."

"Not that much," Ilme said. Valzin did it before, she could do it again—and they weren't prepared, none of them were prepared. She thought of Mei, bright and eager in the library; white-faced and shaking in Falador.

Valzin chuckled. "Are you all right?"

As they mounted the stairs, Ilme dropped her voice. "I know what you did. You killed Zorya."

For a moment, Valzin looked so surprised that Ilme nearly doubted herself—she'd been wrong about Zanmaron, now she'd been wrong about Valzin.

But then Valzin smirked and said "Sorry? I don't remember who that is."

Such a lie—when had Valzin forgotten anything? That was part of what made her so invaluable. Ilme stopped in the middle of the stairs and faced the High Marshal.

"You killed Zorya," Ilme said again, more firmly. "You

summoned the demon."

"Why? Because I'm Zamorakian? That's a very hurtful assumption. I assume you got it from Perior?"

"No," Ilme said. "Because you know how to do all manner of things. I believe you know how to summon a demon."

Valzin tilted her head, still smiling, the fingers of one hand resting lightly on the wall, as if she had no more than paused. "You believe," Valzin chided. "But you don't know. And it sounds like Zanmaron doesn't agree with you." Ilme hesitated and she pressed on. "I do know how to do all manner of things. Like keep this country together, whatever the cost. Like root out the weaknesses, to preserve the core."

Old grief wrapped its claws around Ilme's throat. "How could you?"

"With a summoned demon, apparently." Valzin shifted her coat to her other arm, and started up the stairs again, catching Ilme around the shoulders to guide her up with one strong arm. "Look, let's say, for example, you have a kingdom. It's a solid little kingdom, it has a lot of promise—but it has a lot of problems too. It has nobles that used to rule their own little tribes and now and again they think, 'Well, maybe I should be the king!' It has a neighbour who presumes that they are owed special treatment, and they whisper war over the fact they won't have it. There are greedy merchants, muttering about how they really are the ones who deserve power—after all they have money now that there are runes to sell.

"All of this chaos. Well, our Lord Zamorak loves chaos. Chaos brings change, and change lets the ambitious rise. So, if one loves the little kingdom, if one believes in it, then by all accounts one needs the little kingdom to use the chaos. It's very simple."

Ilme shook her head. "Killing Zorya wasn't anything Asgarnia needed."

"No," Valzin agreed, nodding to several grey-robed wizards who passed by obliviously. "Ideally, when Jarl Viljar heard that you'd tricked him from the Moon Clan itself, he would have cut us off from the essence mine, and we'd have been forced to go to war to reclaim it—everyone would have insisted, and we would have been able to hold it over all their heads. It probably would have gone poorly for Endel, maybe the Green Order on the whole, but you would have managed, Ilme, I'm sure.

"But then that idiot man chose to be angry at the *Moon Clan* for pointing it out, and not Endel for lying! Acted like it would have been no skin off his nose if Endel had told him he had come from the moon itself, so long as the trade was good. That still baffles me."

They reached Ilme's study and stopped before the door. "If it helps," Valzin offered, "I think in this *very hypothetical* example, killing the guardian, while not ideal, still would have achieved its goals. We flushed out the traitors, Misthalin sweetened up, and as a bonus, Al Kharid is out of our hair. So, in the end, in theory anyway, this would be a successful action for a true patriot to take."

Valzin smiled at Ilme, as if she hadn't just laid out exactly how set the whole world into war. "Anyway," she said, "do you still want to play king's table? I got a new board in Misthalin. But we can use yours."

Ilme stared at her. "Are you mad? You *killed* Zorya."

"I didn't say that." Valzin sighed. "You need some time, I understand. I honestly assumed you'd figured this out ages ago, so my apologies."

"You thought I figured this out and… what? I was fine with it?"

"Well, you're practical," Valzin pointed out. "I like that about you. You do what's needed, and you consider unlikely sources and tools—yes, I thought you'd see this was all necessary and make your peace with it. That's how it worked when you were Moranna's spy. I made sure we fed you what would make Moranna dance and when you realised, practically, that you wouldn't survive much longer, you chose Asgarnia."

Suddenly Ilme was thinking back to that conversation in the forest, to the knowing looks Valzin gave her before that in Falador while she scribed for Master Endel. The ones Ilme had been so sure were her own fears playing tricks on her mind. "You... you knew that too. All along?"

"Of course I did," Valzin said. "Though I will give Azris her due, she did try to blackmail you all on her own. Made my job much easier—I had a plan that was going to take months! And look how well it all worked out! You and she are friends, Asgarnia reaps the benefits of your skills, and you've been very helpful to me specifically—your reports of the death of Zorya, the attack on Ardougne, the death of Gunnar. You're very good at detail and plucking people's heartstrings!

"Anyway, try and make your peace with this too," she added, still so calm, so matter of fact. "I think you are well aware that I will crush you like a bug if you decide to be a problem." She patted Ilme's shoulder. "It's nice to see you in person again. Do let me know if you want that game of king's table. I'll go easy on you."

TWENTY-FIVE

The whole of the Wizards' Tower assembled in the great hall for a feast to celebrate the arrival of High Marshal Valzin, who accepted the accolades and ceremony with a gracious smile and the same imperturbability she'd always exuded.

To her right, Azris sipped her wine and kept her mouth shut. It would be a lie to say she didn't admire High Marshal Valzin. But it would an equal lie to say she liked her. Even when she'd been young and convinced of her own cleverness, Azris had given Sanafin Valzin the widest possible berth—a hawk didn't test an eagle's talons.

"What are you working on these days, Master Unaia?" Valzin drawled as she pushed away her empty plate. "Master Zanmaron mentioned some of the orders were working on new weaponry?"

"Yes," Unaia said primly. She sat on Azris's other side, and being trapped between the two of them after the day she'd had was the very limit. "We have several Blue Order wizards enhancing the elemental staves to make them more... combat appropriate. Should such a need arise."

Azris rolled her eyes at Unaia's deliberate omission of Ilme's work. A peacock, that was Unaia. Sharp beak, all show.

But Valzin, sharper still, smiled past Azris at Unaia. "How wonderful to hear the Blue Order is collaborating with the Green. Wizard Ilme is a *treasure*, don't you agree, Azris?"

"Extraordinary," Azris agreed. Reflexively, she found Ilme, sitting at one of the tables near the wall, lost in thought and very clearly sneaking bits of ham to Rue under the table. Azris sipped her wine—she didn't look upset. Pensive, but not upset.

Probably puzzling out something interesting with rune altars, she thought a little sulkily. Ilme didn't have to worry about disbursements or planning banquets or dodging a metaphorical peacock's sharp beak.

"My apprentice, Perien, is working on some enchanted blades," Unaia was saying. "All new theorems. He's quite a remarkable young man."

Azris hid another roll of her eyes in a swig of wine. Perien was a fine enough apprentice, but he had the dullest ideas and he was an abominable suck-up to boot.

"I'll have to see them," Valzin said, sounding fascinated. "Perhaps I'll come by tomorrow."

Unaia hesitated, visibly wrestling between the honour of the High Marshal taking an interest in her apprentice and the highest-ranking Zamorakian doing the same. How could she imply the Blue Order stood above the Red, and still covet Valzin's attention? "I... Yes, High Marshal. I'll be sure he's ready."

Valzin gave her a sharp little smile, then turned her bright gaze to Azris. "You're very quiet, Master Azris. Where's Master Zanmaron?"

The question of the hour, Azris thought. "I assume he's caught up in some project or other. He'll have to explain what he's working on to you." *Since he won't tell me.*

"Always dawdling over his equations," Unaia said under her breath.

Azris shot Unaia a look full of venom. She might not be *wrong* exactly—if the Red Order had a weakness, it was Zanmaron's tendency to forget he was the master of the order, not an independent wizard anymore—but saying so, especially in front of the High Marshal, was beyond the Edicts. At least the High Marshal wouldn't take Unaia's side—

But then, Valzin said, "Isn't that the truth? I worry about him. About the whole order really. I just don't know if this is where wizards dedicated to Zamorak... belong." She smiled at Azris, and Azris felt blood rise into her cheeks. "Unaia tells me you're still... involved? How did you put it?" she asked Unaia.

Unaia seized her own wine glass. "Oh, I think involved is all I said."

"I wonder why in the world that came up," Azris said, still glaring daggers at Unaia. Really, was there nothing better to gossip about?

No, a vicious little voice in her whispered. *There isn't.*

"Truly, an astonishing achievement," Valzin said. "Felicitations. Do you find it difficult to navigate? What with your orders being so different?"

Azris ground her teeth so hard her molars pulsed. "The search for knowledge is a joint effort," she said. "The Green Order—"

"Those are Master Endel's words, no?" Valzin sipped from her wine goblet. "An order's got to have an ethos, or it's not much of an order."

"Our ethos is knowledge in balance."

"Spoken like a Guthixian," Valzin chuckled. "All hope for greater ideas, no practical solutions." Behind Azris, Unaia snickered.

Azris bristled. "Spoken like a Zamorakian in peacetime," she retorted. "No outlet for your chaos but stirring up gossip?"

Valzin's blue eyes had taken on a feral kind of look, as if Azris were doing exactly what she'd wanted, as if she were clutched in the eagle's talons tight. Her gaze flicked up. "Oh, Master Zanmaron. We were just talking about you."

A hand fell on her shoulder. "My apologies," Zanmaron said, from behind her. "We had… We were caught up. Master Azris could I talk to you for a moment? Excuse us, High Marshal."

Valzin gave her the most obnoxiously knowing look as Azris stood, scraping her chair against the stone floor. Azris scowled at Zanmaron's red-robed back as she followed him from the hall, ignoring the many eyes that seemed to be on her. He stopped beneath a tapestry of Guthix bestowing rune magic and raked a hand through his hair.

"Where have you been?" Azris whispered before he could speak. "I got stuck between the High Marshal and Unaia—"

"Forget Unaia," he hissed. "Stop antagonising the High Marshal!"

"What happened to 'Azris, you're so stubborn why would I ever tell you what to do'?" she demanded. "She's antagonising *me* and it's not like anyone else was going to defend me!"

"Are you drunk?"

"You should *wish* I were drunk! I would be a lot less angry," Azris retorted. "While you were fussing in your workshop about rune altars and bookbindings—or whatever was so important—I had to be the one between the two of them. *After* I spent a solid two hours telling Unaia she can't usurp workrooms from the Red Order—which is *not* my job! Start taking care of your own order!"

He raked his hand through his hair again. "I never asked you to do that!"

"What do you expect me to do? *You're* not dealing with it!"

"And you're not leading the Red Order!"

"Neither are you!"

She and Zanmaron had fought so many times through the years, and she never knew exactly when it started, what set them off away from camaraderie and kindness and into conflict. But she knew when it got away from her, when the anger built so high she couldn't stand on it, when he only pushed away, only told her she wasn't enough—there was always a moment where she felt the slip of something, like a cliffside shearing away, and she didn't know how to turn back.

"Azris? Are you out here?" Ilme called. She came through the door to the hall, Rue looping in the air behind her. "Good. I need to talk to you. It's urgent."

"We're busy!" Zanmaron said.

"No!" Azris snapped at him. "*This* is my job." She spun around to face Ilme. "*What?*"

Ilme stopped, as if the force of Azris's anger had frozen her. "I need to go to Falador."

"Why?" Azris demanded, at the same time Zanmaron said, "No!"

Ilme gave Zanmaron a dark look. "I need to talk to the king. Maybe Grand Master Perior."

"No, you *don't*," Zanmaron said. "That's a very bad idea."

"What is?" Azris said, looking back at him. But Zanmaron set his mouth in that stubborn way, and when she turned back, Ilme had gone stone-faced again. "You have to tell me why you're going to Falador, or I don't give permission."

"Bad friend," Rue said.

"Shut up!" Azris snapped. "Tell me why you want to go."

"I told you," Ilme said. "I have to talk to King Raddallin. About… intelligence matters."

"Intelligence matters?" It was all Azris could do to keep her temper leashed—such a lie, such a blatant lie. A lie she couldn't cut down, and Ilme knew it—what she did for the king was outside the order's purview.

"Ilme, don't be stupid," Zanmaron said. "You can't go."

And for all Azris wanted to pin Ilme down, to make her tell Azris what was going on, suddenly she was a thousand times angrier at Zanmaron. "Well, too bad you're not her order's master." To Ilme she said, "Did you choose an apprentice?"

"I narrowed it down?" Ilme offered. "Lumbridge, that Cordelia girl and the Kharidian boy—Faryd, I think."

"Wonderful," Azris said, dizzy with wine and fury. "Congratulations, you now have three apprentices. Find them tasks or else bundle them to Falador and start their lessons on the road."

Ilme blinked. "I don't think that's a good idea."

"It's *not*," Zanmaron interjected.

"I don't think I asked what your opinions were," Azris said. "Either of you. If you're not going to tell me what secrets you're keeping, then you can deal with the consequences. Those three had better have tasks the next time I see them, or I'm cutting your disbursements." She whipped back to Zanmaron. "Give my regards to the High Marshal, for whatever they're worth. Since you're the only one of us doing anything *interesting*."

Azris stormed off and neither of them chased her—which she had the presence of mind enough to appreciate, even if some part of her wanted them to try, wanted to lash out again. She climbed the stairs up and up to her own workrooms near the top of the tower, went in, and locked the door behind her.

For a moment, she imagined Unaia looking over the room, imagined her little digs about how obviously Azris didn't need this space. *How dusty everything is! What do you need that worktable for, arranging your schedule? Couldn't your apprentice handle your correspondence from your study?*

Azris's remaining apprentice never came up here. Sland been one of Master Endel's last apprentices, and she'd taken him on after he'd died. He was polite and good at keeping her calendar straight, solid in his equations. He did not ask for more. He didn't want more.

Azris let out a sigh that took most of her anger with it. She crossed to the shelf over her large slate worktable and pulled down the four books that were her life's work. Four treatises on teleportation—four different and detailed arguments that amounted to what wouldn't work. She laid them side by side on the dusty table.

The first time, she'd been crushed when the equations wouldn't line up, the rune energies wouldn't stabilise. Everything had made sense—in theory. Enough magic and you could move anything— just make yourself the 'anything' and anchor the magic first. But no.

This is part of the process of discovery, Master Endel had told her, as she scowled at her work so hard she could have cried. *You find what* doesn't *work this time, and it tells you where to look for what* will *work. Write it up. If you don't keep at it, someone else will need the notes.*

She'd done as he'd said—and done it again, when it hadn't been a matter of pulling the place to you, or reversing a summoning, or the complex interactions of opposing runes. The problem started feeling more like a beast she was tracking, the path narrowing. She was close.

And then, Master Endel had died. And then, Azris became the Master of the Green Order.

Azris scrubbed her hands over her face, swallowing the lump in her throat—she missed the old man, sudden and sharp as a knife in her chest. She wasn't drunk, but the wine was making her head ache or maybe it was just the dust.

She ran a hand over the row of covers, thinking of what Ilme had said. If the staves pulled rune magic directly from the nexuses of the altars, could they use the raw energy of the altars to pull people through that same connection?

Tomorrow, she would have to give the High Marshal a tour of all the Green wizards' workrooms. Tomorrow, she would have to write letters to secure the coin for the caravan into the Wilderness to rebuild the chaos altar. Tomorrow, she would have to apologise to Zanmaron or make him apologise to her—or maybe both.

But that night, instead, Azris picked up a piece of chalk, brushed the dust from her worktable, and began to describe the world in rune equations.

TWENTY-SIX

◀◆▶

Snow fell, light and flurrying as Ilme rode for Falador, her purpose hanging heavy in her mind. This was the right course—the only course—even if Zanmaron insisted she was only courting trouble.

She'd managed to find tasks in the Tower for her sudden new apprentices: Faryd she set to calculating the angles necessary for the staves to interact with the rune altars at a distance. Cordelia she set to work reading through the ancient texts Master Endel had collected in life, searching for any reference to Zanmaron's theorised plane. The duke's son, Teodnor, copying Zanmaron's proof—which he took to as if she'd told him to find the honey-cake hidden in the library.

"This is a mess!" he said gleefully when she showed him the worktable covered in chalk. "Don't worry, I'll get *all* of it." He set to work writing out the calculations in a neat, narrow hand, under Rue's curious supervision. Zanmaron shot her a look over the boy's head.

"Don't erase anything until Master Zanmaron or I have checked it," Ilme said. "I'll be back in just a few days."

Zanmaron had stopped her in the doorway. "What am I supposed to say if Valzin asks where you are?"

"Honestly?" Ilme said, her stomach knotting. "There's an excellent chance she'll come after me, so it won't be your problem. Which is why I am glad you're keeping an eye on my apprentices, and Rue. I have to go."

"I'm not feeding your dragon!" he'd called after her. "And this is still the worst idea you've ever had!"

Ilme pulled her cloak closer. The king and Valzin had reconciled and what was she going to do but out the High Marshal as a monster? She pulled her cloak closer around her as the wind picked up. She knew what she was about to deliver Raddallin. Like reading Gunnar's letter. Like seeing Gunnar's army descend on Ardougne out of the night. Like Gunnar refusing to believe her that someone else had killed Zorya. Over and over, the complete destruction of a friendship she'd thought unassailable.

No—worse. She and Gunnar had been friends, but Valzin was not merely Raddallin's friend. She was his advisor, his second in so many things. She had built Asgarnia as much as he had. Ilme would need to be careful how she broke the news.

Ilme arrived very late, requested a private audience with King Raddallin as soon as possible, and spent a restless night in guest quarters, before being summoned shortly after dawn to meet the king. She met him over breakfast, in a small private room, not the great audience chamber. He waved the Black and White Knights standing guard over him to leave.

"Tell me," he said gravely, "you've found a way to reach the essence mines safely."

King Raddallin's chestnut hair had faded into grey, his beard more silver than brown. He still had his height and his strength, but there was no denying that the dwindling supply of runes was taking its toll. Gone was the immortal warrior-king, the hero of the Donblas—Raddallin was undeniably only a man.

"I'm afraid not, sire," Ilme said. "Rather, I've discovered something you should know about the High Marshal."

She told him about Thyra's confusion, about confronting Gunnar in his last moments, about Rue's revelation. About Valzin's dancing hypotheticals—her almost-admission.

"Valzin started the war," Ilme said. "She told the Moon Clan about Master Endel's deception. She killed the guardian. She wanted to flush out rivals and betrayers, and she didn't care who got hurt."

Raddallin sat silent for so long a moment, that fear worked its way up Ilme's spine. "Do you have proof of this?" he asked finally.

"She confessed it," Ilme said. "More or less."

Raddallin glanced at the door. "I told you once if you were going to tell me not to trust Sanafin that you had best bring me extraordinary proof."

"Rue saw her," Ilme began.

"You want me to take the word of your pet?"

"Valzin all but admitted…" But she let the words fall away, studying his stern expression. He didn't believe her. It would cost too much to believe her.

"Regardless," he said slowly, carefully, "if what you say is true… then I don't see how it changes matters. You say she started the war—that denies much of our northern neighbours' agency in the matter. No one forced Gunnar Viljarsson to attack the rune altars, no one forced the Fremennik to join them. Even if Sana did what you're saying, I would say history will judge it the wise choice."

"What?" Ilme burst out.

"We are a nation of contradictions after all," he went on, as if she hadn't protested. As if he were convincing himself. "And we are stronger now for having united against that threat. Misthalin has certainly fallen in line."

"She killed a Guardian of Guthix!" Ilme began. But at the same time, she remembered Valzin saying, *The things I have done for you.*

Was Ilme telling him anything he didn't know already? Were there worse things he was afraid of coming out?

"What I recall from your reports," Raddallin said, "was that Gunnar struck the final blow. He remains the killer of the guardian. And I think we should leave that where it is."

"Gunnar is *dead*—"

"All the more reason," he said firmly, folding his hands. "You know—everyone knows—that mistakes were made after the war ended. We nearly lost the Kinshra—and that *cannot* happen. Sanafin has forgiven us for that misstep, and Asgarnia rejoices to have its favoured daughter home."

"Your 'favoured daughter' nearly broke the *world!* If she does it again—"

"Enough," Raddallin shouted. Ilme took a step back. "I cannot *lose* her now—I know better than anyone that what I am, she made me. I would be a warlord in the mud, if not for Sanafin Valzin. Do you understand that?"

Ilme shook her head. "You underestimate yourself, Your Majesty."

He only shook his head. "My dear friend is by my side again, my best advisor is speaking to me," he said. "I will not risk losing her." He cleared his throat. "It won't be announced until later this month, but I intend to adopt Sana and name her my heir."

Ilme stared at him in disbelief. "Does she know?" Valzin had brushed the suggestion off before, insisted it wasn't practical. "Does the council know? They won't like it."

"The council may not appreciate everything she does, and I will admit, I didn't either. But her absence has made very clear that an Asgarnia without Sanafin Valzin is not one that will long survive. I trust her."

Why would Sanafin Valzin, the second-most powerful person in Asgarnia, start a war? Ilme thought. What if she were the most powerful person in Asgarnia? "What if I'm right, Your Majesty?" she said. "What if she does it again?"

"It's not your concern," he turned back to his correspondence. "The rune essence mine and altars are." He waved a hand, dismissing her. "If you leave soon, you should be back at the Wizards' Tower before nightfall."

Ilme left, forgetting to even bow. She felt as if she'd suddenly arrived in a strange world whose edges and truths she couldn't know, whose currents and tides were dangerous and unpredictable. King Raddallin did not care that Valzin had intentionally started the war. Valzin didn't care she had murdered Zorya. Ilme was alone, adrift, and she did not know where she was sailing, except that Sanafin Valzin would now have her eye fixed firmly on Ilme.

TWENTY-SEVEN

Azris's fifth attempt to solve the teleportation problem fizzled out before she got through the second proof. No combination of runes she could hypothesise would create enough energy. No angle would get around the limitations of spell reach. She had been up most of the night and to what end? She threw her chalk across the room and scrubbed her hands over her face.

Take a break, she told herself. *Get some breakfast. Come back later with fresh eyes.* But when would later be when she had a thousand tasks, a thousand more interruptions?

"Master Azris?"

In the door, Zanmaron's wide-eyed apprentice, Kelavan stood, half in, half out, and eyeing her as if she might explode. Azris narrowed her eyes, "If Zanmaron sent you to collect me," she began.

Kelavan held up a hand in a gesture of calm. "No. No, no. He... he doesn't know I'm here. I had a question for you. Mei suggested I should show you something. If that's all right."

Mollified, Azris considered him. Kelavan, she thought privately, was wasted on Zanmaron. The boy was studious, clever even—but he was terrified of making a mistake and Zanmaron's temper made that all the worse.

He probably wouldn't be better with you, Azris admitted to herself. Also, Zanmaron would never forgive her if she poached his apprentice. She gestured at Kelavan to come in. "What do you need?"

He crossed the room and held out a stack of papers. "He gave me a proof that I shouldn't be able to solve. A refutation of Ozzikan's theoretical maximums and directional requirements."

"'You can't hit what you can't see'," Azris paraphrased. She took the offered pages and scanned the proof. "Does it not make sense?"

"Yes and no?" he said, still nervous. "He's… He and Wizard Ilme have been working out a proof involving the elemental staves and the rune altar worlds. He's positing there's a plane connecting this one and the rune altar worlds—a sort of 'glue-plane' holding things together." He hesitated. "I don't know if he's ready to talk about it."

Azris looked up at the boy, frowning. "A 'glue-plane'? That's what they're doing?" Why hadn't he just told her that?

"Yes, I've only been involved in checking his equations over and copying the notes but…" He nodded at the papers she held. "I wondered if you routed a spell through that secondary plane with law runes if you could bypass a barrier. And… my calculations work."

Azris stopped, the meaning of his words filling her like ice cold water.

A spell itself couldn't cross a barrier. A spell aimed at this 'glue-plane' with law runes to reinforce the intention of it could. A spell could then be sent somewhere you couldn't see.

"You think you solved the teleportation problem," she said slowly.

"No," he said in a rush. "No, no. I'm just an apprentice. I think… I think I've made a mistake. And it's not Master Zanmaron's specialty and if I want to improve I should seek out the best sources—and, well, everyone knows you're the expert on the teleportation problem."

The problem, Azris thought, her eyes refusing to take in any more of the proof. *Not the solution.* Suddenly she was so aware of her scrawling, fumbling attempts on the table behind her.

"Master Azris?" Kelavan asked. "Do… Do you see the error?"

"It's very neatly done," she said, keeping a tight control of her voice. "Let me look at it in more detail. I can think of three mistakes you might have made that most people don't notice, but it will involve some… time with the proof. You can leave it with me."

A relieved smile spread over Kelavan's face. "Thank you. I really appreciate your feedback, Master Azris."

She made herself match his smile. There would be errors. It wasn't a simple problem. An apprentice picking it up for the first time couldn't solve it. "Of course," she said. "Leave it with me."

He left, and she tore into the proof. The first page was simply a repeat of Ozzikan's ancient theories, a practice most apprentices had done and she herself had repeated a dozen times. It was one of the primary complications of the teleportation problem, though not as impenetrable as it presented itself. Kelavan's neat script laid out the specifics clearly. The second page, though, added the variable of the 'glue-plane,' effectively bending the energy of the spell. Azris pored over this bit by bit, making notes as she went—she'd tried bending spells before, but only through known planes. Separated spaces. Not this.

It was perfect. Elegant. The addition of the interstitial plane absorbed all the extra power, bent all the angles into true. You would need a ritual akin to the rune altar construction to make anchors that directed the power... but you would have teleportation. You could go anywhere.

Kelavan had done what she'd been incapable of doing.

Azris stood up too fast, suddenly unable to look at the proof, unable to face it. She paced the room, her arms wrapped around herself.

She was a *terrible* wizard—an apprentice had shown her up. A terrible order leader—why had she not spotted Kelavan and claimed him when she could? A terrible partner—Zanmaron hadn't told her any of this, and she had to face the possibility he'd *known* it would be the piece she'd been missing for all of these years.

But... he didn't know Kelavan had found it.

She stopped her pacing, the fallen chalk before her feet in two broken pieces. Nobody knew. Kelavan hadn't shared what he'd found, except with his Grey apprentice friend, who'd said he should show Azris. And Mei certainly didn't *know* that the spell was correct—she'd told Kelavan to have Azris look it over. Only Azris knew what he'd done.

Azris picked up her thrown chalk and went back to the worktable, to the pages scattered over her chalked failure. If she said it was hers...

No. But it still needed a ritual built off of it. She could just... sketch that out. That was the important, practical part anyway. She could just see if that would work—maybe it wouldn't. Maybe none of this would matter.

TWENTY-EIGHT

◆▸

Valzin met Ilme riding when she returned to the Wizards' Tower. "What?" she called merrily, as she reined her horse up close to Ilme's grey gelding. "No White Knights to haul me off to answer for my crimes?" When Ilme didn't answer, she went on, "Did he brush you off?"

"He said if I was going to tell him to not trust you, I would need extraordinary evidence," Ilme told her. "That doesn't sound like he doesn't believe me."

"It sounds like he doesn't *want* to believe you," Valzin pointed out. "Which is functionally the same thing."

"He also told me you convinced him to adopt you. To name you his heir."

"I love how you think that was me. I've been putting him off for years." She flashed a bright grin. "A real pity none of the other options worked out."

Ilme clenched her teeth. "What are you going to do now?"

"Oh, Ilme," Valzin said. "Just because this one thing didn't work out in your favour, doesn't mean everyone's against you. I am sorry you didn't get what you were hoping for. Maybe he'll make it up to you with a sword."

They came the gatehouse and as they waited for the guards to pull the heavy doors open, Ilme considered Valzin, considered the thread of venom in her last words, seeped out as if it couldn't be contained. "You're still angry at him," she said. "I mean why wouldn't you be, I suppose? He didn't understand where he went wrong did he? Giving the council all that power and seating all those Saradominists."

Valzin chuckled as if she'd told a joke. "Where do you get these ideas?"

"You tell me."

"No, those are the sort of chats good friends have. And as your little dragon says, I'm your 'bad friend' now. I think I'll ride on a bit more," she said to the guards as they waved the two women in. She smiled at Ilme. "Let you get settled. Tell me if you want that game of king's table."

Ilme handed her horse off to the stablehands and climbed the winding stairs up to her rooms, tired to the bone, but still worrying at the revelations of the last two days. It would be sensible, a part of her knew, to accept that nothing would bring Zorya back, that Raddallin and Valzin had already set a course for Asgarnia, that the balance would be best kept by not stirring things up.

It would be sensible, she admitted, but it would also risk the same things happening over again. It would mean accepting Zorya's death as necessary. It would mean, in essence, continuing as Valzin's tool.

I will crush you like a bug if you decide to be a problem, Valzin had said.

Once, Valzin had told her she would always be someone else's tool, someone else's weapon, until she had the power to challenge those who would use her, to claim herself for herself. She knew better than to assume Valzin wasn't planning something—what did she do when things grew to settled but sow chaos that forced everyone into action? And so Ilme needed to find out what she was doing and put a stop to it.

You're observant, Moranna of the Narvra had said of Ilme, so long ago. *I can use that.*

I *can use that,* Ilme told herself. She was still observant, still a keen reader of people and now she was much older, much wiser, and she had many more allies.

Let's play, Ilme thought grimly.

✦ ✦ ✦

She went first to Zanmaron's workroom, finding him alone and sitting with multiple open books. She shut the door behind her before saying, "I'm sorry you're in this already, but Raddallin's going to make Valzin his heir and I need your help to figure out why."

Zanmaron scowled up at her from his worktable. "Kelavan and some fraction of your apprentices will be back here any moment—"

"Then I'll talk fast. Did she leave while I was gone?"

"No, she's been annoyingly underfoot," he said. "I assume the White Knights aren't coming to arrest her."

"The king doesn't believe me," Ilme said. "Or maybe he's afraid to move against her."

"Or maybe he doesn't care."

"Did she talk to you? Did she bring up Zorya?"

"Oh, I spent all of our time together convincing her that I have no idea what you're talking about and have never known at any point in our friendship. Mostly she wanted to talk about what a disaster the Blue Order is. Which, all things considered, is a little rich given the state of the Green."

Ilme frowned. "What does that mean?" The door behind her opened, and Kelavan came in with armful of books, trailed by Cordelia and Faryd carrying their own smaller armfuls, and Rue, trying to pounce on the overlong hem of Faryd's green robes.

"It means," he said irritably, "that Azris is locked in her workroom since the banquet, and won't open the door. I went up there to see if she was all right after our fight. It *didn't* go well. She's furious."

Behind Ilme she heard Kelavan suck in a breath. Both wizards turned to look at the apprentice. Kelavan flushed. "I... I might have... I went to talk to her the night of the banquet about..." Here he looked guiltily at Ilme. "I had a problem with one of my proofs and I thought she could fix it."

Zanmaron stood. "What did you *do*?" he demanded.

"It looked... Mei thought it looked like I'd found a way around Ozzikan. That it might have been the answer to the teleportation problem. It wasn't. It couldn't have been. But I figured Master Azris... I wasn't trying to upset her."

"Oh, Kelavan," Ilme sighed. She turned to Zanmaron. "If she was already upset about your fight, thinking about the teleportation problem has probably sunk her even deeper."

Zanmaron cursed. "I don't suppose *you* can talk to her."

"I think you know the answer to that." Valzin was up to something, she was certain of it, and if she succeeded, well, her friends' squabbling, the orders' petty drama wouldn't matter at all. "You have to talk to her. Bring a bottle of wine. Or a pie."

Zanmaron whirled on Kelavan. "The next time you have a question, remember who your master is and *don't*—"

"Leave him alone," Ilme said. "What's done is done. Deal with Azris. And *don't* offer to check her equations." Ilme scooped Rue off the floor. "Stay with Master Zanmaron, will you?" she said to Faryd and Cordelia. "I'll be back as soon as I can."

Rue crawled up over her shoulder, trying to tuck his bearded chin against her neck as she walked. Ilme peeled him off and held him in front of her, where she could see his face. He opened one amber eye to regard her. "Did you bring spiders?" he asked.

"You have spiders here."

"Falador spiders," he said in a pouty voice.

"No," she said. "You'll have to come yourself next time."

"Too cold."

"Did you keep an eye on my bad friend?" Ilme asked.

"Yes," Rue said, trying to tuck his head under her arm.

"Answer some questions and you can nap," she said, pulling him away and laying him over one shoulder. "What did you see?"

"She bothered your small ones. About what they're doing," Rue said. "About the spells. About do they like you. About who are their parents. The Valzin is a master to the Teondor."

"A master?" Ilme asked. "What do you mean?"

"He is from Lumbridge where the duke owns him."

"His father."

"Yes that. And that father has a father. And that father had a father and that is Valzin's father. It was confusing. But she asked if he would like to be a master greater than his father-master some day, and she made him nervous and confused too."

They were related—which made sense. In another time, Valzin could have been the Duchess of Varrock and Misthalanian noble families intermarried as much as anywhere. And Teodnor might become Duke of Lumbridge someday. Perhaps it wasn't so strange to ask about that either.

"She talked to the Mei," Rue said. "And the prig."

"What?"

"The blue prig. That's what your grumpy friend called him."

Ilme racked her thoughts. "Oh. You mean Unaia's apprentice?" What was his name? "Perlen?"

"Maybe." Rue yawned, showing needle teeth. "Can I nap in the vault?"

"They don't like that. You track dust everywhere. Did she talk to anyone else? Did you see?"

"Everybody," Rue said. "The Temrin. The Azris. The Eritona. The Unaia. Can I nap in your rune pouch?"

"You don't fit." Ilme paused, considering.

Of all the names Rue had listed, one stood out as the strangest. Of course, Valzin would speak to the masters of the orders, and she would speak to the Red Order with special attention, given their shared faith. She would also speak with wizards she knew from the early days—Ilme, Eritona.

Ilme could not guess why she would seek out Perien of the Blue, Unaia's favourite apprentice.

She was close to Unaia's workroom. On a pedestal in a niche nearby sat a statue of a coiled snake, another ancient guardian. Ilme tucked Rue into the serpent's bronze coils and gave him an air rune to hug under his chin. "Don't lose that," she told Rue.

"Mine," he hummed, rubbing his jaw against the runestone as Ilme went to find Perien.

✦ ✦ ✦

In Unaia's workroom, she found Perien in conference with one of Azris's apprentices, a heavyset man named Sland. Perien was a sallow-faced young man, lanky and dark-haired, with a perpetually pinched expression. They were standing over a set of weapons: a sword, a spear, and a dagger, in silvery and gleaming blue metals.

"When they're finished," Perien was saying, a little smug, "they're meant to go to Grand Master Perior. But Master Unaia is talking about making them a present to the king."

"How did you finally anchor the lightning spell?" Sland asked, leaning down to look along the length of the spear.

Perien huffed a sigh. "I've only managed on the dagger. It keeps discharging and—Oh! Wizard Ilme. Welcome. Master Unaia isn't here, she's visiting Master Temrin. Or did you come to see…" He trailed off gesturing at the weapons.

"Thank you," she said. "I was actually hoping to talk to you, Perien."

Perien gave her an uncomfortable smile. "Ah, I… I've been asked to keep to my studies. You understand."

Those rumours of her stealing apprentices. "I'm sure Master Unaia would appreciate hearing you honoured my greater age and higher rank by granting me a little time to answer some questions."

Perien, caught between Unaia's clear orders and the edicts of Saradomin, seemed to do some silent calculations, before nodding respectfully to her. "Of course. I'm happy to assist. With questions."

In the hallway outside, where a tapestry depicting the Founding of Falador ran along the walls, Ilme said, "I heard the High Marshal was curious about your work."

He frowned. "Well, yes. I'm told they're very impressive. I didn't let her handle them of course. That would be risky and well… inappropriate."

"So, you showed them to her and she left?"

"Well, we spoke less about my work and more of philosophy. I'm told she enjoys 'verbal sparring' as it were. We debated the role of the king, I believe, what he owes his subjects and what they owe him. She had interesting things to say about ambition and improvement." He glanced past her as if making certain no one was listening to them. "Master Unaia wasn't terribly pleased. But I think she… well, understandably, she's wary of her apprentices consorting with Zamorakian principles."

"Because of Zanmaron." Ilme considered him. "Do you know why he left the Blue Order?"

"I assume," Perien said delicately, "that he was swayed by the temptations of Zamorak. Power and chaos and all that."

"That's not really what they believe."

Perien fidgeted with the cuffs of his robes. "That's what the High Marshal was saying as well. That change is the only true law of life, that trying to resist change brings unhappiness. It's very..." He bit his lip. "Well, really it makes no sense. It asks for destruction."

Ilme looked up at the tapestry around them, the mounted soldiers, the wizards turning runes into blasts of air and fire, the spirits summoned to their armies' sides. "Sometimes you have to destroy something to build a better version in its place," she murmured.

Perien winced. "Or we could improve what we have. Or accept we have what we need."

"'This is the wisdom of Saradomin'," Ilme finished, a little cheekily. "Thank you."

+ ✦ +

She went to find Eritona—if anyone in the Wizards' Tower had heard that changes were coming to Falador, it would be Eritona. Ilme found her sitting in a courtyard with Mei. Her dark braids were piled high on her head, the slightest crinkling of her dark skin at the corners of her eyes the only real sign she was ageing. She waved Ilme over.

"We were just talking about your new apprentices," Mei said.

"Three?" Eritona asked. "And then you run off to Falador?"

"I had a message for King Raddallin," Ilme said. "Can I ask you something? The High Marshal made quite the circuit while I was gone. What is she doing?"

Eritona glanced sidelong at Mei and seemed to decide the younger woman could be let in on this bit of gossip. "It was a little odd. She doesn't usually bother chatting with me beyond the basic pleasantries. Instead, we played king's table and discussed philosophy. It was pleasant," she added. "Although I didn't find out anything *very* interesting. The High Marshal's philosophies are pretty widely known."

Ilme frowned. "Did she talk about the duty of the king?"

Eritona nodded. "Yes—did she put that one to you too? That's interesting. It almost makes me think King Raddallin's chosen a successor, and if I had to guess, the High Marshal doesn't approve."

"She asked me something similar," Mei said. "But I didn't think it was that strange. Might she just be curious?"

Eritona shook her head. "It's the kind of thing I would do if I were trying to prepare an argument for some treaty, back in the day. You want to argue against something, you ask around—get people to make the argument for you. It feels like she's building an argument that the heir isn't appropriate. Whoever they are."

"What if she's arguing *for* the heir?" Ilme asked.

Eritona wrinkled her nose. "I suppose. But then I'd expect her to tell us what she thinks—put us in the right frame of mind. The king's going to want everyone to approve of the choice, not have everyone's minds full of doubts. But she's looking for doubts. She's looking for weak points."

"She was much more interested in what I thought than telling me what she thought," Mei said. "Not like when she wanted to debate the roles of the, um, minor gods as you put it. How Armadyl fits together with Zamorak. But I was warned she likes to talk about that."

"It is what makes Asgarnia great," Eritona said. "I also got to repeat my lessons for her, although admittedly, I'm not a very devout Guthixian. Who is though?"

That made Eritona, Mei, Perien, and perhaps Teodnor of Lumbridge, the targets of Valzin's questions about kingship—why? There would certainly be disagreement when Raddallin announced his decision. But Eritona was right—Valzin already knew all the arguments against herself. Why go fishing for other people's opinions?

+ ✦ +

Ilme sought out Unaia last, expecting to confirm the same conversation, but also worrying at a different puzzle. The Blue Order Master was with Master Temrin, playing a game of king's table in the latter's study.

"About the kingship?" Unaia sounded puzzled when Ilme asked her. "Not at all."

"We talked of my studies," Temrin chimed in. "The history of Gielinor I am writing? I've almost finished the section on the First Age? That's what I've decided we should call the era before the emergence of the faiths of gods other than Guthix and—"

"She admired Perien's work," Unaia interrupted. "And then... well, you can't stop her talking, can you? Zamorak this, Zamorak that. Fortunately, Perien is dedicated to the path of righteousness. And the most brilliant apprentice I've ever had. Such potential." She moved one of her attackers toward Temrin's wall. "He'll certainly go far."

Temrin peered at the board. "You used to say that about Zanmaron, didn't you?" He placed a defender, surrounding Unaia's piece on both sides. "Capture."

"Yes, well..." Unaia sniffed. "Zanmaron is evidence a lack of discipline can stymie even the greatest potential." She shifted another of the peg-like pieces, arranging a row against the castle wall.

Ilme frowned, a thought occurring to her. "Was Valzin the one who convinced Zanmaron to leave the Blue Order?"

"No." Unaia blinked at her. "I don't think. She *was* far too casual with you children—no sense of proper decorum. I can't imagine it *helped*." She picked up a piece, but as if she were unable to leave it alone, she added primly. "If anyone except Zanmaron ruined his prospects, it was Azris. He was perfectly content with my methods of teaching before he started fooling around with that girl. She makes him *wilful*. And now look at them."

"Heads of their orders?" Ilme asked dryly.

Unaia smirked. "Well. For now. Watch your king, Temrin," she warned.

"What is that supposed to mean?" Ilme asked, as Temrin repositioned his king out of danger.

"Perhaps nothing," Unaia said airily. "But… over dinner the High Marshal suggested dissolving the Red Order. She seems to wonder what the purpose is in organising wizards devoted to chaos."

"They're not devoted to chaos," Ilme started.

"Hmm, Zanmaron is very methodical?" Temrin added, puzzled, moving pieces over the board. "Very thorough in his studies?"

"Perhaps that means he ought to come back to the Blue Order," Unaia said. "But I suppose that's up to him."

Ilme left, more puzzled now. Valzin was most definitely working toward *something* but what involved Eritona, Mei, Perien and perhaps Teodnor? And what—if anything—did it have to do with Raddallin's decision to make her his heir?

TWENTY-NINE

THE SEVENTIETH YEAR OF THE REIGN OF KING RADDALLIN
OF ASGARNIA
THE FIFTH DAY OF BENNATH
THE WIZARDS' TOWER

As Ilme had predicted, Raddallin's announcement that Sanafin Valzin would be his heir was met with more than a little surprise and disdain. She was too old, they said. Nearly as old as the king. She had no heirs of her own—this was not the re-founding of a line that had faltered. She was a Zamorakian, which no speaker themselves would name a problem, but, well, it was an issue for *some* people.

Valzin for her part did not gloat, did not wave her good fortune about. She was poised and proper in a regal and ceremonial suit of armour, chased in gold and enamelled with the colours of the kingdom's orders—blue, green, grey, and a tasteful accent of Zamorakian red.

"She's plotting something," Ilme said to Zanmaron, when Valzin returned to the Wizards' Tower on her tour of the country. "I haven't figured out what yet."

"You've certainly been more interested in it than parsing the rune altar connection," Zanmaron said. "Or fixing Azris."

"Azris doesn't need fixing. She's just…" Ilme struggled for the best way to put it. "She's taking some time to work on her own projects."

"She always does this," Zanmaron went on, folding his arms. "Gets upset about something minor and blows it out of proportion. Absolutely refuses to be apologised to."

Ilme looked sideways at him. "*Did* you apologise? Or did you do the thing you always do and try to pretend it had blown over?"

He scowled at her. "It *should* have blown over. I was late for one banquet."

Azris had been avoiding them both, having food brought to her rooms, and delegating the work of running the order's daily business to Eritona or Sland. When Ilme had caught her pacing the halls one night, she'd looked a mess but refused to address it.

"What are your apprentices working on?" she had demanded.

"Settling in?" Ilme said. "Zanmaron's got them checking sums. Are you sleeping?"

Azris's temper had flared. "*You* were told to take those apprentices on, not give them to the Red Order to guide—he'll snatch them up too. Can you never just *listen*?" And she had stormed off again, refusing to answer Ilme's shouted questions of who she meant by saying 'too'.

Zanmaron huffed, scowling at the floor. "There's a rumour going around Unaia's looking to have Azris removed."

"It's not her business."

"When did that ever stop Unaia of the Blue?" he spat. "And if you ask me, it's gotten worse since the war ended and we didn't suddenly get the rune essence mine back." Then, "Azris sent a message around to the other masters. She has a presentation. Did she invite you?"

"No," Ilme said. "What's she presenting?"

"No idea," he said. "But if she's going to make us sit through another explanation of why teleportation doesn't work—"

"If she is, what are you going to do?"

He faltered. "I don't know," he admitted. "She... She's been frustrated with her lack of progress. All the mess of running an order." He paused. "And watching out for mine. She needs a new project. An apprentice she can actually work with."

Ilme's own apprentices were proving to be a complication. Each of them already excelled in areas of the work of a wizard: Teodnor was delighted by the process of collecting notes into an easily read resource. Cordelia was quick at hunting down specific references, and clever about including what Ilme might not have realised she needed. Faryd had a very sharp understanding of how spells functioned in physical space.

And Ilme was the wrong wizard for all of them.

Ilme was searching through correspondence for more clues of what Valzin was planning—nothing from Entrana, nothing from Ardougne, nothing from Varrock—when all three apprentices arranged themselves before her desk. "Wizard Ilme?" Cordelia said. "We have a problem."

"Master Zanmaron says we aren't to come back to his workrooms unless we intend to swear to the Red Order," Faryd announced.

"I *can't* become a Zamorakian," Teodnor said, twisting one cuff in his opposite fingers. "My grandmother would skin me *alive*."

Ilme sighed. "He's joking."

"Perhaps," Cordelia said. "But he did go on to say you are the one who took us on, not him. And if you tried to send us back, we were to tell you that since he's the only one working on your project, he doesn't have time to handle us."

"Oh," Ilme said, a little taken aback. "Well... You can..." She racked her brain—what was she working on before Valzin returned?

"It's obvious," Faryd said, "that you're working on a different problem. We want to help with that." He nodded at the correspondence. "What should we look for?"

For a moment, Ilme thought of Moranna—of how useful an innocent wandering around where they would cause no comment could be. Who could blame her if all of Asgarnia was at risk? Send Cordelia to the stables, have Teodnor write letters to his father, plant Faryd at Valzin's elbow with a wine pitcher—

"No," Ilme said, as much to herself as to them. "This isn't a matter for children."

"All of us are seventeen," Cordelia began.

Ilme wrinkled her nose. "Are you really?

"And we won't be forever," she went on.

"Ideally," Teodnor added.

"You have to prepare us," Cordelia went on. "That's... that's your duty. How are we supposed to become wizards of Asgarnia if all we do is wait for you to notice we're here?"

"If you're not going to teach us anything," Faryd said, "then why retain us at all?"

Because Azris forced my hand, Ilme thought, but she banished it—it was a selfish thought, an unkind thought. A true thought, she admitted, but not one she wanted to hold onto.

She thought of what Azris had said that morning she came to insist Ilme take an apprentice, that morning Ilme had gotten so gloomy about Gunnar and the war: *Would you give it up?* She wouldn't, and likely neither would any of them. She thought of Azris, bringing her the book of rune magic, bringing her in effect into the Green Order. She thought of Master Endel, his drive for knowledge, but in the end, his sacrifice to secure the future. A future she was now responsible for carrying forward. A future Valzin threatened—had always threatened.

"You're right," she said. "I've been… distracted. I have a problem where I think I know the outcome, but I don't know where to begin the proof, so to speak." She stood up. "Who wants to learn how to disassemble and rebuild an elemental staff of fire?"

She spent the afternoon showing them the ins and outs of the elemental staves that had been her own great contribution to wizardry, and she managed to put Valzin and the maddening puzzle of the royal adoption out of mind. Maybe she couldn't outflank Valzin. She couldn't change the past, maybe she was worrying about changing the wrong parts of the future.

When Cordelia managed to burn her eyebrow off, dislodging part of the imbued components, Ilme called a halt to the day. "Write up all your findings," she told them. "And at least three ideas for how the individual pieces might interact with Master Zanmaron's 'glue-plane'."

"Abyss," Cordelia said. "I found a reference that called it the Abyss."

"That *is* a better name." Ilme tidied up the workroom, checking the light through the windows. Azris's presentation was soon, down in the Chamber of Shrines. "I'm going to go look in on Master Azris," she said. "I'll be back shortly." She left them all three, bent over their notes and scrawling furiously. She smiled to herself. Perhaps apprentices weren't so bad.

On her way down to the shrine room, she crossed paths with Valzin coming up the stairs. Valzin had changed into a long tunic of deep-red cloth with a blue brocade overdress pinned at the shoulders over it. She wore an ornamental chestplate, a twin of Raddallin's, a simple tiara perched on her shining black hair, and a sword at her hip.

Overall, she had the look of a wolf pretending to be a sheepdog— something just shy of wrong—and Ilme tensed, prepared to do battle.

"Well met," Valzin said pleasantly. "How is the day treating you?"

"Your Highness," Ilme said, stepping to the side to let her pass.

Valzin moved with her, as if they were keeping the staircase clear by mutual decision. "Oh, don't call me that," she said. "Aren't we old friends? Of some sort anyway." Her blue gaze glittered with amusement. "Where are your little apprentices? Did you interrogate Teodnor about our conversation already?"

Ilme didn't answer. "Are you enjoying your tour of the country? You're back here so soon."

"How can I stay away?" Valzin said. "You all do create such fascinating things. I hear a rumour Azris has managed something very impressive. Perhaps my travels will get a lot simpler?"

"I can't say," Ilme told her. "If you'll excuse me—"

"Of course," Valzin said. "Just one question: what are you digging at?"

"Nothing," Ilme said. "I spent the afternoon showing my apprentices how to build a staff of fire."

Valzin clucked her tongue. "That's disappointing."

"You don't need to mock me," Ilme said. "We both know what you did. We both know I can't forgive it. We both know you have Raddallin's ear and his trust—you've won."

Valzin sighed. "Have I? To be honest, I worry I'm not cut out to hold a throne. It's terribly limiting when you get down to it. If you're going to do it—not cling by your fingernails while you pillage everything until they drag you off to the chopping block—if you're really going to rule a nation, then you have to focus on all sorts of things that don't really serve *you* directly." She smiled and gestured vaguely at Ilme. "Sort of like what's going with you here."

"What do you mean?"

"Well, from what I understand, you're working very hard on that rune altar research. You're running around trying to mend everyone's rifts. Soothe Azris, reassure Zanmaron, calm Unaia down—on and on. And meanwhile you're asking after me. What am I doing? What am I saying? Who am I saying it to?" She laughed. "And you're teaching these apprentices! You're very good at balancing all that mess. The dreaming god would be proud."

"I do what I need to," Ilme said. "This tower is only as strong as the support we give each other."

"Well, I hope *that's* not true," Valzin said. "You haven't really fixed all those rifts after all. His Majesty is arriving soon. Another over-fancy dinner. Tell Rue there will be ham." She stepped around Ilme and paused. "Oh, if His Majesty asks, do tell him we talked." And she continued up the stairs.

Ilme headed down to the council chambers, feeling unsettled, as if Valzin had let her think she was ahead, but was really circling her, like a wolf waiting for its prey to tire out.

Valzin, questioning people in the Wizards' Tower as if she planned to argue against the heir Raddallin chose. Valzin, claiming she was a poor choice for a queen-to-be. Valzin, teasing her, wanting to know what she thought she'd figured out.

Ilme stopped in the hallway outside the council chambers, where apprentices sat on padded benches waiting for their masters within. She marked Perien, Mei, and Sland among them.

Valzin preparing to argue against the heir, who was herself, who she knew no one would countenance. Ilme frowned, a theory coming together.

She sat down next to Perien, who startled at her appearance. "Wizard Ilme," he said, by way of greeting. "Can I help you?"

"Has the High Marshal engaged you in more philosophical discussion since she arrived?"

He pinked. "Well, she only just got here, but I did speak with her briefly and it did turn to the nature of human authority. But nothing untoward. I told her the wisdom of Saradomin," he insisted. "If Master Unaia asked you…"

Valzin knew she wouldn't be queen—not without a great uproar from the Saradominists. She had always known that, so she would be prepared for it. Perhaps even counted on it. Ilme wondered if she had toured Asgarnia not to gain the affection of its inhabitants, but specifically to make certain as many people as possible saw and disapproved of her as possible.

And if she proved an unsuitable heir, and she stepped aside, she would want to present another option. Someone that the Church of Saradomin would approve of… but someone she thought she could control.

What if all these discussions, all these questions, weren't preparations to argue against an heir, but questions meant to test the suitability of an heir? Did Eritona know her place in the scheme of Asgarnian power? Would Mei understand that she must focus on what Valzin pointed her at, and look away from what Valzin wished?

Would Perien, like his predecessor, be lured away from Saradomin once he was in power, a final blow against the church that had thwarted Valzin again and again?

The doors to the shrine room banged open, and Zanmaron stormed out, jaw clenched, eyes blazing. Azris charged out after him.

"Zanmaron, wait," she hissed. "Where are you going?"

He whipped around. "As I said, I'm going to discuss with *my* apprentice what we can add to your framework." He bit off each word. "Unless there's something you ought to tell me about *this*?" He shook a rolled-up parchment at her.

Azris stuck her chin out. "That I worked very, very hard to solve it. That a little acknowledgment might be due?" Her mouth quivered as if she were holding something back. "You can't even be proud of me for this, can you?"

Zanmaron stared at her, jaw pulsing, waiting for something. "You *know* why I left," he spat, turned on his heel and stormed off.

Azris turned to Ilme, flushed and furious. "What are *you* staring at?"

Ilme pulled her away from the apprentices, back into the shrine room. Four statues, idealised wizards of the order, stood in a circle around the room. To one side Master Temrin and Master Unaia were excitedly discussing Azris's spell framework.

Ilme heard the words 'teleportation anchor'.

"You *didn't*," Ilme said.

"Didn't what?" Azris said. But her cheeks were flushed and her eyes wouldn't settle. "I finally made a breakthrough."

"Kelavan told us he went to you with a proof. He solved it, didn't he?"

"No," Azris said. "Of course not. He… he got close. He made a few assumptions. And they… inspired me to build this framework."

"Then why is Zanmaron storming out of here like you spit in his eye?" Ilme thought of his final words. "Oh dreaming god. Unaia used to claim his work. Azris…"

Azris managed to turn even redder. "Look," she hissed, "I have worked on this my entire *life*. Kelavan didn't even know what he had—he was sure it was a mistake. It wasn't finished. It was generalised. I just… I made it functional." She glanced at Unaia and Temrin. "Kelavan is brilliant, all right? He'll do great things. Someday. We need this *now*. The Green Order needs this—*I* need this."

"By repeating all of Unaia's mistakes?" Ilme said. "No—not Unaia. You are being like the worst parts of Master Endel!"

"Brilliant and an excellent teacher?"

"Selfish and focused on the wrong things."

Azris drew back. "How dare you—"

"Tell me I'm wrong," Ilme said. "Endel was complicated—who isn't? He was brilliant, yes, a good teacher, true, and at the end, he did what saved everyone, but you and I know he did it so the ritual would anchor. He did *everything* to advance rune magic—including lie to the Fremennik. Those aren't the parts I'd like to remember, and those aren't the parts I want you to emulate!"

Azris looked away. She folded her arms. "You don't know what it's like," she whispered. "I've worked so hard, too hard to be nobody."

"You're not nobody," Ilme said fiercely. "You're the master of the Green Order. But I'm saying this to you as your friend: you're being horrible. And Kelavan would know *nothing* without what you've already done on the teleportation problem. But Azris, it is beyond the Edicts for you to think you can steal his work."

"It's not..." she started. But she couldn't seem to finish. "Why are you so sure *he* solved it? That I couldn't?"

"Because if you didn't have Kelavan's work in there," Ilme said gently, "then Zanmaron would have been elated, not cursing you." She shook her head. "Figure it out, Azris. Don't be this person."

Valzin's taunts echoed in Ilme's mind as she searched for Zanmaron. She went then to Zanmaron's rooms, his workroom, his private study, and found him there at last, berating Kelavan.

"They *took* your idea. They took it, because you handed it to them. This is why I tell you we no longer trust the other orders. Perhaps this Tower became great precisely because the four orders are in conflict with one another. We of all the orders should remember that."

A pause. "Do you believe that?" Kelavan asked.

"How can I not?" Zanmaron gritted out.

"What are you going to do?"

"What am I going to do about Azris taking your idea? Nothing," Zanmaron said. "I hope this teaches you a lesson you will remember for the rest of your career, spurring you on to greatness: no one will help you but yourself. Perhaps then Zamorak will make something of you." More parchment rustled. "I'm going to complete this. Your solution requires a second plane of existence for the travel to pass through, and it will be based on *my* research. If I can do that then the Red Wizards will take some credit for the ritual, even if, thanks to you, it is not the full credit we deserve."

"I'm sorry," Kelavan said.

"Go. Think about how you can redeem yourself in Zamorak's eyes. I need privacy."

Kelavan came out, shame-faced, and nearly walked into Ilme. "He..." he said, startled. "Master Zanmaron requests privacy."

"Master Zanmaron is being an ass," Ilme said.

"He's right though," Kelavan said. "I just... handed her my work without telling him what I'd found. He should have punished me as soon as he found out."

"No, it should have been fine," Ilme said. "And it *will* be fine—Azris knows she can't leave you out. You will get credit alongside her. She's... not acting her best self. Which can happen to any of us."

Kelavan nodded. "She did do a lot of the important preliminary work."

"Treatises and treatises worth."

He ducked his head. "Perhaps I should have focused more on studies that don't require sharing credit with other orders."

"Don't listen to Zanmaron," Ilme said. "What's he doing in there but collaborating further? We all work together."

Kelavan gave her a rueful smile. "But when does the Red Order get the credit? Master Zanmaron did great work in finding the secondary plane, but when people talk about his research, it's about how it's built from your work with the staves. Master Unaia talks over him and pretends he's not a master. Master Temrin doesn't listen to his suggestions about the altar rebuilding. Even High Marshal Valzin questions his authority. They erase him."

"Azris doesn't," Ilme said. "Which is why I really believe she's messed up, and she'll fix it." She sighed. "Don't take him too much to heart. Everyone thinks you are a very brilliant wizard and whatever gods are watching or dreaming of you, you'll go far. I'm sorry your master is also the most irritable man I've ever met."

Kelavan flushed. "I should go change before the dinner." He started down the hall, then turned back to her. "Thank you. For trying to help."

"Of course," Ilme said.

She blew out a breath and steeled herself before knocking on Zanmaron's study door. "I know you're in there," she called.

The door opened only wide enough for Zanmaron to stick his head out. "I'm not talking to you."

"Not even if I agree Azris messed up?"

"This is out beyond the Edicts—you know, I thought she and I had come to a better understanding but this… this is something else."

Ilme frowned. "Why? Weren't you just telling Kelavan that this is what comes of sharing work?"

"Eavesdropper."

"You're hurt. That's fair. Just… don't do anything rash."

"Why not?" he spat. "That's all we're known for. Or hasn't Unaia bent your ear lately?"

Ilme pursed her mouth, not wanting to ask what she needed to ask. "Has Valzin been talking to you?"

Zanmaron narrowed his eyes. "Why are you *obsessed* with her?"

"Let me in. You're making a mistake."

"No," Zanmaron said. "I'm working. I'm done sharing my knowledge with the Green Order—and tell Azris that's not all I'm through sharing. Her framework is missing details—I'm finishing it for her, and you can see it when I'm done. And then she will have no choice but to put the name of a Red Order wizard on her precious teleportation spell, and we can never speak to each other again."

With that, he slammed the door shut.

✦ ✦ ✦

Rue sat on Ilme's lap during the dinner to welcome King Raddallin, his little purple head peering over her plate. "They are noisy," he said, reaching for a piece of ham. "Most of them."

Azris's teleportation spell was the talk of the evening, everyone bubbling with excitement, trading notes on what the final spells might look like and toasting to the success of the ritual that would anchor teleportation magic. Even the White and Black Knights, who had accompanied the king, seemed easy and relaxed now that the promise of teleportation hung in the air. Raddallin gave a speech honouring their good work, everyone cheered and clapped, and the room was full of merriment.

All except for the sombre Red Order, who had separated themselves at the table along the opposite wall from where Ilme and Azris sat.

Azris kept several seats between herself and Ilme. People kept coming up to congratulate Azris, to talk with wild gesticulations. She would offer them a polite smile, a nod, and then glance over to the table of Red Order wizards, looking for Zanmaron, who had not come down to the dinner. He was still locked in his study, busy with his part of the spell.

Ilme broke off a piece of sour bread, chewed it thoughtfully. Zanmaron and Azris had been fighting and making up since they were nineteen—but this was different.

"You don't seem to be enjoying yourself."

Valzin stood behind Ilme's chair, goblet held loosely in one hand. She'd changed again, now wearing her Kinshra armour, as if she'd given up pretending to be a neutral party. Ilme glanced back at Raddallin, who was speaking with Unaia, trying to reassure her of something while she spoke faster and faster.

"Looks like your ascension isn't going very well," Ilme said.

"Not a bit," Valzin agreed, sipping her wine. "Did Raddallin talk to you?"

"No," Ilme said.

Valzin gave a little snort. "Well, credit where it's due, he trusts me more than I expected—maybe as much as people worry he does. This wine is delicious. Where's it from?"

Ilme seized her own goblet. "I know you're planning to step down. Replace yourself with an heir you've chosen. One you think you have a handle on."

"Oh good," Valzin said. "Then you won't be surprised when it happens. What's wrong with Azris?"

Ilme squeezed her hands into fists—she could never surprise Valzin, why did she bother trying? "She and Zanmaron are fighting—what's new?"

"That." Valzin gestured with her goblet at the subdued Azris. Unaia had left the king's side and gone to Azris instead, expounding at length about something that was making Azris look increasingly uncomfortable. "I have never in all her life seen that woman so quiet."

"It's a momentous occasion," Ilme said flatly.

Valzin chuckled. "You don't know the half of it."

Azris stood and excused herself, edging around the great hall. She paused as she passed the Red Order table, and for a moment, Ilme thought she was going to seek out Kelavan. But then she continued on out of the room.

Ilme stood, scooping Rue up under one arm, intending to follow. "Excuse me, I need—"

Valzin pushed her back down into her chair. "Wait. It's about to get good."

King Raddallin stood and the cacophony of the room ebbed away. He cleared his throat. "Once again, the hospitality of the Wizards' Tower is outmatched only by the ingeniousness of its members' advancements. One can sit here this evening and forget for a time the long dark nightmare that our kingdom had so long lain under. Now we will have even more reason to celebrate as you have resolved our lingering weakness with the forthcoming teleportation ritual. Our dwindling reserves of rune essence will be a thing of the past."

People cheered and raised goblets—except the sombre Red Order. Raddallin waved for quiet again and continued. "However, I have another, bittersweet reason to speak to you here. As you know, after many years and no surviving issue, I declared an heir to my throne—Sanafin Valzin, the High Marshal of Asgarnia." He gestured to Valzin, and a polite smattering of applause followed.

"I have in the time since heard a great many concerns about my choice," Raddallin went on. "I want to be clear: I agree with *none* of them. I chose High Marshal Valzin because of her dedication to this country, her support of this kingship, and her tireless work throughout the war with the Fremennik, which often went unsung. Yet having heard the concerns of the citizens, she and I together have made the decision that she will abdicate this role, and step down in favour of a different heir."

"Wait for it," Valzin murmured. Ilme searched the crowd for the likeliest candidates, for anyone looking nervous or excited—Perien, Mei, little Teodnor, Eritona, who else?

Everyone only looked puzzled.

"Knowing that the future ruler of Asgarnia must be as dedicated, as tireless, as humble and as forthright as Sanafin Valzin, I have decided to establish formal adoption of an existing ward." Raddallin turned and looked at Ilme, full of pride. "Ilme of the Green."

THIRTY

**THE SEVENTIETH YEAR OF THE REIGN OF KING RADDALLIN
OF ASGARNIA**

THE SEVENTH DAY OF THE MONTH OF BENNATH

THE WIZARDS' TOWER

Valzin's hand tightened on Ilme's shoulder.

"Just a friendly warning," she murmured, "if you say 'no' right now, you might well declare a civil war. Which is why I preferred doing it this way—though I was prepared for Rad to ignore me and tell in you in private, let you argue why you're wrong. So much tidier. I recommend standing up and bowing to His Majesty."

Ilme's thoughts raced—she couldn't blindly follow Valzin's orders, but every eye in the room was on her, every one of her colleagues looking as startled as she felt. She could trace the thoughts leaping through the crowd of them—*first he chooses Valzin, then he chooses some Green Order dilettante best known for having been a spy for the Narvra? And did he* say *Narvra? And then what?* Where would their thoughts lead them? There were too many people, too many paths to guess.

So Ilme stood. She bowed to Raddallin. He made a toast to his new heir that she hardly registered. She accepted the well wishes of her colleagues and demurred the requests for private conversations until later. She saw in their faces a hunger for explanation, an envy and a frustration that she longed to make sense of. A whole line of wizards trying to congratulate her—Temrin with stories of ancient queens, Unaia with praises for Saradomin, Eritona with a glass of wine she sorely needed.

She had to talk to Raddallin. She had to talk to Raddallin *right now.*

When she tried to excuse herself to approach him, however, Valzin pulled her aside, "Oh, walk with me first. You'll have plenty of time to talk to your dear lord father." She looped her arm through Ilme's and steered her through a door into one of the galleries that framed the great hall. Valzin shooed away the few wizards who tried to follow, and the Knights stationed at the door moved to block the path. "You *were* surprised. I thought you'd figured it out."

"Why would you suggest me?" Ilme demanded. "I have nothing to do with politics."

"Says the spy. Raddallin very much appreciates your keen political eye."

"I'm a wizard. Not a warlord."

"Do we need a warlord?" Valzin asked, all innocence. "You'll have me. And that's the key part—Raddallin's realised that, without me, he'd be nothing. So when I told him, you were actually perfect, that your ascension wouldn't set off any jealousy in other noble families, given you're… let's go with 'estranged' from yours, well, he was very grateful for the solution." She grinned. "I'm very convincing. Especially when he's panicking. Also I think he feels guilty about the guardian."

"Why me though?" Ilme said. "You're still stuck with me—what's your plan?"

"Simple: all recent events to the contrary, we've always worked well together," Valzin said. "As I told you before, you're practical.

I appreciate that—there's no need to *mould* you the way I might, for example, Perien of the Blue. Moreover, you have always been involved in politics, only in a much quieter sense than Eritona, so people remember you, but don't think of you as the one who stuck them with bad terms in the runecrafting treaties. You are of the Narvra, so anyone who harbours some notion of overthrowing Raddallin will prick up their ears, but you loathe what you come from, so you will never give them what they want.

"And if we do consider recent events, I suspect both of us would prefer the other were kept close enough to keep an eye on. For the good of Asgarnia. Plus, the gossip here and in Falador is that you've been very suspicious of me lately, so no one thinks *I* chose you—especially not the council. You're perfect."

Ilme could guess who had spurred that gossip. "I'll refuse."

"You can," Valzin allowed. "But like I said, you'll get a civil war out of it. How's that going to make Raddallin look? Two heirs in a row that don't work out? A Zamorakian and then a Guthixian— what *will* the Saradominists do? I'm afraid," she said, in a dramatic whisper, "they'll decide to take everything over. Neither of us wants that.

"And really," she went on, "that's your choice: you can do this, let the council vet you, become the queen, and consider my *suggestions* as they arise; or you can refuse, damage Raddallin's legitimacy further, and almost certainly lead this country into civil war."

There it was—the trap and the cliff. She could stay where Valzin had her pinned, or she could leap into the unknown and hope for the best. Ilme could not guess which one Valzin wished for—she just kept offering Ilme that insouciant smile.

There has to be another way, Ilme thought. But she could see nothing. Either she submitted to Valzin's schemes, or threw everything—*everything*—to the wind.

Ilme caught herself.

Fear causes hesitation, Zorya had told her. *Hesitation gains one time to* think.

She needed to stall, to give herself space to find that third path. She couldn't let Valzin trick her into moving too quickly.

Because if Ilme knew one thing, it was that she couldn't read Valzin—if this seemed like the end result of the High Marshal's plans, there were certainly deeper layers she was missing.

"I suppose I should pack for Falador," she said. "I'll need lodging for my apprentices. They travel with me."

"They'll be so sad to miss the teleportation ritual," Valzin said. "But history happens where it happens. Maybe we'll stay a little, give a few afternoons over to letting Master Unaia lecture you, just for good measure. The council would love it if she approved." Valzin wrinkled her nose in an impish way. "Actually, let's make it even tidier—I'll go on a hunting trip. Everyone can think I'm sulking and there'll be no whiff of us working together."

And it would buy Ilme time, she thought, to figure out what exactly Valzin's trap was.

THIRTY-ONE

THE SEVENTIETH YEAR OF THE REIGN OF KING RADDALLIN
OF ASGARNIA
THE SEVENTH DAY OF BENNATH
THE WIZARDS' TOWER

In the same moment that Raddallin's speech unfolded the next stage of Valzin's plan, Azris the Green pounded on the door of Zanmaron's study. "Open this door!" she shouted, afraid her nerves were going to fail her. "Open up, damn it!"

Her fists ached as much as her chest. *If he would just yell back—*

"Go away," Zanmaron's voice came muffled through the door.

She hit the door harder, slapping it with both hands when her fists couldn't take more. "No! Come out here!"

Silence.

Terror crawled up nerves, over her neck, into her brain. No—she swallowed. She was going to say what she came to say. And if they were done—really done—then… then she would deal with that next. She pressed her cheek to the door.

"You can claim the spell," she said. "You and Kelavan. It was his work. He figured it out. He figured it out because he used your work. I… I couldn't see it and I panicked when an *apprentice* could.

I... I just panicked. And now it's your research that's making the actual anchors. I'm... I'm the footnote." She swallowed against the lump building in her throat. "I'm sorry. I should have told you. I should have told Kelavan what he'd found. I should have told everyone." She drew a deep breath and shut her eyes tight. "Please don't hate me."

More silence.

There was her answer. She'd said her piece—she'd been the bigger person. He could do what he liked and that wasn't her problem. It wasn't—it *wasn't*. Azris pushed away from the door, chin high, and told herself she did not care.

She had made it three steps when the door opened. "Wait."

Azris stopped, but refused to turn around—she was *not* going to be the weak one. *You already are the weak one,* a vicious little voice in her hissed.

"You're not a footnote," he said, wearily. "And you're an idiot, but I don't hate you. I couldn't hate you, Azris."

She glanced back over her shoulder—she had to, because if she didn't turn around he would think she was crying and maybe she was... but also it wasn't fair when he talked like that, to keep her back to him. To act like he was no one.

He looked awful—sweaty and tired and sorrowful. His brown hair was sticking up wild, the way it did when he was frustrated with some problem and kept digging his fingers into his hair.

But the problem is you, the vicious little voice said. *Or the problem is him?* But when they kept returning to each other for decades... maybe it wasn't a problem? Maybe it was another problem she couldn't stop trying to solve, even though it turned out wrong again and again.

"Why are we like this?" she asked, and she almost hoped he'd snap back with some insult, some cutting comment about how *she* was the one who had started it.

He sighed instead. "Honestly? Because we're too stubborn for each other and too smart to bother with the rest of these fools."

"*You* didn't get shown up by an apprentice."

"Are you joking? He does that to me constantly, it's infuriating," he said. "If you leave me for him, I'll be very put out."

Azris pressed a hand to her eyes, sudden tears welling there. "Stop it. You're not funny."

"Oh, waiting gods, come here." He pulled her into an embrace, tucking his head against the curve of her neck. He smelled terrible, but she didn't want to be anywhere else.

All the other times they fought, it burned hot and fast, sharp words traded carelessly and quickly until neither of them could sustain it any longer, and then it was just as fast and hot, but more teasing, more coaxing.

This wasn't how they fought—the coldness, the retreat. This wasn't how they made up—the honesty, the *weeping*.

"Dreaming God," she said, disgusted. "I might be in love with you."

"You have been saying that for at least fifteen years now," his muffled voice came. "You might have to accept you can't falsify it. And I love you too." She poked him in the ribs, and he let her go. But his smile softened.

"Every time we fight," he confessed, "I'm afraid it's going to be the last time. And I don't want that, even if in the moment…"

"In the moment," she finished for him, "it feels like if you don't shout no one will hear you?" He nodded. "I know that feeling."

"Yeah, I've been told I don't always listen all that well. I'm sorry about the banquet. About leaving you to fend for yourself. And defend me."

"I'm sorry I took it out on you," she said. "I was… I was just embarrassed." They were all right, she thought. Although it felt so fragile and strange.

"What have you been doing?" She reached up to smooth his sweaty hair down. "Literally wrestling that spell?"

· He raked a hand through his hair mussing it again, and beckoned her wordlessly into the study.

The room smelled foul, of sweat and sulphur and ash. In the corner, where he'd pushed away the furniture, there were lines on the floor and deep grooves in the stone that hadn't been there. Azris closed the door as Zanmaron dropped onto the bench.

"I summoned a demon," he said.

Azris stared at the ruined floor. "For... fun?"

"What? Of course not, you needed a conduit to pass through the secondary plane. That was my theory Kelavan was repurposing—that summonings were bending through a forgotten secondary plane. So... I summoned something that could help anchor the spell through it." He nodded at the corner. "It's still there, just invisible. It will be attached to me until we've finished."

Azris felt her eyes shiver as she considered the corner, as if the air were trying to escape. She sat down next to Zanmaron. "Does it work?"

"I think so," he said. "We'll find out when we cast it. But... I'm an idiot. Unaia won't touch this. *Especially* if she knows I did it—this is the one line I didn't cross that she was so sure I would. And your ritual needs four masters."

"Did it..." She looked up at him. "You're all right? You didn't have to... sacrifice anything?"

"Nothing physical," he said. "But I'll be all right. And it should hold. But first... I don't know how to tell Unaia." He shook his head. "All she will hear is how I failed, utterly, to be anything she wanted. She will hear 'evil' and she will not touch this ritual if she knows there's a demon involved. But we need this—we need the essence mine, and we need to access it safely."

Azris considered the scorched floor, picturing the spell as if it were written down. You could obfuscate the demon, mark it as an amplification source...

"What if... we just don't tell her?"

Zanmaron gave her a sidelong look. "She's not stupid."

"I mean that's up for discussion," Azris said. "But she thinks it's *my* work. Which she will happily tear to pieces, but she won't take it as a personal affront if she goes through this spell and spots the demonic influence. Because it will have nothing to do with you."

Zanmaron slouched against the wall, frowning at the marked floor. "So you'd just... carry on as if the spell were yours."

"For the ritual," Azris said. "I told you, I'll share the credit. They can put Kelavan the Infuriating Genius first in the history books." She leaned against him. "But we'll have teleportation. We can go anywhere. Supply anything."

"Probably reveal all sorts of new things too," he said, putting his arm around her back. "Once we can travel with magic across the continent, and into the rune altars, what else can we do? Can we go to other planes? Can we go beyond the Edicts?"

"To the moon?" she teased. She sighed. "Or maybe we can leave it to the apprentices. Let them show off for a bit."

He kissed the top of her head. "But first this."

"This," she agreed. "It's my spell. I did all of it."

"And if anyone asks," he said. "I told you not to summon a demon."

THIRTY-TWO

◄◆►

The teleportation ritual was postponed until the king, the High Marshal, and Ilme had left for Falador. There was, the masters of the orders agreed, too much risk inherent in performing such a powerful ritual. If anything went wrong, gods beyond the Edicts forfend, they could not risk the king, his heir, or—to a lesser extent—the High Marshal.

"Mind, I don't mean to suggest the High Marshal is expendable," Unaia said to Azris as she worked out which runes would be needed for the teleportation spells, once they'd made the anchor. "Only that I'm pleased the king saw reason. She was *not* a suitable heir." Unaia idly sorted air runes into neat lines. "Though I also find the choice of *Ilme* of all people… perplexing."

"It's infuriating, is what it is," Azris said, sweeping one of Unaia's lines back toward her. Her hand shook as she did, and she cursed to herself. "I needed her *here* for this."

"Oh, I'm sure you'll do fine." Unaia gave her a pinched sort of smile. "Though, if she'd been available, you might have been able to reorganise the ritual a bit."

Azris bit her tongue. It had been a week, and Unaia had tried half a dozen times to convince Azris to cut Zanmaron out of her ritual. The art of pushing back, just enough to keep Unaia from pushing harder—or worse, backing out of the ritual—was wearing Azris down.

Unaia dragged the air runes into a careful circle. "I'm just saying. He acted horribly when you made your announcement. And he's been… distracted since. Do you want that energy in the most important ritual any of us is likely to complete?"

If Zanmaron was distracted, it was the efforts of holding the demon with him for an extra week. Azris didn't like to think about how the demon was draining him. The last three days, he'd hardly gotten out of bed.

"Let it go," she'd told him two nights ago. "Or give it to me. Get your stamina back up. "

"It doesn't work that way," he said. "It's bound up in the framework of the spell—I'm not sure what will happen if I let it go. It might vanish, it might rampage around, it might explode."

She smoothed his hair back. "If they move the ritual again, we're taking a boat and a staff of fire out onto the water, and you're letting it go."

He shut his eyes but nodded. "Did you hide it? In the equations?"

"I stripped down the ritual itself. We'll keep the room dim so no shadows show. If Unaia spots the demon," Azris had said, tucking herself next to him, "it will because we let it rampage around and squash her."

In Azris's workroom, Unaia leaned forward over the runes, as if someone were going to overhear them. "You *can* do better, my dear," she said. "Sometimes we get too comfortable with something… unsuited to us."

Azris smiled at Unaia so broadly she hoped it looked like she was about to take a bite out of the other woman—better than telling her all the ways Azris hated her. "Balance is power," she recited. "Zanmaron's very excited to participate in my ritual. Did you have any questions about it?"

Unaia pursed her mouth. "Is this about that spurious gossip?"

"I have no idea what you mean," Azris said, still thinking it would be very satisfying to unleash a litany of all Unaia's flaws.

"Please," Unaia said witheringly. "I'm not a fool, Azris. I'm sure it brought Zanmaron great joy to hear the White Knights tried to take over the Council of Falador. I still don't believe a word of it."

Azris frowned. "They did what?"

"They did *nothing*," Unaia said primly. "The Council and the White Knights are in perfect harmony and I refuse to believe otherwise—and I most certainly refuse to believe that Sir Perior has hushed it all up."

Privately, Azris thought the Saradominists could do with some spurious gossip. See how they like it, she thought. "Unaia, once again I have no idea what you're talking about. I've been very busy." She swept the runes into individual pouches and swept the pouches into a basket. "I need to make sure everyone's ready. Don't forget your copy of the ritual."

Unaia took the page from her and studied it. "This looks different."

"Your part's at the top," Azris said, quickly. "I left off the extraneous details—just make certain you channel through a law rune, and you're directly opposite Zanmaron." *Where the spell between you should obscure the demon,* she added to herself.

"Simple," Unaia said. "A wonder you didn't solve it ages ago."

"A wonder you didn't step in and do it for me," Azris said, sharply. "I have to go."

She picked up the basket and swept from the room before Unaia could test her fraying temper further. She was still shaking from nerves—they were nearly done, this was nearly finished, and the other side of it held teleportation. It would be worth it. They could deal with the Blue Order and the fragmenting power of the Wizards' Tower afterwards.

In the Chamber of the Four Shrines, she found Zanmaron already waiting, standing against the wall beside the door, speaking to Kelavan. He looked awful—hollow-eyed and feverish. Azris searched beside him, and found the telltale shimmer of the demon.

"It's not complicated," Zanmaron was saying, his voice rough with fatigue. "You just stand between Master Azris and Master Unaia and channel through the fire rune."

"Are you sure you're—" Kelavan spotted Azris, and whatever he was going to say, he swallowed down. She smiled at him.

"Good morning," she said. "Ready to proceed?" She caught Zanmaron's eye, and he gave the smallest shake of his head. Kelavan still didn't know.

They'd opted not to tell Kelavan their plans—which Azris still felt terribly guilty about. But Zanmaron had been firm.

"The boy is smart and he's excellent at drawing surprising conclusions," he said. "But he can't lie to save his life. If he looks suspicious, Unaia will pounce on it."

"So he's going to hate me instead?"

"No, he's going to hate *us*," Zanmaron had said. "For a little bit."

Kelavan was looking at her less with hatred, more with hurt. Zanmaron clapped a hand to his shoulder. "Looks like it's time to begin. Go to your spot."

Azris dropped her voice as the boy left. "You look awful. Are you all right?"

"I'm up," he said. "You look—what was it?—gorgeous and commanding?"

"Funny." She blew out a breath. "I feel as if I'm going to vomit. I think I handled Unaia, but you need to stay far, far from her. It's mostly invisible, but we don't need anyone asking questions." She handed him a copy of the ritual. "Here. You have the chaos rune?"

"Of course." He gave her a lopsided smile, as the others filed in. "Thank you. For managing Unaia."

"The least I could do," she said. "Let's finish this and get you back to normal."

They arranged themselves in a circle as Azris had designed, masters and apprentices, so that the colours of their orders alternated, grey and blue, red and green. The floor had been chalked with the arcane diagram that would help direct the flow of magic as they cast it. Azris went around, checking they had the runes they would need, making certain they had their copies of the ritual. As she passed Unaia, she glanced back at Zanmaron, making certain the shimmer of the demon's presence was hidden in the shadows behind him.

"Is he *drunk?*" Unaia muttered, following Azris's gaze. "I don't think we should proceed if—"

"It's *fine!*" Azris snapped, shoving a law rune toward her. "Master Zanmaron is *tired* and I am done waiting. Just trust me, Unaia."

Zanmaron cleared his throat as Azris took her own spot. "Please remember, once the ritual begins we must all keep our places in the circle. If anyone leaves there could be disastrous consequences." He cleared his throat again, as if it pained him, and began chanting the words of the spell, harsh and halting words that tripped from his throat one after another.

The room swelled with magic, the lines marked on the floor filling with power. Unaia's voice joined Zanmaron's, chanting the same words, and then Temrin's, and lastly Azris picked the chant up, a sliding, sinuous chorus to underpin the first.

Every hair on Azris's skin stood on end, and she felt the pulse of magic bound into the nature rune she held shift and synchronise with the words they spoke. The apprentices took up the spell, a call and response forming. At the centre of the chamber, their shared power manifested, becoming a crackling column of power that grew and grew, flooding the room with bluish light.

Azris cursed to herself and glanced at Zanmaron. The light illuminated him, casting fierce shadows in the angles of his face, pale brightness over his skin.

And tracing the shape of the demon he was anchoring the spell through. Its shadow loomed over Zanmaron, too large, too dark.

Unaia was still on the other side of the column, chanting and ignorant of the demon. But beside Zanmaron, Azris found her error: Perien the Blue flinched back, nearly stepping from the circle. "What is that?"

"Concentrate, Perien!" Unaia snapped, picking up the chant again. The column grew brighter, more solid, a sliding, puckering feeling in the air building, filling Azris's mouth with a taste like old ice.

Nearly there, nearly there, Azris thought.

But then Perien took a step back, stumbling a little as the magic held him in the circle. The spell warped. "It's a demon," he said. "I can see it."

"Don't move!" Azris shouted.

"Do the ritual as written," Zanmaron said through clenched teeth.

"Mei!" Perien called frantically across to Zanmaron's other side. "You can see it, can't you?"

"Get your apprentice under control, Unaia!" Azris snarled. The magic was like a torrent, rushing through her—but it was wobbling, a dangerous imbalance in its frequency. She thought of Master Endel, of how he'd died rather than break the spell in progress. "If you break the circle we all die," she panted.

"It's safe, Perien!" Mei called, feeding runes into the spell. "I studied it—there's demonic power in it but it's safe! Just keep the circle!"

"You knew!" Perien cried. "Demonic power is never safe! We have to stop!"

"I'm sure the demonic influence is minor!" Unaia said. "Azris knows better than to feed something dangerous into a spell. I trust her fully. Hold your place!"

Azris cursed and cursed and cursed as the wobble increased— Mei turned to Unaia, distracted, confused. "Master Azris? No, it was Kelavan's. I was there when he made his breakthrough. This... This was his work."

"It doesn't matter," Kelavan said. "Hold the spell."

Unaia turned to Azris. "What are they talking about?"

"It's my spell!" Azris blurted, trying desperately to keep Unaia's attention on her. "I worked all my life on this problem. Some kid has the idea? No—it's mine! I did this! All of it!"

"Just finish it!" Zanmaron roared. "It doesn't matter whose spell it is, we have to complete the ritual!"

The room was now a cyclone, a storm of power to rival those that pummelled the Northern Sea, and in the flash of magic, Azris could see the demon more clearly, the shadows of wings and horns, the pulse of otherworldly magic. But at the same time the magic was braiding itself together, the anchor was holding.

They'd managed, she realised with a sudden elation. They'd made a teleportation anchor.

But the spell had to finish, had to discharge its building energies. And their focuses were slipping.

"What is *that*?" Unaia demanded. She was looking past the column of magic that now bounced and danced and bent enough to reveal the demon fully.

"You said you trusted me," Azris tried to shout, but Unaia's attention was on Zanmaron.

"'It doesn't matter,'" she sneered. "It certainly does. Never a demon! The one thing I asked you."

"Hardly," Zanmaron managed through gritted teeth. "Nothing was enough."

"I *begged* you to keep to your duty, but you always had to flaunt your disrespect. I always knew you would go to the bad, Zanmaron, but you will not drag me or Perien down with your demon-god!" The righteousness of decades twisted her features— Zanmaron had disappointed her first by failing as her apprentice, and then by not failing at all.

"Don't break the circle, you idiot!" Azris shouted. "You'll kill us all. It's nearly finished!"

They should have told her, she realised. They should have had it out. Because there was no making Unaia see reason, perhaps; but this was too dangerous. Azris glanced to her right, to where Kelavan stood, looking fearful but holding fiercely to his part of the spell, counting down under his breath to the completion. They weren't going to make it if—

"Come, Perien," Unaia said.

And Unaia turned and stepped out of the circle of power.

"No! Don't!" Zanmaron shouted.

Azris turned, all instinct, and shoved Kelavan as hard as she could out of the circle. He landed hard, rolled over and came up on his knees. "Do the teleportation spell!" Azris shouted. "Bottom of the sheet—just like you wrote out." He stared at her confused a moment, but Azris had to trust he'd be sensible.

Crackling veins of purple energy spidered up the column of light. Azris turned, toward Zanmaron, starting to run. She shoved Mei toward Kelavan too, and the purple lightning built and built—

Until a beam shot out with a crack like thunder, skewering Zanmaron through the chest.

A scream ripped itself out of Azris's chest, and the world seemed to slow around her as his head fell back, his knees buckled. She ran as if in a nightmare, as if the room were an eternity wide, as if she would never, ever reach him again. She pulled runes, wove a shield together as she reached him.

You won't, a little voice whispered. *He's gone.*

He couldn't be gone, he wasn't *allowed* to be gone—she reached him and pulled him close, but he was so boneless, so heavy. He had to be all right, she thought. They'd done it. Everything was going to be better now.

She looked behind her, watching the spell break apart, releasing all its energy. Bolts shattered the stone wall, sending cracks up to the vaulted ceiling. Another bolt struck Unaia right in the centre of her back as she fled.

Kelavan, Mei, and Perien clustered together in the corner, and then a flash of brightness consumed them—the spell worked.

Azris smiled as she clutched Zanmaron close, as the purple lightning shattered her shield. It had worked. It had always been possible. She hadn't been wrong.

The magical column thundered again, another burst of energy exploding outward. The room collapsed, the floors above cracking. Everything was thunder and the endless pull of rune magic. When the bolt struck Azris, she felt nothing but that bone-deep pull, saw nothing but endless stars.

THIRTY-THREE

◄►

"You're sure there was no sabotage?" Raddallin asked. Mei stood before him, a shell of herself. A mirror, Ilme thought, of that day in Falador, after the final battle.

Ilme sat beside the king of Asgarnia, this time in a quiet parlour off his private rooms, with Rue attached to her lap as if he were glued there.

Listening to Mei recount the deaths of Ilme's friends and colleagues. Watching this girl stand in the same place she had so many times, giving details of other terrible events. It was not easier to be sitting on this side of the conversation.

"The only sabotage was that the orders didn't trust each other," Mei said. "I believe Master Zanmaron added to the spell without telling anyone, save perhaps Master Azris. And then neither of them explained it fully. Master Unaia…" She swallowed. "I can't say why she did what she did, but I think the bad feelings between the Saradominists and the Zamorakians haven't helped matters."

"But he summoned a demon?" Raddallin clarified.

"Maybe," Mei said. "I don't think that was hurting anyone but him."

Raddallin searched her face, grave. "You understand Perien gives a different version of events."

"As I said," Mei answered, "I don't think the bad feelings between the Saradominists and the Zamorakians have helped matters. But he and Unaia both knew they should not step out of that circle. Regardless of any other deception." She swallowed. "Master Azris saved us. Me and Kelavan, and Perien because she told Kelavan to test the anchor. To use the teleportation spell."

The three apprentices had appeared in the square outside the palace, panicking and covered in stone dust. They had gone first for the barracks, and the White Knights and the Kinshra had raced for the Wizards' Tower. They were still waiting for them to return. To find out who had survived beyond these three.

"Thank you for your answers," Raddallin said, dismissing Mei. He looked up as he did, and let out a sigh of relief. "Sana. Thank goodness. We've had terrible news."

"I heard," Valzin said, her expression grave as she strode into the parlour. One of her arms hung in a sling. Mei looked up, curious, as they passed each other, but said nothing.

Ilme's thoughts whirled. The tower had fallen while Valzin wasn't in Falador. All she'd found in the week she'd been in Falador was rumours—of her own unsuitability, of the White Knights plotting insurrection, of the Kinshra threatening rebellion.

And Zanmaron was dead. Azris was almost certainly dead. She wanted to weep, but she couldn't let herself. It felt unsafe.

"What happened?" Raddallin asked.

Valzin waved him away. "It's embarrassing. My horse spooked at a fox and threw me. It's just sprained." She sighed. "A terrible time for me to be away. How are you, Ilme?"

"Bad," Rue said, curling his claws into the fabric of her skirt. "She is very bad-feeling."

It stung, really, how Valzin still spoke to her as if they were friends and comrades, as if she hadn't openly and explicitly made Ilme her tool. "How you'd expect. Where were you riding when you fell off your horse?"

Valzin shrugged. "Near Misthalin. Was it sabotage?"

"Unclear," Raddallin said. "The grey apprentice says it was an accident. The blue says the Red Order Master intended something nefarious."

"Given Zanmaron is the one who died first, I doubt that, sire," Ilme said. "Unaia broke the circle. That's all."

Something like sorrow flashed over Valzin's features—quick as a swallow dipping over a field. "Sounds like perhaps the apprentice is covering for the master. What about Kelavan? I heard three made it out."

"The boy is... insensible at the moment," Raddallin said.

"To be expected." She turned to Ilme. "Have you tried talking to him? You and his master were close after all. And you are his future queen."

Nothing had changed. Valzin's choice still lay before her: accept her role as Raddallin's heir, or refuse it and damage his legitimacy. She had tried to talk the king out of this, but he refused to discuss it.

The only thing that had changed was that she wanted even less to chase Valzin in circles. She felt as if she could lie down and never get up again...

Ilme frowned. That would serve Valzin very well, wouldn't it? If she didn't have the will to fight her?

"Oh my dear," Raddallin said, misunderstanding her long silence for grief swelling up in her. "I know you've suffered very greatly—you must believe me when I say you *can* bear it. You must. That is what a ruler is for."

"Yes of course," Ilme said. "I'll go... I'll go find Kelavan now."

"I'll come with you," Valzin said.

Ilme left the king, promising to a schedule of preparation before the Council and the representatives of the tribes approved of her adoption, as Rue settled around her shoulders. It wasn't now—so Ilme pushed it out of her mind. She could not lie down, she could not give up—and she could not waste time.

If you are going to tell me not to trust Sanafin, Raddallin had said once, *then I expect you to have extraordinary reasons.*

I think she lied about being in the place where she is supposed to be, Ilme thought *doing what she is supposed to do. I think she hurt her arm because she was in the tower and is planning something nefarious.*

This did not, she knew, qualify as extraordinary reasons.

"How do you want to do this?" Valzin asked as they walked.

"Kindly," Ilme said. "You were with the Kinshra while you were hunting?"

"For a fox? No. I went off on my own a bit. Why?" she added. "Were you going to ask them all if they also saw the fox?"

"I cannot think of anything I care less about than a fox."

"That's fair," Valzin said, her smile spreading. "It's certainly an interesting time to be alive, wouldn't you say? So many things in flux."

Ilme said a little prayer for balance and blew out a breath. Nothing would be gained by tossing Valzin across the courtyard with a fistful of runes. Rue growled and she reached up to scratch his cheek. "The king seems sobered. Perhaps you should have convinced him to choose an heir less likely to be in the middle of a magical catastrophe."

Valzin's smile froze, a hint of something sharp and furious behind it. "It's temporary," she said. "Being forced to reckon with his own fragility always makes him falter."

"I don't know if that's true."

"That's because you've always seen the public face," she said. "You've never been the steel that props him up. That absorbs the strikes he can't take."

The anger that threaded Valzin's words made Ilme turn cold. "I think you ought to leave Kelavan alone. He's got nothing you want."

"At the moment anyway," Valzin said, light again and cheerful. "Keep an eye on him. That one's simmering into something... interesting."

Ilme hoped. She crossed the palace to the guest quarters where the apprentices were staying on the other side of the palace green. Before she could reach the door, Faryd came flying out.

"Wizard Ilme!" he shouted. "Wizard Ilme, come quickly! They're going to kill each other!" Ilme chased him up the stairs, two at a time, following the sounds of crashing pottery and young men shouting. Rue launched himself from her shoulder to hover around Faryd.

Perien flew from a doorway ahead of her to slam against the opposite wall. Kelavan launched himself after. "You *bastard!* You killed them all and you have the nerve—"

Perien struggled, swinging at the other young man. "I—was— trying—to—"

Ilme aimed a small air spell between them, throwing Kelavan back, away from Perien. He was up on his feet a moment later, but Ilme had interposed herself. "No!" she said. "No! We don't *do* that! Especially now!"

Kelavan pointed a shaking finger at Perien. "He said it was for the best. He said Master Zanmaron made the mistake—*you* made the mistake! You and *your* master! He said don't stop, don't break the circle! You've killed them all!"

"I *offered* to let him join the Blue Order," Perien said. "I was trying to help."

"I'd rather burn it to the *ground!*"

"Kelavan!" Ilme cried. "Enough! Perien, he has an order, you're being cruel. Kelavan, stop *fighting!*" She shoved him back into the room they'd come out of, and held up a pair of runes, ready to knock him down again. "Sit down," she panted. "*Calm* down. I will deal with him, and you will make yourself ready to talk to the king."

"Why?" Kelavan demanded, and there was no sign of the timid young man he'd been. "Because he wants to dissolve the Red Order too?"

"Because you were there and you know what happened, and—" Ilme's voice cracked, her thoughts full of her lost friends, full of these poor young souls' grief. "Did she ever tell you?" Ilme asked, more quietly. "Azris. Did she apologise at least?"

Kelavan hesitated. "She saved me in the end, she told me... I think she and Master Zanmaron were protecting me. Protecting each other. From *Unaia!*" he snarled past Ilme into the hallway.

Ilme pushed him back further, and shut the door. "You're not bringing them back by hurting him. You're not saving the Red Order by washing it in Saradominist blood."

"There's no saving it," he spat. "They already talk like it died with Master Zanmaron."

"It only dies if you turn on it," Ilme said. "It only dies if you play into these *stupid* games. I don't doubt for a moment Mei's version is true. Unaia was exactly as narrow-minded and fragile as to break that circle because she thought she was teaching a lesson— she was never anything less."

"They're not going to blame her," Kelavan said. "They're going to blame Master Zanmaron. They're always looking for a Zamorakian to blame. They're the ones trying to take over Falador and oust the council and—"

"What?" Ilme interrupted. "Who's doing that?"

He shrugged. "Everyone's talking about it. There was some sort of uprising with the White Knights. Sir Perior shut it all down. But they were going to eject the council if they succeeded." He scowled at the floor. "And then probably they would have blamed it on the Kinshra."

"Don't paint them all with Unaia's brush—that was never about Zamorak and Saradomin. That was about her wanting to be right, about wanting her wounded pride to have purpose and not being able to admit for half a century that Zanmaron *hurt* her feelings. That's not about gods, it's about people."

Kelavan shook his head. He looked so very young. "You don't get it."

Ilme wanted to scream that she understood far better than Kelavan did—perhaps far better than he ever would. She had watched her country unite and splinter, watched her friends fight and die, only for the country to unite and splinter, unite and splinter.

"You think," she said, "that this is all of you—being Zamorakian. That it defines *everything*. But your god doesn't even claim this— what does Lord Zamorak say? Change is constant, change is opportunity. Show strength in adversity and be ready to strike. Where does He say, 'hold a grudge until it's cold, make an enemy of those who disagree'? Even the most devout Zamorakians have *allies*, Kelavan—it's in your creed to use the strengths of others to advance your cause."

But the young man only gazed at her, hard and angry. "Change is inevitable," he said. "And maybe what we need to change is to finally wake up and see that the Saradominists will end us all if they have the chance."

Ilme cursed. "Sit down. I will come find you later."

She left, shutting the door too hard, and found Perien on the stairs, pressing his sleeve to his bleeding nose. "If I hear," she said, low and furious, "another word of you carrying on your master's tradition of claiming the Red Order ought to be dissolved, Perien, I will drag you to the ice shelves myself. I am sorry for your loss. I am sorry Unaia let her temper get the better of her good sense—"

"That isn't what happened," Perien said, but he couldn't meet her eyes. "There was a demon."

"And you know, under no circumstances do you break a circle once a ritual's started," she said more gently. He was, she knew, no more or less than what he had been taught—he'd known only Unaia and her strict rules of magic and hierarchy that said a demon was a transgression so foul it must be stopped, lest they risk their souls and selves. "Your allies don't all kneel before the same altar, Perien. They never will."

"They didn't tell us what was happening," he said, sullenly. "Master Unaia would have seen the summoning—she had to have. They hid it."

"They were foolish," Ilme said. "But they were my friends. They were heroes of Asgarnia many times over—Unaia too. Nobody was wicked here. Just foolish."

She started to leave, but then Perien said, "She didn't. Master Unaia. She didn't say the Red Order should be dissolved."

Ilme lolled back, frowning. "What do you mean?"

"She didn't say that. She... The High Marshal said it. Twice or more, I think. The first time... Master Unaia was appalled that she would talk about her own... about an order related to her church like that. But then, well, it made a little sense. They'd all rather work alone. I mean, that's what the... that's what their church says."

"No, it doesn't," Ilme said. "But thank you. I'll remember that."

"Do you know when the Knights are expected to return?" he asked. "It's... it's silly, but... my weapons set. The one I was working on. I was hoping that it might be recovered from the Tower. Or what's left of the Tower." He paused. "I would like something to do right now."

"I'll find out. Go back to your room," she said, nodding up the stairs. "And don't talk to Kelavan right now."

Ilme left him, adding this piece to the suspicions tumbling over in her mind. Valzin had suggested the Red Order be disbanded. Someone had been spreading rumours of insurrection among the White Knights—insurrection that no one had warned Ilme of when she was now so close to the king?

If chaos is only a crucible…

You have too many variables, she could almost hear Master Endel's ghost saying to her. *Winnow them down.*

Make a guess, Zanmaron's voice said. *If it could be anything, what could it be?*

Pretend, she told herself, that Valzin had started the rumours of Saradominist rebels. Pretend, she told herself, that Valzin hurt her arm in the tower collapse…

She didn't kill the others, she hadn't sabotaged the ritual—Ilme believed that, so why was she there. What else had she been interested in?

Perien's weapons set, those shining blades meant for Grand Master Perior. That Valzin had gone out of her way to admire multiple times.

Pretend, she told herself, that Valzin wanted Perien's weapons set.

There will be a pattern? Master Temrin offered. *There is knowledge in every piece.*

If, Ilme thought, you predisposed people—your allies, in particular—to believe in rebels who might harm the king, then they would not be surprised if the king died. If there was a weapon that pointed inexorably toward said rebels, you wouldn't even need them to do the deed. If you waited for a distraction big enough—say, a once-in-an-age magical ritual—you could slip in and steal said weapon—though it would be a pity if the ritual fell apart and brought the building down on you.

Ilme thought of Valzin moving through the Wizards' Tower all those times—through Red, Green, Grey, and even Blue. She might not have engineered the ritual to fail, but she had turned them firmly against each other as she went—she would have to, if she was preparing for the Saradominists to be blamed.

Blamed, Ilme thought, for assassinating Raddallin.

That's not proof, Azris said. *You know perfectly well that's not proof.*

It wasn't, Ilme knew. But if she could find one of Perien's weapons it would be extraordinary proof. She pulled Rue off her shoulder again and held the little purple dragon so his eyes were even with hers.

"Rue," she said, "I need your help."

✦ ✦ ✦

The first place Ilme looked was Valzin's study. She stood in the hall ready to intercept Valzin, and slipped Rue inside to hunt for the blue and silver blades behind tapestries or under rugs, hidden in caskets or inside cushions. But even with his keen sense for magical emanations, he found nothing.

"Spiders," he offered. "Six spiders."

"That's all right," Ilme said. "We have other places to look."

They searched the Kinshra's barracks on the pretence of inventorying any runes they had kept. They knew her, and were very accommodating, and had many kind words to say about her fallen friends.

"Have you heard about any threats against the king?" Ilme asked one, a young woman with curly brown hair cropped short.

She looked askance at her fellow knights, as if she weren't sure what Ilme meant. Or unsure if she ought to tell Ilme? "I'm sure if there were, we'd stop it."

"Some talk about more internal rebels," a man with a short dark beard said. "Maybe Grand Master Perior's got some trouble with his troops. But they run a strict force. They'll find the problem."

They searched Valzin's rooms while she was hunting with the king, and when again they found nothing, Ilme had a sudden panic that Valzin was doing it *now*, out in the forests where confusion would obscure the deed. She had raced down to the stables herself, hurrying the grooms to ready the fastest horse left, when they'd come riding back, Valzin and Raddallin in good spirits.

"Why, Ilme," Valzin said, "you look like you've seen a ghost." She leaned in. "I'm assuming you left my rooms in good order?"

"Why would I be in your rooms?" Ilme asked.

"That's a very good question," Valzin said. "Aren't you late for your fitting? You can't be presented in those old robes."

Would Valzin do it then? Ilme tasked a reluctant Rue to stay close to the High Marshal while she was measured and draped and discussed. But when she found him again, Rue had nothing to report.

"She gave an apple," he said. "To me. I ate it."

"Did she go anywhere?" Ilme asked. "Anywhere odd? Anywhere she might have hidden the sword?"

Rue flew in an agitated loop. "Big castle. I don't know."

He was right—Falador was enormous, and Valzin had watched it being built around her. Ilme couldn't hope to find the stolen blades when Valzin was the one who'd hidden them. If she'd hidden them. Ilme pressed her hands to her eyes—she felt as if she were jumping at shadows.

The Knights returned with survivors from the Tower collapse, Eritona among them, and Ilme reunited with her old friend with many tears and embraces. There *were* weapons and staves and even runes pulled from the tower's wreckage—but not, as Ilme feared, Perien's treasured weapons.

"Maybe don't find the sword," Rue said. "Maybe find something the sword wants to poke and look there. Like for me, you look for where there's good napping. Or spiders."

Ilme frowned. "The sword doesn't…" But she let the thought trail away.

Ilme could chase her up and down the castle, and Valzin would only smile and chuckle at her determination because Valzin was so much smarter and so much more prepared.

But if she was right, Ilme knew exactly where the weapon was going to end up.

THIRTY-FOUR

———◄◆►———

The night was warm and full of the songs of insects. The king had retired early, weary from a long day of discussing the fallout of the Wizards' Tower collapse, the plans for his succession and the rumours of agitators in his most loyal ranks. Too much of the day, they said, had been spent locked away and arguing with his heir, who was proving high-strung and difficult in the aftermath of her colleagues' deaths.

Ilme of the Green, of the Narvra—people were still testing which epithet to choose, gauging their companions to see which identity won out—had also retired, eyes heavy with lack of sleep, features drawn. Poor thing, people said. Too much too fast, but at least we'll see how she manages before she is queen, and at least it's not the High Marshal we're watching.

Sanafin Valzin strolled through the corridors of Falador, unbothered, the sword gifted to her by King Raddallin strapped across her back. The night was warm, the country safe, and anyone who watched her would say she patrolled without a care in the

348

world. She came to the king's door, to the White and the Black Knights stationed there. They saluted as she arrived.

"I'll be taking a shift, Gilbert," she said to the Black Knight. "You can head back. Plenty of evening left to spend."

He held her gaze a moment, then nodded. "Zamorak grant you mastery over all obstacles."

"Well, hopefully it stays a quiet night." She turned to the White Knight. "Sorry I'm late. Don't let it reflect badly on the order."

The man shifted uneasily. "I'm actually meant to go off-duty as well. Did you see another White Knight headed this way?"

"No," Valzin said, frowning. "Perhaps they've been detained." She took the place of the Kinshra knight, who saluted again and departed.

The insects sang, the moon shone down. The White Knight's replacement didn't come.

"I don't want to tell you your business," Valzin said. "But—"

"I'm concerned too," the White Knight said. He looked down the hallway. "You... Would you mind, High Marshal, if I ran down to the barracks to grab someone? Find out what's happened?"

Valzin looked troubled. "I suppose." She unsheathed her sword and tested her injured arm. "I don't like it," she confessed, "but at least he's safe in his own bed. Go quickly."

The White Knight offered her a hasty salute and took off down the hall.

When the clatter of his armour had passed out of earshot, Valzin relaxed. She took off the harness that held the sword Raddallin had gifted her, and opened a slim pocket stitched into the scabbard where it lay against her back. She drew out a blue and silver dagger that shivered with magic and opened the door.

It was darker still in the king's bedchambers, but the slow rhythm of Raddallin's breath filled the room. Valzin moved carefully toward it, drawing a small number of runestones from her own pocket.

She paused beside Raddallin's bed, the moonlight enough to trace the long bulk of the king at rest there.

"The things I have done for you," she whispered. She brought the runes close and unlocked the magic in them, greenish light pouring from her fingers to draw vines out of nothing to wrap Raddallin tight.

He woke, startled. He cried, "Sana?"

"Raddallin," she said flatly, and raised the dagger.

In the same moment, another pulse of magic flooded the room. Stronger vines erupted from the floor, seizing Valzin and folding her arm, bent back to strike, so that her hand was trapped against her armoured shoulder.

Ilme lit the lantern beside her, illuminating the shadowed corner where she'd been waiting, night after night, for Valzin to strike.

"What took you so long?" Ilme said, as she climbed onto the bed to free the king. "I assume this is evidence enough, Your Majesty."

Nothing about Valzin was smiling now. Here was the cold, hard anger that had flashed free that day after the White Knights had been rewarded. "Interesting," she said.

Raddallin broke free of the vines and stood, the bed between him and Valzin. "Sana, what beyond the Edicts? How could you? How *could you?*"

Valzin said nothing a moment, as if she were calculating any and all paths out of this and finding them wanting. "Does it matter?" she said at last.

"You were done with him," Ilme said. "You saw your influence fading. For all he loves you, he listens too much to the Saradominists."

"That's a lie," Raddallin snapped.

"Oh, it is *not*," Valzin spat. "I built you. I guided you. I made this kingdom through you. And for what? You're turning it into Misthalin to rot in its own self-satisfaction, and you won't hear a word about it."

"You're jealous—"

"Think that," Valzin said. "Think that all you like. That I am tender and weak and I need the love of the masses—they don't love me, they cannot love me. They have *never loved me.* Never mind, I am the reason for their good fortune."

Raddallin shook his head sadly. "You are telling yourself a story, Sana. We made something wonderful, and you deserve credit for all you've done. But don't pretend you did everything for power—remember the early days, the plans, the discussions. We made a place that drew on the best of all of us. That was the goal, and if you want to tell me that all of this time, my dear friend, my brilliant companion, my stalwart sword was a mask on a suffering betrayer all these years, then I *will* call you a liar."

Valzin looked away. "Well. The past is past, isn't it? Here we are now. Your White Knights will return soon enough, and they will not find me weeping over your corpse with a Saradominist's dagger in your heart. My Kinshra won't step in to seize the traitors. So what will happen?"

Raddallin moved so that she was forced to look at him again. He reached up and twisted the dagger out of her grip. "Would you really have done it?"

Valzin smiled, false and vicious. "I would do anything for Asgarnia," she said, a touch of insouciance in her words.

Ilme watched, an ache deep in her heart. Raddallin was right and he was wrong—he'd lost Valzin when he'd let the Saradominists erase her. Maybe she needed that recognition, that love, but Ilme felt certain the greater part was that she needed to see she would not be cast out of the country she'd built up. Like Azris's fear of being remembered only as a failure, like Zanmaron afraid the ones he loved might turn on him, Valzin had reacted to protect herself—and what she thought Asgarnia needed.

But that wasn't her decision, Ilme knew. The magical vines fell away, and Valzin stood, wary but weaponless, cornered like an animal.

"You will leave," Raddallin said. "Take your knights and never return here."

"Exile?" Valzin said, amused.

"Your Majesty, I still think that's a bad idea," Ilme began. If they could send her to another continent, another plane, maybe—

"I never thought you were bloodthirsty," Valzin said, brushing off her sleeves. "Or foolish. If he has a trial now, with all the rumours racing around, there might be an uprising among the Zamorakians. I'm the only one getting punished—that feels like we're not really equal after all."

"Not that," Raddallin said. "You're right. You've done more for me than anyone alive or dead. So this balances the scales. Take the Kinshra, take a horse, and never come back. If you do, know that I owe you nothing."

They were like two leaves, Ilme thought, caught in a whirlpool and swirling around each other. Raddallin could pretend Valzin might take exile honourably, but the glint in her eye said it was only a matter of time before she'd be back.

Then again, Ilme thought, perhaps this was the cliff she leapt off. Perhaps something greater—or worse—lay on the other side of this for Sanafin Valzin.

Valzin looked up at Raddallin, considering "I'm not wrong, you know. This won't be easy for you. What do you think will happen when all the Kinshra and I disappear into the night? Do you imagine everyone will shrug? Do you imagine my warnings about the Saradominists are all in my imagination? You will embolden that council and Misthalin—I have held back more threats than you can imagine. I still think it will be a Saradominist's blade that takes you one day and now I will wager they'll put it in a

Zamorakian's hand to seal the deal. Chaos is coming."

"Like your plan? Only reversed?" Ilme pointed out.

She was fuming—not only at Valzin's taunts, but at the fact she wasn't wrong. Ilme could see such a thing happening so easily, the tenuous peace of Asgarnia's many sects fracturing as the Saradominists and the Zamorakians turned fully against each other. But whereas through the many years it was a matter of constant repair, constant balance, Valzin's bold path through the nation shed enough sparks to start a wildfire, and Ilme wasn't sure they could snuff them all out safely.

"I will do what I need to do to hold this kingdom together," Raddallin said solemnly.

Valzin snorted. "And I guess without me, you'll find out what that really means."

There was a rap on the door and then it opened to admit the White Knights tasked to check in on the king: Perior and two other knights. Ilme nodded at the grand master, grimly.

Raddallin shook his head. "You always see the worst in people."

"Someone has to," Valzin said to Raddallin. "You never could. And you're not going to live forever, Rad, no matter how hard you try. Good evening, Perior," she said, looking past the king. "Welcome to the show."

Perior regarded her with only sorrow. "I was so sure Ilme was wrong."

"Yes, well. 'To each to the extent of their own abilities, for the price of their own sacrifices'," Valzin quoted, but there was suddenly something thick about her voice, as if perhaps this weren't so easy. Ilme studied her, no closer to truly understanding Sanafin Valzin.

Perior took hold of her by the arm, the White Knights taking up position on either side with swords drawn. Valzin ignored them. She nodded to the king, as if she were only leaving. "Raddallin, I hope that blade is quick when it gets you."

He shook his head. "Find peace, Sana. I will remember you as you were."

She flashed that teasing smile at Ilme then, as the White Knights came forward to escort her into exile. "Best of luck," she said. "You're going to need it." And the marched her from the space.

For a long moment after the knights left the room, neither Ilmeshe nor Raddallin spoke. Where did they even go from here? Who did they trust? How did they rebuild and how did they keep Asgarnia together?

"I think," he said, his low voice heavy with sorrow, "it would be wise for you to leave now. Tomorrow we will need to discuss how to... manage Valzin's disappearance, and how to move forward. You're certain you won't stay?"

"I maintain, Your Majesty, that you have far better choices for a successor than me," she said. "Valzin only suggested me because she thought I was controllable."

"And you bested her."

"Which I will concede might be a skill for a warlord, but not a queen." He looked away, and she went on. "I will stay and help you assess them before I go. Perhaps set them up as my own successor, before I... depart in an untimely fashion. That I can do."

"We will discuss it," Raddallin said, and she knew he intended to try to talk her out of it. But through these long nights of waiting, Ilme had thought back over her life and the moments she was truly happy, and very few of them had come in service to a lord or lady, very few of them had anything at all to do with service to a mere nation.

She went down to the chapel of Guthix. It was not the same place she had been jailed when she was sixteen—that fortress had been swallowed and remade by the citadel Falador had become— but it had reused the same stained glass, the tears of Guthix glowing faintly green as the sun rose outside. Ilme walked the path around the chapel, slowing her breathing, stilling her mind.

Balance in all things, she thought. *Peace in all matters.* There was nothing simple in that, nothing easy. Valzin had not been wrong, only change was constant, and it could not be resisted simply because it was different from what came before. The balance had to be remade constantly. Peace had to be reassessed moment to moment.

You have been at this so long, she thought, *and you are still a tadpole in the mud.*

Best of luck, Valzin's voice taunted in her thoughts. *You're going to need it.*

Her apprentices found her there, an anxious Rue leading them. When he saw her, he ploughed into her chest, burrowing into her arm. "I'm all right!" she said. "Calm down!"

"Your bad friend?" he said. "Your bad friend?"

"Rue was very worried," Cordelia said. "He dragged us out of bed."

"There was an incident," Ilme said delicately. "I will need to see to the king for a few days."

"Of course," Teodnor said. "He's important."

"Should we study with Wizard Eritona then?" Faryd asked.

Ilme moved Rue under one arm and considered the three of them. They had promise and she wanted *this* for the world—more wizards, more magic, more tools to aid the balance. They were tired and worried, but she could still see the spark of interest in them, the excitement for what lay ahead.

She thought of being just a little older than them, about the times she was happiest.

"No. I think," Ilme said, "you all ought to prepare for a journey. What do you know about the rune essence mine?"

ACKNOWLEDGMENTS

From *Erin M. Evans*:

Much gratitude to my editor, Michael Beale, whose keen eye and good humor helped shape this story into what it is. Thank you to my agent, Bridget Smith, for her hard work and support.

Many thanks to the friends and colleagues who helped out with this story when it got stuck—Shanna Germain, Treavor Bettis, B. Dave Walters, Rhiannon Held, Lana Wood Johnson, and Yang Yang Wang. You guys are fantastic.

Thank you to the folks at Jagex for making sure I did right by your lore. Thank you to Tim Fletcher for the long conversations about how to bring life to the past of Gielinor and to Aeternus Lux and others for their fact-checking.

Thank you to Paul Simpson and Kevin Eddy for polishing this book to a shine. Thank you to Mark Montague and Terence Abbott for the best giant frog demigod a girl could hope for. Thank you to Daquan Cadogan for the continuing editorial support.

Thank you to my family, Kevin, Idris, and Ned, who put up with me cranking out a second this year. Thank you to my sisters, Kristen and Julia, who, among many other gifts, rectified the situation when I said "What's *Point Break*?" This is all your fault.

From *Jagex Ltd*:

Many thanks to all those who assisted in the development of this book.

At Jagex Ltd, in particular: Terence Abbott, Kate Blacklock, Tim Fletcher, Matt Parrish, Andrew Macdonald, Mark Montague, Ed Pilkington, and Stuart Walpole.

Plus all those who read and inputted into various drafts of the manuscript including Aeternus Lux.

With additional thanks to B-hive Associates Ltd.

ABOUT THE AUTHOR

Erin M. Evans is the author of the Books of the Usurper series, beginning with *Empire of Exiles*, and the award-winning Brimstone Angels Saga, set in the Forgotten Realms. She is a co-host of the podcast *Writing About Dragons and Shit* and a cast member of the actual play series *Dungeon Scrawlers*. Erin lives in the Seattle area with her husband and sons.

For more fantastic fiction, author events,
exclusive excerpts, competitions, limited editions and more

VISIT OUR WEBSITE
titanbooks.com

LIKE US ON FACEBOOK
facebook.com/titanbooks

FOLLOW US ON TWITTER AND INSTAGRAM
@TitanBooks

EMAIL US
readerfeedback@titanemail.com